It is early in the 15th Century and a strange

way up a mountainside on a small Greek island, is witnessed by a

young goat herd, Ioánnis. He can see that something is being

carried but has no idea what this covert ascension is all about.

As he grows up on the island he comes under the influence of an

old priest who opens the young boy's eyes to perceptions that are

quite new.

All this is disrupted by a cataclysmic event which pitches

Ioánnis into a lifetime's odyssey throughout the turbulent world of

the Near East, a journey of the mind which brings him, in the end,

to a revelation and a startling conclusion.

Andrew Chapman was once a doctor but, for the past fifteen

years, has devoted his time to writing and composing. His first

novel, *Beyond the Silence*, was published in 2010.

Andrew Chapman

For Christine .

Ikon

Best wishes .

Andrew Chapman .

Pilrig Publishing

PILRIG PUBLISHING

First published in Great Britain in May 2012 by
Pilrig Publishing

A CIP catalogue record for this book is available from
the British Library

ISBN: 978-0-9564421-1-6

Printed and bound in Great Britain by the MPG Books Group, Bodmin and King's Lynn

PILRIG PUBLISHING

STONECROFT

BREDON

TEWKESBURY

GL20 7EL

www.pilrigpublishing.com

For Ed

who, inadvertently, gave me the idea for this book

Ikon

Map

The Eastern Mediterranean and Near East in the 15th C

Venice
Ferrara
Florence

Mediterranean Sea

Adrianople
Constantinople

Aegean Sea

The Islands

Bursa

Anatolia

The Black Sea

The Cappadocian Desert
The Taurus Mountains
The Gates of Cilicia

Aleppo
The Lebanese Mountains
Damascus
(Dimashq)

PROLOGOS

The Monastery of Ayios Ioánnis Theologos. 1474

The bells ring well before dawn. Five of them, each calling at its own rhythm, neglecting the timing of its fellows. Cracked tones, nearer to the clang of a billy-goat bell than anything else, a cacophony of sound floating out over the island. Not like the sounding of the great bells of Ayia Sofia in Constantinople that I knew before the Apokalypse (which is how we termed it then). These are bells that define the edge of the day, the first movements of the Monastery. I could be anywhere on this earth until they root me back in the familiar, the God-enclosed space.

I lie still. During the night the rough blanket has slipped to the floor. I was hot enough not to want to retrieve it. I lie still and allow the gentle light of the dawn to creep into my white cell. Through the high window opposite it comes, there is no stopping it. I let my head fall back on the hard pillow. The Abbot has been good to me, considering my age as an excusable sin. But yes, he has been good to me, granting me dispensation from the early office. I lie still and let the words of the Jesus prayer sidle into the vagueness of my early morning consciousness. 'Lord Jesus Christ, son of the living God, have mercy on me.' Again and again, just in the way I was taught by Gerasimos all those years ago. 'Lord Jesus Christ, son of the living God, have mercy on me.' Words so familiar that any meaning soon slips away. 'Lord Jesus Christ, son of the living God, have mercy on me.' Now I know not to hunt down meaning when I pray. Years of practice. I contain my focus within the confines of my old body, practising the hesychast spirituality, becoming my unself.

A mosquito lands on my right forearm, breaking into my meditation. I reach over to bat it away but already its proboscis has perforated my frail skin, thin as paper and just as defenceless. A

1

futile attempt which weakens me in my mind. Pointless to try. My beard is itching. It usually does at this time of day. With the fingers of my right hand I gently scrape the skin of my jowls, pulling down to straighten the bushiness of the growth. No longer the blackness of my heyday, now the greyness of mortality.

And then, unwanted but as regular as the sounding of the matins bells comes the urgency. Low in my belly. My hand runs over my bladder, wrinkling the sparse grey hair. The urgency that compels me to rise. I have to pee.

And I know that, however much sought after, it is not going to come. Not unless I catch it at the right moment. As if I could trick the obstruction when it's not looking and piss away my distended bladder.

Slowly, very slowly, I push myself up until I am perched on the edge of the bed. I sit, panting, my arms spread out like two bastions, buttressing the upright of my weak body. I look around the cell. Sparse, whitewashed, empty mostly. A small ikon on the wall, a reed mat on the floor, a jug on a low shelf and there, across the cell, the pot.

It is a good-sized, earthenware pot; it needs to be sometimes. Just because I can't always pee it out doesn't mean I can't produce as much as the next man. I can fill it on a good day (and, then, that really is a good day).

Today I'm not optimistic. I heave myself to my feet, creaking audibly, and shuffle across the room. Shuffle, why do I shuffle? It seems to be expected of me. The oldest monk in the community should shuffle; it defines the vigour of the younger men. So I shuffle away and cross the room to the pot. I lift it by its two handles and carry it back, placing it carefully on the edge of the bed. I pull my shift up above my waist. I contemplate the swelling in my belly, the scraggy thinness of my thighs; Holy Father, I need to pee. The urgency, excited by the prospect of possible relief, becomes stronger.

I commence the ritual. Making a weak fist with my left hand I beat my swollen abdomen in a gentle rhythm, not too hard.

With my right hand I grasp the shrivelled foreskin of my penis and pull downwards, firmly, continuously. Sometimes it helps to try and straighten it.

Nothing happens.

I can hear the cicadas now. Their sound can cut through the singing in my old ears. The voices of angels, that's what the Abbot calls my singing, "You are blessed, Father, to hear the sound of the heavenly host." Maybe he's right but sometimes I wish they would shut up for a while.

But now all my focus is on my bladder, oblivious of sound. I try standing and nearly drop the pot. Still nothing. From where I am standing I can see through the high window to the outside world, I can see but what can I see; the roofs of the town, the harbour far below, the small church perched on the top of Mt Profitis Ilias, across the valley, high up in the dawn haze. I see all this but it cannot be incorporated. It is a jumble of unrelated images. The effect of a nearly bursting bladder is to disjoint my world. Existence is distilled down to the imperative of obtaining relief; only that.

I know that it will have to be the tubes. The boy collected them for me last week. My instructions were clear, only pick stems that have two hands breadths of length between knots. No stems that are thicker than your little finger, none that have been tainted with goat shit. Centuries ago, or so it seems, I cut these for whistles; playing simple tunes to the goats. That's what we did. All over the island.

He's a good boy. He collected a bundle for me, washed them well and brought a knife from the kitchens. I trimmed and cut until I had a selection of lengths and thicknesses. I pared down one end of each stalk so that there were no sharp edges, nothing to tear the inner linings. Now, for the first time, I have to use them. The urgency from below my waist has become a scream; long and unvaried.

I select a small, thin one. Standing up and crouching forward I peel back my foreskin. I spit on the end of the tube and

3

introduce it into the floppy opening at the end of my penis. I expect pain but, surprisingly, there is none. It slips in a short distance and then sticks. Now I do feel a pain, a sharp pain that seems to come from deep underneath me. I force the tube on until it has nearly disappeared inside. The pain increases.

Nothing flows. I pull the tube out and bright blood, not much of it, follows. I drop the tube to the floor.

It needs to be a longer, thicker one. I pick up the longest I have and repeat the procedure. This time there is length to spare when I reach the painful spot. I push hard but there is no progress, only an increase in pain.

I picture the anatomy of the bladder in my mind, I have seen the drawings, and pull on my foreskin with my left hand, steadying the tube with my right. I pull directly downwards and, at the same time, the tube moves up inside me. I bring the angle of penis, foreskin and tube to its former position and, blessings to the Great Pantokrator, a flow of urine emanates from the tube. A strong, increasing jet that seems as strong as the fountains of the Sultan's Palace in Bursa. I aim at the pot, for most of the deluge is flowing on to the floor of the cell. My aim is true and the pot is half full before the flow comes to an end. Gingerly I remove the blessed tube and stand upright. All the pain, the urgency, the disjointedness has gone. I look at the new day and see, with joy, that it is the only one available. No recriminations, no shadows of the past; no apprehensions for the future for there is no past, no future. I am redeemed into the immediacy of the present moment, a present that is now empty of meaning, empty of God. I am eternally glad of this moment.

I fall to my knees on the piss-covered floor and pray.

MEROS PROTON

Chapter 1
The Island. 1408

It was some time before he noticed that one of the goats was gone. The black and white kid; always an adventurous little bugger, the boy told himself. The little beast had lost its mother, taken by God knows what when her kid was not yet weaned. He had found her carcass down a ravine, torn apart and stinking in the high sun. Probably town dogs; they roamed in packs. Enough of them and they could bring down a nanny-goat with no difficulty. He had fed the kid with milk from the other females, succouring the little black and white runt until it grew into this independent, wayward adolescent.

The boy had been sitting on the rock for a while. Daydreaming and forgetting his charges in the tight, middle of the day heat. Now he was in trouble. It would mean another beating, returning with one kid less.

"And how do you think we live when you keep losing our goats, stupid layabout?" He could hear his Baba now, the roughened tone betraying no affection, the arm raised to beat him. A familiar enough event for the boy but, even so, and even though he did not recognise it, the violence was eating into his soul.

The rest of the flock were quiet. Not moving too much, gently cropping the desiccated thistles, impervious to the heat of the day. He could risk leaving them, it would be no more than a few minutes. He had lived with these animals for so long, he knew their ways. He knew they would not move from good grazing; instinctively he knew which way the missing kid would have gone.

He slipped off the rock and landed on the dusty path. Picking up his long stick he set off up the slope, heading for the skyline. The thistles scratched his ankles but he was used to that.

5

The thick leather of his sandals protected his soles, he was at ease. He knew his way around this island.

He reached the top of a rise. Now he was looking across a hidden valley to the sloping skyline. His eye followed it upwards to the small white block on the summit; familiar to him, that building. The Holy Kathisma and church of Profitis Ilias. Mama had told him about it. There was no hermit there nowadays. It was empty throughout the year.

He shifted his gaze to the valley and immediately spotted a movement. There he was, the little bastard. A flood of relief drenched him when he saw the black and white shape under a thorn bush, quietly grazing on the few remaining leaves. The landscape was barren, there were no trees, just rocks and scrub; precious little good land and therefore precious little wealth on this island.

He made his way down to the valley, careful not to alert the jumpy kid. Even though he had reared this little fellow the young goat was still capable of making a run for it. The boy slipped down behind a rock, only a few paces from the animal. He stilled his breathing and took stock. The slope behind the bush was steep, a goat could skip up it but not a boy. If he made a rush for the kid it would be up that slope with no difficulty.

It dawned on him that his options were limited. Either he left the kid where it was in the hope that it would return later or else he had to find some means to catch it. The former was attractive except that he knew that the chances of the little animal making it back alone were negligible. Almost certainly the foxes would have it, even an eagle would tackle a little creature like that. More than his affection for the beast he feared his father's reaction to the news that another valuable kid had gone. He felt tears in his eyes, frustration dissolved into fear and anger.

There was one chance. He reached in his pocket for the thin pipe. He had fashioned this himself. It had taken him days to complete but, in the end, he was proud of his handiwork. At first he could blow a few notes only. As time went on he could sound phrases that eventually led into tunes. Haunting tunes incorporating trills, falling intervals. Tunes of the country, tunes from the rocks, the wheeling crows, the calls of the goats.

He started to play. As the snatches of melody echoed around the valley he watched the kid. Its head rose from feeding, looking across to where the boy sat playing his pipe. And then it froze, as if the music of the pipe had reached its waywardness. He felt a surge of relief, but continued to play. After a few moments the animal took a few tentative steps towards the boy. It stopped in the full sunlight, sniffing the air, seeming to judge how safe it was to continue this move. Goats are very aware of danger, he thought; that caution and an ability to eat almost anything around was what made them so successful on this island.

The boy watched and continued to play. He searched for his most entrancing tunes. Music of attraction representing safety. Come, little goat, he thought. Come on. Save me from a belting, come on. He played on.

At first he did not notice. He was so absorbed with playing in the little truant that he failed to see movement on the skyline. The kid had stopped three paces from him. He stopped playing and at that moment he did see something on the ridge. He looked up. The sun was directly in his eyes. He lifted his arm to shield the light and screwed up his eyes.

The figures were silhouetted. They formed a line along the slope. Five of them. The one in the front was carrying a pole. Following on, at a laboured pace, were two other figures. They seemed to be dressed in black but the sun was in his eyes, he was unsure. The fourth one was not in black, he was sure of that. Dressed like his father, like any other man on the island who was not a monk. He was carrying something. It was rectangular, not large, it was difficult to make it out; sunshine glistened off gold but that moment of iridescence was soon gone.

For a brief interval a cloud covered the sun. It was then that the boy could make out the fifth figure. He was some distance away but his long, grey beard, his clothing, the hat that he wore, all

7

these were recognisable to the boy who had spent all of his short life in the shadow of the Monastery, who had been taken to the Holy Week and Easter celebrations every year since ever he could remember. It was the Abbot of the Monastery of Ayios Ioánnis Theologos, the Monastery that dominated the island from its perch on the hill opposite. There was no mistaking him.

The boy stood rock-still as he watched the slow progress of this strange procession, moving steadily up the slope. Sounds of a chant floated down to him in the still afternoon air. Chants like those that he heard in church though he could not make them out clearly enough to identify them. And then he did; *Kýrie eléison*, no mistaking that. 'Lord have mercy'. What were they doing?

Time passed, though he was oblivious of it, as the procession ascended the steep slope to the summit. They were heading for the white, block shaped building that was the church of Profitis Ilias. He had often been in that church. It was little more than a shed. A rough bench along one wall, a primitive ikonostasis and little else apart from a worn fresco on the side wall. They only had one service a year in that church; on the commemoration day, attended by the Abbot, a few monks and the occasional man from the town.

But, it was not that day today, he was sure of that. What was happening? The monk in front lowered his crucifix (the boy could now see what the pole was) and ducked into the church, the others followed. They disappeared.

He felt a softness against his leg. It was the kid, muzzling up to the one human that it knew it could trust. The boy slipped a braid around the neck of the small creature and breathed a sigh of relief. He became aware that, whatever it was that was happening in that small church, the participants would not welcome being observed by a scruffy goatherd. Gently tugging on the braid he led the kid back to the herd. He was relieved to see that the rest had not wandered off in his absence, With a twitch of his long stick he drove them down to the path, leading them towards the small town.

Again a meandering chant drifted down to him on the gentle breeze. He looked back. The sun had shifted a bit and he could see them more clearly now. Coming down the ridge, the same procession but without the object. The man, no longer encumbered by his load, was helping the Abbot over the rough ground. Whatever his former burden was he had left it behind.

The boy turned back down the track. Soon he reached the shed where the goats were housed. It was a tumble-down affair made of rough hewn stones. Grass sprouted from the roof. Inside the stench would have been unbearable to most people; he barely noticed it.

It was nowhere near nightfall but he needed to leave them secure. His Baba was out with the fishing boat and would not be back until after dark. He closed the latch on the shed and turned back up the path.

It was hot for an ascent. No shelter, no shade; those people must have sweated in those robes. But the boy was driven on by his curiosity, he was oblivious of discomfort. It was a rocky climb to the summit, a jagged ascent.

Soon he was standing in front of the small church. He found that he was panting, now he began to feel the heat. No shelter up here; poised on a pinnacle like a stylite there was no escape from the sun. Sweat was running off him, he felt light-headed, the white building seemed to sway on its rock foundation. Now it was more than curiosity. Whatever was inside this church, whatever it was that had been carried up the mountain by that strange procession began to assume an overriding importance for him. It had become vital that he should unravel this strange secret. At that moment more vital to his life than anything else. Not that he ever thought much about his life. What was there to think about? The same most days, tending the goats, milking the nannies, delivering the kids, putting the billies, stinking of lust and copulation, to tup the females in season. He never imagined it could be different. Even his father's beltings made a change from the sameness of his days.

9

But now there was a mystery. He had to look so he took a few steps forward. Now he was standing in the entrance to the church; he pushed open the door.

The light overtook him and illuminated the far wall. He stepped over the threshold and screwed up his eyes for a few seconds. A trick he had learnt when he lost goats in a cave. Opening his eyes slowly his sight was adapted to the shade. He looked around, careful not to look into the bright light flooding through the door.

It appeared that nothing had changed. No sign of a rectangular object. Nowhere. He scrabbled around behind the ikonostasis. Nothing there at all.

The church was empty. He sat down on the dirt floor; mystified.

The afternoon sun begins to lose its intensity as it sinks towards the skyline. My fingers, as if they have an existence of their own, scan the fibres of the net, searching out breaks. So many things can damage a net; jagged stones on the bottom, floating debris, even rough handling by the fishermen. Not that I am like that, I have been taught to be careful. The school of hard belts, that's my Baba.

"Ioánnis, you have to learn" I have learnt all right.

I can work without watching my fingers, leaving them to get on with the job. Calloused fingers, more like an old man than the boy that I am. My eyes scan the harbour, restful in the familiar scene. It is well sheltered, this harbour. The land at its head takes a wide sweep round and that creates a protected entrance like an encompassing arm. The Meltemi can blow up a wild sea around the island but there's little more than a gentle swell in the harbour. The sun is shimmering on the water now. Descending fast these summer days, time to go.

I pack up the net. Not fully repaired but it will do. So we lose a few little fish through the holes, there are plenty more. This has been a good year for fishing. We've all eaten well.

It's a good enough job, I suppose. Three years now since Father gave the goats to my little brother Stefanos and put me to the fishing. God's only trade, he calls it. "Ioánnis, you're following the disciples. The profession of saints!" He laughs uproariously at that, every time he says it, which is often. I suppose that's why I have his name, Ioánnis. After Ayios Ioánnis, son of Thunder, the disciple that our Lord loved, the old man who was exiled to the cave up the hill, here on our very island, the venerated evangelist that gives his name to the Monastery high up above the town.

11

That's what they told us about him, the monks. I wonder how one man can accomplish so much but I would never dare to question them. In the severity of their holiness they never appear receptive to any dissent. I keep my doubts to myself.

I stack the net in the bow of the kaiki We shall be out before dawn so I must have everything ready. Once I am sure that I have forgotten nothing I set off for home.

Why doesn't my father get us a home down by the shore? Every day we have to climb up to our house in the town and it's a long, tiring climb. All the other fishermen live near the quay in a jumble of makeshift huts, stinking of fish and latrines. Perhaps I do understand why that has no appeal but we could live a little further from the shore and still be close by. We do well from the fishing, he could afford it. But Baba says we have to be up in the town in order to be near the Monastery. They buy most of our fish and so most of our income comes from them.

I put my shoulder to the donkey cart, loaded with the day's catch slipping and sliding in the wickerwork baskets. The donkey needs one tap with my stick and he's away. He knows the route. I walk behind, quietly.

We meander between small fields, fertile here at the foot of the hill. Soon we reach the start of the paved path. Baba says that this path is five hundred years old.

"Built by the monks, they say." He spits and curses, "built by us poor peasants more like, not those lazy bastards." I hate it when Baba talks like that. I think he ought to respect the monks. I would never dare say anything though. That would be too dangerous.

It is a good wide path which zigzags its way to the very gates of the Monastery. The stones are polished smooth by centuries of use. Sometimes I have to help the cart over the steps but they are spaced far apart and none of them is too steep. Tall eucalyptus trees on either side of the path provide shade and aroma until we meet the change of scent which marks the pine plantations. It is cool here in the shade of the trees. I stop the

12

donkey and rest. There is a stream running through the little wood so I fill a small bucket with water and take it to the donkey. The sound of his drinking is all that I hear.

Emerging from the wood I see the Cave, the cave of Ayios Ioánnis Theologos. There is a low protecting wall, painted white, in front of the entrance. Small medallions and roughly painted ikons are hung on the vegetation around. The Cave of the Apokalypse is what Father Ignatios calls it. Holy ground.

We take the steep bend in the path and leave the Cave behind. By now I can see the houses of the town and, above and dominating, the grey walls of the fortress-like Monastery. They rise from the houses like an apparition. A solid, well-protected apparition. A holy apparition. The Monastery of Ayios Ioánnis Theologos, the same John that shivered in his cave of exile, the same John that had fantastical visions. Father Ignatios has told me about them, revelations he calls them. They have pictures of them in the Monastery but I have never been allowed to see them. They are protected, sealed up by the grey stone walls, secure.

I turn a bend and there is home. Mother is sitting under the olive tree shelling peas. The old familiar smell of goat wafts across from the shed. Stefanos has brought them in early today. He is sitting on the ground, whittling away at a green stick. Eleni is playing in the dust, disturbing the scrabbling chicks and perturbing the mother hen. No sign of Baba.

Mother smiles at me. "A good catch?"

"Not bad. Five baskets full. Where's Baba?"

"He's out. I haven't seen him since this morning."

I need him to tell me how much of the catch to sell. I have done it myself in the past but he always grumbles. "You could get more if you sold it to Stavros; you'll ruin us if you go on like this." Somehow never quite pleasing him. In any case we always sell the first three baskets to the Monastery. I set off up the lane.

The monks never like me to come in to the Monastery. The business is done at the gate. The steward comes down and is fingering the fish. "Not bad, Ioánnis. A good catch today," but he

13

never gives me any more for it. I cannot bargain, I feel intimidated under these grey walls. It would be like making a deal with God, a figure almost as intimidating as my Baba.

Stavros, who runs the taverna in the town, takes the rest. We do a deal which should satisfy Baba. I like Stavros, he has a twinkle in his eye and he always give me a cheese pie to take home, not that it goes far once I have shared it with Stefanos and Eleni, but it is a kind gesture.

"Markos at home?" Markos, his son, and I are old friends, way back to my days as a goatherd. Stavros has a large flock and Markos is a natural when it comes to goats. He taught me all I know; where to find strays, how to deal with injuries when the stupid beasts fall down ravines. Many are the times that we have reduced dislocations, splinted fractures and saved valuable animals that otherwise would have ended up in the pot. But nowadays I have graduated to fishing whilst Markos, in the absence of a younger brother, is stuck with the goats.

"Not home yet. I'll tell him you've been."

I make my way back down the narrow paved streets and unhitch the donkey from the cart. He trots around the small field, shits and lets out a bellowing bray, glad to be free of the burden. I've never liked donkeys. Goats are far more intelligent. For one thing billy goats never behave like our stupid donkey, frequently wandering around the field with an embarrassingly long erection dangling from his hindquarters and never a female in sight. At least the billy goat will wait until the last moment before producing his erection, ready to stuff it into the receptive female. I hope I'm more like a goat than a donkey though there are times when I wake at night, mystified by strange sensations, the cover lifted like an Arab's tent by my unexpected tent pole.

"Ioánnis?" It is Markos, reeking of goat, "you coming out?"

"I'm going out, Mama, Markos is here."

"The meal will be ready in an hour, Ioánnis. Your Baba should be home by then."

"I won't be late." I sling an arm around Markos's shoulders and we stride off down the lane. Eleni is calling after us but I do not catch what she is saying, choosing not to turn back to find out.

Soon we leave the town and take a path through the scrub. It winds around the head of a valley and then up to a ridge. From here we can watch the sea on three sides of the island. In the far distance, illuminated by the reddening sun we can see the mountains of the mainland. I have never sailed that far. Baba has warned me, it is far too dangerous. There are corsairs with fearsome reputations and the mainland is now the territory of the Ottoman Turks. Father Ignatios, our local priest, has told me of this; bit by bit they have swallowed up the Byzantine Empire. Only the centre, Constantinople and a few nearby territories, are left.

Not that the corsairs have bothered us, though. We go on fishing and living off the land. Nothing interferes with that. Baba says that the Monastery does all right. They have three trading ships. I can see one now, tied up in the harbour down below us. Large, round, ships with triangular sails that carry plenty of goods to trade.

"And the lucky bastards pay no taxes, just because they're fucking monks" my father would say. Not that he can complain. He pays no tax on the fish that we drag out of the plentiful waters around the island. Easy money, to my mind, but I would never dare say it to Baba. I may be fifteen and taller than he is but he is still ready to give me a beating for insolence.

I turn back from the view, Markos is sitting on a rock, the sun is sinking fast. Behind him the ridge runs steeply up to the summit. Mt Profitis Ilias, the hill from which the prophet Elijah was lifted into the heavens, so Father Ignatios says. A considerate old prophet, though. At the last minute he remembered to drop his mantle down to his successor, Elisha. I guess he wouldn't be wanting it in heaven. No heat, no cold up there. No need for a cloak.

I could never understand why the old prophet was here, on the island, when he was taken up. Surely he was over there in the

Holy Land, roughing up the prophets of Baal and lighting fires without a tinder. I am nervous about asking Father Ignatios. He is such a gentle old man, I feel I can't upset him.

Markos has taken to throwing stones at the lizards.

"Come on, Markos, I'll race you to the top." I point to the Kathisma, the white building on the point of the hill. It's quite a way.

"Are you crazy?"

"Are you chicken? Come on." I am already running up the path whilst Markos follows me, complaining but laughing. He can't keep up with me now that I have grown as tall as a man. It's cool now and the run is no effort.

We reach the top, panting. It is only then that I remember the last time that I was here, that strange procession. I stand still, staring at the door of the small chapel, trying to recall. It was so long ago.

And then the feeling returns. The feeling that, somehow or another, what happened here is important to my life. The feeling disturbs me, turning over something that is deep down within me, rocking the stability that I imagined had been there.

I turn and stare across the valley at the Monastery. It's powerful, grey walls seem even more forbidding in this light. Is that where God lives? Bastioned by those solid walls, impenetrable and unmovable?

The sun is well down into the sea by now. There is a chill in the air.

"Let's have a look inside, Ioánnis." I am hesitant. He steps up and pushes on the door. It is locked. Without knowing why I am relieved. I want to go.

"Let's go home." I am already thirty paces down the track before he follows. I can see smoke, rising like lazy serpents from the households. Meals prepared, men returning. Predictable, dependable, untroubled life.

I run towards it.

Chapter 3

As expected Baba grumbles.

"The Monastery only gave you this?" He holds up the small bag of coins. "You should have asked for twice as much."

"I tried to get more out of them but they wouldn't have it. They always give us the same."

"What use are you to me, stupid Ioánnis? We shall be ruined if you go on like this." I am tempted to tell him to sell the fish himself if he thinks he can do better but previous experience prompts me to keep quiet. To talk like that to my Baba will only earn me a belt.

"I'm really sorry, Baba. I'll try and do better next time." He grunts and turns.

This is how it is. Always an air of tension, living with a threatening volcano. He is the same with Stefanos, though I have never seen him beat my brother, and he has no time for little Eleni. Worse than that is my suspicion that he beats Mama; I have seen the marks. She tries to hide them but I can still see weals on her neck that she cannot conceal with the rough scarf that she wears.

I can talk to Markos. "Does your Baba hit you, Markos?"

He looks shocked. "No. Never. He never has." We are sitting on the edge of the drinking trough in the main square. Stavros's taverna is over in the corner. He has a few customers.

"Why do you ask, Ioánnis?"

Now I wish I hadn't. "Oh, it's nothing. Forget I asked."

"Come on, Ioánnis. Something's on your mind."

I stir the water with my stick, staring at the ripples. There is a long pause. I am aware of the gentle murmurings of the drinkers across the square, a donkey brays somewhere down below us, flies are buzzing around a small heap of goat turd. It is the hottest, and the quietest, time of day.

"Would your Baba hit a woman? Ever?"

"Course not. What a question? What's up with you, Ioánnis?" He reaches across to give me a cuff on my arm. He is fooling about but I catch hold of his wrist and hold it so tight that he winces. I look him straight in the eye. My voice is hushed.

"My Baba beats me. He uses his belt." Markos looks shocked but there is more I have to tell him, "and I know he beats Mama." Markos's eyes widen at this, I look away. "I hate him, Markos, I wish he were dead. I'm frightened that one day I shall kill him."

Markos's jaw has dropped now. I lower my gaze and loosen my grip on his wrist. He puts his arm around my shoulders, "I'm sorry, Ioánnis, I never realised."

A shout comes from the taverna. "Markos! I need your help over here. Come on boy."

Markos squeezes my shoulder, as if there is much more that he wants to say, then stands up. "Coming, Baba." He runs across the square leaving me on my own. I know that Markos and his younger sister Anna love their father but then Stavros is a gentle, mild man. My Baba thinks he is a fool. He says he allows himself to be short-changed. Baba thinks that is a weakness but is very ready to exploit it.

I can talk to Father Ignatios about Baba. The old man listens patiently but he doesn't say much. Sometimes he will say "Ioánnis, he is your father and you owe him the same respect and reverence that you owe your heavenly Father. Remember, even when he behaves in a way that offends and hurts you, that these are failings in him. They can be redeemed though our Lord Jesus Christ. Remember your Baba in your prayers and never lose hope for his, and your, redemption." From anyone else such advice would seem pious nonsense. From Father Ignatios it has enough wisdom to nearly convince me.

Yet how can my Baba be equated with my heavenly Father. Surely God would not allow my Baba to behave as he does. I know that I can love God but how do I love my violent, angry Baba?

Father Ignatios is a gentle man. He lives in the Convent of the Evangelismos which lies down a narrow valley by the sea. He has his own cell in the convent which he allowed me to see once; empty except for a bed, an ikon and a washstand. He is the priest to the convent and spiritual advisor to the nuns. Markos has told me that they make ikons in that convent. The nuns are known to be greatly gifted in their skills. Their ikons are sent far and wide, even as far as Constantinople; from a tiny convent on this small island to the great Imperial City.

Father Ignatios usually takes the services in the Church of Ayios Ioánnis Prodromos, near our house. He used to tease me with this name.

"Ioánnis the Forerunner, that's you. Always running everywhere" This was in the days when I was a goatherd. I had to run in those days, catching up with the strays, rounding up the escapees. Sure-footed over the rough ground.

Mama takes us to church there, all three of us. Baba never comes. The service is long and Stefanos and I stand throughout. Mama and Eleni can sit for part of the service.

Stavros, Markos's father, is the cantor. I like the sound of his light, high voice. The sound of it fills the small space, intermingling with the smoke of incense that Father Ignatios burns with unrestricted abandon.

"This is our prayer, floating to heaven," he would say. It makes Eleni sneeze.

Sometimes we sing as well, mostly *Kýrie eléison* and *Amen* but delivered with gusto, nonetheless.

But it is Father Ignatios's homilies that I like best. He will take the gospel passage of the day and set off on a journey that often seems as if it is a digression. Today it is the Gospel story of the wedding at Cana.

19

"Dear children, imagine, if you can, this wedding feast. The bride and groom and all the guests gathered in a small house. How crowded it must be. I expect there are chickens running around the floor," (it could have been our house,) "dogs, too. Everyone is happy." He pauses for a moment; I wonder if he has lost his way. At times like these he seems like a very old man. But no, he is off again.

"We are not told by the Gospel writer, the Blessed Ioánnis Theologos how it came about that Our Lord was present at this wedding. It seems that no one knew who he really was; no one except the Blessed Theotokos, Maria his mother, the God-bearer.

"So when the wine runs out - that's a familiar state of affairs, is it not?" he chuckles into his beard, "when the wine runs out his mother immediately goes to him. Not because she knows what he might do. At this stage she knows nothing of his miraculous powers, they have yet to be revealed. But she does know that he is the Messiah, the Christos. She was told that by the Archangel, thirty years before that bibulous wedding. And she believed it.

"So what does Our Lord say? 'My time has not yet come' Almost irritated by his mother's attempts to make him reveal himself. Nevertheless he acts. And so the party is saved when twelve pitchers of the best wine are produced. Almost certainly a good party with that quantity of wine on top of what had already been drunk." He chuckles again.

"So why was our blessed Saviour's first miracle such an unconventional, even an irreverent one? This was not raising from the dead, healing from the palsy, even feeding the five thousand. This was making the party go with a swing."

There is absolute silence at this irreverence on the part of the old priest. I hear a donkey bray in the distance.

"But remember, dear children, that this is a story of Ayios Ioánnis Theologos. It does not appear in any of the other three Gospels. What does that tell us? It is a story with a meaning, it is there for a definite reason. The Blessed Evangelist is using the

20

language of a story to tell us of a truth, a truth much more significant than how to organise a good wedding feast. Ayios Ioánnis is creating language to tell of a truth that is hard to apprehend with language. A truth about God's love, poured upon us like the new wine of Cana. That is how Ayios Ioánnis speaks to us, in stories."

He ends and shuffles back behind the ikonostasis. The service continues but I cannot follow it. My mind is tumbling over with the words of his homily. Usually homilies are straightforward and boring. A recitation of what was in scripture with no reflection nor interpretation. Father Ignatios has surprised and shocked me and I do not understand. I am confused by this talk of creating language. Up until now I had been taught that Holy Scripture was the unalterable word of God, that Ioánnis and the other Evangelists were the means by which God spread his word to humans. Now Father Ignatios seems to be suggesting that they were creators themselves, that they made it up. This is very shocking and, whilst it disturbs me, at the same time I find it exciting. I am aroused by a feeling that is almost physical. I can feel my heart racing in my chest. This is a new feeling.

I try to talk to Mama about it but it becomes apparent that she was not listening.

"Eleni was fretful, Ioánnis. I could not pay attention to what he was saying. Was it interesting?" I do not answer.

As I walk back home I am overtaken by Markos. He puts his arm around my shoulder and kicks at a pebble in the path. His sister Anna is with him. She is two years younger than Markos and me with silken, straight dark hair and dark eyes. She wears a long skirt decorated with small, highly coloured metallic discs and a deep blue blouse. She is smiling.

"Hello, Ioánnis. What did you think of Father Ignatios?"

I look at Markos, nervous about how to reply. He seems more absorbed in kicking pebbles. I move away from him. Now I am walking beside Anna.

21

"I am not sure. I was confused by what he said. I have never heard that sort of thing before." She laughs and her delight is apparent.

"Neither have I but isn't it wonderful. I always thought that was a silly story but dear old Father Iggy has changed that."

"Did it make sense to you?"

"I think so. It's certainly better than the old ideas about Ayios Ioánnis and his gospel." I ponder this, remembering that it was just down the road from here that the Blessed Theologian wrote that other incomprehensible book, his Revelation.

"You know what he used to say when he was an old man?" I jerk out of my reverie.

"I'm sorry. Who used to say?"

She laughs again. "Wake up, Ioánnis. What Ioánnis Theologos used to say when he was very old and living in Ephesus."

I shake my head. I have no idea.

"Father Iggy told me. They would ask him for a sermon or some other words of wisdom. All he would say was 'Little children. Love one another.' Just that. Nothing else."

She has stopped walking and stands on the path in front of me; facing and staring straight at me. Her legs are set slightly apart, hands on her hips and her lips are opened a fraction. She holds her head on one side as she smiles at me. The light in her eyes reawakens that feeling of excitement that I had experienced when listening to Father Ignatios's homily; yet this is a different form of arousal. I am seeing her, no longer as a girl, Markos's little sister, but as someone quite different, a young woman. A woman excited by the same things that excite me, a desirable woman. I have never seen that in Anna before and it confuses me. The depth of her gaze discomforts me.

In a moment she turns and runs down the path after the retreating back of her brother. I remain motionless until I hear a slow footfall behind me. I turn, it is Father Ignatios. He is smiling. It is as if he knows what is happening. He might know but I don't.

22

That look occupies my head for days afterwards. I know of the frivolity of other village girls, giggling and talking behind their hands. They flirt with Markos and he is always ready to respond. I cannot. It is not what I want. This encounter with Anna was something quite different, more serious, more challenging. Quite unexpected.

I am out in the bay, hauling in the nets. The sun is low in the sky, moving from gold to red. Reflections bounce off the wavelets, matching the glistening of the fishes as the net drags them from the water, emptying them flapping in resignation on to the deck of the kaiki. I work automatically for my mind is on Anna and that look. Why does it discomfort me? What was it that Father Ignatios could see? She is different from all the other girls, more serious, wiser. A kind of wisdom that I want to share

I have landed all the fish and stowed the net on board. Just as I start to row back to the shore, I hear a call.

"Ioánnis! Ioánnis!" Up on the headland there is a small figure calling and waving. The sun, now near the horizon, is right behind the calling figure making it difficult for me to see who it is.

"Ioánnis! Come quickly." I recognise the caller now. It is Stefanos. His small figure is jumping and waving, urging a reply.

"Stefanos! Is that you? What's the trouble? Why all the fuss?" My voice echoes around the small bay.

"Ioánnis, come quickly. It's Eleni." He turns on his heel and runs down to the shoreline. With a few strong pulls on the oars I ground the kaiki on to the beach. Stefanos is frantically pulling on the bow. Two old fishermen come across and between us we heave the heavily laden boat up the shingle beach. Stefanos is panting.

"You must come now. Mama sent me. Come on." He is pulling at my sleeve.

"Hold on, what about the fish? I have to unload the boat." One of the fishermen steps forward and spits on the ground.

"Leave that to us, boy. We'll pack 'em up." I hesitate, unsure as to whether I should trust these men but Stefanos is pleading.

"It's Eleni. She has fallen over the cliff edge. She's badly hurt. Baba is nowhere to be found. Mama said to fetch you. Ioánnis, come quickly!"

I turn to the fishermen. I know them well enough. "Thanks, I'll be back later." They nod, almost unwilling to accept my thanks, and set to, loading the fish into baskets.

Stefanos sets a fast pace up the paved road that takes us up to the town. I can just about keep up but he has the agility of a goatherd so it is a struggle. I know the cliff edge that he means, where the land falls away at the end of the town. I've lost goats down there in the past. It's a fall of about twenty cubits but the ground at the base is soft earth and vegetation which is fortunate. Nevertheless it's a long way for a small girl to fall.

Now we are running through the narrow streets of the town, all arranged in an irregular pattern so there is much ducking around corners, running up steps, not many straight lines. Baba says they were built all higgledy-piggledy like this to slow up raiders who come to attack the Monastery. Not that any have ever breached its vast, grey walls in the three hundred years since they were built.

As we approach the cliff edge I am relieved to hear a cry. It could have been a young goat but I recognise it. It is Eleni; in pain but conscious enough to be able to cry out.

We peer over the edge of the cliff. Mama is there and beside her is Eleni, lying awkwardly and crying in a mixture of pain and fear. Mama glances up and a look of relief floods her face when she sees me.

"Oh, thank the Lord, Ioánnis. You're here." I know this cliff edge well. There is a quick way down if you are nimble and fearless. I am down at the base in a few seconds, Stefanos close behind me.

I kneel down beside Eleni. She looks at me in fear. I need to calm her. It is the same as the goats. Calm them first.

"All right, Little Elly. You're going to be all right. Don't be frightened." It isn't the words that I use that matter, it's the tone of voice. I try hard to sound confident, unhurried. It works. She visibly relaxes.

I move to check her for injuries. Mama intervenes. "Careful, Ioánnis. Do you think we should touch her? I've sent for Lula."

Lula. I know this Lula. She regards herself as the healer in the town. She uses herbs and potions in an indiscriminate manner. She does not impress me. When I had the mumps she prescribed a poultice of fermented vine leaves and goats' dung. I can still smell it to this day.

"Don't worry, Mama. I won't hurt her. I know what I'm doing."

I turn back to little Eleni; it is clear that she is breathing satisfactorily, enough to produce her cries.

"Do you know where you are, Helly?"

"Yes" her voice was weak but clear, "at the cliff."

"What happened?"

"I was standing at the top and Jason ran into my legs and knocked me over." Jason is one of our livelier dogs, a stupid cur.

"Can you remember falling?"

"Yes, yes I can."

"Have you been awake all the time?"

"Yes."

"Are you sure?"

"Yes. I'm sure." She speaks more confidently now. I survey her obvious injuries. She has a large gash across her scalp. It is bleeding profusely, some of the blood has run down over her face but I know that it will not bleed for long, scalp wounds rarely do. She is holding her left wrist with her right hand. It does not look too misshapen at first glance.

But her right leg is bent up under her at a peculiar angle. When I touch it she screams. Mother is upset, she snaps "Ioánnis, be careful. You'll hurt her."

I have seen this often enough with goats, the dislocated joint. Further inspection confirms it, Eleni has dislocated her right hip. I will have to work fast. Very soon the muscles will tighten up and then it will be impossible to do what I am about to do.

"Mama. We have to lie her down. Lay your shawl out on the ground." The earth is soft under the cliff here, It is comfortable enough to lie on. Mama complies but still looks suspiciously at me. I ignore her, time is short.

"Stefanos, I want you to come beside her and support her pelvis. Put your arm around her and hold her firmly. Don't be afraid. Just there. That's right." I show him how to do it then slowly straighten Eleni's leg at the knee. She whimpers a little but does not protest. I slip my hand up the outside of her thigh until I can feel the distorted shape. The top of her thigh bone is in the wrong place.

"Now, Eleni, for a short moment this will hurt but afterwards you will feel much better." I try to sound confident. I've done this on goats, within a few minutes they are skipping about again. But my own little sister, that is altogether different. Mama turns to me, fear in her eyes.

"No, Ioánnis! You mustn't do this. You'll hurt her. You don't know what you are doing." I look her in the eyes. I know she wants to protect her little girl but we cannot wait. Certainly not wait for old Lula with her shitty poultices.

"Mama. Hold her hand and don't watch." I take hold of Eleni's lower leg and steadily and surely start to pull; nothing jerky just a long continuous pull. Eleni is quiet. I can feel the muscles resisting but they are not in full spasm yet. I increase the pull, harder and harder. Eleni screams and as she does so I feel the

26

clunk as the round head of the thigh bone slips back into its socket. I release the pressure slowly, bit by bit, until I can lay her leg out straight.

"Well done, Eleni. It's over." I am rewarded with a weak smile. She is a brave girl. Mama makes no more protest while I look her over for any more injuries. There is a simple fracture of her left wrist. I send Stefanos back to the house to get some linen strips to bind it up. There appear to be no broken ribs, as far as I can tell. Mama produces a small white scarf. We use it to staunch the flow of blood from her scalp.

"We shall have to carry her home, Mama. We need to make a stretcher." Stavros is with us by this time, Markos as well.

"I can get something" he volunteers. He and Markos are soon back with an old door, padded out with blankets and cushions. Having strapped up the little girl's wrist we lay her on the makeshift stretcher and, with one of us on each corner, make our way back up to home. Mama is walking beside me, holding Eleni's good hand.

"Will she ever walk again, Ioánnis, it looked so bad?"

"I think she will." Her look of surprised admiration shows me that a change has occurred. The change from deep suspicion of my competence to a trust that is almost too unquestioning. All catalysed by a single act. For a short moment I feel like a man.

We reach the house. Outside is the hunched figure of old Lula. She hurries towards the small child huddled on the old door. "Come here, little one. Let me get at you. I have balm for your wounds."

Suddenly she is interrupted. Mama has turned to face her, fire in her eyes. "Get away, you old charlatan!" she hisses. I can see her fists clenched, "and take away your revolting potions. You are not needed here."

"Holy Mother of God. Are you mad? She is badly hurt. She needs help."

"We have all the help we need. Lula. Just go, please." The old woman looks about her, sizing up the situation. She is remarkably astute.

"It's the boy, isn't it. Are you going to rely on a mere boy, who only knows about goats?"

"Yes!" Mama's face stiffens. "that's about it" I cannot look at the old lady. She turns on her heel and shuffles away. Eleni is whimpering.

"Mama, let's get her into the house."

We set up a bunk for Eleni in the main room, near the fire. Wrapped up and warm she seems better. I notice that she moves her right leg a little. I have been out to collect some herbs. I know the ones that injured goats instinctively go for. Perhaps they will help Eleni.

Suddenly the door crashes open. Sunlight floods in until the frame is filled with the shape of Baba.

"Ioánnis!" he bellows. "Where are you, you stupid, lazy piece of shit." I can smell the drink on him from across the room. He strides over and grabs me by the throat. His fingers hold me so tight that I nearly faint.

"Where's the bloody fish?" I try to speak but can only feebly gesticulate with my right arm. I try to point to Eleni.

"Yiorgos, leave the boy alone," my mother is on her feet. "Eleni has been hurt and he came to help. I sent for him."

"So how long has this little cur been a doctor? What's wrong with Lula?"

"Lula cannot do anything for Eleni. Ioánnis has put her right. See for yourself."

There is a moment of stillness in the small, smoky room. Baba lets go of my throat. His head is slowly swinging from side to side. He appears not to see Eleni.

I don't like the signs. I've not seen this behaviour before but it frightens me. I call out in warning, "Mama!" but at the same moment his right arm is swinging out in a wide curve. His hand is open so that when he hits Mama on the side of the head there is a

28

loud, sharp clap. The force of the blow is brutal. Mama makes no sound but staggers back and then falls to her knees. I see the look in Baba's eyes, unfocussed, dead. I know that this is dangerous. Stefanos is crying, hunched in the corner.

Baba steps forward and grasps Mama by her long hair. Now she cries out and Eleni screams. Roughly, he pulls her across the room and throws her to the floor. She lies still. She does not try to escape. It is as if this were a well-rehearsed routine, familiar to the two of them. This scenario has to be completed to allow his anger to pass. I am desperate now. I am not going to stand by and allow this vicious performance to continue.

I run at Baba, fists flailing. At first he appears not to notice me. His gaze is fixed on the whimpering figure of Mama, rolled up on the floor. But I persist which makes him turn towards me.

"Baba. Leave her alone. She has done nothing. Stop it right now."

He stares at me and then roars, "Get out of here! Get out and take your feeble brother with you."

"I'm not going 'til you stop. Stop it, now!"

"Are you ordering me about in my own house, you good-for-nothing young cur. I'll see to you!" With that he strides across the room and grabs the large leather belt that hangs across a wooden chair in the corner. I know this belt. It is too familiar.

He reaches out to grasp me. His large hand grabs my right arm and twists it behind my back. At the same time, he forces me face down on to the table. I hear the rush of air as the belt swings in a wide sweep before it hits me, hard, across the top of my thighs. The pain shocks me and I do not have time to move before the wide belt swings down once more and hits me on the buttocks this time. I cry out.

As I do I see Mama rising from the floor. She moves slowly, hesitantly, dazed by the blows. The pattern of events is altered. With a great roar Baba charges across the room, his attention turned from me to her. He aims a huge kick and his heavy, workaday boot hits her in the shins, just below the knee.

29

She collapses like a bundle of rags. He is aiming a second kick to her head so, despite the searing pain in my buttocks and legs, I throw myself at him from behind. My fingers scrabble to find his eyes. I must have reached them because he blunders into the table and crashes it over. There is a sound of broken pottery.

Perhaps it the smashing sound, perhaps it would have happened anyway but the anger seems to siphon out of him. He shrugs me off and strides for the door. He says nothing. In a moment he has gone.

Mama gets up from the floor, bleeding from a wound over her eye. She stumbles across to comfort Eleni who is crying silently. Stefanos comes out of the corner and helps me put the table upright again. We clear up the shards of broken pots. Nobody says anything but inside I burn with fury. Now I feel murderous towards my Baba It's all very well for Father Ignatios to say what he said. He has not witnessed what I have witnessed. My father is evil, there can be no salvation for a man who does such things. I can never forgive him. I don't even think of forgiveness. My anger is an all-enveloping passion; I am shocked at its strength.

I think that Mama can read my mind. "Don't feel bad at him, Ioánnis. He has worries and then he takes to the drink. He doesn't mean it."

I cannot believe it. Here is Mama, unable to stand upright, blood rolling down her face to congeal with the dust of the floor, excusing him? I cannot believe it.

"Mama. Are you crazy? He will kill you one day. Why do you put up with it?" Her gaze drops, she looks ashamed. "I will never let him do that to you again." I muster as much false confidence as I can. "I will never let him do it."

She hobbles over to me and puts her arms around me. She is sobbing. I hold her firmly, aware of how much things have changed in the space of but two hours. I doubt whether I am ready for that change.

Chapter 5

On the following morning the sun is just clear of the sea when it finds me slipping down the narrow streets of the town. Few people are up this early. I seek out the church of Ayios Ioánnis Prodromos. The door is closed. There is no one around

I spoke to the old fishermen last night. They had packed my catch into the baskets. Three of them they had marked for the Monastery and the others they sold down on the quay. I thanked them as they handed over the money.

"How is little Eleni?"

"She was badly hurt but I think she will recover."

Did Yiorgos come home?" They seemed to know more than I thought they did.

"Yes." I was not going to elaborate.

The older of the two spoke. "He's a wild man when he has the drink in him."

I avoided his gaze, slipped them a few coins and retreated. This was not a conversation that I wanted. As I walked away I could feel my ears redden. I knew they were watching me but I would not turn around. It was enough to have a violent, drunken father without the added hurt of the whole island knowing it.

But an uncomfortable thought has crept up on me. I have seen something different, something far more shocking. It feels as if I have watched the enactment of a well-worn drama. A violent, sacrificial drama that has become the only means to bring the devil out of him. Each stage, each movement as clear as if it had been rehearsed to perfection. The thought sickens me. Surely she would not collude in this way.

Last night I found my bed as soon as I returned from the quay. Eleni and Stefanos were both asleep. Mama was busying

31

herself with the pots in the kitchen. She had a large bruise over her left eye but the laceration had stopped bleeding. She kissed me as I went to bed.

"Sleep well, my boy. It's all over." But for how long, I thought.

Later I heard Baba return. The two of them were talking in low tones. Soon they went to bed as well. Within minutes I heard the rhythmic creaking of the bed frame, the ursine grunts from Baba and the gasps from Mama before silence descended. All familiar to me.

I push on the door of the church and it opens. The sun illuminates the dull gold of the ikonostasis. I stand at the entrance. Floating dust particles delineate the slash of the sun's rays. The scent of old incense is comforting. There is no one about.

I sit on one of the benches by the back wall. From here I have a clear view of the ikon of Ioánnis Prodomos. I still myself, control my breathing until I am attuned to my surroundings. Ayios Ioánnis is looking straight at me. His hair is straggly and long, suggestive of a life outdoors, in the desert; sleeping under thorn bushes, scrabbling for water from underground springs, feet worn with walking on rough stones. A wild man, it is said. Some people, so Father Ignatios tells me, thought that he was the prophet Elijah returned. Perhaps he came back, perhaps the chariot delivered him to the top of our mountain. But no, he was in the Judaean desert. There is no doubt of that.

But his clothes are not ragged. An orange tunic and a blue-green cloak. His right hand is held in the position of blessing, facing towards me. Thumb opposed to middle finger, index finger erect, fourth finger curled over and little finger upright but curved. Hanging by my side, my own fingers move into the same position. They are short and stubby, they have none of the eloquence of the saint's elegant, long digits; it is difficult to make the shape.

In his left hand he holds a scroll. He holds it firmly as if reluctant to let it go. What is written on it? There is nothing that can tell me. I look at his eyes again. The look is kind. He may be a

32

wild man but he has a cool kindness about him. It is reassuring. I expect him to be censorious, this man who called on everyone to repent. I expect passion, even condemnation. But what I see is none of this. What I receive at this moment is knowing and understanding. How can he know what I am going through, inside me? But he seems to and that brings me relief. I am still.

There is a faint click from the latch of the door. I do not move. Slowly, quietly the door opens. I turn to see the hunched shape of Father Ignatios stepping over the portal. He carries a large bag as well as the stick which is his constant companion nowadays. He does not seem surprised to see me.

"Ah, there you are Ioánnis. Come to see your saint, eh?" He chuckles into his beard. "I've always thought he was a rather cultured Ioánnis Prodromos, don't you agree? The nuns have tried to smarten him up a bit, make him a bit more respectable. I tried to tell them. I said 'even saints get dirt under their finger nails' but they don't listen," another chuckle. "You're up here early my boy" it was more a question than an observation.

"I wanted to think, Father".

"And have you?" his question was abrupt.

"Have I what?"

"Thought."

"Not really. I can't get my mind in order."

"Quite right. Thinking is highly overrated. As if we could sit on our backsides and make the world come right. Don't get me wrong there's a great place for thinking; thank goodness for Aristotle, for Jerome, for Ayios Basilios and all the Fathers, but sometimes what we need to do is feel. And we're not very good at that." I had no idea what he was talking about so could not respond.

"Do you notice the scroll that he is carrying? What do you think that is?"

"I don't know. I can't read what is written on it."

"No. It's meant to be hidden. Unlikely thing to come out of the desert, isn't it? What can it signify?" I was silent. "Some people say it represents the Old Testament. The Prodromos as the last of the Old Testament prophets. Others say it symbolises Ioánnis's message to the people of Israel. Written down in case he forgets it or gets it wrong." His old laughter bounces around the small church.

"What do you think, Father?"

"Me? I'm just an old fool. What use is my view?"

"I want to know, Father. You are no fool."

"Well, thanks for that, young Ioánnis, but actually I really am unsure. Sometimes I think that it is a significator." He can see my tortured expression. "Well, that's got you thoroughly confused, hasn't it? Never mind, a significator explains who or what this man, this straggly-haired saint, is. And, in this case, it states that he is message, message embodied, message personified, *a voice crying in the wilderness.* Message which comes to us as language and helps us towards meaning, towards forming our world." He stops, staring at the ikon for a few moments.

"So let's venerate him." He shuffles down the church to the ikonostasis and kisses the ikon. I follow him and do the same. He goes around to the back of the ikonostasis.

"Come around here, Ioánnis. You can give me a hand."

I have never been behind the holy barrier. The idea of doing so seems a bit shocking. As if reading my mind he calls "it's all right. It doesn't matter when there is no service. Come on."

I am surprised at what I see. Somehow I expected a jewel bedecked space filled with holy ornaments. Instead there is a rough and ready table, some vestments hanging on hooks, a container of incense, an old mug of water, a comb and a clutter of bits and pieces that seem to be stored here as there is nowhere else to put them.

Father Ignatios smiles as he notices the look of incredulity on my face. "Don't be mistaken, Ioánnis. It is not things that make for holiness. It's what we do with them, what we ascribe to them." He picks up a pot of incense. "Just a pot of funny coloured crystals, aren't they? But when, in the Holy Eucharist, we burn

34

them on the coals they become holy, a holy cloud of prayer, because that is the value that we give them."

I am not certain whether I understand what he is saying. I know that it is very different from what I hear from the monks. But then, Father Ignatios is different. There are two poles of existence on our island. At one end the monks in their solid fortress, remote, unapproachable and impossibly holy. At the other end are the ordinary people, the fishermen, my father, the people who work in the fields, coarse, rough, common and very unholy. The monks need the proximity of the coarse, the sinful, to delineate their holiness. The ordinary people need the holiness and prayers of the Monastery to redeem their inadequacies. A balance, then, which will never change because none of them will let it change. Both sides would have too much to lose.

But Father Ignatios is to be found in neither of these two groups. He seems to shuffle between the two without belonging to either. A maverick, almost, but a holy maverick. He has the true holiness of a man who is comfortable with God and comfortable with his fellow human beings. He could speak the truth to the Abbot, he could speak the truth to my Baba. He has the licence and the authority of the outsider, a resident in neither camp.

"Are you coming for your lessons today, young Ioánnis?" He is heading for the door now. Father Ignatios has been teaching me for two years now. Mama knows but Baba does not. I don't want him to know. He is bound to be angry.

"Yes, Father, I'll be here just after sunset." I need to get down to the boat. Time is moving on.

"I've a bit of a surprise for you today, my boy. A bit of a surprise." He is already shuffling down the street, chuckling away. A dog barks.

He has been teaching me to read, not just our ordinary script but the writings of the ancients as well. He is teaching me mathematics, logic, natural philosophy. Some I understand but much remains beyond me.

We meet in the church of the Prodromos. Rarely are we interrupted there. He is a good teacher. "Knowledge is the key, young Ioánnis," he would say, "you can open up the world with what you are learning. You can stay a fisherman all your life, if you want to, but without knowledge you have no choice. Learning frees you."

He is a hard taskmaster, not always the twinkly-eyed old rascal. Sometimes quite severe. "How can you hope to understand if you don't work at it? Nobody is going to hand it to you on a plate, Ioánnis. The cosseted life is not for you, young man. It's either the hard graft of a fisherman or the intense toil of the scholar. Which do you want?"

I know what I want. I want the means to break out from the life that seems ordained for me. Day after day of hunting fish from the sea, hands calloused from the rough twine of the nets; backbreaking work and endlessly monotonous.

But the life of learning is hard, too. Hard on my brain. I struggle with Aristotelian logic. What can this have to do with anything in my life? Father Ignatios is insistent.

"You have to understand how the ancients think, dear Ioánnis. They formed the way we think, they created our world. If we are to understand our world we have to understand what they say."

"But that is so difficult to accept, Father. Surely our world was created by God. He made the earth, the sea around us, the fishes, the animals, us as well."

"Yes. True, Ioánnis. That is how we speak of it but, if you study, you will find that there are other ways to speak of it. Other languages that express our world."

"What languages? Can you not teach me?"

"Would that I could, young man. They remain unclear to me. But you will discover them in good time. You will find your way into your world."

This had me even more confused but I can see that the old man cannot say, or is unwilling to say, anything more. Perhaps he really does not know, is limited by the outer stretches of his understanding. I sense that there is no point in pressing him.

It is especially hot out in the boat today. Not a trace of the Meltemi, water like glass. Never good conditions for fishing. I work away all day until I hear the bells of the Monastery ringing for Vespers. Time to stop. I row, as quickly as I can, back to the quay. I have an assignment with Father Ignatios and his mystery. It is more than an hour before I have got rid of the fish. Only three baskets today. Baba will be cross but what can I do about it. I take all three to the Monastery and receive the usual price.

I clean up at home. Luckily Baba is not there.

"Are you going to your lesson, Ioánnis?" whispers Mama conspiratorially, not that there is anyone to hear.

"Yes. I'll be home in two hours." She smiles.

I slip out of the door and soon reach the small church. The door is ajar and I can hear Father Ignatios talking inside, his usual, gentle, lilting speech that he uses when he teaches. I push open the door and he looks up.

"Ah, Ioánnis. Come and meet the surprise," he beams. In the shadow, behind the door I can make out a shape. A person. Before my eyes adapt to the dark the shape speaks. A light, immediately recognisable voice.

"Hello, Ioánnis. How are you today?"

It is Anna.

Chapter 6

"There you are, my dear Anna. The perfect example of a young man struck dumb." The old priest chortles away, clearly enjoying his surprise. "Come on, young man. Have you nothing to say to this beautiful young lady?" He beams and Anna looks at me.

She is wearing a long cloak with a dark hood. As I stare at her face, the surprise on my own quite undisguised, she smiles, seemingly amused at her part in this subterfuge.

"How is little Eleni, Ioánnis? Markos told me all about it."

"She, she's going to be all right, I think, I hope" I stammer. "Thank you".

"Now come on you two. We can't be standing here all night. Sit down, sit down." The old priest scurries down the church to retrieve a book from behind the ikonostasis. He calls back to us "I've something special for you today, especially you, young Doctor Ioánnis." This is accompanied by more chortles.

I am beginning to relax. I sit down next to Anna.

"How long have you been?" my voice runs out so I indicate the inside of the church with a gesture.

"Been coming to Father Ignatios? About a year. Didn't you know?"

The old man has returned. He is carrying the book and a small stool.

"We've kept it quiet, haven't we my dear. Not even Stavros knows. Only Maria."

"Yes, mother knows."

"Though I think we're going to have to make it public before too long. She's a very bright pupil, Ioánnis. Oh, there's no need for you to look so crestfallen, you're no dunce yourself. But she is making fast progress. One day she will need more than I can

39

give her," he allows his head to droop a bit, "poor, old dullard that I am." I am beginning to recognise that he enjoys play acting of this type.

Anna jumps up and gives his arm a squeeze.

"No, you're not, Father Iggy." I am shocked that she uses this diminutive but he seems unaffected by it, "you're a wonderful teacher and I don't want anyone else." Father Ignatios mumbles away into his beard and turns his attention to the book that he is carrying. Anna sits down again and slips off her cloak. Her long, dark hair, held by a small comb, falls down her back. I notice the smoothness of the skin of her forearm as she rests her hands in her lap, patiently waiting.

My capacity for coherent speech seems to be returning.

"So what have you studied so far, Anna?"

"A little of most things, I suppose. I could read a bit before I came so that has been the easiest." Father Ignatios looks up from his book.

"Her reading is exceptional. She can master all the old documents that I show her. I think we have read all the Gospels, most of the Pentateuch and the Book of Revelation of course." No longer did I feel a competitor. This was out of my class.

"Why have you not told your father? Wouldn't he be proud of you?"

A cloud passes across her face. "I don't know. He is very proud of his involvement with the church but he has a clear idea about where women, girls, should be in the scheme of things. I think it will disturb him to know that I am taking on all this learning. He'll worry that it will make me less attractive as a wife, more suited to be a nun and I know he doesn't want that for me."

"I think she's right, young Ioánnis. Best to keep this a secret between us."

For a moment I experience a conspiratorial thrill; a secret between myself, Anna and the old priest. It brings with it an unfamiliar feeling, a sense of discovery, of elation, almost of danger.

40

"So, as she's been coming on marvellously well, and so have you my downhearted young friend, it made sense for us all to learn together. Shall we get on?"

"Yes, of course" says Anna. I nod.

"All right. Now Ioánnis. What do you know of Aristotle?"

"Er, Aristotle. A philosopher who was a pupil of Plato but who denied the immortality of the soul. He believed in the value of," I struggle for the words, "of empirical observation. You start with material objects from which you infer spiritual reality. He was a great believer in reason and much of his work on logic was used by the Fathers and also by that Latin scholar you told me about, whose name I have forgotten." I look for help.

"Thomas Aquinas" says Anna, as cool as a cucumber and she smiles at me in friendly confrontation.

"Oh, yes, Thomas Aquinas, that's it."

"Well done, Ioánnis. But what does this 'empirical observation' mean, Anna?"

"I think it means that first of all you observe material things, wind, stone, animal behaviour, human illnesses and from these observations you make up your theory."

"That's about it. But why was that idea so special. Surely it's obvious, isn't it?"

"Well no, not really. Plato, Hippocrates and many others had theories based on nothing more than the ideas that they dreamt up in their own heads. Aristotle's views opposed that way of going about thinking altogether."

I am overcome. Here is a beautiful fifteen year old girl, sitting and quietly expounding knowledge and ideas that would mystify her mother and father, knowledge that is kept from all but the monks and nuns in their segregated isolation. It occurs to me that Father Ignatios is taking the cork out of a particularly explosive bottle. Does he know what he is doing? I only have to take one look at him to know that he does. Father Ignatios is smiling. He wants things to change.

He is opening a book now.

41

"This is Aristotle's *Physics*. It doesn't often get an airing, this book, but I've had it for years." He reads slowly, the light is getting dim and age must be affecting his vision, Anna and I are still as we listen. Eventually he ends with

"Plainly, therefore, in the science of Nature, as in other branches of study, our first task will be to try and determine what relates to its principles." He closes the book.

"So what does that tell you, young people?" I am silent, so is Anna.

"I'll tell you a story, then. The story is of a young man who lives with his herd of goats. He lives with them for years, summer and winter, cold and warm, wet and dry. He finds them grazing, he delivers their young; when they injure themselves he teaches himself how to put them right." I know what is coming now.

"One day he comes across an injured child. Badly injured and in pain. All the world says 'leave it to those who know' and those people would have fanciful theories about cures and potions. They would say 'she has too much black bile' or 'there is an excess of phlegm', they would drain her precious blood from her and do nothing but make her worse.

"But the young man has *seen this before*. He knows this type of injury, albeit in a goat. He knows enough about the anatomical structure of a goat to know that it is not all that different from a human child. He knows what to do.

"And here is the crucial part of the story. Not only does he know what to do but he does it. Who or what does he trust in? God? His guesswork? No, he trusts in his empirical experience. His understanding of Aristotle's first principles. He has done this sort of thing before." He pauses to get his breath. "It takes courage." He repeats again, "It takes courage."

There is silence. My face flushes and Anna's hand creeps across to mine and squeezes it. She takes it away. Father Ignatios gets up, tucks the book under his arm, picks up his stool and slowly makes his way down the church. Without turning, he calls

42

out "'til next time," and disappears behind the ikonostasis. Anna rises, bends over, lightly kisses my cheek and goes. I am left alone at the back of the church. I feel exhausted.

In the weeks that follow we meet many times, Anna, Father Ignatios and I but there is never the degree of intimacy that I experienced that first time. We study hard. As there are two of us ideas bounce around with more energy. As a consequence we learn faster.

There have been no further violent episodes with Baba and Mama. Baba stays away for most of the time, returning very late most nights. I am busy with the fishing. Markos often joins me.

We are fishing out of the main bay, round the headland and in a smaller bay that sometimes attracts large shoals. It is a long haul to row but with two of us it is much easier. As we round the headland I look out to sea. There is a shoal of dolphins playing about a mile offshore. This looks encouraging. We row into the bay and set the net then row in a large arc. Once the net is out we rest on our oars and wait. Markos passes me some water. It is a hot day and we both need it.

"Ioánnis. Have you seen Anna recently?" How was I going to tell him that we were together last night. I lied.

"No, not for quite a while. Was she in church last Sunday?" I knew she was. There was little else that I looked at.

"Yes, I think so. I think she was. Anyway I wondered what you thought of her." I can feel my ears begin to redden. Desperately I try to control them.

"Thought of her?"

"Yes. She's behaving real strange at the moment."

"How?"

"I dunno. Moody, quiet. She's no fun like she used to be. She and Baba have huge arguments." This sounds usual for a fifteen year old. I say so.

43

"Yes, I know. But it's not like Anna. I wondered if you knew. Perhaps there is something bothering her, something on her mind." Markos knows more than he is letting on. I have to distract him. I am saved by fortune.

"Look!" I point out to sea. The school of dolphins has moved in closer to shore. They are clearly hunting fish for the water has taken on a silvery sheen, punctuated by thousands of flapping fish, thronging on the surface. The whole shoal is coming our way, straight towards our net. Within minutes the net is bowed down with the weight of fish, the bow of the kaiki is dipping towards the surface of the water. Markos and I set to pull in the net and deposit mass upon mass of squirming silver fish into the well of the boat. Once we have hauled them on board we are low down in the water.

Markos calls from the bow. "We'll never get around the headland loaded like this".

"You're right. Let's pull in here and get some help."
Gingerly we row towards the shore of the small bay. We ground the boat as gently as we can and make it fast.

There is no one about. There is a fisherman's hut above the beach but it is deserted. We take the track over the headland, back to the quay side. It is more populated here. I find our baskets and borrow three more. I find the two fishermen who helped me out the day of Eleni's accident. We negotiate a deal which is both generous to them and gets me the help I need. The four of us make our way back to the boat.

"Holy Maria!" The older fisherman spits on the ground. "What a catch."

We load the baskets. Markos has managed to find a handcart so we are able to get the whole catch back to the quay side. I earmark three baskets for the Monastery, as usual, and go to look for buyers for the rest.

"Baba will take three this time, I'm sure," says Markos. It is easy to sell the rest.

The donkey cart is loaded. The donkey is the only one of us unenthusiastic about the bumper catch. He needs constant goading to keep him going up the hill. For once I feel sorry for him.

I take the three baskets to the Monastery. The steward says nothing, just gives me the money. We make our way to Markos's house. Stavros takes the three baskets with no query, and he gives me a good price for them.

"Good quality fish, Ioánnis. You're becoming a real expert." I grin with pride, but know that it had more to do with the dolphins than with me.

I am just turning the donkey around when Anna comes out of the house. She looks at me without recognition. No smile. She walks off down the lane.

Markos looks across at me, "see what I mean?"

I don't understand.

Chapter 7

I am pretty sure that Baba is beginning to notice my absences. Even though he is seldom to be seen when I return from the fishing, and frequently not there when I return late after my sessions with Father Ignatios, yet somehow I sense his suspicion.

It is early evening. Today's was a poor catch. Just enough for the Monastery with none to spare for Stavros. Poor fish at that. Young ones with very little flesh on them. I am cleaning myself up outside the back door. Little Eleni hobbles out, her arm in a sling, a stick in her other hand to steady her. She is progressing well. Secretly I am very pleased. In a way I see her as a walking embodiment of my competence, there for all to see. It makes me feel proud.

"Ioánnis. Baba is home. He wants you." I look at her, interrogating her expression to see what I can expect. She smiles and winks.

Inside Baba is seated in the large chair. For once he does not smell of drink. Mama is preparing food in the kitchen area. "Come here, boy" he orders gruffly but there is no violence in his manner. I walk across the room and stand in front of him.

I am off my guard. I do not even see his arm swing out, only feel the enormous blow to my head. I fall to my knees, dazed and confused.

"Baba. What are you doing? What's that for?" My head is ringing.

The only reply I get is another blow. I fall forward on all fours. Where is Mama? Where is Eleni? As if they could protect me.

"Get up, you young whelp" growls Baba. I wince, expecting more blows but there are none. Slowly I climb to my

47

feet. My head is beginning to clear. I look at Baba and see that he is holding a rough sheet of paper. It has writing on it, my writing.

"What is this?" he shouts as he waves it in front of me.

"I don't know. I really don't. Where did you get it?"

"I found it under your bed. Are you saying it is not yours?"

"Yes. No. No, it's not mine. I found it."

"Found it? Where?"

"In the street; it was lying in the street." His face is close to mine.

"What's it say?" I look at it. It is my notes about Aristotle. I can read it perfectly clearly.

"You know I can't read, Baba. It must be something to do with the monks. They must have dropped it."

"Well it's mine now. I shall keep it. Maybe I'll ask Stavros to read this bit of monk-shit for me." I know Stavros can read. What I do not know is whether he will give me away.

"I'm sorry, Baba."

"Sorry? Why sorry? You say it's not yours."

"I'm sorry it makes you angry." His only response is a grunt.

"Go on, get out. I've seen enough of you."

I make for the door. As I run off down the street. I notice that Mama has slipped out through the back of the house. She is going up the hill, towards the square.

After a bit I slow down to a walk. I am crying but my tears are tears of anger. The thought, the fear, that he would stop my learning. I would rather kill him. I could do it, just give me a knife and I would plunge it into his black heart. I don't care what Father Ignatios says, I cannot honour him, even respect him. He is evil. Why do I let him beat me?. I am taller than he is now and I am strong. Hauling in the nets day after day has given me powerful muscles. I could stop him but yet I do not. Violence is boiling up within me and it is a violence that frightens me.

These thoughts are still rattling around inside my head when I push open the door of the church. Anna is there already.

Father Ignatios is sitting opposite her, talking quietly. They both look up. Anna says nothing. Father Ignatios looks me in the eyes.

"Well, now. Something's up again, isn't it, Ioánnis?" I slump down, my head in my hands and start to cry again. I hate myself for doing it, in front of him, in front of Anna.

Her hand is on my arm.

"Steady down, Ioánnis." I turn to look at her. Her face is composed, not smiling. Father Ignatios says nothing. We all remain still. Eventually I stop crying.

After a gap whose length I cannot measure, it may be a minute, it could be an hour, I manage to speak.

"Father Ignatios. How can I love my father when he is so evil?"

"Why evil, young man?"

"I'm afraid he's going to stop me coming here."

"Why do you think that, Ioánnis?" says Anna. Her voice is gentle. It steadies the turmoil inside me.

"He found one of my sheets of notes. I lied and said it wasn't mine but I'm sure he didn't believe me." I turn to Father Ignatios. "What can I do?"

"There is nothing you can do, dear boy. Nothing except trust in the work of the Holy Spirit. And that's a very significant exception." He smiles a little. I think he recognises that his answer does not satisfy me. "Now it's time for study and today it looks as if it may be particularly relevant." He hands us the large book of the Gospels and Acts.

"Here you are then. Can you find the doctrine of the Trinity in this book? Come on then, have a look." For once Anna is as mystified as I am. For the next ten minutes all is quiet whilst we search.

"Well, have you found it yet?" he cannot resist a chuckle.

Anna looks up. "No, but there is the passage at the beginning of John's Gospel about Jesus as Word."

"Oh yes," I say, "In the beginning was the Word."

"Quite right, Anna, but it is not the doctrine of the Trinity as we understand it, is it? Now what about the Spirit? What have you found?"

I know this bit.

"The Spirit came down on the Apostles at Pentecost. In other places there are references to the spirit of Jesus, or the Spirit of the Lord."

"Yes, quite right. And at the beginning, in Genesis, you have the Spirit moving over the waters."

"Well doesn't all that add up to the Trinity?" Anna is a little irritated now.

"Yes, I see what you mean. There is mention of the three components but nothing, and this is crucial, about the nature and relationship of each one of the three to the other. It is that relationship which is the doctrine of the Trinity." I am beginning to get confused. Father Ignatios can see this.

"The doctrine was agreed upon three centuries after the death of Jesus. I can tell you there was a big dust-up, yes, physical violence, before the delegates to the Council of Nicaea agreed to the formula that we have today. I think there was considerable pressure from old Constantine, the Roman Emperor, to get something agreed. I don't suppose he cared what it was, just so long as everyone agreed on a party line." Father Ignatios delights in shocking us from time to time. "But it stuck so there you are, it must be a workable doctrine. I don't know if we really understand what it means but that's the orthodox faith, sometimes it is better not to think too much, accepting is more important." He paused, his eyes unfocussed, "I think that's enough for today, you both look knocked out. Off you go, you two." He chuckles and we can still hear his giggles as we close the door behind us.

Anna has pulled her hood up. She whispers to me, "Ioánnis, follow where I go," and slips away down a narrow side street. I check that there is no one about, wait a few seconds and follow her.

She follows a convoluted route through the little town, a route that is even unfamiliar to me. Soon we are out of the houses and walking across a plateau to where three windmills stand. The air is still so there is no movement from them. From here we can see the sun sinking into the sea behind us and night creeping up from the eastern horizon. We sit on a large boulder. Hooded crows are tumbling around the cliff below us, mobbing a small falcon. In the far distance it is possible to make out the line of mountains on the mainland. Occupied by the Turks now. No one dares go near there these days.

Still, clear weather like this means that there is a storm on the way. Fishing will have to be close in tomorrow if I can get out at all.

Anna turns to me. "Ioánnis, I need to know something." I turn my head towards her but she continues to look out towards the distant horizon. "Are you serious in your studies with Father Ignatios?"

I feel affronted by this. "Of course I'm serious. What do you mean?"

"What I mean is, do they matter to you?"

"I don't understand; matter to me?"

"Don't be difficult, Ioánnis. I'm trying to be clear. I need to know that this learning is the most important thing in your life."

"Well, I've never thought of it like that but, yes, I think it is. Do you doubt that?"

Her eyes are on fire now.

"It *really* matters to me, Ioánnis. Matters desperately. I cannot settle for being a fisherman's wife, or a farmer's for that matter, I want something different."

"Yes. So do I, but, "

She interrupts, "I doubted it. When you came back with that big catch. You looked so proud, as if what was really important to you was being a brilliant fisherman and making lots of money. I thought you had forgotten about the learning." I blush at the memory. Yes, I had been over-jubilant.

51

She continues. "The Ioánnis I know is sensitive, clever and prepared to study, I thought I had lost him," she starts to cry, quite quietly, quite gently.

Without thinking I put my arm around her. She does not draw away.

It is dark by the time I reach home. Judging by the snores Baba is already asleep. Mama is sitting beside the fire. She is knitting a dark garment. From its size I guess it must be for Eleni. She looks up as I come in.

"Hello, son" her voice is quiet. She smiles at me.

"Are things all right Mama?" I indicate towards the bedroom.

"Yes. All right, Ioánnis. He took that paper up to Stavros." I had forgotten the paper. Apprehension drops like a stone inside me. She can see my expression.

"Don't worry. I got to Stavros first. He didn't give you away." Relief propels me across the room and I fling my arms around her.

"Thank you, Mama. Thank you a million times."

"No need to thank me, my darling. It was the only thing to do." She looks sad now.

I go to bed but I cannot sleep. The storm that was predicted by the clear air of the evening arrives in the depth of the night. It is signalled by an unnatural stillness. The usual sounds of night are silenced as a prelude to the cataclysm that is to follow. Now it is upon us; the wind howls, rain beats hard on the flat roof of our house. I can hear Eleni calling out, fearful of the thunder. Mama goes to her.

The stupid donkey is kicking out in his stall and braying incessantly. This sets off the goats who bleat away in their lock-up shed. There won't be so much milk tomorrow. Disturbances like this always affect them.

The one thing that remains undisturbed is Baba's snores. The storm does not wake him. I am relieved at that.

But it is more than the storm that keeps me from sleep. Weather never frightens me unless I am out at sea and caught up in it. It is Anna. It is what she said this evening. I cannot leave it alone. I know that what we are learning with Father Ignatios is important. The thought that Baba might stop it, may prevent it happening, has disturbed me much more than I would have believed. But what I have not faced, and what Anna has exposed, is the inescapable and obvious question; what am I going to do with it? I suppose I thought that learning was worth it for its own sake but can that actually be true? Learning leads to change, that should be obvious. I have not looked at that clearly enough.

For what place is there for learning here? As I lie awake thinking about it I can see that the only place for it on this island is in the Monastery or in the Convent. Knowledge, learning finds its way inexorably to the religious institution. Is that where I want to be? I do not share Baba's contempt of the monks yet I don't believe I have a vocation to shut myself away behind those oppressive walls.

By now I am not only confused but also disturbed. The image of Anna returns. She was so passionate. Fiercely passionate about learning, quite unwilling to accept the usual role of a young woman. Will she go into a convent? I find the idea ridiculous. Anna as a nun, pious, retiring, quiet? I cannot see it.

The storm is reaching its maximum now. The noise is intense. It does not stop me falling asleep, my brain is exhausted.

A hand is shaking my shoulder, gripping hard, roughly. I wake with a start. Sunlight streams into the house but I can still hear the wind howling. I look up. It is Baba.

"Wake up, boy! There's work to do." He leaves me to get dressed and then pulls me outside. He is still rough in the way he handles me but there is no aggression in it now.

"Look at this mess!" He gestures to indicate the damage that the storm has done. The whole side of the donkey's shed has blown down. I can stare right in to see the beast cowering down in some filthy straw in the corner.

53

"Take the beast, Ioánnis. Put it in the field and hobble it."
I do as he tells me. Even though I have little time for the donkey I
hate to use the hobble. Baba insists,

"You shouldn't be so squeamish, boy. They don't know any
better. They're used to it." It is the kind of casual cruelty which is
characteristic of nearly all the men on the island.

With the donkey hobbled and braying away in indignation
we start work on the repair. Most of the wood has been cracked
and splintered by the wind but we find other pieces to cobble up
the damage. All the time the wind is roaring around us but, with
the sun now warming up, I am working up quite a sweat.

I stare down at the bay. It is rough.

"I don't think I can take the boat out today, Baba."

"Why the hell not?"

"Just look, Baba. Even if I could get out in that swell
there'd be no fish to catch." He stops what he is doing and stares
down at the bay, a hand shielding his eyes from the sun. He stays
like that for at least a minute.

Please, I implore in my head, please don't make an issue of
this. My plea must have been heard. He grunts and turns back to
the job in hand.

"You're probably right. But we can't have you lazing about
all day. You can clear out the goats' shed, help Stefanos. It needs
doing."

I think I'd rather risk the stormy sea than shovel all that
goat shit. I say nothing but go indoors. Mama gives me some
bread and a mug of goat's milk. I am angry. I thought that not
having to go fishing would give me more time to meet Father
Ignatios. And of course, Anna.

It must be months since the goat shed was last cleaned
out. The stench is unbearable, particularly as the day warms up.
Stefanos and I carry out cartload after cartload until we have a
large, steaming pile of dung at the bottom of the field. Then we
lay down new straw on the shed floor. The wind is still blowing

54

hard but with less of its previous intensity. There are two hours before nightfall.

"See you later, Stefanos." I turn to walk away.

"Ioánnis." I look back. He is standing by the gate of the field. He is a slight boy, a quiet boy who seems most happy when he is out with his goats.

"Where are you going?"

"About." I wasn't sure myself.

"Don't leave me here," he starts to cry, then wipes away his tears with the arm of his filthy jerkin.

"What's up, Stefanos?"

"I'm frightened of him" he looks back over his shoulder at the house.

"Baba, you mean? He won't hurt you. It's only me he goes for."

"But when you go, he'll turn on me." He may be young but he's perceptive.

"Go?"

"Yes, go. You're sure to go. Soon." What does he know, my little brother? More than I know myself?

"I'm not going, Stefanos. I've got the fishing to do." He looks at me. I can see that he is not convinced.

"In any case, where could I go? There's nowhere on this island." I see him look up at the Monastery, rising above the town. I laugh, unconvincingly.

"On no, brother of mine. I'm not going to become a monk. No hope of that."

"Are you sure?" he squints at me against the sunlight.

"Absolutely, Stefanos. Don't worry, I'll be around for a good long time, long enough to keep Baba off you." I try to sound as confident, as dependable as I can. I think it has an effect. The fear-fuelled droop of his shoulders has gone. He is back to the carefree young boy.

"Thanks, Ioánnis." He turns and runs back to the house. In a moment I hear Eleni and him laughing together. I am left standing in the small field. A billy gives me a half-hearted butt for which he earns a kick up the backside. I leave the field and shut the gate.

It only takes a couple of minutes to reach the little church of Ayios Ioánnis Prodromos. I know that Father Ignatios will not be there yet, actually quite glad to have the place to myself. I push open the door and am greeted by the familiar smell and the cool, dark interior. I sit at my usual place at the back of the church, staring at the ikonostasis. The Prodromos seems the same as ever, straggly hair but rich clothes, the scroll in his left hand. If that scroll is a symbol of knowledge, a signifier, then the prophet is like me. Living his life in rough surroundings, acquainted with animals, with hardship but now blessed, or cursed, with knowledge and learning. Carrying a disturbing message but not just that. He is the forerunner. He comes to announce change, earth-shattering, mind-shattering change.

And he is not a simple messenger. There is nothing in the ikon to say where the message comes from; he is not Hermes. It is as if he wrote it himself. It is his message, his words.

He stares at me. He is not frightening, not at all; wild when I look into his eyes, for sure, yet he is giving me assurance; that is what I see. But he is challenging me, too. I am going to have to make a choice, sooner or later. The prophet does not let me off the hook; neither does he help me see what that choice could be. If only it were so easy, knowing the choices and deciding.

It is attractive to think that I could simply carry on, fishing all day, learning in the evenings, seeing Anna. Would that it could carry on like that. But the Prodromos is gentle but firm, he does not allow that. Change is happening already. I cannot stand still but yet I am too paralysed to move. And the leaving has started.

I hear voices outside. The door opens. It is Father Ignatios and Anna. It is time for study.

"Ah, there you are Ioánnis." He looks at me quizzically, "time to stretch your brains, young man." I look down at my hands, resting on my lap.

Anna giggles and sits beside me. As Father Ignatios goes to get some books from behind the ikonostasis, she whispers in my ear.

"He took me to see the convent this afternoon." I look at her, there is a question in my look. She laughs.

"No, silly! I'm not becoming a nun. He took me to see the ikons that the nuns paint. They're quite beautiful, Ioánnis. Bright colours and plenty of gold and, do you know, they're all the same. This is one of theirs," she indicates the Prodromos "though the nun who made it has died now. Father Iggy says that she was reckoned to be one of the best ikon painters between here and Constantinople. He also said that her last one, made just before she died, went missing. None of the Sisters knew where it had gone and none of them had ever seen it. She was a very secretive person. Quite a mystery, eh?"

I do not reply for I am beginning to remember. A hot day, a procession up the ridge of Mt Profitis Ilias. I was a young boy then, never sure of what I was seeing but overcome with that strange sense that it had importance for me.

Father Ignatios has returned. "Let's get started. Now, Socrates."

Old Socrates. We have never really looked at him up until now. Never wrote a single word, it was all written down by Plato, but he stood under the shade of the Athenian olive trees and single-handedly changed the course of the world. I feel very proud to be Greek like Socrates but Anna seems disturbed.

"Why should such a good man be told to commit suicide? It seems all wrong."

"The powers that be said that he was corrupting the young. They passed the sentence."

"And he did it voluntarily, drank the hemlock without any protest?"

"Yes, my dear Anna. He accepted the judgement without a single complaint." He chuckled. "I suppose it's a risk run by all old men who pervert young people with new ideas. Do you think the

57

Abbot will be coming after me with a cup of hemlock?" He is laughing away now, entranced with his fantasy, light-hearted about it, as if living or dying was of little concern. Just like Socrates. I wish he wouldn't treat it so flippantly. I feel myself getting cross so I glance across at Anna, looking to see that she is affected as I am. She turns away from my gaze. Father Ignatios stops laughing.

"It's too much levity, isn't it Ioánnis. I'm sorry, it cannot seem so funny to you."

I blush. "I don't know, Father. It seems terrible that such a great man should let himself be killed so easily. I cannot understand it."

"Perhaps he knew it was his destiny and so accepted it. He was a man at peace with himself, you know. But it seems different when you are young. I would have reacted just like you at your age, just the same."

"Jesus was the same," Anna speaks up.

I don't follow this. "How do you mean?"

"He allowed himself to be killed. He never argued. He could have stopped it at any point but he didn't."

"You are quite right and very perceptive Anna. Jesus is sometimes spoken of as the sacrificial lamb but sacrificial lambs have no say in whether they are slaughtered or not. They are passive."

Anna is warming to the theme now. "Yes, but Jesus was not passive. He was active, he willed the whole arrest, trial and execution."

I interrupt. "Just like Socrates. Neither of them were in the power of the people who dealt with them. They went to their deaths in control of events, not controlled by events."

"But" Anna's face screws up with concentration in an expression that has an effect on me which is both exciting and unexpected, "didn't Jesus call out on the cross *My God, my God, why have you forsaken me?*".

"That's true, but do you know where those words came from?"

I don't know the answer to this. Anna is equally silent. Father Ignatios gets up and disappears behind the ikonostasis, emerging a few moments later with a heavy, bound copy of the Psalms. He passes it over to us. "Take a look at Psalm 22." We turn through the pages and there it is. The first verse of the Psalm, *My God, my God, why have you forsaken me.* Jesus was quoting the Psalm.

"He would have known it very well," Father Ignatios went on, "a Rabbi like him would be very familiar with the whole psalm. Let's read it ourselves."

Between us we read through the psalm, verse by verse; when we have finished he closes the bible.

"Well?"

We are both silenced by what we have just read. Eventually Anna finds her voice.

"It is all there, isn't it? The whole crucifixion story, even the casting lots for his clothing. It's, it's uncanny." Father Ignatios smiles but says nothing.

"Yes," I feel excited by this revelation "there's that bit about *all who see me laugh me to scorn,* that happened, didn't it?" Father Ignatios still says nothing.

"But how can it be?" Anna's perplexity shows in her furrowed brow; she holds her hands, half-cupped and still over the bible on her lap. "Surely all the people involved were not using the psalm as an actor's script. The Roman soldiers certainly wouldn't have known the psalm."

"Then it must be God who directed things," I say. I look at Father Ignatios and immediately feel less convinced. He is stroking his beard.

"Well, that could be. With God nothing is impossible but I wonder if it is likely. Look at verse two, *but you do not answer.* The psalmist seems to be speaking of a God who is absent. Unseen and unheard. Not the sort of God who would act as puppet-master to all those events of the crucifixion." He pauses for a moment, making those quiet grumbling noises that old people do

59

from time to time. "No, I believe that God stands back, yet flows unremitting love on us at the same time, like the new wine of Cana. How would you feel if you knew that everything that happened, everything you did was pre-ordained by a God who intervenes here, there and everywhere?" I think I know.

Anna answers for me. "Less than human."

"You're quite right, young Anna, less than human." There is a pause, a moment when silence is appropriate. As I sit there I feel animated by what has happened, as if, for a short moment, my life has moved to a different level. It is an exhilarating feeling. This is a new kind of God for me.

Father Ignatios is continuing. "It was the same with Socrates. He left his students to find their own way. He never told them how to do it, or what to do."

I think about the old Greek, still unable to understand how he let himself be cajoled into swallowing the poison. Yet his name, his work, comes down to us where so many others have been forgotten.

"He makes us think, doesn't he?" says Anna. "Even now he makes us think."

"Yes Anna, that's right. And what does it do to you, making you think in this way?" Father Ignatios is leading her on.

"I don't know, it's difficult to say. It's as if he makes your mind shift. Just a bit, so that you see things differently, from a different," she pauses,

" Perspective?" I complete her sentence. I am beginning to grasp it now. The excitement grows. We are travelling into new country here. Anna smiles at me, her hand slips across and squeezes mine, out of sight of Father Ignatios. It feels warm and a little moist.

"Yes, a shift. Not always a large shift but a small, yet significant shift in our perception. He encourages us to step back, to look at the words we use and how we use them. Socrates, you see, marked a major turning point in philosophy, in how we see the world, a step forward from which there is no turning back. That

60

may be why he so readily drank the hemlock. He knew what he had done to the world and that it would never be reversed. He could safely leave, knowing his work was done."

No one moves. I can hear the bells of the Monastery ringing to announce Vespers. For a brief moment the idea of a regulated day, reliable and predictable, has an attraction for me, a refuge from the shifting sands of uncertainty. But it is no more than a passing thought. The old man has stood up. He leans forward and pats Anna, then me, on the head.

"That's quite enough for today, young people." It seems as if he wants to say more; he hesitates, then turns and shuffles off down the small church.

In a low voice Anna says to me

"Ioánnis, does your Baba know you come here?"

I look surprised, "No, of course not. He'd be wild if he knew. Surely Stavros doesn't know; I mean, about you?"

She smiles. "Yes he does. And he knows about you too."
"Oh no! He's bound to tell Baba." A flush of fear rises within me.

She looks at me kindly. "Don't worry. He won't. Mama and I talked to him about it. He won't give you away." I calm down a little. "Your Mama came to see my Baba and told him about the discovered paper."

"Did Baba bring it to Stavros?"

"Yes. He wanted him to read it. Baba did read it out for him and said it must have come from one of the monks." I am relieved now. A feeling of warmth for Stavros and Maria is translated into a hug for Anna. She does not resist.

"Oh, thank you. Thank you. You don't know how relieved I am to hear that. Thank you, Anna." I release her but she does not move away. Instead she turns her face to me. I hold my breath, lean forward and kiss her on the lips. The softness is unexpected, then excitement as the moistness of our lips intermingles. For a moment her tongue slips into my mouth and then withdraws. I am still holding my breath.

61

She laughs. "Breathe, Ioánnis, breathe! You'll pass out if you don't" I blush and allow a huge intake of breath. As I sigh out, an exhalation that echoes around the church, Father Ignatios emerges from behind the ikonostasis.

"Not gone yet?" There is a twinkle in his eye, a very knowing twinkle.

We turn and leave. "Good night, Father." Outside it is dark. Anna takes my hand and leads me down a side alley.

"Ioánnis. You're not fishing tomorrow, are you?"

"No. Of course not. It's Sunday."

"Can you meet me? You know the hermitage of Petra?" Of course I did. I had fished every bay of this island. There was not a piece of the coastline that was unfamiliar to me.

"Yes. I'll meet you there. After Holy Eucharist?" I'd have to construct a story to explain my absence. That would not be very difficult.

"That's lovely. See you then." Once again a flutter across my lips and she has gone, leaving me in a state that is quite novel. I cannot get her out of my mind, the taste of her, the feel of her firm body, the sheen of her long black hair. I make my way home, stupidly grinning at passing cats. They appear not to notice.

Chapter 8

The hermitage of Petra is situated in a large rock, known as Kalikatsoú, the Cormorant, which stands as high as a two-storey house on the end of a spit of sand in one of the quietest bays in the island. There are no houses nearby. Father Ignatios told me that this solitude was one reason why the rock was chosen as a site for a hermit's residence in the past. In addition it combines a honeycomb of caves, enough to make it a very luxurious hermitage. No one lives there now, as far as I know.

This morning I speak to Mama as we walk down to church.

"I shan't be around until this evening, Mama."

"Oh? Why, Ioánnis? Where are you going?"

"Stefanos has told me that some of the goats have gone missing." I had already primed Stefanos, without letting him know the full truth. "I said I'd look for them. I know the sort of places that we're likely to find them. I know the island better than him." That was true. Stefanos was a dreamy young man, not really cut out to be a goatherd.

"In that case I'll save some food for you for this evening."

"Thanks, Mama. I'll take some bread and cheese with me."

There is no need to speak to Baba. He usually leaves me alone on Sunday, saving his harassment for the other six days of the week. Still, I've been in his good books since that huge catch the other day. We all benefited from that.

The walk from the town down to the little, deserted bay is not far but the lightness in my step suggests that I could have bounced from one end of the island to the other and hardly have noticed it. As I reach the shore I stare at the smooth spit of sand that sweeps out in a gentle curve to the Kalikatsoú itself. The intense blue of the sky is complemented by the deep blue of the water. The air is still, the surface of the sea smooth; the warmth of the sun enhances my elated mood.

I turn to look back. There above lies the town, clinging to the edge of the grey, protecting walls of the Monastery. The white walls of the houses shimmer in the haze, the blue of the church domes merges into the azure sky. From here I can look at my town from a distance, a distance that encourages detachment. I can view my life, the fishing, Baba, Father Ignatios all with that small degree of detachment which puts them all in a different light. I become aware of a new sense, a sense that there is no permanence. Nothing will carry on for ever; it is a thought that is both exciting and frightening, at the same time.

I shift my gaze to the left, across the valley to the straight, steep slopes of Mt Profilis Ilias. The small church on the summit gleaming white in the sun reminds me of that strange procession, the procession that I chanced upon years ago when I was a young goatherd. I have not thought of it much since then, not until Anna told me of her visit to the Convent of the Evangelismos. Now I wonder what that procession meant all those years ago. Was it an ikon that was being carried up to the summit? It must have been important for the Abbot was there. Some day I must try and find out. Perhaps I will ask Father Ignatios though, if it is indeed an important secret, he may not tell me. He can be an enigmatic old man if he wants to be.

I step out along the sand towards the rock. As I approach it looms large and massive in my path. There is no one around. Has Anna changed her mind? For a moment I panic. That would be too much to bear.

But then I see her. She is sitting on the rock, about halfway up. There is a kind of natural stone terrace at the entrance of one of the caves. She is hugging her knees and staring out to sea. Her long, dark hair falls freely behind her. She is wearing a simple white shift and appears not to have seen me. For a moment I want her not to notice that I am there. I want time to stare, to absorb her. Now, at last, I appreciate how beautiful she is; her olive skin, her delicately sculptured face, a quiet, striking beauty that overtakes me. I break the spell.

"Anna!" She turns at the sound of my voice, then waves.

"How did you get up there?" I could see no handholds.

"Wait there" she commands and disappears into the cave. In a few moments she emerges from a tunnel at the base of the rock.

She laughs. "An upstairs and a downstairs. Those hermits had a very smart house." She runs across to me and throws her arms around me. I hold her around the waist.

"Come on, then, Ioánnis. Kiss me" and we return, in a moment, to the intimacy of the previous evening. Except that this time our kissing goes on for much longer.

"Anna" I murmur.

"Ssh. Quiet." She closes her eyes as she opens her lips to mine once more.

After a few minutes, she pulls away from me. "Come on. Let's swim! " and standing at the very edge of the water she pulls her shift over her head, shakes out her long black hair with a toss of her head and stands with her arms out to the warmth of the sun, totally naked.

I cannot move. I cannot breathe. The smoothness of her skin, the gentle curve of her back, her dark hair tumbling over her shoulders, I cannot take it all in. I want the world to stop at this moment. She turns her olive-tanned body towards me and giggles,

"Are you going to swim in your clothes, Ioánnis?" her taunt is softened by an understanding smile. She seems to recognise how shy I am.

"Anna, you are beautiful." I start to unbutton my clothes. She walks over to me and pulls off my shirt.

"So, darling Ioánnis, are you. Look at you. What a powerful body you have now." She takes a step towards me and runs her right hand through my dark, curly hair. She murmurs quietly, "What a beautiful body has my Ioánnis." She links both her hands together around my waist. Her head rests on my shoulder and I smell the warm musk that emanates from her. By this time I am naked as well. I close my eyes as she lets her hand slip down my chest, my belly until she strokes my penis. As it rises she sinks to her knees and kisses the tip. I am almost overcome. I pull her to her feet.

"Let's swim." I run ahead of her, my tumescent organ embarrassingly as ridiculous as the donkey's. She runs after me and soon we are splashing around in the warm, supporting water. I grab her by the waist and shower kisses over her breasts. I close my mouth over each of her erect nipples and caress them with my tongue. She moans with pleasure.

Then we swim, far out into the bay. She is as a lithe as a mermaid and slips through the silvery water as if it were her natural medium. I follow her as we head for a small island that lies in the bay. I can see a beach backed by a grove of tamarisk trees that surround an old, ruined hut.

I am almost unbearably happy. I never expected to find myself this way with Anna. I could swim to the Turkish mainland with her, were it what she desired.

We reach the beach and run, dripping, to the shade of the tamarisks. I sit on a rock and watch Anna squeeze the water from her hair. Within minutes we are both dried in the warmth of the midday sun.

She walks across to me and stands in front of me, her legs are apart. She bends down and takes my right hand. I wonder what she intends, my penis stirs. She places my hand between her legs.

"Rub me, gently, Ioánnis." With her hand she shows me what to do. Then she falls to her knees and pushes me down so that she is astride my naked body. Gradually she begins to writhe in rhythm with my hand. She emits little, low groans which become louder and louder. Suddenly she knocks my hand away and takes my erect penis in both hands. She rubs her hands up and down until it is huge. My breathing becomes stertorous, my desire unbearable.

I lie back on a cushion of dried sea weed. It crackles under my weight but makes a comfortable bed. There is an urgency in her movements now as she lets herself down on top of me, guiding my penis inside her. I gasp as it slips deep into her pelvis, her juices lubricating its penetration. She starts to move up and down on me, faster and faster. I grasp her around her hips and begin to thrust, I cannot control myself. We are both crying out now, more and more until I realise that I can contain myself no longer; I hear a roaring and wonder who it is. Then I realise it is me. With huge upward thrusts I erupt inside her. At the same moment her eyes roll up in their sockets and with a huge convulsion she lets her weight fall down on me. I make a slight movement of my pelvis and she reacts with a small spasm, a momentary after-shock.

Her head is slumped on my shoulder.

"Ioánnis, Ioánnis. I love you."

There are no words that I can find to say. We remain still as the sounds of the shore, the waves, the call of a gull, cement us in our fusion of love. Eventually we separate and I stand up. I lift her in my arms and find the softest bed of dried seaweed on which to lie. She curls up and falls asleep under the benevolent afternoon sun.

I sit beside her, unable to take my eyes off the beauty of her naked form. Happiness overwhelms me. She has transformed my life, transformed it for ever. I do not want this moment to end.

There is a straggling oleander growing out of the ruined cottage behind us. Bursts of pink flowers that seem out of place on this wild beach. I walk up the beach and collect an armful to bring them back to Anna. She is still asleep, lying on her back with her arms outstretched, a gentle smile on her lips. I lie the flowers on her recumbent body, in her hair, decorating my loved one.

The wind stirs and she wakes. She looks down at her flower-bedecked body and smiles at me. I bend forward to kiss her on the lips and again begin to feel a stirring within me. Anna pulls me down to her and within moments I am inside her again, scattering the oleander flowers on to the dried seaweed. This time our love-making is even more exquisite; we take our time, time to explore and enjoy each other. Eventually, sated with passion, we fall asleep.

I do not know how long we sleep but it must be a few hours because, when I wake, the sun has shifted and lowered in the sky. Anna is still asleep. I stand up and stare at her beautiful shape, the peace in her face as she sleeps. I am overcome with love as I wander down to the shoreline.

From here I can see across the water to the Kalikatsoú, guarding the mainland. To my right I can see out to sea. I scan the horizon, not expecting to see anyone fishing today. Then I spot it.

Way out to sea, near the horizon. A large, long shape. I stare and stare, shielding my eyes with my hand in an effort to make it out. Gradually I become aware that it is coming closer. I begin to notice movement. What is it?

After a few more minutes it is definitely closer. Now, with mounting horror, I begin to see what it is. A large vessel, high out of the water and at least a hundred cubits in length. The movement that I spotted is oars; now I can see that it has three banks of oars. This is no trading vessel. I know the look of them. This is a trireme, a fighting ship It can only mean one thing; corsairs.

We have to act, and act quickly. What I know of corsairs tells me that they are not approaching the island on a peaceful mission. They probably have over a hundred fighting men on board, bent on piracy and destruction. I have heard about these raids but there has never been one on the island in my lifetime.

"Anna! Wake up! Quick!" she is immediately alert. I point out the approaching vessel.

"We must get back and warn the town." Already she is running for the water. We make a fast pace to the beach where our clothes are left. Soon we are running up the track to the town.

"They won't have seen it from the town," I pant, "they won't see it until it appears at the harbour mouth."

"Come on, Ioánnis. Don't waste your breath talking."

"You go to your father," I call, "I'll go up to the Monastery." We split up, no time for farewells.

The Monastery door is closed and locked. I beat on it furiously. Come on. Come on. It swings open. A young monk stares querulously out.

"Hey! What's this all about, boy? What do you think you're doing?"

I don't even bother to reply but slip past him and run up the steps, oblivious to his shouts from behind me. Now I am in the courtyard opposite the Monastery church. An older monk emerges accompanied, I am relieved to see, by the steward who knows me well. It is the latter who speaks.

"What on earth is it, Ioánnis? Why all this commotion?"

"Corsairs, corsairs are coming. I saw them. They will be in the harbour before long." The steward is a sensible man. He turns to the elderly monk.

"Go and tell the Abbot at once." He turns to the young monk who let me in, who has followed me up the steps.

"Find two others and ring the alarm. Ring like there's no tomorrow!" The monk hesitates, "Go on! Move!" Soon all the bells are ringing furiously. I run to the battlements of the Monastery and stare out to sea. As I look the trireme heaves into view and turns to enter the harbour. It is going to be too late.

I leave the Monastery and sprint home. Baba, Mama, Stefanos and Eleni are standing outside, staring up at the Monastery bells. Baba calls to me

"Boy! What's all this fuss? What's going on?" I explain as quickly as possible.

"Mama, you must take Stefanos and Eleni up to the Monastery. You'll be safe there." Stefanos begins to protest. "No, Stefanos, you must go. You can look after Mama and Eleni."

Baba is already striding down the road in the direction of the harbour. He is carrying a large fence post. A feeling of despair overtakes me. I overtake him.

"Baba. You can't fight. They will be heavily armed."

"Don't stop me, boy. No one invades our island." His manifest courage is surprising. Together we head for the port.

I am much faster than Baba and arrive at the quayside before the trireme has disembarked. Small boats are being let down the vast hull of the boat. Men are jumping into the boats; swarthy, muscular men carrying cutlasses and knives. Some have round shields. They are shouting to each other, a language that I don't recognise.

Baba arrives with his fence pole. Men from the port, fishermen, merchants are milling around, uncertain what to do. Baba bellows.

"Follow me! Form up in three ranks by the shore here." He shepherds them into a semblance of order. The first small boat is heading straight towards them. As it grounds the armed corsairs leap into the shallow water and wade to the shoreline. With a roar Baba charges towards them. Other men follow. He swings his fence pole above his head and, as the corsairs approach, mows two of them down with one sweep. The other armed men head for the fishermen who defend themselves with light sticks. Two or three go down, blood spilling on to the sand.

A second boat grounds. In the gunwales stands an enormous Turk, bald headed with long, black twin moustaches. He is naked from the waist up and carries an enormous sabre. With an agility that is surprising in a man of his bulk he leaps out of the boat and soon reaches the shore, just at the point where Baba is embroiled with two other invaders. He pushes them aside and I see him lift his weapon.

"Baba!" I scream but my scream is cut off in horror as the blade of the large man's sabre cuts into my father's neck. There is an immediate fountain of bright red blood that describes an arc against the blue sky before falling to the sand. Baba falls. I run towards him.

The corsairs are moving past us, going up the shore and into the port. The fishermen have fled. I kneel down next to Baba.

Blood is pouring from his neck. As he breathes a red froth is foaming and bubbling from the wound and from his mouth. I tear off my shirt and stuff it hard against the wound. His eyes are glazing over and his breathing is getting weaker.

"Baba! Baba! Don't die. You mustn't die." He looks at me, a focussed gaze held only for a moment. He does not speak. Within a few moments his breathing stops, his face becomes ashen and his eyes close. Still trying to hold my blood-soaked shirt to his neck I lay my ear to his chest wall. There is silence.

I step back and stare, through my tears, at the husk of this man who terrorised my life. But I loved him, even though I was never able to tell him so. I want to know whether it was the same for him, want to ask him but now I never shall. Now it is too late.

I turn and run, back uphill to the town. I have to see that Mama and the others are safe. And Anna, where is Anna? Why have they come to our small island? There is no plunder worth the taking. We are poor fishermen and farmers.

I look again at the men swimming ashore. In the fading light I can just make out some long objects being carried ashore, ladders. There can only be one reason to bring ladders on a raid like this. They are after the Monastery. There would be plenty of plunder there. Gold in abundance, precious art works, plenty of materials to be traded back on the mainland.

I must make for the Monastery. Mama, Eleni and Stefanos are there. Now Baba is gone the responsibility for them all falls to me. As I weave my way through the town streets I can see fires starting up in the houses around the quay. Flames penetrate the dusk. I can hear the cries of women and children even up here. The corsairs have not reached the town but it won't be long.

The doors of the Monastery are closed. I beat on them as I did earlier. The bells are still ringing. No one answers. I am about to beat again when I see figures huddled in the shadows in the corner of the square.

"Hello," I call "who's there?" A figure in black moves out of the shadow.

71

"Ioánnis?"

"Mama! Why aren't you inside? You are not safe here."

"They refused us entry. We couldn't get in."

"What? I don't believe it."

"It's true, Ioánnis," Stefanos has emerged from the shadows, "They said they did not have enough supplies to take in the townspeople. They sent us away." I turn to stare at the implacable battlements.

"Bastards!" I scream but the sound echoes away unheard. In my anger I determine that I am not going to warn them of the men with ladders. "You can rot in your own fucking mess!"

"Ioánnis! You must not say such things." Mama is shocked.

"Mama. We cannot stay here. Follow me back to the house." I spot torchlight flickering at the foot of the paved walkway up to the town. There is no time to spare.

Back at the house I can hear the goats bleating in their shed. Stefanos goes to see to them.

"Mama. Listen carefully. Take Eleni and Stefanos and find your way to the convent of the Evangelismos. You should be safe there. Tell them that Father Ignatios sent you. Now go; quickly, go."

Mama kisses me on the forehead and leaves. I have to find Anna. As I leave the house I notice that the goats are quieter. Screams from lower in the town indicate that the corsairs are near. I go to the donkey's shed and find a long-bladed knife. I tuck in into my belt and set off towards Stavros's house in the square. As I turn a corner I come up against a trio of corsairs, one carrying a ladder, the other two well-armed. They stop and in that moment of surprise I am on them. Years of slaughtering and butchering goats guides the thrust of my knife. The first one goes down with hardly a sound. The second swings his blade at me but I duck and it whistles over my head, almost parting my long, black hair. I bring my knife up through his soft abdominal wall and into his chest cavity. Bright red blood wells up from the entry wound. He falls to his side, groaning.

"Baba, that's for you," I mutter to myself. The third man drops his ladder, turns and runs. I am amused at how easy it is to kill, almost relishing in the simplicity of it. It releases something within me, something atavistic. I look around for other corsairs that I can despatch but now there are none around.

I carry on uphill. Just as I am about to enter the square in front of Stavros's house a figure blunders into me. It is Markos. He is agitated, gibbering.

"Ioánnis, Ioánnis. The house is on fire!" I run into the square. Stavros's house is on the opposite side from where I am standing. Flames pour from the windows, the roof is alight.

"Where's Anna?" I scream.

"I don't know. They're all in there I think. I don't know."

I run forward but the heat throws me back. Anna, not Anna.

"Come away, Ioánnis. There's nothing you can do. We have to get away."

Fires are breaking out all over the town now. I run back to our house. The house is not on fire but the donkey's shed is ablaze. I hear the wild brays of the beast as flames shoot up through the roof. I cannot do anything about it. The donkey will die.

And then I notice, in front of the goat shed, a huddled figure; on the ground. I run across and turn it over. It is Stefanos, a deep wound in his arm and a hole in his chest wall. Dead.

I fall to my knees. My father, my lover and now my brother. It is not just too much to bear, it is even more than I can acknowledge. Now I have no courage, no cowardice. I act automatically, as if one act leads inexorably to another. I have no choice.

I stand up. The shed door is open and the goats have gone. Provisions for the galley, I suppose. I run back into town. People everywhere, screaming, fighting. I see the first ladders going up against the Monastery walls. In a moment of wry amusement I notice that they are too short, they cannot reach the battlements.

73

Monks are scuttling about on the top of the walls throwing over rocks, heavy implements, boiling water. I can see that the assault on the Monastery is going to fail. Just at this moment I wish it were otherwise.

I meet Markos again. "Come with me, Markos." He follows down a narrow street. Only then do I realise it is a dead end.

Quickly I turn to escape but it is too late. A bunch of corsairs has followed us down the street and is obstructing our exit. I pull out my knife and threaten the lead man. He swings at me with a heavy truncheon but misses. I knee him hard in the groin and he goes down. The others are laughing at the sight of their comrade rolling around in the dust. Two of them come forward and grasp Markos. They tie his arms behind his back and drag him away.

Only then do I notice who is there. It is the huge man that killed Baba; bald head, black moustaches, blood staining his cutlass. I am fairly certain that my time has come but I am not going without a fight. I leap forward with my knife. He laughs and with a quick swing of his weapon cuts into my arm and knocks the knife from my grasp. I close my eyes and await the final blow. My arm is numb.

But it doesn't come. Suddenly my arms are held by two of his companions. He is shouting orders to them. They drag me to the end of the cul-de-sac. There is a water trough at the side of the road. They bend me forward over it. Am I going to be beheaded? That same detachment predominates, I don't really mind just so long as his blade is sharp and his aim true.

There is more shouting and suddenly I feel my trousers being gripped by the waistband and ripped off me. At the same moment I feel my legs dragged apart, one man on each leg. The awful truth dawns on me, no longer am I detached. I crane my neck to look behind me.

What I see is a terrible sight. The huge Turk is standing in the middle of the street, a few cubits from me. He is roaring through his nostrils, his face is red and pulsating. I look downwards and see the explanation. He has his organ out, in his hand, and is masturbating vigorously. I jerk my head back and struggle and scream but I am held firmly by the two strong men. This cannot be happening to me; all detachment has gone now leaving only naked fear.

I feel a huge, searing pain in my arse as he forces himself in. I almost faint with the tearing agony but am soon pulled back to full consciousness by the thrusting of his pelvis, each thrust hitting me like a sledge hammer. The pain is unrelenting. I am screaming. The men holding me are laughing, jeering, egging the Turkish corsair on. At last, with a huge convulsion which bangs my head against the stone trough, he is done. He pulls back and the thrusting stops. The pain is still exquisite. The other men let go of me and I slump to the ground. I expect a slash of the cutlass to finish me off. I cannot care but no merciful blow comes. Within moments I am on my own.

I am lying in the dust of the narrow street. Sounds of the rain, screams, shouts, the crackle of flames continue but I cannot move. I am crying tears of anguish, not just for the pain; if it were just that I could bear it. I cry for the humiliation, I cry for the death of Baba and Stefanos, I cry for the loss of Anna, I cry for the destruction of a world that is gone in an instant.

Still lying there I remember Mama and Eleni. Will they have made it to the convent? Suddenly I am alerted. I get to my feet and retrieve my torn trousers. They are just about able to preserve my dignity but in any case by now I do not care. Dignity has long since gone. I notice blood dripping down my thighs from the forced penetration. There is some water in the trough so I bathe myself. Some of the pain eases. The slash on my arm is still bleeding, I have nothing to dress it with since soaking my shirt in Baba's blood. I look around. There is a small house close by with the door swung open. I step inside. The looters have been here. I remember it as a small weaver's house. The inside is a mess; there is no one around. I root around and find a length of white

75

material with which I can bind my arm. It is hurting much more now. Strewn over the bed are some old clothes. I find a shirt and fresh trousers.

I hobble up into the town square, the pain in my arse makes it difficult to walk properly. The shouts and screams are receding now. Clearly the assault on the Monastery has been abandoned.

Suddenly a group of corsairs come into the square. They are shepherding a small group of women and children. The raiders have tied their captives' wrists together and then tied them to each other. The women are quiet but some of the children are crying. I duck back into the shadows as they drive them across the square. At that moment I see Mama, and Eleni. I almost call out but stop myself before I do. There is nothing I can do. Mama looks exhausted, Eleni is crying. In a moment they are gone.

So quickly do these things happen. In a moment your mother, your sister are gone from your life. And here you are, powerless to prevent it. Now I experience a depth of desolation that is deeper than I could have ever imagined. Everything that had constituted my life has gone.

My steps take me to the church of the Prodromos, the oft-trodden road. There are still corsairs about so I must be careful. I push open the door of the church.

They have been in here. The interior is wrecked, ikons torn down, furniture scattered. The gold of the ikonostasis has been ripped off and taken away. It is chaos.

And then I notice a bundle on the floor, behind the ikonostasis. I edge forward and kneel down beside it. It is Father Ignatios. Gently, I roll him over and then see a large, bright red pool of blood on the floor. He has lost a great deal of blood yet he is still alive. I can feel a weak pulse in his neck. His eyes flicker open. For a moment they stare at me vacantly and then recognition dawns.

"Ioánnis?"

"Yes, Father, it's me. Keep still and I will try and help you."

"There's no point, Ioánnis. I am dying. I know that." I realise that he is right. Even a young man could not survive that degree of loss of blood.

"Father, Father, don't leave me."

"I have little choice, my boy, but come now" his tone brightens a little, "you must get away to somewhere safe." He is fumbling in his robes for something. The effort is exhausting him. Eventually his hand comes out with a small key on a length of frayed cord. He holds it out to me. I can hardly hear what he is saying. I lean my ear to his mouth.

"Key. Profitis Ilias. Key. Go, boy. Take Anna, go." His eyes close and for a second time in this terrible night I watch a man that I love die in front of me. I close his eyelids and kiss his forehead. I know I had my Baba but this old man was the true Father to me. I clutch the key in my hand and, still on my knees, am torn apart with sobbing.

Chapter 9

There is enough moonlight for me to make my way up the mountain. Despite that I frequently stumble, tripping over hard rocks in the rough path. By now I am emptied of purpose. I do not really understand why I am making this climb. Father Ignatios's dying mandate is all that keeps me going.

I stop for breath. Below me is spread a panorama of destruction. Flames are leaping up from the torched houses both in the town and down by the port. Little sound reaches me up here, the screams of the wounded and the captured have quietened down. Now the only sign of activity is the movement of torches carried by the corsairs down on the shoreline. I can just make out bunches of people being forced into the boats and then I realise that this is what they have come for; slaves. The looting of houses and churches was an incidental bonus for these brigands. They were after people, young men for fighters, women and children, I cannot bear to think for what. Mama and Eleni must be amongst them but not Anna. At the thought of her burning to death in their family home, a scream of anguish forces itself from deep within me but is lost in the blackness of the night, emptied into oblivion.

My gaze moves along the coast. In the moonlight I can see the rock of Kalikatsoú. The memories of Anna and me, of the passion and the tenderness, run the risk of being obliterated by the carnage of the last few hours. So is this decimation of the island is a punishment for us, a retribution for our illicit love?

But nothing registers any more. I turn and automatically, wearily continue the climb.

When I reach the top I can see the corsair trireme beginning to move out into the bay. I watch the oars moving as one, like some vast sea-centipede. Soon, it is rounding the headland and setting a course for the mainland.

I look across at the town. Nearly half the buildings are alight. The air is still and the smoke billows upwards in a mute appeal to the heavens. Through the smoke I can see the Monastery, there is no smoke rising there. I feel a rage as bitter as gall inside me. They could have given shelter to the women and children at least. Yet they refused refuge to Mama, Eleni and all the others. The bastards, the fucking bastards! I shall never look at that Monastery in the same way ever again. If that is the love of God I want nothing to do with it.

Then I think of Father Ignatios. He did not seek to hide away behind the stone walls. He must have been in the church when the corsairs burst through the door. I can see the poor old man trying to protect his church, only to be rewarded by a sword thrust through his guts. Just one blow of the sabre can wipe out all that knowledge, that wisdom, that love. The loss twists my insides, I choke on my despair.

And then I remember his words. "Profitis Ilias, go boy, take Anna, safe". I feel the key in my hand. Why did he send me up here? Far enough away, I suppose. The corsairs would not be bothered to chase a slim young man all the way up this craggy path. But he gave me the key, he wanted me to go into the church.

The church is small and balances on the pinnacle of Mt Profitis Ilias. It is surrounded by a low, stone battlement. On one side the mountain drops away precipitously. I edge around to find the door and push it open. As I stand in the doorway I remember that time, many years ago, when I entered this church; part of another life it seems. It has no connection with me now.

Moonlight floods into the church yet it is still difficult to make out any detail. My eyes adjust and only then do I discern the painting on the wall, the picture of the prophet Elijah, ascending in a chariot of fire; taken up by a whirlwind from beside the Jordan. Elisha stands below him, receiving the cloak that floats down from the departing prophet.

It is as if Father Ignatios is speaking to me. "Come on now, Ioánnis my son. It's up to you now. I am leaving. You must continue the work." Is this why he told me to come up here? Is this the message? I fall to my knees. "How can I, Father? I don't know enough. I am frightened. How can I?" There is no answer.

"Show me what to do. Please. I can't go on." I remain on my knees in this little church on the pinnacle of the mountain. Through the open door I feel the stirrings of a breeze. In the end I climb to my feet and, with no purpose in mind, wander around the small space. I move behind the ikonostasis. The floor is carved from the smooth rock of the mountain top, it feels cool under my feet.

Then I stub my toe on something hard. Bending down to feel what it is my fingers encounter metal, pitted with age. It is a large ring set into the floor. I could have missed it on any other occasion. I bend down and, grasping it with both hands, pull.

Nothing moves. There is no sound. I search the floor around with my fingers. It is clear that the ring is attached to a round, flat plate of stone. My fingers locate a small keyhole. I produce the key from my pocket and slip it in. It turns easily. I grasp the ring and pull hard but then scream out loud as pain shoots up from the sabre wound in my arm. I drop the ring and allow the pain to settle before reapplying myself. With as large an effort as I can muster the whole plate moves. It is hinged and I can just swing it upwards to the vertical where it rests, precariously balanced.

It has revealed a space, not very large, like a small pit. There is something inside; I reach down to lift it out, nearly dislodging the balanced plate. It is rectangular, wrapped in sacking. I carry the parcel outside so that I can examine it better in the moonlight.

Sitting on a rock I remove the sacking with care. It is an ikon.

A strange place to store an ikon. Why is it not hanging in the church? I turn it to catch the moonlight. Reflection bounces

81

from the richness of the gold background. It is not an old ikon, it must have been made recently.

Of course. The gold reminds me. I remember the flash of sunlight on the gold, the strange procession all those years ago. This was their special burden, this must be it, carried up the mountain and then hidden in the stone floor. My mind is a turmoil of different images. I cannot put them together, make sense of them. It will not work.

I stare at the ikon. Time passes. I cannot make my brain understand what I am gazing at; my perceptions are too disjointed. The moon is high in the sky now. Light floods down on the pinnacle of the mountain. I look away, look out at the bay. The trireme has gone. Only the smouldering remains of the burned houses tell of what has happened in this violent, destructive night. The breeze is still picking up, blowing from the north; signs of a Meltemi developing. It will be blowing hard by the morning.

I look at the ikon again. Now I can appreciate what I am seeing. It is an ikon of Ayios Ioánnis Theologos, our Ioánnis who lived in the cave below the Monastery. He is looking upwards and across the ikon. In his hands he holds a quill with which he is writing on a parchment. I can read the words on the parchment, Θεὸν οὐδεὶς ἑώρακεν πώποτε, *no one has seen God*. I recognise these words from Ioánnis's gospel. He is looking upwards but looking at nothing, his gaze is vacant, unattached as if his attention was not external but internal. His inspiration is coming from within himself.

I remember the usual ikon of Ayios Ioánnis, seated in the cave, his scribe beside him, attention focussed on the revelations that were being shown to him. Dictating what he saw. A vessel for the transmission of God's revelation. The ikon I have here is quite different.

I tilt it to allow the moonlight to illuminate the surface fully. Only then do I notice, in thin black letters, further script. They are written on the top right hand side of the ikon, away from where the saint is looking. It is easy to read, Ἐν ἀρχῇ ἦν ὁ

82

λόγος, *In the beginning was the Word*. The start of Ayios Ioánnis's gospel. The passage that describes the word, the logos, language.

Something about this ikon unsettles me. Without understanding it I can, at least, recognise that this is a disturbing image. Now I realise what that procession was about; a need to hide it away. But why with such ceremony? Chanting, the Abbot following behind, hidden away but with a degree of reverence which would be strange if it was simply an anathematised ikon.

My mind has had all it can take. I become aware of an overpowering feeling, a feeling that is fanned by the steadily building breeze that is blowing around me. A need to go, to get away, to escape. To leave.

Quickly I wrap the ikon in its sacking and place it back in its hiding place. I lower the heavy slab, turn the lock and escape from the little church.

I run down the mountain track, surprising myself at my agility. Soon I reach the town. I cannot stop, not even when I come across bodies in my path. The monks have emerged from the Monastery and are tending to the wounded.

I reach the shore. Will it still be there? Many of the fishing kaikis are gone; commandeered, no doubt, by the corsairs. Please let mine be there. I run to the end of the beach. There it is. Hauled up under the tamarisks, partly hidden away. My determination gives me extra strength. I haul the heavy kaiki down to the water's edge. I climb in to check that the oars are inside. They are, as is the simple sail. The water container lies in the base of the boat, empty. I grab it and run to the well. The whirr of the mechanism echoes across the bay. There are few other sounds. I can see no sign of human activity. Once it is full I heave it along the sand to the boat.

In the dark I do not see a dark obstruction that is in my way, not until I trip over it and fall heavily. Luckily none of the water spills. I get up and look down at the obstacle.

Now I can see what it is. It is Baba, the sand stained deep with his blood, his body still warm. Now at last it reaches me, the horror of all that has happened. Baba, Anna, Stefanos, Father Ignatios, the violation. I fall forward on to my arms and vomit into the sand, a tearing, aching vomit that seeks to rip the whole of my insides through my throat. My eyes stream with tears, the burning in my arms becomes intense. I am immobilised.

I lift my head and, like some wild creature, howl to the moon.

Nothing changes. Nothing moves. I must get away. I struggle the last short distance to the boat and heave the water container on board. With a strength that surprises me I haul the kaiki into the water, reach for the oars and set out. I have no idea where, all I know is that I have to go. I have to leave.

I row vigorously and soon I am out in the wide bay. The Meltemi is picking up in strength so I raise the simple sail. The kaiki runs well before the wind. I can sit in the stern and steady the tiller. We are making good speed. Southwards, a direction that I have never sailed before. We sail out, my little kaiki and I, out into the open sea. There is a gentle swell running from behind us.

I look back. The shape of the island, so familiar to me, is receding. Still a few lights of burning houses, torches lit on the Monastery battlements. The island is slipping out of me, inexorably, unconsciously. I am being emptied. Emptied by the horror, emptied by this journey of escape. It is as if I am being wiped clean; not just my mind but my whole self. My story has come to an end in the events of this terrible night. All I can know at this moment is the compulsion to go, to travel before the wind. Never to return. Empty.

My eyes begin to droop as exhaustion overcomes me. I lash the tiller to stay on a straight course and slip down into the gunwales of the boat, seeking rest. In the moment before I sleep I notice the first glimmerings of sunlight in the east but nothing can keep me awake now.

PERIIGIS PROTI

I feel the sun's heat on my back. I have no inclination to move for I am trying to understand where I am and what has happened. Events of the night have been evaporated by the burnishing light of the morning sun. I stay still, trying to remember. I am suspended, unaware of the gentle pitch of the boat, the rattling of the sail in the wind. I am cocooned in a moment of present; there is no past, no future. I am held in the exact moment.

Then I open my eyes and, to my horror, I see another figure in the boat. Another person? Did I fail to see them slip on board as I heaved the kaiki into the water.

The figure is sitting in the bow. I stare at her white shift, the long dark hair. Her face is away from me, her hand trails languidly in the water leaving a trail of ripples. It is Anna.

I shake my head as I pull myself up from my lying position. With a clearer brain I look up.

She is gone.

"Anna!" I call as if there were the slightest possibility that she might answer. But there is no reply. I look around. I am on my own, far out at sea. I can see no land, not even the smallest islet. The Meltemi is driving me south. I am resigned to running before the wind. Now the wind and the sea can have me, do with me what they will. I have lost Anna again, my desolation is complete. That momentary vision, no, not a vision, I could swear that she was real, puts a seal on the depths of my misery. Blow me, wind. I no longer care.

Hours pass and the sun moves towards the west. The sea is beginning to grow, the waves are larger. I have to guide the kaiki carefully to keep its stern to the mounting sea. Grey clouds are climbing up from the northern horizon like distant battalions. Normally I would be frightened but the impending storm does not concern me. If it takes me, overturns the kaiki and drowns me in the depths I do not mind. I can wait to see what my fate is to be. I feel disinterested in my outcome. I am emptied, a husk; there is no sense in looking for meaning in my life if it is about to end in a meaningless way; that thought causes me no concern at all.

A crack of lighting bisects the black northern sky. Thunder rumbles around the horizon. It starts to rain; steadily at first but then, with mounting intensity, accelerating into a downpour. In a moment I am soaked to the skin. It is a warm, hard rain that flattens the surface of the sea; not completely but enough to make the pitching of the kaiki more bearable.

I look behind me in the direction of the threatening sea. A grey mass is rolling up towards me, a huge wave that builds and builds. Already it blots out the horizon; I can hear its roar. The surface of the sea in front of the wave is being sucked up by the vast leviathan. It is only a short distance off. I am frightened now. I struggle to keep the stern of the boat head on to the wave, it must not catch me sideways on.

For a moment we are still. The wave towers above me like a huge rock face, frozen and overpowering. Then the boat is flung upwards and forwards. I find myself thrown into the bow, nearly hurled overboard. Water crashes down into the little boat, now spinning around and around. But still upright, we have not capsized.

And then it has passed. The sea resumes its usual pattern. I can see the retreating monster, rolling south, on and on to the African coast.

I struggle back to the centre of the boat. There is shipped water half way up the gunwales, the oars have gone but my water container is still there. With an old bucket I start to bail out the sea water. But now it is getting dark so I lower the sail and tie the tiller. The sea will take us now. I am exhausted, my arm burns like fire. Sleep overcomes me.

I awake before sunrise. The wind has eased and the sea is calmer now. We are making no progress so I raise the sail and continue the journey south. Thirst drives me to find the water container. I take a drink only to spit it out immediately. It is contaminated with brine. Seawater must have got in during the storm. I must have failed to seal it properly.

No water; that is serious. I was prepared for anything to happen to me but my reaction to the giant wave has shown me that there still remains a desire to survive. I cannot help myself. My reactions to events are bound to be those that will help preserve my life. There is no getting away from it. Even though my life has no purpose, no meaning, I am still forced to survive. All that I thought my life was about, my family, Anna, my studies with Father Ignatios, may have gone but there remains an animal-like urge to stay alive.

I have to find water; as the dawn comes up I scan the horizon. Nothing but sea, then, away to the south-west I spot a low shape in the far distance. I turn the tiller and set a course towards it. As I get closer I see it is a small islet. It cannot possibly be inhabited but I can make out some green. Vegetation; that must mean there is water. I urge the little craft forward.

As I approach my heart sinks. The shoreline is rocky. There is nowhere that I can put ashore. I sail around the island in a fog of frustration. Then, suddenly, I see a small beach of sand. I drive the kaiki in and jump out to pull it up the strand.

The vegetation turns out to be scrub, mostly thistles. There is no sign of any habitation. I climb a few rocks which form the highest point of the islet. Over the other side I am surprised to see a small herd of wild goats. They are gathered around a muddy spring, drinking from it in peaceful contentment. I still have enough skills from my days as a goatherd to know how to approach them unseen. I reach for my knife and single out a kid that should make good eating.

In a moment I bound down upon them and have the kid, bleating furiously, in my grasp. The others have scattered to goat-cries of protest. With my knife I slit its throat and allow the blood to drain on to the ground. I lay its lifeless body down and fill up my water container with the muddy water. Carrying both burdens I make my way back to the boat.

By now the sun is high in the sky. The Meltemi is blowing but more gently than before. The prospect of food reminds me that I have not eaten for two days. A driving, demanding hunger comes over me as I skin and gut the young goat. Leaving a pile of entrails steaming on the ground I search around for fuel for a fire. Soon the little body is roasting on the hot stones.

I survey the scene. It is going to be hard to get the kaiki off the sand without oars. Luckily this is a southward facing beach. Just so long as the wind holds it should be possible.

I eat my fill of the goat meat. The rest I store in the boat. I push and pull the kaiki until it is half in the water. Then I set the sail and with a huge heave set it off in a southerly direction. I only just manage to throw myself in the stern before the wind catches the sail and it heads off from the shore. That frightens me for a moment; to have been abandoned on that tiny islet would be stupid. And fatal.

We sail on. A gentle breeze keeps us moving southwards and I doze off.

I am awoken by a change. I sit up and look about. Far off on the horizon to my left I can make out a large land mass. It is a long way away. I look up at the sky, the wind has changed. We are now moving east. I have no choice, I shall go where the wind takes me.

I find some fishing line in one of the lockers, bait it with bits of goat meat then sling it overboard. Soon I am pulling in some good fish. I select the largest and throw the rest back. I am quite used to eating raw fish. I eat my fill as the sun descends into the sea.

I begin to lose track of the days as we sail on. I have finished all the goat but there are plenty of fish to catch. My supply of fresh water is getting low.

It is late one afternoon. We are making slow progress with a light wind behind. I am sitting in the stern, guiding the tiller, there is nothing to see in any direction.

Gradually everything that I can see, the bow of the kaiki, the water container, the sea around, seems to take on an increased intensity. A strange feeling comes over me. It is as if this were the best possible kaiki in the world, that this were the most perfect, most delectable sky. I feel lifted up, held. I have an overpowering sense of happiness, as if everything that is must be right. I feel at peace. All things are held together.

Within a time interval that I cannot determine but which must be brief, the feeling goes. Now I am left with a sensation of wonder, a wonder that I cannot understand. I want Father Ignatios here. He would explain it to me. Is this what he means by the love of God poured out like the new wine of Cana?

And the thought of my beloved old teacher, and of what has happened to him, brings me back to this world like a stab in the back, the world of contingency, where one thing leads to another. There is no escaping it. We sail on.

I have taken to lowering the sail whilst I sleep. The little boat rocks gently on the swell. It is a comforting movement, it allows me to rest. The pain from my arm is easing, the wound is healing with a livid scar. The violation is becoming a memory now. I have no pain from where I was penetrated. But I am still overcome with disgust and shame when I think of what was done to me by that brigand. The memory of his pole-like cock thrusting up inside my arse distorts my mind. It desecrates all that happened between Anna and me that same day. The tearing of his rape rips apart the tenderness of our love-making, despoils it, destroys it.

The burning is of a different kind now, a burning hatred of that man, a hatred that pulls in other, older hatreds. The Turk begins to occupy the same space in my mind as my Baba. Both

89

were violent towards me. Perhaps this is a violence that I attract. Baba never beat Stefanos and the Turk did not rape Markos. Love and hatred find themselves in close juxtaposition within me but now I am impregnated with hate; violence and hate. It threatens to overpower me.

Over to my left in the far, far distance. I can see a line of high mountains, covered in white. Snow; I have seen this before, in winter, on the mountains of the mainland. It is possible to see them on a very clear day. I have never seen snow close to, though. Later in the day I see mountains, again white covered, ahead of me now. We are travelling towards them; we are being taken towards land.

As night comes I keep the sail up. The prospect of land is exciting me. In any case the water container is nearly empty. I must make landfall. I sail on in the darkness, following a course in the stars.

At some time before dawn I become aware of the flat low shape of land. I can hear a gentle surf, breaking on the beach. I strain my eyes in the dark as the wind takes us in towards the shore. Now I can make out a long sward of beach, gleaming yellow in the starlight. Within moments the kaiki grounds. I run forward to the prow, grasp the rope and jump ashore. The sand is soft and deep and my feel sink in, up to my ankles. I haul the boat up the sand until it is safe.

I stop and look around me. It is an empty shore, as far as I can see. Inland from the beach is lush vegetation; not at all like the island, thick-stalked plants that rise above my head. A stream runs through the greenery. I collect the water container from the kaiki and fill it up. Beautiful, clear water, cool and refreshing, a pleasant change from the muddy liquid I had to steal from the goats. I drink deeply and settle down to wait for dawn.

As I sit there, hugging my knees, I think back. My escape from the ravaged island, the long sea voyage, the storm, all these seem to have been outside my control, my determination. But now I sense that my own initiative is returning. No longer am I in the

90

lap of the gods, or the fates or what you will. Now I am rediscovering Ioánnis and my first feeling is of panic. Here I am, stranded on the shore of a country of which I have no knowledge, with no plan of action. Should I try and return to the island if that were possible? It is quite apparent to me that this is not an option. The island has left me, it has slipped away and I am becoming a new person. There is a new story of Ioánnis that is beginning to develop. Not that I can perceive much of it at the moment. All I can be sure of is that I want to go on, I want to allow that story to develop. From the recent disinterestedness I am discovering a need to remake my life, to recreate a story, my story.

But I do not start with a blank sheet. I bring to the story my restlessness, my need to act, my desire to know, a violence and a loss, loss of the love that could have changed me yet again.

The sun has come up, shining over the mountains in the east. Now that there is daylight I can see how the land lies. Inland are olive groves, vast olive groves that stretch as far as the foothills of the mountains. And the mountains, what mountains! I can make out gorges, little valleys and then, high above, vast ranges of peaks. The whole vista covered in snow that gleams in the rising sunlight. I thought that our Mt Profitis Ilias was high but these mountains dwarf the island's little hill. The view is breathtaking. I stand in awe, staring at the sight. As I stare a purpose is growing within me, a sense of urgency that is compelling me to enter these mountains. It is not the same urge which drove me from the island, it is different from that. No longer is it escape; it is part of that sense of completeness that I experienced when I was in the boat, the sense that it is right to act, right to make this journey.. There is nothing to hold me back, indeed there is no other choice. I neither feel elated nor cast down by this certainty. Picking up the water container, I set off, heading for the mountains.

MEROS DEFTERON

Chapter 11
The Lebanese Mountains

I don't understand why this land is so empty. I have trudged through olive groves for hours now but have yet to meet a single person, nor have I seen any sign of habitation. Where am I? I know that my journey must have taken me out of the deep blue Aegean sea into the vast Mediterranean. Is this Cyprus? I have heard of the island but it cannot be as large as this land mass, nor can it have such high mountains. Baba used to tell me stories of the Frankish armies that sailed this way to the Holy City, but that was two hundred years or more ago.

Those were the days when Baba was gentle to me, when I was much younger. The memory of that time fills my eyes with tears. However vicious he was to me I want him back; he was my Baba. The memory of him is of violence but that earlier, more distant time is deeper within me. The Baba who, despite it all, I loved.

After a few hours walking I leave the coastal plain as the land begins to rise towards the hills and mountains. From a raised vantage point I can now see a small village some leagues away. White, flat-topped houses, a little church with a reddish dome. I do not want to meet anyone so I pick up my pace as I steadily gain height.

Soon I have reached the snowline. This landscape is unfamiliar to me. The sun is bright in a deep blue sky above me but the air is chilly. The snow glistens in the light, my feet crunch their way up a simple path, climbing towards trees, a whole forest of trees.

And what trees they are. Tall and evergreen with massive trunks. Branches sprout out at a right angle and their splayed

93

foliage forms a platform for the falling snow as well as a shelter underneath. I have seen a tree like this before, although much smaller. On the little islet of Ayios Yiorgos, just off the north of our island there was one of these trees. The fishermen up there said that in days gone by hermits lived under that tree. They had come from the east carrying seed which they planted in order to grow these enormous, protective trees. Only one survived and that was stunted by the barren, rocky soil.

I know these trees. Cedars, cedars of Lebanon. The same trees that were used to build Solomon's temple (I can remember Father Ignatios telling us the story). So this forest must be in Lebanon, that must be where I am, Lebanon.

I am not sure that knowing this is helpful. If I am found will I be treated well, or slaughtered as an interloping infidel? I shall have to be careful.

It is beginning to get dark. I find a sheltered area under one of the trees where the ground is free of snow. I wrap my cloak around me and settle down to wait for the dawn. Only now do I become aware of my growing hunger. Up here there is nothing I can find to eat so I turn my thoughts to anything that will distract me from the gnawing pain in my stomach. Inevitably the events of that terrible night predominate. I think of all those things that Father Ignatios taught us about a loving God. Yet that night God appeared to be locked away within the hard walls of the Monastery with the monks. Is that what God is like, protecting himself? Not at all like the loving father that we had been told about. The new Ioánnis begins to doubt as sleep overtakes me.

I am awake before dawn. The night is not quiet. I can hear something deeper in the forest, further up the mountain. A low grunting sound, heavy breathing. My blood turns to water as I realise that the sound is coming towards me. I tense myself for possible flight and peer, pupils widely dilated, into the darkness. I can discern a faint cloud in the blackness, exhaled breath. Making as little movement as possible, I reach around me on the ground until I have found a moderate sized rock, big enough to fit easily in

94

my hand. The noise is getting closer. I tense myself, my insides taut, my throat dried to sawdust, my heart pounding in my chest.

It shuffles into sight. A large, grey bear. I have never seen such a creature before but I know its appearance from drawings. It stares at me, its eyes are small and expressionless. Its head swings from side to side. For a moment it reminds me of Baba. It seems to be working out whether I am worth eating.

Years of practice with the goats have given me a good arm and an accurate eye. With as terrifying a shout as I can muster, I hurl the rock hard, directly at the animal. My aim is good, it hits him right between the eyes. It is never going to damage him but it should hurt. It certainly seems to because he lets out a howl, turns around and lumbers off into the forest.

I stand where I am and laugh. I laugh and laugh out of sheer relief, out of pent-up fear, at the banality of the encounter. Eventually the laughter stops. I sink to my knees, shivering uncontrollably. It is obvious that I must get away from here so I gather up my things and climb upwards through the forest.

As I emerge at the top the sun is appearing above the skyline high above me. I welcome its weak warmth. Over to my left I see what appears to be a way into the mountains. It is a rocky gorge, obviously sheltered because there is little snow there. It is a walk of about two hours to find my way to the entry of the gorge. I peer upwards into the cleft in the mountains. A huge jumble of rocks and boulders stretches upwards. There appears to be a trace of a path through the chasm of rocks so I follow it. Bit by bit I rise higher until I can see that the gorge is taking me up to a hanging valley, a valley hidden in the high mountains. I heave myself over the last few boulders and stand upright.

What I see is completely unexpected. There is no snow here. The valley floor is about four field-widths across and stretches away into the distance. It is green and full of foliage; olive trees, apricots, apples. Only after a while do I realise that it is all cultivated. I see green crops, vegetables all in well-ordered fields. I look into the distance and there I see a small village of single-storey stone houses, some rising up the cliff that marks the end of the hanging valley. Smoke is rising from the morning fires. I can make out a few people moving about.

I have no choice. I cannot go any further up the mountain, the way is quite impassable. If I go back down I am very likely to meet a bear with a painful head and a taste for vengeance. I have to risk it with these people. I cannot believe that they are bloodthirsty Christian slayers so I set out towards the village with such small amount of confidence, bolstered by my innate optimism.

The path takes me through the fields, zigzagging between the irrigation ditches. Water off the mountain must keep this land fertile, the little rivulets and culverts are cleverly arranged so that all the fields are well watered. I am getting close to the village now.

A dog rushes out towards me, barking fiercely. I turn my head away and ignore it. That is usually enough to quieten it down. A small boy follows the dog. He is dressed shabbily and two rivers of snot dribble down from his nostrils. He says nothing, just stares.

"Hello, boy. What's your name?" With a shock I realise that he is the first human being I have spoken to for days. But he is not to know that. There is no response from him apart from an increase in the gape of his mouth. He wipes his nose on his sleeve.

"Where is this place? Can you tell me?" This has an effect, but not the one that I had hoped for. He turns and runs back into the village, shouting wildly.

Within moments two women and an old man appear. He is carrying a wooden-handled hoe which he brandishes in my direction. They are calling things out to me but I cannot understand their language. I have heard the language of the Turks when they traded at the island, Arabs as well, on occasions. This language was nothing like theirs.

"I'm sorry," I call out, "I do not understand you. All I want is something to eat." I point to my open mouth in the universal gesture of demanding food but that only agitates them further.

96

The old man is waving me away, indicating that I should leave the village. I stand my ground.

"I cannot go back. I have to stay here. Please give me something to eat." Obviously they cannot understand what I am saying but perhaps they have picked up the tone of my plea. The old man stops waving me off and the three of them retire into a little huddle, still speaking unintelligibly but at least their tone is less agitated. One of the women disappears, soon to return with half a loaf of bread and a cup of olive oil. Nervously she hands them to me.

"Thank you. You are very kind." I sit on a rock and assuage my hunger with the bread and the oil. The bread is a bit hard but the oil is fresh and delicious. They watch me carefully from a safe distance. Once I have finished I stand up and hand the container back to the woman. I smile at her and this time she smiles back.

"Is there anywhere that I can stay? Just for a day or two? I have some money" though as I say this I realise that my few coins will be of no value here. The old man mutters something and disappears back into the village. The women follow.

By now I have collected a considerable audience of children of all shapes and sizes. Mostly as ragged and as snotty as the boy I first encountered. Some of the boys, not all, wear spotted head-dresses, scarves tied around their head and hanging down over their shoulders. They are all silent. They stare at me, I look at them; the sun beats down.

We must have been frozen in this state of mutual gaze for quite a few minutes. I am not aware that anyone else has appeared until a voice behind me, a gentle, unthreatening voice, speaks to me in my own language.

"Greetings, brother. Can we help you?"

Unable to hide my surprise I turn at this voice and am confronted by a young man, taller than me, with dark hair and dark features. His deep blue eyes, hooded by generous eyebrows, are nonetheless friendly. He is smiling at me.

"Who are you?" I stammer. He should have been asking me.

"My name is Ibn al-Hassif, my friend. And do you have a name?" He is still smiling.

"I'm sorry. Yes of course. My name is Ioánnis."

"Ioánnis, John, welcome to Kashaya".

"Kashaya, that's this village is it? Is this Lebanon?"

"Yes. You're right, but not many people know of this village. We're well hidden away up here." The effect of this amicable conversation is dramatic. Suddenly I am overwhelmed with a mixture of grief, happiness and exhaustion. My head begins to swim.

"Careful," calls Hassif and he steps forward to hold me before I collapse. "Sit down here." He switches languages and calls out orders to the children who surround us. They scatter as Hassif helps me to sit down on a low wall. Within minutes they are back with fruit, apricots, peaches and a flagon of wine. As I eat and drink I begin to feel better, less faint.

And then I look at myself. What must they make of me? Old cord sandals, breeches that are torn in many places and a filthy white shirt, stained with blood: my blood, goat's blood, the blood from my Baba. Despite my appearance Hassif does not seem to be concerned as to how I have come to be there. He seems to accept my arrival as a natural turn of events.

"Come, we must find somewhere for you to rest. You look exhausted and," he chuckles at this "you could do with a change of clothes. Here, take my arm." Supported by his strong arm we make our way into the village.

It is an orderly village. Small houses, some built of stone, some of clay bricks, all with flat roofs. As we pass people watch us with interest but no hostility. Again I hear snatches of a language that I cannot understand.

"Here we are. This is my house. Please enter." I stoop to pass through the doorway. It is dark inside. I can just make out a figure in the corner wearing a dark shawl.

"This is my wife, Soraya and this", he reaches down to pick up a small child, "is my little boy, Ibrahim." The child squirms in his arms so Hassif puts him down. Ibrahim runs to hide behind his mother's skirts. Hassif speaks again, this time to his wife. I recognise the language this time, it is Arabic but I still cannot understand it.

"Come, Ioánnis. We have a bed for you. I think you need to sleep." He leads me through to a small room at the back. It is bare but clean. The walls are white-washed. A single bed with a firm mattress runs along one wall, blanket folded at the end. Soraya appears with a bowl of water and towels. Hassif smiles at me.

"We'll leave you to wash and then sleep. When you wake I shall bring you fresh clothes." He closes the door and I am alone.

I sit on the edge of the bed. What is this place with its strange language and this gentle, hospitable Arab and his family? I had always been told that Arabs were bloodthirsty, anti-Christian and warlike. These were the stories that the men of the island told me about them. Can I trust Hassif? I am so tired I have no option. I pull off my clothes, wash in the clear, cold water and settle down in the bed.

But my sleep is troubled with dreams. I am back on the island, there is fighting and bloodshed all around me. Then Baba is in front of me, pulling off his belt, raising his arm to flail me with it. With my knife I slash at his throat. His blood covers me. I am screaming and screaming. I wake, still with the cry in my throat but just in time I stifle it. It is dark so I lie still; there's no sound apart from a gentle breathing from the room next door.

The dream has terrified me but now I am overcome with a sense of calmness, almost of relief. I drift off to sleep again.

When I wake it is light once more. I can hear sounds from the village; chickens, the occasional bray of a donkey, children playing in the street. There is someone moving around in the main room of the house, probably Soraya. I smell the welcoming tang of baking bread.

From further up the village I hear a strong, wooden hammering sound. Rhythmic and constant, it continues for about two minutes then stops. I feel so comfortable. I am content to lie back in bed and let all these sensations roll over me. This is the first time I have felt like this since before the raid on the island. And with that thought I am once more robbed of any peace, remembering everything that happened on that night. Now all I can think of is Anna, my Anna; torn away from me just at the moment when we had discovered each other, gone forever. Feeling like this I have no wish to go on. My heart is emptied.

There is a knock on the door and Hassif enters. He is carrying a bundle.

"Here are some fresh clothes for you, Ioánnis. They may not be the most perfect fit but I think they'll do."

Now I have a chance to notice how he is dressed. A tunic and cloak and a spotted head dress, held on by a red cord.

"Hassif, you dress like an Arab."

He laughs. "That's because I am an Arab, brother Ioánnis."

"But you don't seem like an Arab."

"And what should an Arab seem like, pray?" he says still smiling.

"Oh, I don't know "

"I know. Bloodthirsty, war-like." I blush at my prejudices. He laughs again. "Put these on, Ioánnis. Then come and have some breakfast with a bloodthirsty Arab." His laugh is open and infectious. I smile as he leaves the room.

We breakfast on bread, goat's milk, raisins and dates. It is wonderful to eat fresh food again. I feel the strength returning to my body. When the food is cleared away Hassif turns to me.

"I think I should show you all the village, now."

"I'd welcome that. I have many questions."

"Well, we'll take them bit by bit. Come, let's go" and he ducks under the front door, out into the street.

I was to discover that it is later in the morning before the sun's rays reach the village. The huge mass of the mountain rising from the edge of the valley keeps the small commune in the shade until well on in the morning. It is just appearing now. I welcome the warmth for we are high up here, the night has been cold.

I stare up at the mountains, rising like massive cupped hands above us, enclosing our hidden valley. There is snow on all the slopes of the mountains except where the rock is too steep to allow it to accumulate. Ice shines off the rock in the morning sun. Every now and then I hear a distant crack and low roar as small avalanches slip down the face, high up above us.

The snow comes to an end at the foot of the mountain side, not intruding on the fertile greenness of the level ground. Hassif notices me looking.

"It hardly ever snows here; and we get very little rain too. We rely on the melt water in winter and mountain streams in the summer."

"Have you lived here all your life, Hassif?"

"No, not me. I came here a few years ago."

"With Soraya?"

"Yes. Soon after Ibrahim was born. Her family came from this village originally."

"So why?"

He smiles but there is a hardness in his eyes. "You've got a lot of questions, haven't you, my friend." I look abashed. Have I upset him? I think he senses my concern.

"No, you've a right to ask. All this must seem very strange to you. Ask away." His permission is reassuring.

"Is this an Arab village, or it is Christian? I can't make it out; and what is this strange language that everyone speaks; and how can you, an Arab, speak in Greek, my language?"

"Hold on! Hold on." He is laughing again. "Let's take it slowly Ioánnis. A dullard like me cannot keep up."

We have been walking through the village and, at this moment, we turn a bend. Up ahead is a larger stone building. It is

101

a church, built in the old style, a rectangular space, no dome. Hassif leads me in through the narthex into the body of the building. I stare at the ceiling which is formed from massive beams of cedar.

The interior is plain. No ikonostasis, just a simple stone altar. No ikons that I can see but behind the altar is a wall-painting. The figures are primitive and the colours have faded but there is enough for me to make out the scene. I recognise the oak leaf, an old man and three figures with wings. Abraham at the oak of Mamre. There was a similar ikon in the church of Ioánnis Prodomos, back home on the island. This painting is old; certainly much older than the ikon that I knew. Hassif has come up behind me.

"Ibrahim" he murmurs softly, "our ancestor and your ancestor." My gaze is fixed on the painting. "This is a Christian church, Ioánnis but in our language, the language of the village we have the same word for God, Alah. We worship differently but we worship the same God."

"So where is your mosque?" I have not seen any domes or minarets.

He smiles. "It is here. Here where you are standing. Here we meet for prayer. We share, Arab and Christian alike. Sometimes you cannot tell the difference."

"But surely" I am confused by what he is saying "surely we believe completely different things."

He shrugs his shoulders. "Perhaps, but up here, living like this it is what we do that is more important than what we believe. We need to get along in order to survive," I notice a darker look cross his face, "there has been too much of the other way down there," he indicates, with a nod of the head, the way down the mountain. " I escaped from there, but only just. I was lucky to find this village."

I stare at him for I cannot begin to know what has been happening, what is happening. But I do have a moment of identification; both of us are refugees from violence. Once again I feel a sense of relief.

"Let's go outside, Ioánnis. I need a drink."

We sit in the shade of a large holm oak that grows just outside the church. Hassif produces two mugs and scoops clear water from a small aqueduct that runs alongside the square. "Now you must tell me something of yourself, Ioánnis." His enquiry seems natural, I am not offended. "Where do you come from?"

"My home is a small island in the Aegean Sea, not far from the mainland. It is a wild island but there is a large Monastery above the town. The Monastery owns most of the island. I'm a fisherman. I catch fish with my father's boat." I feel a claw reaching for my throat, making it is hard to speak. Hassif is silent but attentive. "Corsairs, brigands arrived one day. We had no defence against them. They slaughtered many people, including my Baba," I start to cry but he does not move "and they burnt down many of the houses. Families were burnt to death, families that I knew." I pause for I doubt whether I can continue. There is a silence before he speaks.

"Families you knew?"

I look at him. What is he asking? "Yes," I hesitate, knowing that I have to go on "including Anna." My voice falters.

"Anna, who is Anna?"

"I loved her. I loved her and those bastards burned her to death." I feel as if my chest will burst. I need to swallow but my throat is dried up.

"Here, take a drink," he is offering me a mug. I drink and it helps.

"Go on, Ioánnis. Did the brigands catch you?" I turn to face him; has he guessed? "I think perhaps they did, brother. Did they hurt you badly?" I cannot speak but I nod, not daring to look at him.

"I know these people and their ways. You must feel a great hurt; and anger." I cannot look at him but suddenly the anger is too much.

"How do you know? You can't know. How do you know?" Quite involuntarily I am shouting.

"It's all right. Anyone would feel angry. Perhaps ashamed, too?" There is another pause. The midday air is still. I feel desolate and start to cry again, quietly but insistently. I feel his arm go around my shoulders. I can feel his warmth alongside me. We stay like this for some minutes until the tears have stopped. Hassif stands up.

"I think we need to eat. Come, my friend," he offers his arm. It is accepted.

Chapter 12

It is many months since I arrived in the village of Kashaya. Almost unconsciously I have slipped into the gentle way of life of the people here. I have no sense that this tall, dark-haired Greek is seen as an intruder.

I have met most of the inhabitants of the village by now, even though our conversation is only in signals and mime. The language that they use in Kashaya is Aramaic. It used to be widespread throughout the region, even as far as Persia. Now there are only a few villages that retain it. It is the language that Jesus and the disciples used. Now I remember. It appears a few times in the gospels including Jesus' cry of desolation from the cross, 'Eili, eili, L'mana shurektain'. *'My God, My God, why have you forsaken me?'*

Most of the villagers are Christian but a significant minority are Muslim, like Hassif. Nevertheless the Arabs speak Aramaic except during their prayers when they use Arabic. I find it hard to believe that Christians and Muslims can share the same church but there seems to be no difficulty for them. There is an imam, a young man who leads the prayers four times each day. Otherwise he farms like everyone else. He also has a large herd of goats but the milk and cheese from these animals appears to be freely available for all, as does most of the produce from the fields.

Hassif introduced me, early in my stay, to Father Mouannes, the village priest, the only other person, apart from Hassif, who speaks my language. He explained to me that they were Maronite Christians, followers of St Maron. They were similar to other orthodox churches but had been cruelly persecuted by the Byzantine Emperors in the past. For this reason some had hidden in the mountains and established the village in this out of the way spot. Arabs and Christians had always lived happily together in ancient times. In Kashaya that had continued.

I asked Father Mouannes how it was that Christians and Arabs shared their worship. I had seen Arabs attending Christian feast days, Christians joining Arabs in their prayers. He gave me the same answer as Hassif.

"It is not so much what we say or believe, it is what we do that matters. We speak the same language, the language of Abraham, the language of Jesus and we all call God Alah. There is more that binds us together than divides us."

As I walk back to Hassif's house these words go over and over in my mind. So many people, myself included, are too ready to identify with one way, one understanding. I've heard it said time and time again, "You're either Christian or you're damned." Baba used to talk like that. He, and many men on the island used to hate Muslims (not that they ever met any). It was a deep seated prejudice. Perhaps there are Muslims who hate Christians too. Here, in this outpost of tolerance such small-mindedness seems stupid. His words echo around my brain, "There is more that binds us together than divides us."

In such a peaceful place it could be hard for me to remember what has happened in my life. The wound in my arm is well healed by now and I sense that change is occurring with the wound in my heart. The sense of the loss of Anna and of my family is just as acute as it has always been but from time to time the pain that that loss engenders is not as intense. The gentleness of this village is allowing that change to happen. So do my talks with Hassif.

One morning he brings water into my room for me to wash.

"How do you feel today, Ioánnis my friend?"

"All right. I am sleeping better now."

"Still dreaming?" A pause.

"Sometimes."

"Good dreams?"

"I dream about Anna mostly." I pause again, needing to collect my feelings. "I hate those dreams." My voice falters.

"Hate them, brother?"

"They torment me. In my dreams she is still here but I know she isn't. She's gone. Gone for ever."

"It makes you angry."

"Yes, of course, it does. Why shouldn't it?" He smiles gently but says nothing. "I feel really angry and that doesn't help."

"Angry with yourself, perhaps."

How does he know? I don't want to admit it. My voice takes on an aggressive edge, "What do you mean? With myself?"

"It's easy enough to be angry with those brigands, much harder to be angry with yourself."

"But I'm not to blame." I am blustering now. He sits silently. "How can I be to blame?" Tears of frustration begin to well up. I cannot look at him.

Another pause, then he speaks. "Listen, Ioánnis. It's not about blame. It's about anger. I say again, the hardest anger is with yourself. I know you couldn't do more to save her but your knowing that, for you, makes no difference to the power of the feeling, the feeling of anger towards yourself. Perhaps that is the feeling that you have to acknowledge."

I can look at him now. I look directly at those deep blue eyes. A shift has occurred, not just in me but also a shift in him. He knows me more and I have allowed that to happen.

"I think you're right, Hassif." It is a relief to say it. For the moment I can feel the anger draining away.

Over the weeks we have many talks. He takes me on walks out of the valley, on to the slopes of the mountains. There are countless little paths that can take us high up the declivity. The snow line is higher now as the year extends. He shows me a path that would take us over the skyline and down the other side.

"It's an ancient track, this one. Only passable in summer. It is the only way out of the valley if you want to get to Damascus or Antioch. That's many days walking on the other side."

"Have you been there, Hassif?"

"What? Dimashq? Yes, I've been there. A lovely city. Always has been, of course. Quite a Christian heritage." I remember the story of St Paul and his conversion. Hassif could read my mind. "Yes, the place where Paul went after his conversion experience Mind you, in one account he went off to live with the southern Arabs, the Nabuteans, for three years. You see how intermingled our cultures are." He broke into one of his uproarious laughs. We stopped to sit on a rock. The view was magnificent, sunlight on snow and the blue of the Mediterranean glittering in the distance.

"Have you heard of your namesake Ayios Ioánnis of Damascus?" I shake my head.

"He lived there, amongst the Muslims, a few hundred years ago. A very wise and saintly man. He was one of the principal opponents of the ikonoclasts." I was being treated to another example of my friend's erudition.

"Ikonoclasts?"

"That's right. Haven't you heard about them? The movement lasted for over one hundred years. They convinced themselves that ikons were idols and therefore should be destroyed. There was widespread destruction before the Church came to its senses, partly thanks to Ioánnis Damascene. And did your old Father Ignatios tell you about apophatic theology?" Again I shake my head. "Ioánnis was one of the main exponents of apophatic theology."

"Apo-what?"

"Apophatic theology? It is what the Latins call the via negativa." I am getting more confused.

"I don't know any Latin. Slow down a bit, Hassif, and explain." He smiles.

"Sorry, Ioánnis, I get carried away at times. Apophatic theology asserts that there is nothing that can be said about Alah in his essence. He is quite unknowable so that the only things that can be said are negatives, what he is not; infinite, immeasurable

108

and so on. Ioánnis Damascene showed us that. He also said that Alah can be known only by his actions, for example his redeeming love through his Son, Jesus Christ. There are good biblical precedents for this, mostly in the gospel of that other Ioánnis, Ioánnis Theologos" I am trying hard to follow this whilst he continues "and for us Muslims, there is a similar position. Alah cannot be described, he is only evident through his attributes and the word expressed by the Prophet in the Qur'an. We have a Sufist philosopher, a mystic, who propounds similar ideas to Ioánnis of Damascus; al-Ghazali, a very wise man."

We sit in silence and I try and assimilate what he has been telling me. God is unknowable. That is a strange thought. In my old understanding God has always been very much there, underpinning and controlling the world and my life. But now I begin to think about what Hassif is saying about apophatic theology I remember some of the ideas that Father Ignatios showed us. A God who controls everything would make us less than human. In his gentle way was old Ignatios taking us towards Ioánnis of Damascus? Taking us towards a God who is becoming ever more distant.

Later that evening I am alone, sitting on a large rock that rises out of the centre of the valley. Hassif tells me that it is known as 'The Seat of the Prophet' by the Muslim villagers and 'The Chair of St. Maron' by the Christians. It is a good place to sit and contemplate. Quiet evening sounds drift across from the village, goats bleating, children calling, somewhere a mother is singing her child into peaceful sleep. Smoke rises vertically from a number of fires, smudging the clear evening air.

I do not think that I could ever find a more peaceful, gentle place to live. Now I can see that it has helped to heal my heart. Not only the conversations with Hassif but the gentle hospitality of Soraya and the tolerant friendliness of all the people of the village. It has enabled me to rediscover my life, a life that was destroyed by all that happened on the island. This extraordinary village of Kashaya could become, for me, a separated Paradise, if I were to let it.

And so I know I have to leave. I climb down from the rock and seek out Hassif.

He does not seem surprised at my request.

"Certainly, Ioánnis. I knew that you would need to go. I could recognise it."

"Part of me would prefer to stay for ever. There is such peace here."

"Yes. I can believe that. But you are healed now, compared with the ragged traveller that found his way to us four months ago. Yet healed for a purpose. You have much to do, brother. Journeys to make, secrets to uncover, perhaps even people to find."

"Yes." My throat tightens. "I want to try and find Mama and Eleni. I know it may not be possible but I have to try."

He sits opposite me with his hands on his lap. Little Ibrahim is playing with some wooden blocks in the corner.

"You cannot go back the way you came. By now your boat will have been requisitioned, or wrecked. You have to go over the mountain. I will take you tomorrow, if the weather is right. I can put you on the road down to the plain." He smiles "I think we need to dress you better for travel, though."

The following morning he comes into my room with a bundle of clothing and a shoulder bag. There are stout sandals, a tunic and a cloak and, most surprising of all, a head-dress.

"Here, I'll show you how to wear it." He can see the doubt in my eyes. "Don't worry. You'll be safer on the road if you look like an Arab. Come on, put it on." He shows me how to fold and tie it, then packs my bag with fruit, bread, oil, cheese and a water bottle. Finally he hands me a purse. "Tie it to your waistband. You'll need it." It is weighed down with heavy coinage. I look up at him, quizzically. "Don't worry you can pay me back when you've made your fortune."

110

Soraya has prepared a good breakfast, knowing the endeavours that the day will bring. Soon afterwards we are striding out the village with the farewell calls of the people ringing in our ears but only after I make time to meet Father Mouannes in the church and to receive his blessing.

"Alah go with you, young man. You may forget all of us but never forget how all of Alah's children can live together in peace." I promise that I will, there is no doubt of that.

Hassif knows the paths well. He picks a route that zigzags up the huge sweep of the mountain's wall. The sun beats down on us as we slowly gain height. The village grows smaller and smaller whilst the high peak of the mountain towers above us. I begin to feel dizzy so avoid looking down.

After about two hours climbing we reach the ridge. It is a saddle between two peaks of the mountain. High pinnacles rise above us. Broken rock and scree slopes tumble away on either side. I take one last look at Kashaya far, far below. A momentary sadness tightens my throat. Will I ever see it again? Why am I leaving? For a moment I am tempted to retrace my steps, to walk back into the village and announce that I am staying for ever. But then, would I be made as welcome?

I turn back to Hassif. He has already started on the path that weaves down the other side. I look out to the east. There is nothing but heat haze and the white, limestone barrenness of the hinterland that stretches away into the distance. The contrast with my green valley is extreme. Is this really where I want to go, into this wilderness? I have no idea how I am going to search for the remnants of my family. No idea where they might be. Do I really want to be going on like this?

Without answering myself I set off down the path.

Chapter 13

It is some hours before we reach flat land. By now the sun has passed its zenith but the heat is still intense. Hassif is leading me through scrubby land, vineyards and olive groves. The trees are stunted and gnarled, the olives are green and hard with more time needed for them to ripen. By a small stream we take a rest and refill our water containers. Hassif turns to me.

"I think you should make your own way to Dimashq, my brother. I can set you on the road, it is not far from here. It'll take you another day to reach the city so you'll need to sleep under the stars." Hearing this makes me glad of the good cloak that he has given me. He is reaching into his bag for something.

"Here is the name and the address of a man who will take you in but be sure to give him this letter. Don't speak to anyone along the way, keep your scarf up over your face and guard that purse," he pointed to my waistband.

"Is it so unsafe, Hassif?" My nervousness is betrayed in my voice.

"You just need to be careful. The city was sacked by Timur and his Mongol warriors less than twenty years ago. You can still see the heap of skulls of the people of the city, piled up in a field outside the walls. But the Mongols didn't stay and the Mamluk Sultan from Egypt has assumed control. It is more peaceful than it was but you'll still find bands of armed men roaming the streets. You need to be careful and," he is burrowing in his bag again, "you need to take this."

From his bag he produces a long-bladed dagger, safely enclosed in its sheath. My eyes widen with both excitement and horror. I am appalled that he would think that I could use this weapon. He hands it to me and I withdraw it from its sheath. The blade is straight and sharp, the metal glistens in the sun. For the first time I experience the thrill of being armed, of being protected. I realise that, should the need arise, I could use this blade.

"Damascus steel, my friend. The best in the world. Guard it well."

The handle is ornamented but shaped to fit my hand perfectly. Along the length of the blade runs a blood channel. It is an awesome weapon, just holding it awakens something within me, something covert and exciting.

"Well now, fisherman, you've moved into a different world now. Only use it when all else fails. Just showing it should protect you most of the time. Keep it well hidden in your tunic." He looks up at the sun. "Come on, we must move" and within a moment he is striding off again down a track that meanders through the olive groves.

Soon we are out in the open. There is less vegetation here. The sun has dried the ground to cracked rock and dust. Lizards dart from under our feet.

And then we are upon it. A wide road. Some of it is paved, some is dust. It looks ancient, running from north to south across our path. I turn and look back at the mountains behind us. Away to the north is another range. To the east and to the south is barren emptiness. A sense of panic rises in me as I stare at the at the desolation of this vista. Hassif has turned to me.

"Take the road to the south. That will take you to Dimashq by the end of tomorrow. Alah go with you, Ioánnis my brother." He is standing still, no longer the jovial guide. I look straight at him. "Goodbye, Ioánnis, he says gently. "I know it will go well with you." Tears fill my eyes as he puts his arms around me and holds me in a firm grasp.

The last person to hold me like this was Anna.

"Thank you, Hassif" I cannot find other words to say. He lets go of me and points to the south.

114

"Go. Go now, Ioánnis. Go." I set off along the road. I sense that I should not look back. When I do he has gone. The road is empty.

He was right. It is towards evening of the next day that I see, through the haze, the walls of the city. I have seen a few people on the road but they take no notice of me, a tall, hooded Arab who makes for the other side of the road. As I approach the city there are a few fields, the occasional low house. The ground is dry but there are irrigation ditches, although they are empty at the moment. Away to the right I see a large patch of land that is green. Tall trees that I do not recognise are scattered amongst the vegetation. That must be the source of water. As I approach, I can see that a river runs through it and out along the foot of the city walls.

And what walls. Higher and even more solid than the walls of the Monastery back on the island but as I get closer I can see that parts of the defences have been damaged. Some of the damage has been repaired with lighter coloured stone. In some places, though, there are gaps, as prominent as the missing teeth in an old man's mouth.

My road is taking me to the north-east side of the city, entering through a large, open gate. As I approach the city the road begins to fill up with people, chattering, shouting, some pushing and shoving. I can hear the calls of market sellers just inside the gate. I am swept along by the crowd and carried though the gate.

Unable to help myself I bump into a bent old man carrying water containers. He turns towards me, ready to complain. He is looking straight at me with a quizzical gaze. I tighten my hand around the handle of the hidden knife, not knowing what to expect. A moment later his expression changes. Something in what he sees in me causes him to grin broadly. I stare at his edentate face and wonder what has brought on this change.

115

"Al salaam a'alaykum, brother." He accompanies this greeting with a large, mock bow that causes his water carriers to rattle. The crowd surges and carries me away.

It is obvious to me that trying to pass myself off as an Arab is fruitless but so long as no one mistakes me for a Mongol I should be reasonably safe.

There are food sellers in the market. The pungent smells remind me how long it has been since I last ate properly. Immediately, as if called up by the aromas that hang in the air of the suk, I experience a huge hunger that needs to be sated now.

At one stall I see an array of colourful and tasty looking foods. I choose half a chicken that has been cooked in spices that I have never seen, or smelt, before. I wolf it down along with a flagon of sweet white wine. The effect is marvellous, intoxicating; all hunger is dissipated, my well-being is restored.

I reach in my bag for the name and address that Hassif gave me. It gives me a shock when I read it. 'Dimitrios Papadikis, Straight Street.' A Greek here in this Arabic city? I have to find him. I have learnt enough Arabic from Hassif to be able to ask my way. I approach a tall man in an Arabic head-dress.

"Al salaam a'alaykum. Can you tell me how to find Straight Street?" He stares at me and replies in Greek.

"You want the Christian quarter, young man. Follow this road here to the bottom. Then turn left and you'll find it." I thank him and make off.

He calls after me; his tone is rough. "Hey! Who you looking for?" I glance down at my piece of paper.

"Dimitrios Papadikis, sir. If Alah so wills." For a moment he pauses, then his stern expression cracks as he laughs.

"Dimitrios? Ha! The best of luck to you, young sir" and in a moment he has gone

I follow the directions. Soon I find myself in an open, paved street that stretches across the width of the city. This must be the street called Straight. I remember it in the story of St Paul's conversion. Somewhere along here must be the house of Ananias and somewhere here must be Dimitrios Papadikis. I am not sure if I am looking forward to meeting this Dimitrios. My encounter with the tall man back in the bazaar has unnerved me. But I cannot avoid it. I have to trust Hassif.

I wander up and down the street. This is certainly the Christian quarter judging by the crucifixes and the small shrines set into alcoves in the houses. I spot the blue dome of a church, only one street away.

There are only a few people about which seems strange. Only then do I remember. This is a Sunday; of course there would be few people about in a Christian quarter. My heart sinks at the prospect of finding nowhere to stay in this large city. Night is coming on. I slump down on a stone bench at the side of the road.

As always happens it is a few small children that are first to appear. They stand in a semi-circle, staring at me, keeping a safe distance from this weary Arab.

"Dimitrios Papadikis?" My voice is tired but I repeat the name, "Dimitrios Papadikis? Where can I find him?"

A little girl giggles which sets the rest of them off into peals of childish laughter. Then they start to chant. "Dimitrios Papadikis, Dimitrios Papadikis. Papa, Papa, Papa, dikis!" They start to dance up and down. My heart sinks; they are going to be no help.

"Scram!" I shout and they disappear in a moment. Except for one, a young boy who had remained quiet throughout. He stares at me with a solemn expression. Then, in Arabic, he speaks,

"Follow me, please, sir."

"Do you know Dimitrios Papadikis, young man?"

"Follow me, please, sir." I get to my feet and follow him. He sets off down the street. After a bit he dives off down an alleyway and soon we are standing in front of a solid wooden door. Halfway up there is a knocker in the shape of a long-fingered hand. The boy points at the door.

"Dimitrios Papadikis." I am staring at the disembodied hand. When I look up he has gone.

There's no turning back now. With trepidation I seize the knocker and beat a summons on the wooden door.

Silence. I wait. Still nothing. I beat again. My hand is still on the metal hand of the knocker when the door swings open. I nearly fall inside but manage to steady myself in front of an old woman, dressed entirely in black. She stares at me.

"Dimitrios Papadikis?" Her expression, which is blank and uninvolved, changes not one tiny bit. She turns on her heel and mutters something. I assume, correctly, that she means me to follow.

The house is well furnished. There are hangings of beautiful coloured silks, furniture of elaborate design and an air of opulence everywhere. She leads me to a large reception room and points me to a chair. I sit down on its extravagantly upholstered seat and wait. She disappears.

The air is still. Through an open window I can hear church bells, and further off, the sound of the muezzin. This is a cool room and I relax a little in its ambience.

The atmosphere is broken by the opening of a door at the far end of the room. A man enters, pausing a moment as his eyes adapt to the dim light of the room. He has black, curly hair and a strong face. He is no taller than me but much more corpulent. He must be at least fifty years old. His clothes are as opulent as the furnishings and I notice a ring bearing a large green emerald on one of his fingers.

"You're not much more than a boy. What's your name?"

"Ioánnis, sir. Are you Dimitrios Papadikis, please sir?"

"And if I am, what of it?"

"If you are, sir, I have this letter for you." I pull Hassif's paper out of from my bag and hold it out. At first he just stares at it, limply held in my hand. "It's for you, sir."

His face is expressionless as he takes it from me and opens it. His movements, as he unfolds the crumpled parchment, are slow and deliberate. Then he reads it. It does not take him long; within a few moments he looks up and stares into my face.

"Well, well. So you are a friend of Hassif, then. That is very interesting. Was he good to you?"

"Yes, sir. Very good to me. A real friend."

"Did he tell you about himself? How he came to be in that God-forsaken village up in the mountains?"

"No, not really. He just looked after me. I owe him my life."

"Your life?" he laughs. "So what about your life? Are you going to tell me?"

I begin to feel desperate. "Kýrie Papadikis, can you possibly put me up for a while? I know nobody in this city. I can work and once I do I can find a place of my own."

He interrupts me, sharply. "Young Ioánnis, of course you will stay here. That is what my friend Hassif asks and I never refuse a friend's request. Wait here." He has gone but within a few minutes a solemn looking man in his thirties appears. He is dressed in a loose tunic and wears a turban.

"The Master would like you to follow me, sir." I do as bidden and am taken across a courtyard and up some stairs. He shows me to a small bedroom. Through the windows I can see across the city, minarets catching the fading sun, the solid block of the citadel and beyond, stretching up into the sky, the mountains that I crossed only yesterday.

The room is simple; bed, chair and a simple desk. The decorations are Arabic, the only reminder that this is a Christian household is a small ikon hanging on the far wall. I step closer to look at it. An old man with a long grey beard and wearing an Arab head-dress. His hands rest on a scroll. It is Ayios Ioánnis Damascene. I smile to myself. He seems to embody the easy relationship between Arab and Christian that I found in Kashaya. And perhaps here in Damascus as well.

119

I sit on the bed and remove my sandals. My feet are sore and the cool air allows them to breathe for a while. I lie back and drift into a sleep.

Later, I cannot gauge what the time is but it is now dark, I am wakened by the servant returning. He carries a tray of dishes containing nuts, honey, goats milk and small oranges. He puts it down on the desk and leaves without speaking a word. The food is good and I soon devour it. I wander across to the window. It is very cool now, the sounds of the city are quietening. The moon is rising over the distant desert, a pale scimitar in the star-filled sky. I used to watch the night sky back home on the island, sometimes clambering up Mt Profitis Ilias in the dark to get the best view. Looking up now I recognise that the night sky is just the same here; stars, planets and moon. That recognition brings a brief comfort. Yet I am still a refugee, a fugitive from my home. Running from what and where I am going? I have no idea. My only option is to follow.

Dimitrios Papadikis is another mystery. It is obvious that he is a rich man, powerful as well. Why should he shelter me? And what is his relationship to Hassif?

There is much for me to discover but tiredness claims me so I make for my bed and for a long, deep sleep.

The keening call of the muezzin awakens me. The sound drifts across the rooftops, penetrating and enveloping the houses of the Christian quarter. Already there is activity in the suk. I can hear the calls of the vendors, the bleating of goats, the occasional juvenile bellow of a steer.

There is a knock on the door and the young man from last night enters. He brings water, towels and a complete set of clothing. He looks at me dispassionately.

"The Master would like you to wear these."

"Thank you. What should I call you, sir?"

"Not sir, for a start. My name is Abdul-Malik."

120

"Thank you, Abdul-Malik" he says nothing in response "and thank you for these clothes. I will be down shortly." With a peremptory nod he turns and leaves, closing the door behind him. The clothes are well made and of good material. No longer do I need to wear Arab dress. I wash and dress quickly, a white blouse and a red scarf, a pair of baggy trousers secured with a wide leather belt and leather sandals. I stare at myself in the tall mirror of polished steel that stands in the corner of my room. The clothes suit me. I stand tall these days and have taken on the musculature of an active young man. Dark hair, somewhat curly and untended and a dark beard that, at last, I have been able to trim with scissors left in the bedroom. I look into my eyes, fruitlessly searching out a clue. Perhaps within these dark eyes, I can make sense of the new Ioánnis, can discern the new line of his life.

Downstairs, I find a large table laid out with a profusion of foods, dates, fruit, cheeses, cool milk. I am surveying the cornucopia with ever-widening eyes when I am aware that someone else has joined me in the room. I turn to see a woman, elegantly dressed who is standing and perusing me. I would say that she was in her thirties; she has long dark hair which immediately reminds me of Anna, and expensive jewellery around her neck and on her fingers. She smiles at me in a confident way and holds out her hand. I stoop down and brush my lips over her outstretched fingers.

"So this is the new refugee from the mountains. Welcome, young man. My name is Constantina Papadiki. I believe you met my husband yesterday evening." I nod but cannot, for the moment, find my voice. "Well, are you going to introduce yourself?"

I pull myself together. Mama would not be impressed by my rudeness. "I am sorry, Kýria Papadiki. I am Ioánnis."

"Just Ioánnis? No other name?" and suddenly I realise that I have not used my patronymic since I left the island.

121

"No, madam. Just Ioánnis." She laughs; a high-pitched but gentle laugh, not unpleasant.

"Well, that is very singular but I expect we shall manage. Come and eat."

We settle down to eat and are soon joined by her two children, Kristos and Xanthe. Kristos is fourteen but Xanthe is only seven, the same age as Eleni. Looking at the little girl reawakens the pain of losing my little sister. And the deeper pain is to know that I have lost my Baba for ever and, with even greater anguish, my beloved Anna, burnt to death by those bastard brigands. Sadness and remorse so quickly turns to anger. I must not let it. Not here, not with these people.

Kýria Papadikis quizzes me during the meal. It is apparent that her husband has told her very little about me; not that he knows much himself, the letter from Hassif was not very long.

As the meal comes to an end Abdul-Malik appears and beckons me over. "The Master would like to see you. Please follow me." We weave our way through the labyrinthine corridors, anterooms and courtyards. Finally he shows me into a large room with light streaming through the tall windows. In the centre of the room is a writing desk; all around the edges of the room are sofas, cushions, drapes. The floor is tiled and the coolness is pleasant to my feet. There is a scent of jasmine in the air.

Dimitrios Papadikis is seated on a large chair next to the desk, he indicates that I should sit close to him, on an ornate stool. I comply.

"Well now, young Ioánnis. Did you sleep well?"

"Yes, very well, thank you sir."

"We need to decide what to do with you, young man." I am shocked by this. His hospitality has been kind, much welcomed by me, but I have assumed that it is temporary. I will have to be on my way. I look confused and he looks at my face and laughs.

"Ha! We cannot just throw you out into this city of Arabs living on the edge of a desert. Where could you go? Do you have a plan?" My head hangs a little lower, my voice is less distinct.

122

"No. No, sir. I have no plan."

"Well, let's put all thought of leaving out of your head for the time being." Abruptly he stands up. "Come with me," and he does not wait to see if I am following, he is already through the door and striding along the corridor. I catch up with him just as he arrives at the large outer door that opens on to the street, the door with the disembodied hand. A servant pulls the door open for him and soon we are out of the house and marching down Straight Street. I notice that we have been joined by a large Arab wearing a long sword. Kýrie Papadikis is speaking to him rapidly in Arabic, too fast for my limited knowledge of the language to understand.

"Keep up, Ioánnis. We don't want to lose you on your first day."

After ten minutes walking we arrive at what seems to be our destination. A large, square stone building. It must be some kind of a warehouse. There are large double doors on the ground floor, they seem well secured. At first floor level there is a wide pair of doors that open out on to a platform that protrudes from the building, overhanging the street below. Above the platform is a gantry with block and tackle. Definitely a warehouse.

The large Arab beats on the door with the handle of his sword. After a few moment I can hear the rattle of chains, the turning of a large key and the doors swing inwards revealing a dark space beyond. The door keeper is old and bent up yet surprisingly nimble. He bows to the Master.

"Al salaam a'alaykum, Kýri Papadikis." He bows.

"Good morning, Mustafa. Is all well?"

"Very well, Master. We have no problems." Kýrie Papadikis leads the way in the warehouse. As my eyes accustom themselves to the light I become aware of a treasure trove of goods. There are bales of material, cotton, silks, damask; artefacts of all kinds, statues, pictures; sacks of spices that perfume the air; furniture, hangings, all in a vast profusion. For a fisherman like me, just arrived from a small island, such wealth is difficult to comprehend.

"Well, what do you think, Ioánnis?" He has turned to me.

123

"I, it's, I mean, it's incredible. Where does it come from?" He laughs again; a rolling, rumbustious eruption that causes his whole frame to shake.

"Mostly from the East. It's not all for me. I just help it along its way until it ends up with a willing buyer."

"So you're a trader, is that right?"

"I suppose you could call me that. But I don't do the travelling and transporting. All this just passes through my hands. I am but a humble link in the chain."

I look at him, humble was the last thing that he seemed to me. "So why does it come through here, through Damascus."

"Always has. This is a very old city and cities survive on trade. A little bit of the value of everything here goes into the city's coffers. Meant to improve the place but I suspect that most goes to the Caliph in Cairo." He spits. "But I must keep quiet about that." Now he rubs the side of his nose, "Got to keep my nose clean," and he winks before letting out a huge guffaw. Mustafa giggles but the large Arab remains stony-faced.

Kýrie Papadikis lowers his voice and bring his face closer to mine. "The truth is there are many people in this city who would like to see Dimitrios Papadikis eliminated," and here he draws his finger across this throat to indicate how that might happen, "jealous people who do not like to see me, a mere Christian, succeed. But they also know that they need me. No-one else knows all the ins and outs, how to deal with the traders, how to find the markets for all these goods. Get rid of me and that source of revenue, for which they have to do nothing except sit on their fat arses, would dry up. But I have to be careful. That's why I always have this hunk of meat with me whenever I got out." He breaks into Arabic and calls, "Isn't that so, Hussein. You look after your Master." Hussein bows but does not smile. I can appreciate the protection his imposing presence, and his large sword, affords.

The Master leads us through to a room at the back. There are three upright desks and at two of them sit young men, Arabs, industriously scribbling on large ledgers. They look up as we enter but soon return to their work.

"Come and look at this, Ioánnis." Kýrie Papadikis is indicating one of the ledgers. I take a look. It is covered in Arabic script and numbers. "This records everything that arrived last week, its value, how much was charged in tax and how much went out again. Later on we enter how much it was sold for. That way I know how much profit has been made, out of which profit I have to pay all these people" his arm waves in a wide sweep "as well as keep my wife in the best dresses that she can buy." He pulls a comical sad face, "What a poor man I am, Ioánnis" and, once again, he roars with laughter.

After we have returned home he takes me up to his study. He is more serious now.

"Ioánnis, I have a proposal. I have been thinking hard about it and in the light of what Hassif told me, and what I can see with my own eyes, you are an intelligent and trustworthy young man. How a young fisherman came to be so clever is something I must hear on another occasion but, for now, I'll accept it. I would like you to work for me, in the office of my warehouse. The two boys there seem to do a reasonable job but they are Arabs and I don't altogether trust them. I need someone I can trust to oversee all the paperwork. Could you do that?"

For a moment I have to collect myself. Offering me a job like this, something I have never done before. Could I do it? I begin to feel elated.

"Yes, Kýri Papadikis. I think I could do it." He looks relieved.

"Well, that is good. You can live here. We have far more rooms than we need. But you are going to improve your Arabic first. I'll find you a tutor."

The following morning a gentle, elderly Arab man arrives. His name is Ibn al-Aziz, he is to be my tutor. He has a profuse grey beard and penetratingly blue eyes. It turns out that he is the imam of the mosque further down Straight Street from our house.

It is also apparent that he and the Master are good friends. I can sense the warmth between them.

"Well now, Aziz. This is the young student. We need him to speak Arabic like any young man in this city in precisely four weeks' time."

The old man smiles, "Dimitrios, my friend, that is a tall order. Some people never grasp the language."

"But this is not some person, Aziz, I can assure you. He's a promising young man. He'll do it, you'll see," and he left us to it.

Almost immediately I discover how hard it is to grasp the language. Aziz is very patient but I doubt whether I can manage the task, Kýrie Papadikis's confidence in me seems misplaced. Then, after a while, we begin to make headway; within three weeks I am reading most of the simple texts that he shows me. A week later I can manage to write the commonest hieroglyphs.

"There is much more to learn than the language, though, Ioánnis" said the old man. "I can see you have a broad knowledge in many areas, most surprising in a fisherman." I smile to myself. Old Father Ignatios' work had paid dividends.

After four weeks there is a conference. Aziz, Kýrie Papadikis and me. It is decided that I am ready to take up my post in the warehouse. The Master takes me down there one morning. I am surprised to find the office empty. I turn to Kýrie Papadikis.

"Where are the clerks?"

He smiles. "They've gone. I decided that you could do their job as well as the two of them." My face drops. Straight in as the only clerk. I can't possibly do it.

He can read my mind. "You can do it, Ioánnis. Take your time. I will not harass you," somehow I find that hard to believe but I swallow hard and set to.

"There are no deliveries expected, nor any to go out, during this week. You will have a chance to get your bearings."
That is some reassurance. I am also pleased that I am to continue my lessons with Aziz, twice a week. There is much more to learn,

126

not just how to speak Arabic. I enjoy learning with Aziz, in many ways he reminds me of Father Ignatios.

One afternoon we are sitting in the cool of the courtyard. Aziz has begun to teach me about the Holy Qur'an. He points out Surat 87, Al-Alah the attributes of God.

"You realise, of course, that we can never hope to describe God. He can never be spoken of except in his attributes."

"Yes. I know a bit about the philosophy of al-Ghazali." His eyebrows rise in surprise.

"You know of al-Ghazali? That is surprising."

"Yes, my friend Hassif told me of it. Similar to the apophatic theology of Ioánnis Damascene."

"Well, well! You are quite an exceptional young man. It is proving to be quite a challenge to teach you." He smiles gently.

Over the weeks that follow I work hard. At the warehouse I comb through the books, soon revealing that my predecessors had been cheating Kýrie Papadikis. Petty pilfering at the most so the Master has no need to cause a stir. I restore some order to the records and soon introduce a system which simplifies the whole process. He is pleased with the result and enjoys boasting to all and sundry about his brilliant young fisherman.

Aziz and I range far and wide in our studies. Mathematics is useful for my work. Aziz is very proud to open my eyes to Arabic mathematics.

"Nothing you Franks have ever seen, eh?" He always lumps me in with 'Franks', I suppose because I am Greek.

Or am I? I begin to wonder who I am. Yes, I come from a small island in the Greek sea but here I am in an Arab city being taught by a Muslim imam. My identity is being diluted. I am beginning to think like an Arab, questioning and exploring. Back on the island I was expected to accept things as they were, as they were given to me. This was particularly true in my dealings with priests and monks. The only exception was Father Ignatios. What he taught me has prepared me for my present studies. Every single day I bless him for it.

127

I attend the Church of the Holy Virgin Mary every Sunday. The Eucharist is identical with the service I was used to back home on the island, except that the singing is different and, of course, the language used is the same as in the little mountain village of Kashaya, Aramaic. On one or two occasions Aziz has taken me to his mosque. I am attracted to the cool atmosphere, the group devotion and the shared prayers.

But none of this helps me to understand who I am. I have a feeling that my "self" is being dissolved away in the face of a nameless, ineffable Alah whom I can never, ever hope to comprehend. In the past that perception would have frightened me, nowadays it begins to have attractions.

Late one afternoon I am returning home from the warehouse. As I push open the door of the house I sense that all is not well. In the hallway I meet Kýrie Papadikis looking deeply worried. He hardly seems to notice me.

"Is there something wrong, Master?" He starts at the sound of my voice.

"Oh, hello Ioánnis. Yes there is, my boy. The mistress is not well. She has the fever."

"Has the doctor been?"

"Yes, one of ours. He didn't seem to know what the trouble was. He is returning later to bleed her."

I don't like the sound of this. It has never seemed to me that draining an ill person of their lifeblood can do any good. It makes very little sense to me.

"Can I see the mistress, sir? Just for a moment." He looks at me dubiously, his eyes narrowed.

"I suppose so, Ioánnis. But only for a moment. She is very ill."

I am shown in to her bedchamber. Immediately I can detect the smell of sickness in the air. One of the maid servants is standing at the head of the bed, sponging her brow with tepid water. The mistress is hardly aware of me. I place the back of my hand on her forehead. It is burning hot. Her pulse is rapid but strong. I notice that a rash has spread over her face, all over except for around her mouth. That area remains quite pale. I am aware that the master is standing behind me. I turn to him.

"Well, Ioánnis?" he says no more than that but in his eyes I can see that he trusts me. For a moment that is frightening. "Is it smallpox? Or the plague? What's the matter with her?"

"Neither of those, master. It is a nasty fever but she will recover. She is strong. She needs plenty of fluids to drink, iced water if you can get it. She also needs some extract of willow bark. You can get that from a stall in the suk. I have seen it there. What she does not need is to be bled. That will only make things worse."

The scarlet fever. The pallor around the mouth gives it away. I have seen it before, on the island. Stefanos had it once. Only the very frail succumbed to it. The willow bark extract reduces the fever, the fluids replace all that is lost in the perspiration. That, and gentle, competent nursing is all that is needed.

Kýrie Papadikis thanks me briefly and sends off for ice which is brought down to the city from the mountains and stored in deep caves and cellars.

When the doctor returns with his lancets he is peremptorily dismissed. The master pays him off and sends him packing. I keep out of sight. Although I know I am right about Kýria Papadikis's illness I am nervous about sticking my neck out in this way.

The fever waxes and wanes over the next few days which causes me some worry. Perhaps I was wrong. I am reassured when, within a week, the mistress appears much better. Soon she is up and resting in the courtyard, lying out on a soft divan. It is there, one morning, that I come to her.

"Ioánnis my dear, I understand that I have you to thank for my recovery."

"Your recovery was in God's hands, madam. I merely aided the process."

"I am intrigued, young man. Where did you learn these skills?"

"We lived on a small island, madam. There were no doctors so I had to learn something about illness."

"Well, thank heavens you did. You really are an exceptional young man, exceptional and gifted." I blush, unused to compliments like these.

"It is pleasure enough to see you returning to health, my lady. That is all." I leave her to rest for I have to go to the warehouse. A caravan is due to arrive this afternoon. I need to be ready.

Chapter 14
Damascus 1421

I am sitting on a cold stone bench, trying to recall those events of three years ago but the memories are distant and vague. Yet their consequence is what has brought me to this shady courtyard; my mouth dry with fear, waiting to be summoned.

A few days after my mistress had recovered, I was ordered to attend on Kýrie Papadikis. I found him in his study. Aziz was with him.

"Come in, Ioánnis. Sit down here." With a peremptory wave he indicated a hard chair in front of his desk. Aziz smiled at me. "Aziz and I have been discussing your future." I wasn't sure whether I liked the sound of this but he read my expression, "No, no, don't worry. This is nothing unpleasant. As you know I am deeply indebted to you for your intervention in my wife's illness. It was truly impressive."

"So, young man" Aziz had taken up the reins, "we have discussed how your considerable skills might be developed. I have spoken to my friend who is a teacher at the al-Nuri School of Medicine," I had seen this madrasa, up near the Grand Mosque, "and they are willing to take you on as a student at the beginning of the year."

The School of Medicine Surely they did not imagine that I could manage that.

"But, but sirs, I could not possibly do that. I am ignorant, I have no money, I'm just a fisherman."

Kýrie Papadikis laughed. "Ignorant! Not according to Aziz here. And as for money, do not worry. I shall meet your fees. I am told that you should still be able to work for me for two half days each week. We can get in an assistant for you. There is time to train him up before you start your medical studies." I am silenced by this. After a few moments I find my voice.

"Thank you, sir. And thank you Aziz. I hope that I will not let you down."

The old man was smiling. "Of course you won't We have the greatest confidence in you." Once again I found myself propelled along by events. It never occurred to me at the time that I could refuse.

Time passed very quickly. There was so much to learn. My teachers, all of them Arab physicians, made no concessions for my lack of education. I was thrown into chemistry, pharmacology and physiology, subjects of which I knew nothing, and was expected to master them as quickly as my Arab fellow students. I was taught anatomy from the texts of Galen but there was no dissecting of cadavers. An ancient professor demonstrated distillation. Liquids were produced by this method that had powerful effects, particularly in inducing sleep during surgical procedures. Those of our teachers who were ophthamologists insisted that we learnt a technique of treating cataract that was special to Arabic medicine. A hollow needle is inserted through the white of the eye and the lens is sucked out. This gives the patient at least partial sight, for which they are usually grateful.

When it came to Mathematics I was on easier ground and once I reached diagnosis and therapeutics I was even more at home. It was hard work but I loved it. I was discovering a new world and a new sense of purpose. I could understand the scientific basis of the few things about illnesses and injury that I had stumbled on empirically. Now I could understand how and why they happened. There was much from my experience such as Eleni's dislocated hip and the scarlet fever that Kýria Papadiki suffered, which appeared in my studies. I was enthralled. Now there was nothing more that I wanted than to become a doctor. Not just to heal and cure but particularly to understand for there was still so much that even the greatest physicians did not know.

And I had come to admit to myself that trying to find Mama and Eleni was a hopeless task. Now I am struggling to come to terms with the idea that they are gone for ever. Perhaps I should have appreciated that before but there has been part of me which has always hoped that one day I should see them again. I need to be realistic and close down that hope now. There has been enough, more than enough, work to take my mind off them and the past in which they dwell as memories only.

I continued to live with Kýrie Papadikis and his family. The master let me use his library for study; a beautiful, peaceful room. The assistant that he found for me was a young Christian boy, Arab not Greek. He turned out to be very quick to learn and quite trustworthy so that my supervision was very simple. The master's business seemed to be flourishing, goods moved in and out of the warehouse briskly so his fortunes prospered. He still had his bodyguard whenever he went out but there never seemed to be a need for his protection.

I had noticed that there was another building abutting on to the warehouse. The windows were always shuttered so I had never seen inside. One night I had gone to my office in the warehouse quite late. There was a consignment going out early in the morning and I had to be at the al-Nuri madrasa at dawn. I was checking the roster so that I could leave a note for Ibrahim, my assistant. As I left and was locking up I was sure that I heard a sound from the next door building. I stood still to hear better. It was sobbing; quiet, gentle sobbing. A woman by the sound of it. I walked around the building but the sound soon stopped, to be replaced by silence. I waited but there was nothing else to hear so I made my way home.

I suppose that was six months ago. I soon forgot about it, being sunk in the multiplicity of my studies. It is only now, sitting here, that I have remembered it.

Sometimes I despaired at all that I had to learn. Aziz may have had confidence in me but even he could not have known how much there was to absorb. I was reassured when I passed the basic sciences exam, but chemical science was an even larger field. At times my head seemed unable to assimilate any more. As soon as something new was taken in, something old tumbled out of the back.

And so here I am at the end of the road. Sitting in this courtyard, waiting to be called in for my final examination. This is a new kind of fear for me; I who has faced the greatest extremes of physical threat. This is new, and unpleasant. I spent all of yesterday in the library re-reading the whole of Avicenna's *Canon of Medicine* but I know that it is probably not enough. My hands are cold and my mouth is dry. Why will they not come for me?

In the end it went through in a flash. Three of my teachers, each in turn questioning me. Now that it's over I cannot remember what I said; please God that it made sense. All of us taking the exam are waiting in the courtyard in the cool of the evening, waiting to hear our fate.

A door opens and the senior teacher walks out into the courtyard. With him is a servant carrying a scroll of papyrus. The teacher stops in front of us.

"Alah akbar!"

"Alah akbar!" we reply, as one voice. With no preamble at all he takes the scroll from his servant and unrolls it. He starts to read out names. After each name he indicates either to his left or to his right. The servant copies the signal so each student knows where to stand. After ten or so names have been read out there is only one poor unfortunate on his left, the rest are on his right. It is obvious that the successful go to the right, the failures to the left. He continues reading out names and the right hand group swells. Three others have joined the group on the left. By now they realise their fate and are looking deeply disconsolate. The moment arrives.

"Ioánnis Papadikis" (I have adopted my patron's patronymic); his hand hovers in front of him. I cannot breathe.

He points to the right.

In a daze I stumble to the large group and am received with smiles, muted congratulations and a few back-slaps. A few more names are read out and the ordeal is over. The teacher speaks to the group on his right.

"Attend tomorrow at noon and you will be issued with your degrees." His voice softens and he nearly smiles. "Congratulations, gentlemen." He turns to the left group. "I am sorry that you have not yet achieved the standard required. I am confident that, with diligent study, you will do so on the next occasion. Allah akbar!" We all respond once more. For me at this particular moment, there is absolutely no doubt that God is great.

Back home I am received like a conquering hero. Kýrie Papadikis pumps my hand in congratulations. Aziz beams, Kýria Papadiki hugs me in a huge embrace, reeking of oils and perfumes. A great feast has been prepared and the wine flows like the Barada river that circles the city. I am overcome by it all. I do not notice that Kýrie Papadikis has slipped out. I turn to Abdul-Malik.

"Where is the master? I can't see him here." For once Abdul-Malik looks a little shifty.

"I don't know, Ioánnis. Perhaps there is some matter that he has to attend to." Even though my head is humming with wine and excitement, his answer prompts a moment of anxiety. But I choose to ignore it. The steward fills my goblet again. I am soon swimming in a happy alcoholic haze.

Eventually the party quietens down. Tables are cleared. People take their leave of the master, who has returned by this time. Kýria Papadiki has retired to bed.

I need to clear my head. I slip out of the house to get some fresh night air. As I walk down the street I stagger a little, there is no purposefulness in my walking. I am quite unaware of where I am going, it could be anywhere. It is therefore a surprise when I find myself outside the master's warehouse. It is dark and the doors are secured, naturally. I stop to pee in the gutter, disturbing a rat that has been gnawing on a bit of rubbish. I

135

wander around the warehouse and find myself in front of the adjacent building.

In a moment I am hoisted out of my alcoholic fuddle. There is light in the building. I can hear sounds, human sounds. Not sobbing this time but moans and, interspersed, a low threatening rumble of a voice. Not a language that I recognise.

And then I hear the bolts on the door being drawn back. Quickly I slip into the shadow, hidden yet still able to watch the door.

It opens and a large form is framed in the doorway. It is a man, bald-headed, long moustaches and huge muscles. With a remarkable agility for one of his size he slips off down the street. The door is closed and bolted behind him.

I am frozen in terror. I cannot imagine what is happening in that house, what it has to do with the master. I cannot think of any of this for I have recognised that man. I know him. My mind has returned to the night of the corsair raid, in a recall so vivid that I can barely breathe. To the dark alley, to rough hands holding me.

There is no doubt in my mind. This is bastard who raped me. Fear transfixes me at this momentary glimpse of the man who so violently buggered me. I remain in the shadows but then, with the insane compulsion of a hunted animal, I find myself following him. He has disappeared down a dark alley. My fear should make me turn and run but instead it is leading me to seek him out. What am I doing? What do I want from him?

At the end of the alley I glance to left and right. Nothing to see. Then I hear the gentle splatter of water on stone. I peer in the direction of the sound and can just about make out his vast bulk in the gloom. He is pissing against the wall. He does not know I am here. Would he recognise me, in any case? Have I been one among many that he has raped and assaulted over the years. Would he remember me? Would I be special to him?

I shake my head in an attempt to obliterate such thinking. Without willing it I find Hassif's dagger in my hand. Now I am right behind him. I can see he wears a sword on his belt. I move to his left side, as silent as a cat.

I clear my throat. He is still pissing; a heavy, persistent steam. At my sound he wheels around but still has his hands on his penis. There is no time to think. With one firm stroke I run the dagger in through his left side. Underneath the ribcage and pushing it upwards and inwards, its razor-sharp tip seeking the large, left chamber of his heart. I feel the resistance as I pass through his diaphragm but the desire within me gives me the strength to drive it in. When I am certain that I have penetrated deep enough I let out a loud wail, a cry of triumph, a cry of completeness and I let go of the dagger.

He looks at me with a stare of amazement. His hands are scrabbling for his sword but then, with a gasp, his mouth falls open and a torrent of bright red blood cascades out on to the floor of the street, bouncing off the cobbles and splattering my tunic. Now I know my Damascus steel has found its target. Almost immediately he falls backwards. With a loud thud and clatter his body hits the ground. He makes no sound now but his limbs convulse for a moment and then are still. Blood flows from his side and from his mouth. I reach down to pull out my dagger and step back to avoid contamination. Now I feel no emotion at all. I have killed in cold blood and I feel nothing.

Then, for no conscious reason that I can understand, I step forward. His circumcised penis still lies outside his tunic, large and flaccid. I grasp it in my left hand and, with one stroke of my dagger, I sever it at its base. It is still warm in my hand, a drop of yellow urine falls to the pavement. I stare down at this miserable piece of flesh that has destroyed my life. Now it comes. The dam bursts and anger floods over me in great waves. I speak to him now.

"This is for you, you bastard!" My tone is steely, hard. I stand astride him and reach down. His mouth lies open, his eyes stare unseeing. I thrust the severed member into his mouth. It stands there, a wilted, grotesque, obscene monument.

Now my brain wakes up. I have to get away. Quickly I wipe my blade on his tunic and slip down the alleyway. He will not be discovered until morning but that is only three hours away. As I take a circuitous route to Kýrie Papadikis's house my mind races. I have to get away but where to go? With this one inexplicable act I am once again a refugee but this time a fugitive. I know my fate if I stay. I have heard of the beheadings in this city square. I can imagine it, one slice of the scimitar and my head rolling in the dust of the afternoon sun. Now I am terrified.

Back at the house I quickly find my room. Making as little sound as possible I start to pack up those things that I need to take. During the last three years I have acquired various medical instruments and supplies, I must take these. I change in to the Arabic dress that Hassif gave me four years ago. There is little else that I need to take. I turn to the door.

Kýrie Papadikis is standing there, unsmiling. He is fully dressed even though it is two hours before dawn.

"Well, Ioánnis?" What can he know?

"I'm sorry, Kýri. I thought I would go out for some air."

"Dressed like an Arab?" He takes a step towards me, "and why do you need that?" He points to my dagger.

"I'm, I'm not sure. Night time, dangerous" I stammer.

"Are you sure that it is not you that is the danger, young man?"

"What do you mean, Kýri? I don't understand."

"Then I'll tell you. Abdul-Malik has been to me with disturbing, very disturbing, news. I wasn't sure that I could believe him." I remain silent but my mind is racing. "There is a man with whom I sometimes do a little business, a Turk called Mahmout." I can feel my face reddening. "Not a very pleasant man but quite useful to me. It seems that Abdul-Malik discovered him dead in the street just half an hour ago. Not just dead but mutilated in a most barbaric fashion."

"But why are you telling me this, Kýri? I know no Turk called Mahmout." His eyes narrow as he looks at me carefully.

138

"Are you sure about that, Ioánnis? Only Ibrahim also found this lying near the body" and he produces a red scarf from behind his back. I knew it at once.

"Funny, isn't it. Just like the one that you wear. Perhaps you can produce yours so we can compare." There is no point in fabricating any further, my legs have turned to jelly. I sit back on the edge of my bed.

His tone is gentler now. "I think that, perhaps, you do know about this. Would you like to tell me?"

So I recount what has happened this evening. I tell him about the people in the building next to the warehouse. I tell him how I killed Mahmout.

"But why Mahmout? I know he is not the most likeable of characters but you are not a violent man. What do you have against him?"

I pause. I have told this story to no one other than Hassif but I have to tell it now.

"If I tell you will you tell me what is going on with those people in the building next to the warehouse?"

"No promises, Ioánnis. You are hardly in a position to make deals."

I swallow hard. "As you know I escaped from an island after corsairs raided and killed and captured the inhabitants. The leader was that man, Mahmout."

"So this was revenge?"

"Please be patient; there is more but it is hard to talk about it." He is silent as, bit by bit, I relate the events of that night culminating in my rape by the Turk, Mahmout. When I have finished he remains silent for a good minute before speaking.

"Now I understand."

"Understand?"

"The mutilation. I can see why you did it." His understanding takes the wind out of my sails. I begin to weep.

"Come on, Ioánnis. You have got to get away."

139

I put up a hand. "Wait. You said you would tell me about those people."

He hesitated for a moment, as if unsure, then relented. "No, I have to tell you." He sits down on the edge of the bed. "Mahmout is one of a number of people who trade in people, not goods."

"Slaves, you mean."

He winces. "I suppose so. I provide a trading post for them."

"But where do they go?"

"Lots of places, China, Persia but most go to the Ottoman Turks. They are well treated there, I believe. Some get to rise to quite important positions and the life for the women in the harem is not nearly as unpleasant as you might think."

With mounting horror I understand, for the first time, what may have happened to Mother and Eleni. At once I am filled with loathing for this slave-trader.

"I cannot believe this. How can you take part in this despicable trade?"

"Hold on Ioánnis", there is a flash of anger across his face, "you are in no position to take the moral high ground. In addition to which you need my help now." His voice takes on a steely edge. "It would be an easy task to hand you over to the city guard."

I am on dangerous ground but I still persist, my voice is trembling, "You could have sold my mother and my sister. Does that mean nothing to you?"

"I have to make a living. If I didn't do it there would be others who would. At least I treat them decently, see that they go to good owners."

I would like to believe this but I have my doubts.

His tone lightens as he reaches inside his tunic. He hands me a bag of money and smiles. "Here, take this, Ioánnis. We shall miss you about the place but go now." He escorts me to the main door and let me out into the early dawn. "God go with you. Despite all you are a good man."

140

I walk away without looking back, a fugitive with no destination.

PERIIGIS DEFTERI

Chapter 15

I manage to get away from the city without being detected. It seems wise to avoid the main gates so I slip out through a breach in the walls made by Timur the Lame the year before I was born. The level of the River Barada is low enough for me to wade across.

Which way to go? I cannot go back to Kashaya, I know that. To the east is dry desert. Only a camel caravan would make it through there. South is unknown to me but I do know the road north. I have made the northbound journey with the Master's caravans on more than one occasion, travelling as far as Aleppo where he has another warehouse. The trouble is the road is always busy. I need to put some distance between me and the city without being met by other travellers who might have heard of the bizarre murder in Damascus. And apart from the Mamluk police, who are sure to be searching for me, there are bound to be Mahmout's men, thirsty for revenge. So I have to avoid the road but yet travel north. The only way is to strike off to the west until I am in the foothills of the mountains. Then I can make my way more safely, crossing valleys and water courses, avoiding other travellers.

In the foothills it is refreshingly cool compared with the burnishing heat of the plain and desert. I pass through olive groves and orchards; cross streams that cascade from the heights above. I collect all the food I need, there is no shortage. My water skin is full.

Nevertheless my heart is distraught. With a single, fatal knife thrust I have torn my world apart. There was no anger, no fury, it was an act of impulse but also of coldness. I could have turned away, left him to his pissing. Why didn't I?

143

And I did not speak. He died not knowing who it was that was attacking him in that dark, Damascus alley; a silent assailant with an unknown grudge. I could have walked away but some impulse within me drove me to the extremity of that act. It frightens me to think that I incorporate such a germ of violence which part of me is nursing to fruition. Just when my new life was opening up for me I have destroyed it. Just one day ago I was prosperous, had a well-paid job for a good employer, had acquired the basics of a new profession, a new life far beyond the aspirations of a fisherman. Now I am a fugitive, not knowing where to go, not knowing who to trust; a murderer whose own life could be snuffed out in a moment.

My mind wanders as I walk on. I realise that over the last three years I had begun to think differently about Eleni and Mama. I had come to realise that finding them was an impossible task. In my mind I was beginning to let them go. But all that has changed since I have discovered the true nature of Kýrie Papadikis' business; the slave trade. All the old feelings of outrage and despair have reawakened and, with them the burning, desperate need to find what remains of my family. But now, as a murderer, I am on my own. I need them, Mama and Eleni. I need what might remain of my family.

But would they understand what I have done? Even I cannot comprehend why I did what I did. I am not a vicious person. How I could thrust my Damascus steel into the heart of the Turk, let alone deface him as I did? But, and this is strange, I feel no remorse. The two acts, killing and defacement, have a kind of logical compulsion, a fitting way to complete the story. It is appropriate that the pirate should end his life in a Damascus back alley with his cock stuck in his mouth. No, I feel no remorse.

I have been two days away from the city. Apart from a herd of goats and a few solitary dogs I have not met a single living thing. It is evening now and so I rest underneath a large boulder beside a stream. The sun has long since disappeared over the mountain skyline. A chill is setting in. I wrap myself tightly in my cloak and settle down for the night.

It is Father Ignatios who is on my mind now. What would he say if I were to tell him what I have done? Now I feel ashamed; yet I have no sense of censure from God. I would expect to feel guilty in the face of the Almighty. It is not that I do not feel guilty rather it is that, sitting here in this chill, quiet night, I have little sense of God. Very little sense at all. It is the first time that I have experienced such absence of feeling. I feel the absence of God; not just God gone away for a while but a complete absence. It is strange because for all my life, at least for as long as I can remember, there has always been God; sitting behind events, watching out for me, ever-present. That has evaporated like the morning dew. It is not a fearful feeling, just new. I do not know what to make of it. I need Father Ignatios but then I remember that he is dead. I shall never be able to speak with him, to debate these things at length, to learn from his wisdom and understanding.

And, inexorably, I begin to remember Anna and then the pain breaks through to me like an old wound opening. A searing, splitting, agonising pain that brings from me a great cry of anguish. The sound bounces off the mountain side behind me, replicating into a repeated animal cry of desolation. I have not felt pain like this since I was on the boat. I thought it had gone. Now I know that it hasn't. I am both guilty and desolate.

After a while I manage to sleep, a few hours of oblivion, but when the warmth of the sun wakes me I wake to a world that is empty, both within and without. I make myself eat a bit, even though I have no hunger. A few olives and apricots. I wash my face in the stream and set off. For two days I travel like this, still unsure as to where I am going and what I am going to do. I know Aleppo but have never travelled beyond there. The road goes up from there through the Taurus mountains and the Cilician gates; I know that. Beyond there it is an unknown world.

145

By now I have convinced myself that there is nowhere I can go. I will just have to take my chance in the city. Aleppo is a Mamluk city like Damascus but perhaps word of the murder will have not been passed on. I suppose that I shall have to risk it and if I am discovered one flash of the scimitar would be a quick way to go. I have nothing to live for now.

As I approach the city I can see the tall square minaret rising from the Great Mosque. The walls of the city, like those of Damascus, still have gaps in them. Damage wreaked by the Mongol invaders twenty or so years before has only been partially repaired. I remember liking Aleppo when I made trips here for the master. There was an easy atmosphere which was lacking in the more serious Damascus. Perhaps they will be kind to a fugitive.

The muezzin's call to evening prayer is echoing over the city as I make my way through the streets towards the mosque. In my Arab apparel no one will wonder why I am attending prayers. My lessons with Al-Aziz have taught me what to do. I enter the mosque to join the faithful at prayer.

Once inside I walk across the black and white paving of the wide courtyard towards the ablution fountains. Suddenly I stop because I have spotted someone I know. Just by one of the fountains stands a man who works for the master. I know him well, even though he is infrequently in Damascus. And there, standing in the courtyard of the mosque I see who it is that he is addressing. It is Hassif, I am sure of that even though it is four years since I last saw him. Hassif, from the village of Kashaya; I am certain it is him, the dark hair, the beetling eyebrows.

What is he doing in Aleppo? And why is he deep in conversation with the master's man? I am about to run forward to greet them when an instinctive sense of danger overtakes me. For no reason that I can discern I am convinced that he should not see me.

I turn away and melt into the anonymous throng that is moving into the mosque but I do not join them. I skirt around the edge of the courtyard so that I can watch Hassif without being

146

seen. In the shadows of the evening I am well concealed. I watch until he has finished with the man. I see something pass between them which Hassif slips inside his tunic. The man goes.

Hassif stands there for a while. For a moment I think he is going to join the throng at prayers but then he quickly makes for the exit. I follow him, far enough behind not to be recognised. He disappears into the city, down streets and alleys; it is hard to keep up. Then he turns into a narrow alley and by the time I reach the entrance he has disappeared. Briskly I walk down the dark passage. Suddenly a strong arm goes around my throat and I feel something sharp pressed into my lower back. Fear floods over me as a low voice says, "Well, brother. Why are you following me?"

I stammer out. "Hassif. It's me. Ioánnis. I mean no harm." The arm is removed from my throat and he spins me round.

"Ioánnis, allahu akbar! What are you doing here?"

"Put that knife away, please, Hassif. It's making me nervous." He slips it into his sheath.

"I could ask you the same." He looks around nervously. "We're not safe here, Ioánnis. Cover your face and follow me: only this time stay closer." I am relieved to hear the familiar sound of his laugh.

It is a job to keep up with him but within ten minutes we are outside a bolted door in a quiet street. He produces a key from under his tunic and ushers me into a cool, clean house. There are large cushions on the floor of the living area. Through a small, arched window I can glimpse an enclosed courtyard. A fountain is playing in the centre. Hassif indicates the cushions.

"Rest, Ioánnis. I suspect you have had a hard journey." He disappears and returns with a dish of sweetmeats and small glasses of tea. "You have things to tell me, my friend." His tone is more serious.

"Perhaps, Hassif, but I want to know why you are here. Is this your house? Have you left the village?" I can see that he is offended though he tries to conceal it. Clumsy questions like mine would be deeply offensive to an Arab host. "I'm sorry, Hassif. I shouldn't interrogate you."

"That's all right, Christian brother. Understandable in the circumstances." We are silent for a while. The tinkle of the fountain permeates the quiet. Finally he speaks.

"Ioánnis. I know about the Turk. I am amazed you had it in you but I understand why you did it. I am an Arab so that is not so difficult for me." I say nothing, my head held low. "But you are in great danger. The Mamluk police are after you; not just in Damascus but here in Aleppo." It is as I feared. The road is going to end here.

"I will help you get away. You must go north, through the Taurus mountains and the Cilician gates. I can take you that far. After that you are on your own. You will be in less danger from the Mamluks up there but you will be in Ottoman lands. There are civil wars and battles going on, you will have to be very careful."

I am at one and the same time relieved yet terrified of this further flight. Hassif senses it. "I can see how you feel but to stay here and give yourself up is not an option, Ioánnis my friend. I have heard how you have passed through the al-Nuri madrasa. You, a budding doctor, eh!" he chuckles at this. "You cannot let that go to waste. We have to keep that clever head on those shoulders, don't we?" I nod but a shiver of fear goes through me.

"You must rest now, Ioánnis. We shall leave at midnight so that we can get well way from the city before dawn."

I nod my acquiescence, then raise one hand a little. "But Hassif, I want you to tell me what you are doing here. You haven't told me yet."

He looks serious again. "I will tell you, Ioánnis, but not tonight. We will have time enough when we are on the road. Now rest, my friend. I will call you when it is time to leave." With that he slips out of the room.

I settle down on the cushions, the softest bed I have had for many nights. The fountain splatters a gentle tune. Soon I am asleep.

148

Chapter 16
The Gates of Cilicia

It is hard climbing in this gorge. The track winds and turns, sometimes close to the edge of the torrent, sometimes far above it. We teeter on shelved ledges, at times only a small cart's width across. Once or twice we cross the river on wooden bridges that look dangerously precarious to me. Hassif tells me that Persian armies passed this way but that was centuries ago. In places I notice strange markings on the rock face, letters that I cannot read. I ask Hassif but he does not reply. Always we are climbing, upwards and upwards. At times I can see distant snowy peaks. They must be the same ones that I saw from the boat in my voyage from the island. A vast wall of mountains that blocks the way to the plains of Anatolia; no way through except by the Gates of Cilicia.

It is many days since we crept out of Aleppo in the early dawn. For the first day we travelled quickly. Hassif seemed reluctant to talk, concerned only to put as much distance between us and that city. There were a few people on the trail, families with donkeys, the occasional baggage train but Hassif pulled his scarf around his face and made no contact. Obediently I did the same.

It was when we were approaching Tarsus that he started to talk. We could see the small city in the distance, smoke smudges against an evening sky.

"I think we had better avoid this place, Ioánnis." I didn't ask why, he knew what he was about. "We'll stop for the night here." We had found a small clump of trees, enough to give us shelter. I set a fire to burn and when the sun had gone down we huddled over it for some warmth. We had dried fruit and Hassif made tea in a small cooking pot. Nothing was said. I looked up at Hassif. He looked tired and distracted.

149

"Are you all right, Hassif?"

He sighed. "No, if you want honesty, my friend. My heart is weary."

"What is it? Can you not tell me now?" He stared at me for a few moments.

"Perhaps I can, Christian brother, perhaps I can." There was a pause. I shifted my position so that I could see him clearly. "You deserve to know the story, Ioánnis, but in the end you may regret asking." I indicated, without speaking, that he should continue.

"I am a Nabutean Arab, Ioánnis. We come from far south of here, in the rocks of the desert. It is said that it was Nabuteans that Saul, your apostle Paul, lived with after his conversion; I am sure you remember the story." I inclined my head in recognition.

"I came north, seeking work. This was long before I met Soraya. At that time the cities and the countryside were still devastated by the conquest of the Mongols and their cruel leader, Timur the Lame. Everywhere you came across piles of skulls, heaped up in gruesome pyramids. Life was very difficult, businesses had been ruined. The Mamluks were in power but they seemed unconcerned about this corner of their empire. It was a desolate time.

Eventually I ended up in Dimashq. It was a sad sight but the authorities were making some attempts to restore the walls and rebuild the damaged houses. It was very poor; there were shortages of everything, food, materials, even water." He stood up to put more camel dung on the fire.

"There was not much camel shit, either" he chuckled "because trade was almost non-existent. Then I met Dimitrios Papadikis." He paused, as if remembering. "He was a remarkable man. A Greek, and a Christian of course. But he seemed to know the answer to reviving the city. Trade. He took me on as his chief steward, the same post that you held, and between us we worked night and day to establish Dimashq as a major centre of trade to and from the East. More and more goods passed in and out of

150

that warehouse of his. On every item there was a little levy, not much but then, of course, you know all this. Bit by bit we prospered. And with us the city prospered. Kýrie Papadikis paid all his dues, he is an honest man, and life was breathed back into the suk. He rewarded me well. He used to call me 'my indispensable Arab.' We set up other branches of the business, including the warehouse in Halab, Aleppo."

He fell silent for a while. Beyond the ring of the fire the night was deep black. I heard the call of an owl; for a moment I thought he had fallen asleep but then he stirred.

"A few years passed and everything continued to prosper. I met Soraya and we were soon married. Little Ibrahim came along within a year. We had a comfortable house in Dimashq but, perhaps it is the nomad in me, I was restless. Then something happened that cured my restlessness." I think I know what he was going to tell me but I held my tongue.

"After a few years the business began to deteriorate. There was far less trade through Dimashq and Halab. People say it was the new sea routes. Goods were going by sea rather than the long haul over the Silk Road. Whatever the reason Kýrie Papadikis began to look permanently worried. I kept the books and I could see how much profits were declining. We had to lay off some assistants, the master had to reduce his support of the Church of the Virgin Mary in the city. It was not looking good. Then one day he called me to visit him at home. I found him in his study and with him a huge, swarthy Turk with long moustaches."

"Not him?"

"Yes, Mahmout. The very same. As soon as I saw him, an ugly brute, I thought. He spoke a rough Greek tongue. Kýrie introduced me and said 'this is the man who is going to save our fortunes.' I found that hard to believe but then the master outlined his plan, which you know by now, his plan to start trading in people. 'Hassif, my friend' he said to me, 'there are plenty of people who need servants (he would not use the word slave). We can provide what they want in a kind, humane way.'" I could not stifle a sharp intake of breath. Hassif glanced at me, then continued. "I honestly believe that that is what the master believed but in the presence of that ghastly Turk I had my doubts. Kýrie Papadikis went on to explain how it would be organised. Mahmout, and his associates, would be responsible for bringing the people in and the master would hold them until there were enough to make a camel train which would take them on to whatever destination had a need for them. There was no shortage of customers, Egypt, Baghdad and, above all, the Ottoman Turks.

I was so horrified that at first I could not speak. But then an anger rose within me; a fierce, uncompromising Arab anger. I told the master that what he was doing was evil, and probably outside the law and that I wanted nothing to do with it. Surprisingly he smiled at me and said 'I thought that is what you would say, Hassif, which is why I am releasing you from my service. You are free to go.' This was a stab in the heart. I knew that I would be unlikely to find other employment and now I had a wife and small son to support. I looked at him. I could see that he had already guessed how I would react. He is a very crafty man. 'You need no longer work from here. Find somewhere in the hills to live. From time to time I will have need of you for special duties. Then I will send for you. In the meantime you will still receive your salary.' I could do nothing other than assent. And so Soraya and I settled in the mountains, in Kashaya. He did not explain to me what 'special duties' were. I was soon to find out."

It was very late now and my eyelids were drooping.

"Come on, Ioánnis. That is quite enough for one night. You must sleep." Despite wanting to know the whole story I could not resist this suggestion. We settled down for the night. I slept fitfully, slipping in and out of dreams in which Mahmout figured prominently. On one occasion I dreamt of Anna. She was being held from behind by Kýrie Papadikis whilst the lascivious Turk was advancing on her, his erect organ in his hand. I cried out, enough to wake myself. When I looked around I could see that Hassif was still sleeping,

152

The next day we skirted around Tarsus and headed north for the mountains. The air was clear and sweet as we rose above the plain. After a while Hassif spoke.

"I didn't tell you everything last night, did I?" I was silent, waiting for him. "The special duties that the master wanted me for. It's quite simply really. Mahmout could not provide all the goods that our customers needed. Kýrie Papadikis uses me to find other Mahmouts, and they'll be needed now since you intervened with your bit of steel. It means I travel a great deal, sometimes over the sea. Many of them are corsairs like Mahmout but some come from battles between the different states and factions. There is no shortage."

"You mean you take part in this grisly trade?"

"No. I don't take people. I find people who will."

"Isn't that as bad, Hassif?"

For a moment his voice was raised, the tone more steely. "Perhaps you can't understand. You don't know what it's like." Then he regained his equanimity. "Just thank Alah that you are never faced with such a dilemma, Ioánnis."

There was nothing that I could say. We walked on in silence which he broke eventually. "There's one thing more."

"What else?"

"I don't know if you noticed, when we were in the village, some people came and went." I hadn't noticed but now he mentions it I can remember seeing people who appeared for a while, then disappeared.

"Yes, I think I do. Who were they?"

"This is the last piece of the story that I have to tell you. I found myself compromised by the master's action. I resolved that I would do something to counteract it."

"Counteract?"

"Yes. I started to release the prisoners. Bit by bit. I could not do it for many. It was hard enough to conceal it as it was but I did, and still do, regularly select a few. I take them back to the

153

village and then find ways to return them to their homes. I have many helpers, we have quite a network now."

This stunned me into silence. Returned to their homes. That could mean that Eleni and Mama could be back on the island. But then I remembered that they probably did not pass through Papadikis' hands. I returned to thinking about Hassif and his network. Perhaps that was where he was last night but it seemed wise not to ask him.

"So you are both working for Papadikis and also working against him."

"That's about it. I have to retain his trust, otherwise the whole thing is likely to fall apart."

"Wouldn't that be the best thing?"

He stopped and turned to face me. "Ioánnis. If Kýrie Papadikis didn't run this, someone else would. And they wouldn't be nearly as humane."

I remembered hearing this argument from the master himself. I was more convinced by it, hearing it from Hassif, but the young man in me still found it hard to see things in other than black and white. Yet there was one more thing that I needed to know.

"Hassif, knowing what you knew, why did you send me to Kýrie Papadikis' house all those years ago?"

"It seemed the only possible way to help you, Ioánnis. After all he is not an evil man. He was good to you, wasn't he. And generous?"

I waited.

"So it was not such a bad idea, after all. You see, Ioánnis, the world that we create for ourselves is, at best, good enough. It is never perfect. We make of it what we will. I know your world was torn apart by the corsair raid but you have never experienced what the people here suffered from Timur the Lame. Destruction and heads severed in their thousands. In the end, in the face of such an atrocity, we can only make do as best we can. Nothing is ever completely straightforward."

154

I felt embarrassed. In my head I had judged my friend, and judged him harshly.

"I'm sorry, Hassif. I just didn't understand." He smiled broadly and clapped me on the back.

"Come on, Christian. To the mountains!"

And so we find ourselves in this gorge. The light is beginning to fade but up ahead we can see a cleft in the mountain wall. The red, evening sunlight illuminates it from behind.

"We'll camp here tonight, Ioánnis. Tomorrow you go through the Gates of Cilicia", he indicates up ahead, "and then you are on your own. I go no further."

I sleep very little that night. My conversation with Hassif goes over and over in my brain but is soon overtaken by speculation of what lies ahead. I am to pass through this gap into the unknown. I leave Hassif behind for a second time and now a new awareness is creeping up on me. To pass through this narrow cleft in the mountains is a rebirth that will leave behind all that has constituted my life thus far. This is a pivotal moment for me; there is no turning back.

MEROS TRITON

Chapter 17
The Cappadocian Desert . 1424

It is cool in this cave. Not dark for the afternoon sun angles in through the wide, round opening where I sit. The hard, barren landscape stretches away remorselessly until mountains rise out of the horizon. It is now three years since I first saw this land. It was hard to comprehend what I was seeing at the time. The arid desert, full of these strange rock formations, was quite unlike the one that stretches away from Damascus. Here were pillars of orange rock, some quite small, no higher than a man; others towering away and as high as the minaret of a mosque. Most were triangular and rose to a pointed top. And in the larger ones I could see cave openings. Some rough but others quite symmetrical and neat. A bizarre honeycomb of inhabitable caves. I remembered cave houses back on the island but they were set into cliff-faces and the inhabitants had built frontages on them. From the exterior they seemed like ordinary houses; once you penetrated inside you found yourself in a cave. In the summer heat they were good, cool places to be, though you often had to share the space with animals. Almost impossible to get animals into these caves, though. The entrances are all high above ground. Complicated networks of ledges allow you to clamber up but it is a precipitous climb negotiated only by courageous people and nimble goats.

I sit in the entrance looking west. Gerasimos has given me a task. To repeat the Jesus prayer, over and over, until the sun has disappeared beyond the horizon. I sit with my legs crossed, my hands resting on my knees, palms upwards. My eyes are closed. In my head I recite, over and over again, "Lord Jesus Christ, son of the living God, have mercy on me." I try to time it with my

157

breathing. Breathe in on "Lord Jesus Christ, son of the living God," breathe out on "have mercy on me."

I expect a response. Perhaps a vision, perhaps a voice. Surely some response to my devotions.

There is none. I shift my position slightly. My limbs are becoming stiff. I am becoming impatient, the sun is descending so slowly. "Lord Jesus Christ, son of the living God, have mercy on me. Lord Jesus Christ, son of the living God, have mercy on me."

Gerasimos is a frustrating man. Not a priest but a monk. He will seldom talk of his past. At first I had no idea where he came from. All I knew was that, some three years ago, he was here when I first stumbled, weak and emaciated, into this bizarre landscape. Staggering through the mountains, unsure of the path, I had run short of food. In the end I was scavenging roots, bitter fruit, even the stinking carcass of a mountain goat that had fallen from a high ledge. Then, when I reached the high Anatolian plain, came the enervating heat and constant thirst. I had slumped down in the shadow of one of the pinnacles and must have passed out. When I came to there was this strange little man, staring at me.

He was an extraordinary sight. Dressed sparsely in animal skins. His hair was long and straggly, matted by sweat and dirt. He was barefoot and carried a long thin staff. In my bemused state I struggled to resolve this apparition. An image from the past floated into my mind but I could not, at first, identify it. Then it came to me. The Forerunner. The ikon of Ayios Ioánnis Prodromos, John the Baptist. Taller than this little man but with the same wild hair. This prodomos bent forward. He was holding a cup of water. He spoke to me in Greek.

"Drink, my son." I later came to learn that Gerasimos was a man of few words. I took the cup and drank. The water was like the sweetest wine. I began to recover.

Gerasimos motioned me to follow and led me up a series of ledges, up to a wide cave opening. He disappeared inside. For a moment I hesitated, then ducked my head and followed him. The sight that greeted me elicited a gasp of astonishment. The cave was large and cruciform shaped. There were frescoes painted on the walls and, at one end, a richly decorated ikonostasis. The ikons appeared to be very old, much older than those that I had seen back on the island. I recognised most of the subjects but the style was different. They appeared much more human. I am used to our ethereal style of representation in ikon painting, figures like angels; these were different. They were ordinary people such as you might meet on any day in the market or by the harbour. Their realism was arresting.

What was obvious from the state of the cave contents was that this church, if indeed it was a church, was no longer in use. Gerasimos kissed an ikon, crossed himself and turned to leave. I delayed, entranced by this cave. It brought back to me memories of the Cave of the Apokalypse on the island, the cave that was the refuge of Ioánnis Theologos, John the Divine, the cave where he dictated his revelation. It formed a link with my past, albeit tenuous, which relieved my disjointed soul for a moment

So Gerasimos took me in. He showed me a small cave that I could use. It was spartan but habitable, indeed it still is. It has been my home for three years but now I have improved the interior. I have a bed, I have a place to keep my instruments. I am as settled as ever I was in the Papadikis household back in Damascus.

And my appearance has changed. Now I have a full, black beard, my long hair is plaited and my body has filled out with muscle as a result of living in this hard environment. In the first weeks I wondered where Gerasimos obtained the food which he shared with me. Not a great deal, it has to be said, but adequate for us both. Fruit, rough cheese and occasional meat, usually fowl. Later I was to discover its source. Three hours from the cave there was a great cleft in the plain. Settled into the cleft was a small town. I feared to go near for I still worried that word of the Turk's murder might have spread this far, unlikely though it might seem. I was cautious and watched from afar. Later I asked Gerasimos about the village.

"They are good people. Muslims, but peaceable. They bring me food."

"How is it that Muslims support a Christian hermit?"

Gerasimos was evasive. "It is only right and proper." I could not see why it was so but, equally, I could see there was no point in persisting with my questions.

Neither was Gerasimos more forthcoming about his spiritual life. Bit by bit I learnt that he was a monk from a monastery, far to the north. A monastery which was one of a number to be found on a holy mountain.

"I settled well into the monastic life but soon found the presence of the other monks more of a hindrance than a help. I approached the Abbot for permission to pursue the life of a hermit. He paused to scratch himself. I waited patiently. At first he offered me a cave on the mountain, near the Monastery. I would return every Sunday to worship with the monks who stayed in the Monastery, the cenobitic brothers. I prayed long and hard about this because I felt sure it was not for me."

"But did you have any choice? Surely you had to go where the Abbot sent you."

"That's true, but in prayer you sometimes discover what it is that the Lord wants of you. I was becoming quite sure that I needed to go elsewhere to be a hermit."

"So how did you find your way here?" He stood up and shuffled around before sitting again.

"I was studying the works of the early Church Fathers and found myself reading Ayios Gregorios Naziansos. The words seemed to jump off the page and then I remembered, he was one of the Cappadocian Fathers. He came here," with a sweep of his hand he indicated the whole landscape, "and so I resolved that here was where I was meant to be. I spoke to the Abbot and, when he saw how serious I was, he agreed. That was thirty years ago."

It was difficult for me, a man who was becoming accustomed to moving on, to think of him spending thirty years in this bleak spot.

"But what do you do here?" As I said it I wondered whether Gerasimos could detect the trace of anger in my question that I had tried to conceal. If he had he ignored it.

"Nothing. I do nothing. There is nothing to do." He was an exasperating man.

"I don't understand. Surely you must do something."

"Ioánnis. The world is full of people doing things. Most of them do nothing to improve human lives, in fact they are more likely to destroy them. I do nothing but I am." By now I was on the point of screaming at him. I resisted the impulse.

"How do you mean 'I am'? I really do not understand."

"I am. I contemplate on that. I am in the eyes of God, I am in the whole of creation. I am in the life and death of our Lord Jesus Christ. There is enough contemplation there to last for a lifetime. That is what I do." At last I had an answer. The only trouble was that I was not sure if I began to understand it. We went no further.

I was beginning to plan my departure but to where I had no idea. Perhaps I should try to get back to the island. But I was different now, a man and a doctor, even though I had yet to use what I had learnt. My journey to this point had been almost accidental. I had not planned it. Mostly it had been flight; flight from the island, flight from Damascus. Now I was faced with finding a purpose, a purpose that would restart my travels. Yet it was difficult to discern. I was becoming aware how this bizarre resting place might have more to offer me than I could have ever expected.

Surprisingly Gerasimos never asked me anything about my past, about how I had ended up in his desert domain. He appeared to live entirely in the present. His reluctance to talk about his past stemmed only from the perception that it was of no consequence, no more than was his concern with the future. He lived a life of receptive immediacy.

Then, one day about three months after my arrival, an event happened which determined my future. Apart from

161

Gerasimos there was no one else living in the caves, no other hermits nor anyone else for that matter. From time to time Gerasimos disappeared for a day or two. He never announced his departure. When he returned he never spoke of where he had been. I knew that it was pointless to interrogate him. One day, however, returning from another of his absences, he did speak.

"Ioánnis. It is true that you are a doctor". This was not a question.

"Yes, though I have never practised. Not yet, anyway."

"Tomorrow morning I want you to come with me. Bring your instruments." I wanted to interrogate him but he had already turned on his heel and disappeared. I watched him hop, as agile as a goat, up to his cave. An exasperating old troglodyte.

In the morning we set off whilst it was still cool. No words passed between us as we crossed the barren plain. After about three hours he stopped me.

"Ioánnis. There are people who need your help. Follow me." People? In this barren desert? He walked on at a brisk pace. Soon he stopped. Only then did I see that there was a large opening in the ground, large enough to allow us to stoop inside. It was well hidden in scrubby undergrowth. If I had been on my own I could easily have missed it. He bent down and led the way inside.

He had taken me to a network of underground caves, mostly man-made. Later I was to discover that they were the size of a small village. At first I thought that they were deserted but then, beyond an inner opening we met two men, neither of them much older than me.

"Kalimera" said Gerasimos and they replied in the same way. They were Greeks.

"Follow us, please." They led us further into the earth. The caves were all inhabited. They were clean and cool. A few children played on the floor. My eyes widened with astonishment. Gerasimos turned to me.

"I'll tell you more later but we need your help now."

162

In the back of one of the caves, lying on a bed and covered in animal skins, was a young girl. She must have been eleven or twelve. She was obviously severely ill. Her face was ashen, the skin was taut across her cheekbones, shiny and dry. Her breathing was rapid with a catch in every breath. Beside her stood her mother. She said nothing but her eyes told all as she looked at me. Save my daughter. She is going to die. I shrank from her gaze, my confidence draining away in the face of severe illness. I felt my heart tighten in my chest.

Gerasimos looked at me. "Is there anything that you can do, Ioánnis? What is the trouble with her?"

I looked around at the crowded cave; friends, relations had found their way in, having heard that a physician had arrived. They were all Greeks.

"Empty the room, please, Gerasimos. I need to examine her." The little monk ushered out all except the child's mother. I turned to the seated women. "What is her name, Kýria?"

The woman's voice was low. "Irini. She is called Irini."

I drew back the bedcovers. I listened to her breathing. I felt her abdomen and then I uncovered her legs. A foul stench rose from the bed. My heart fell at the sight that greeted me. The whole of her lower left leg was black, green and purulent. I could see the source of the infection, a huge gash that ran diagonally across her calf muscle, from ankle to knee. I had seen this before, gas gangrene. The smell was unmistakable. There was a case at the al-Nuri. I knew that she would be dead within two hours for the toxins were spreading through her body. She was barely conscious now.

I was horrified. For this to be my first case as a doctor was cruel. A different matter to deal with it in the confines of a hospital with senior colleagues to advise. But here, down in the bowels of the earth in the heart of a barren plain, how was I expected to do anything? I turned to her mother.

"I am afraid she is seriously ill with this infected wound. I fear she will die." The mother flinched at these words. "It is a terrible infection. How did she get the wound?"

The woman spat.

"It was the bastard Turks. The ones who sacked our village." She did not need to go on, I could imagine the scene. I had a thousand other questions but they would have to wait. There was only one course to take.

"We can only save her life if we amputate the leg. That is our only hope."

The woman screamed. "No! No! You cannot do that!"

"If I do not she will die. If I do she may still die but at least she will have a chance. I can do it. I have the instruments and I can also make her unconscious. She will not feel it." At the al-Nuri we had been taught the technique of anaesthesia. I had the distilled agents in my bag.

Whilst we had been talking Gerasimos had been busy outside. He returned and whispered in my ear. "We have a place set up, Ioánnis. Will the mother agree?"

I glanced over to her. She was kneeling beside her daughter and stroking her forehead.

"Well, Kýria, what do you say?"

She paused, then swallowed hard. She was not looking at me. Her voice was quiet.

"Go ahead, doctor. Please do your best."

Whilst she was moved to the prepared cave I sought out an assistant. Gerasimos did not seem to be an appropriate choice but a young Greek, Andros, came forward. He looked nervous but despite that appeared willing. I searched in my bag for the small bottle of opiate mixture that I had carried from Damascus. Leaning over the girl I put the container to her lips.

"Swallow this, Irini. It does not taste good but it will help you." She said nothing but her eyes, wide with fear, stared directly at mine. "Come on, Irini," I continued, "you can trust me." She swallowed and, for a moment, her face curled up in distaste. Nevertheless she downed the whole draught.

I prepared my instruments; I had enough to be able to amputate through the knee. When all was ready I brought out my small bottle of anaesthetic agent, a thick liquid distilled from the mandrake root. Then I selected a clean porous rag from my equipment and poured some of the anaesthetic liquid on to the rag. I put it aside and held the bottle near the girl's nose.

"Take a deep sniff now." She obeyed and almost immediately sneezed. It's pungent smell filled the small cave.

"Try and take deep breaths through your nose, Irini." She complied and almost immediately her eyes closed in sleep. I held the bottle close until she was no longer conscious enough to keep co-operating. Then I picked up the rag and held it over her nose, fashioning it into a shape that covered her nose yet did not smother her. With my left hand I lifted her jaw in order to keep her mouth closed. Her small body felt limp under me.

Her breathing became steadier and slower. Every now and then I would lift the rag to allow her to breathe fresh air. The last thing that I wanted was for her to stop breathing altogether. They had taught us carefully at the al-Nuri. It was all coming back to me.

When things seemed stable I called Andros over. "This is how to hold the mask. Every now and then pour a few more drops on the rag. Don't worry, I'll keep an eye on you in case you get into difficulties. In any case it won't take long."

Now it was my turn to be nervous. The instruments were prepared. Andros was watching me like a hawk. Gerasimos had taken Irini's mother out of the cell; there was just the two of us, and the patient, left alone. I picked up the scalpel and made a long incision around the knee, above the level of the green, black skin. I wanted to leave the kneecap in place, it could act as a buffer on the end of the stump. I needed to take enough skin to make a flap which meant cutting perilously close to the infected area.

Blood flowed into the wound. I staunched it with a wad of lint, then divided the thick tendon that attached the kneecap to the lower leg. With another sweeping incision I opened the joint capsule to be greeted by a flood of thick, sticky synovial fluid. Bit by bit the lower limb was separating. Now I could tie the large artery that ran down behind the knee. I had some stout ligatures on my tray. I tied off the vessel with two of them.

Irini was beginning to stir. "More drops on your mask, please, Andros." He did as I bade and she settled down.

Now just to divide the artery. The ligatures held and I tied off the stump of the vessel with another strong tie. I divided the rest of the soft tissues; fortunately I had removed all the infected tissue in my first cut, and extended my incision through the skin at the back of the knee. The lower leg came away and I placed it down on a mat covered by a thick sheet. It was now but a few minutes work to close the wound with a few sutures and bind it in thick dressings. Once done I wrapped up the purulent, diseased limb and turned to Andros.

"You can let her wake up now. Remove your mask. Well done, Andros."

The young man stood up, his relief clearly obvious, "Will she be all right, doctor?

"The next few days will be crucial. She is not out of the woods yet. Perhaps you could take this and get the men to bury it" I handed him the gangrenous limb, wrapped in cloth. He swallowed hard then took it from me and left the cave. I called Irini's mother in and instructed her how to care for Irini in the subsequent hours. "Don't worry. I shall be staying here until she is out of danger. You only have to call for me if you are worried." She smiled at me as she stroked the brow of her reawakening daughter.

I left them and made my way to a larger cave where some of the men were gathered. They were subdued, almost suspicious of the black-bearded Greek doctor who performed strange acts with strange potions. Nevertheless they were good enough to give me some food and drink. I needed that, my hand was still shaking.

166

And it was from them that I gleaned the whole story of this community. An old man spoke to me. "We have all, at different times, been rescued from our captors, the bastard Turks. Hassif and the others guided us here and here we have stayed until a safe route back to our homes can be found. Some of us have been here for three or four years. " The other men nodded. I had already begun to wonder if the hand of Hassif was behind this colony. He had confirmed my suspicions.

A younger man handed me a glass of wine. He spoke with urgency. "War in Anatolia has been making travel much more difficult in the past year. The Ottoman Sultan is dealing with a vicious civil war and the local Anatolian leaders are taking the opportunity to break away from Turkish domination. We are safe here as long as we keep quiet about it. We have means of gathering supplies so we do not starve."

Bit by bit they lost their distrust of me. I stayed with them through the first stormy days of the girl's recovery. After a while it became obvious that she was going to survive. The amputation wound healed well, a sight that I was pleased to see, and soon she was hopping around on a pair of home-made crutches.

Gerasimos had gone back before me but he returned after a week. By then I had acquired a number of patients with minor ailments.

"You are becoming indispensable, Doctor Ioánnis. They will not want you to leave." And, indeed, as time went on there was more and more to do with this community of refugees. Eventually I agreed to move in to the cave-town. But I missed the peace of my old habitation, and the presence of the enigmatic Brother Gerasimos. In the end I settled on the arrangement that exists now. A week with them and a few days on my own with Gerasimos. The monk was set on teaching me more and more about the contemplative life but I was a slow pupil.

So here I am, immersing myself in the Jesus Prayer, tied up in a life that I never expected. It seems as if nothing will change now.

Chapter 18

I could grow to love this cave. Its privations and its discomforts no longer bother me, not like they did in the first year or so of my residence. I am beginning to tire of my weekly absence to visit the underground dwellers, their demands on me are becoming more and more insistent; I am most at ease when returning here, back on my own. There is space enough for me and a place to lie down at night. I spend my days sitting at the oval entrance, staring across the strange landscape into the distance, staring at nothing.

I do not see Gerasimos much; just when there is food to be divided between us, simple food such as bread, olives, oil and fruit; hardly ever meat. I don't think I've eaten any meat for two months now. Doesn't seem to have done me any harm, my muscles are well-toned and my strength is undiminished.

I hear a rustle behind me, inside the cave. I turn and, in the gloom, I can make out the shape of Gerasimos, wizened, poker-thin. He grins at me.

"Blessings, brother Ioánnis," he always likes to address me as brother, even though he knows that I have never taken vows.

"Gerasimos. What brings you here?" He is staring around my cell, not that there is much to see.

"You seem to have taken to the simple life, brother. Quite the hermit now, aren't you?" He chuckles with a sound like the rustling of dry leaves. For a moment I am annoyed at his intrusion.

"Shouldn't I be, Gerasimos? It was what you taught me."

He nods. "Yes, yes. That's true. You are a diligent follower of the Hesychast, a good novice." He is being obscure again. It is a favourite posture of his, challenging me to think.

"Hesychast, what do you mean by that?"

169

"That's you and I, boy. Simple, open to God. It is a good tradition whatever those scholastics say." He spits in the dust. I am slightly taken aback by this.

"I don't understand you. What scholastics? Who are you talking about?"

"Westerners mostly. In our orthodox tradition it is given to us to hold that God can never be known in his essence, only in his energies." He was off on one of his tangents again. I try to follow him.

"You mean, in his actions?"

"Precisely. And what is his main action?" I am being tutored now. Unusual from Gerasimos who prefers to remain obscure. In this new approach of his I am reminded of Father Ignatios.

"I suppose," I pause as I am uncertain, "I suppose in the outpouring of his love." I wait for him to respond, anxious at his reaction. I find all this very hard to grasp.

"Ha! Well done. Quite right, young novice. Love outpoured, energy flowing from the Godhead. That's what we experience."

"So why are the scholastics different? Don't they believe that?" He is mumbling into his scraggy beard as he looks around for somewhere to sit. I shift along the ledge and he settles down beside me. What a picture we must make. A muscular young man with dark hair and beard and this wizened little hermit. Only there is no one to see us.

"Scholastics, those westerners and that accursed Calabrian, Barlaam, think that you can reach God by reason alone. You can know him in his essence by logical argument. Pah!" He spits in the sand. I have seldom seen him so animated, his head rocks from side to side, he makes curious little grunting noises under his breath

I remember my discussions with Hassif about Ioánnis Damascene. Strangely enough I had not thought about these since leaving that city. Now they were coming back to me; the talk of

170

apophatic theology, God only describable by the negative. We cannot say what God is, only what he is not, infinite, immeasurable, transcendent. God is not, in fact, any of the things that he is called. I found such ideas hard to understand at the time, they are no easier now.

Gerasimos' agitation seems to have settled down. He stares out at the blank horizon. "I suppose I must be charitable. It is no fault of theirs that they have veered from true orthodoxy. We must pray that the Spirit will bring them back to the true enlightenment."

"True enlightenment?" I am beginning to feel angry. "But what is that?" His face shows that he has recognised my annoyance but he makes no concession.

"To strive to know the unknowable, little brother, and thereby to find emptiness." I shake my head in confusion. I have lived with him in this rock strewn desert for three years now and it feels as if I haven't begun to understand a single thing. He looks at me and smiles; no longer is he mocking me. In that smile I recognise a genuine concern.

"I know, Ioánnis. It is hard, but remember, when it is hardest then you are closest. Don't despair." In a moment he stands up and disappears into the cave. I watch him leave from the opening at ground level and make his way in the direction of his own cave. I swear, for a moment, that I see him take a little skip.

Alone again my mind runs over what he has been saying. It confuses me but along with that confusion I begin to experience a feeling of deep excitement. That is strange. Now Gerasimos is beginning to help me perceive a dual journey in my life; the outward, physical journey that has brought me to this place and, running alongside, an inner journey, a journey represented by a dimly perceived understanding which brings that feeling of excitement. Neither journey has direction but I cannot abandon either however much I fail to see where either is taking me. What I do see is that the God that is not is becoming more real to me than the God that is. It is a kind of thinking that is making me dizzy.

My trips to the underground community have established a pattern now. I have become accustomed to the day's journey each way. Rarely do I meet anyone on the road; my travelling companions are rabbits, the occasional deer and the vultures that circle overhead. They disturb me, those great birds with their magnificent wings that soar them through the high air. Sometimes I come across them scrabbling and fighting over a carcass, their cadaverous, ugly heads an undignified contrast to their lofty flight.

There has been no episode as dramatic as Irini's amputation. I have learnt to use my medical skills in the common, annoying disturbances of life, only occasionally being faced with more serious illness. That suits me. Diagnosis is what excites me, the way it was taught at the al-Nuri. I always want to understand what is going on, even if I have little to offer in the way of treatment.

Today I am making my regular weekly visit. The journey has been long and I arrive as the sun is nearly set. As usual they have a room ready for me, somewhere to sleep and eat a meal. As I make my way down from the surface I am met by Irini. She limps towards me on the artificial leg that one of the men fashioned for her, her face wreathed in smiles.

"Welcome, Doctor Ioánnis. Are you tired from your journey?"

"A little, Irini. How are you? Is the stump behaving itself?"

"It's fine, doctor. I can run nearly as fast as my brother." She smiles proudly.

"Well, that's fine, Irini. But be careful not to wear it too hard. The skin is always a bit sensitive there."

She looks at me solemnly. "I would not do that, Doctor Ioánnis. I wouldn't spoil all the good work you did for me." I ruffle her hair, finding myself embarrassed by the compliment.

"Well, there we are. Now, where's my list?" She always had a list for me. People who want to consult me the following morning. I settle down as she reels off a list of names and complaints, all from memory. Sore throats, abdominal pain, headaches; a fair representation of minor illness which I have come to recognise are the staple of a doctor's life.

"You make a good physician's assistant, Irini. I'd be in a mess without you."

She beams at me with pride and turns on her heel. "See you tomorrow morning, Doctor Ioánnis" and within a moment she is gone.

I eat my meal alone. It is strange that this is how I have come to practise the skills that I learnt back in Damascus. I never imagined that it would be like this. I suppose I expected to be building a practice amongst the Greeks of Damascus, becoming prosperous and important, but now here I am, half a hermit and half a physician to a secret community of refugees who live in a hole in the ground.

There have been many comings and goings in the subterranean community. On rare occasions there have been visits from Hassif although it is at least a year since I last saw him. On that occasion he told me that the hue and cry for the murderer of the Turk had died down. Somehow the police knew that the perpetrator was the young man who worked for Kýrie Papadikis but my old master and Hassif denied any knowledge of my whereabouts. In any case I was in Cappadocia, well out of range of the Mamluk police.

Every so often a group of the refugees would leave. Hassif was usually involved although sometimes it would be one or other of his helpers, both Arabs, that would escort a party away. Always at night so as not to attract attention from the inhabitants of the small town that was half a day's walk away. I skirt that town, keeping out of sight, when I make the journey back and forth for this is a restless land. Over the last ten years, there has been fighting, conquest and reconquest. The Ottoman princes are at war with each other and the local leaders, the Karamanids have sought to capitalise on the discord. It is not a safe place to travel. Luckily Gerasimos and I seem isolated from it all.

My morning's work has been frustrating. Whilst none of the people that I have seen have any serious illness, I have little that I can offer them in the way of medicine. I can diagnose. I can inform but when they ask for relief there is little that I can offer. It leads to frustration and resentment at times. I could do more if I was working in a city. I could send them to an apothecary for the medicines that they wanted. Secretly I knew that most of them are going to get better whatever I do or do not do but it is difficult to persuade them to patience.

The following day sees me back on the road; the sun is high in the sky and my old companions, the vultures, circle in the shimmering heat. The two halves of my life are separated by this walk. I am two people. One active and involved, and the other increasingly passive and detached. Maybe I prefer the latter for it distances me from my previous life; goatherd, fisherman, refugee, student, doctor and now murderer. Not often do I like to confront that fact, I am a murderer, but I do now. I killed a man. It was not self-defence, I could have turned and slipped away into the dark of the alleyways but no, I killed him. Was it the power of my rage, my resentment that drew me to it? The one thing that I remember was that I could not stop myself; in that sense it was an involuntary act. That is what I tell myself but at a deeper level I am not convinced. I am guilty but I think I have buried that guilt.

Perhaps that is why the solitary life attracts me so much. Perhaps I can undo it in my mind, take apart the meaningless actions. I pray over and over again. "Lord Jesus Christ, son of the living God, have mercy on me." Asking for mercy, mercy for me, a murderer, an unrepentant killer. Nothing comes back. I cannot believe that I should ever receive mercy, let alone how such mercy could possibly be mediated. All concepts, all the elaborations of traditional dogmas are falling away. Perhaps that is what Gerasimos means in finding emptiness. Perhaps I am on that road.

It does nothing for the feeling, though. Nor for the hard fact of being a murderer. Could I ever tell Gerasimos that I am a murderer? Hassif knows, Kýrie Papadikis knows. I could never tell anyone else. To talk of why I did it, that would be the hardest task. I did tell Hassif. He knows what that man did to me but what he does not know is that I still feel tainted, marked for ever by what happened that night. Neither does he know that it came so soon after Anna and I discovered each other in the erotic passion of our love-making, the unexpected joy of our love. It destroyed all that. I shall never know that joy again. That was the real depredation that that Turk, Mahmout, wreaked upon me.

It is not that it is good or gratifying to lead the solitary life. It is becoming the only appropriate way to be. Yes, I can be a doctor for part of the time but my reality, my right place is to be here in this desert, in my rocky cave. The sun is setting as I reach my goal. The cave is empty. I enter, if not with joy, with resignation.

Stillness. A particular stillness as if the air could be carved and divided. The sun is high. All day I have sat here. At first restless. I was trying too hard, praying too fervently. Still only the words of the Jesus prayer but I was trying to force meaning on to them. Now that has gone and I reside in the stillness. I can feel my pulse slowing. Staring out into the blank landscape. Letting go, but every so often watching myself in my mind's eye. This is a backward step. I ease the grip on my consciousness. Revert to stillness.

Empty. Now no awareness. Not just of myself but no awareness of God. Empty. Aware only of non-God. This is new.

Across my vision darts the shape of a little falcon. Acrobatically it wheels between the rooks that struggle to mob it. Its scimitar wings cut through the stillness. The precision of its flight returns me to myself. Now I am on the further side of emptiness, beyond silence. My view is the same, my vision is the same, but I am aware that my consciousness has moved. I cannot say what it is; but in saying just that to myself I have created, in my

175

mind, words; language. Language falls in to create where there was emptiness before. Language does not represent the darting falcon. Language is primary, it creates my world for me. For a moment I experience thankfulness but with an overwhelming sense of having no-one to thank. It is a feeling of bliss. To be in the eternity of the present moment.

This is new.

Later that day Gerasimos appears. I see his little shape weaving its way amongst the boulders towards my cave. He stops below and calls up. "Brother Ioánnis!" His tone is urgent.

"I am here, Gerasimos. What is the trouble?"

"Come here, with me, you must come." In a few seconds I join him outside. He tugs at my sleeve.

"Come, come quickly. You must see this." I follow at his insistence for there is something troubled in his tone. "Up here, quick." We clamber up a rocky ridge and he points to the west. "Look. Do you see?"

At first all seems as it always does. There is little change in this landscape that I can discern; but then I see what has attracted his attention, a smudge of smoke. He speaks urgently.

"That's the town, isn't it? There's a fire." It was certainly in the direction of the town. The pall of smoke indicates a substantial fire. I am quite clear what we should do.

"We have to go there, Gerasimos. They may need help."

"Go? But what can we do?" There was fear in his voice now.

"We can't just sit back and ignore it," the active part of me has woken up, "Come on!"

Little Gerasimos looks agitated. "You go, Ioánnis. I cannot. I'm too old, too weak. What help could I be?"

I look at him, annoyed at his response. At first I don't see him as he is, an old man, a solitary. What can a man like him do in a crisis? I smile at him. "You're right, Gerasimos. You stay here. I'll go."

Usually it is a good hour's walk to the town but the urgency is on me. I gather up my medical supplies and run all the way. Within half an hour I breast a small hill from which I can see the town, set in the gorge below me. There are houses on fire; I can hear screams and the bellowing of donkeys and cattle. The sight, the sounds take me back to the island. I have few illusions about the horror that awaits me if I continue. For a moment I hesitate, thinking of turning away. Then I hear the clear scream of a child. I drop down a path towards the town, my feet kicking up the dust in my haste.

It is beginning to get dark but the fires light up my way. I can see lanterns and torches moving about below me but cannot make out who is carrying them. I round a corner. In a moment a strong arm is round my throat. I see the glint of a blade out of the corner of my eye. My assailant mutters something in my ear. I am frozen with fear. With a strong shove he pushes me to the floor and I feel the weight of his foot on my back. Expertly he ties my hands together. The cords bite into the flesh of my wrists and they hurt abominably. I am hauled to my feet and a lantern is held up to illuminate my face. By its light I can see my attackers. They are soldiers. Each one carries a curved sabre; on their heads they wear tall, round hats with a length of material hanging from the brim to fall over their neck. They do not look to be Turks as far as I can tell. As they speak I am sure I can discern Turkish, though. I have heard enough of it to know.

And then one comes forward to take a closer look at me. He examines my face and laughs. The next moment he addresses me in Greek.

"Who the hell are you, brother? You look like a Greek to me?" I say nothing, which earns me a kick in the groin from one of the others. I fall to my knees, the pain throbs up inside me.

"Leave him be" said the first. He bends down to me and pulls my head back by the hair, "answer me or one of these beauties will chop your balls off for you. Who are you? You don't look like one of these cursed Turkomen." I get to my feet.

"My name is Ioánnis. I am a doctor." He looks surprised.

"A doctor indeed, in this godforsaken place? Do you expect me to believe that?"

"I am telling the truth. Look in my bag; there are my instruments, my medicines."

"Doctor, eh. Well that could be useful. You're coming with us." They tie a rope to my wrists and with a kick indicate that I should walk on. One of them picks up my bag and together we make our way out of the gorge and on to the plain. Here we meet up with many more troops and a large collection of prisoners. I notice that they are all women and children. No men. At the head of the column are a few mounted soldiers. They have hats decorated with tall, resplendent plumes. With a signal from one of these the whole column moves off towards the west. I stumble along amongst my captors.

We walk for most of the night. The road is rough but passable. As we move along I try to assess this company. They are clearly more disciplined than the pirate raiders. They must be a military unit, but whose?

Our path is taking us well away from Gerasimos and the caves. A sadness overwhelms me as I realise that I might never see him again. He has been a good companion and teacher to me over the last few years. Were it not for him I would never have discovered the Hesychast way. Now, just as I am beginning to grow into it, it is being torn from me just as Anna was torn from me, just as the possibility of a career as a doctor in Damascus disappeared in a trice. Were I to think that God controlled my life I would be driven to defy him as a malevolent dictator. But that is not how I think about God, not any more.

The soldier who spoke Greek to me is walking alongside. I take a risk and speak to him.

"Excuse me, brother." He turns sharply. He is no older than me, possibly younger.

"Can you tell me who you are? Where are you taking us?" For a moment I expect a blow but instead he grins.

178

"Yeah, I can tell you. We're the Janissary Corps. The Sultan's crack troops." He laughs.

Janissaries. Of course. Now I remember. The Turks capture Christian boys and turn them into soldiers to serve in the Janissary Corps. Loyal to the Sultan and legendary fighters. That's how this man speaks Greek.

"So where are we going?" He laughs at me.

"Can't tell you that, doctor. Military secret". He laughs again and his two companions join in.

So we are going west with prisoners, women and children only, and one man; me.

Just before dawn we reach a little wooded area with shelter from some trees. The order is given to stop and us prisoners are allowed to sit on the ground. A few stale loaves and some water are distributed amongst us. Tiredness overcomes me and I drift off into sleep.

My slumber is disturbed by a kick from my Greek captor.

"On your feet, doctor. The Captain wants to see you." I struggle up for my wrists are still tied behind my back.

"Come on. Follow me." We pick a way through the resting prisoners towards where the horses are tethered. Some of the officers are standing around in a bunch. One stands away from them, looking out over the plain. All I can see is his broad back. I am led up to him.

"Excuse me, sir" he still speaks in Greek, "here is the doctor."

The officer turns slowly and looks me in the face. I stare back at him, not believing what I see but there is no doubting it. It is my old friend from the Island, Anna's brother.

It is Markos.

In that first glance I can see that he recognises me. Both of us are changed from the slim, clean-shaven boys of the island. Now I have a black beard and he has an impressive reddish moustache. Both have faces burnished by the sun, mine from eremitic contemplation, his from military service. We are both changed but we both recognise the other.

I read a warning in his eyes. Don't say anything. It is not safe so I keep silent. He speaks. "Well, sir. I hear that you are a doctor."

"That's correct, Kýri Captain. I was trained in Arabic medicine at the al-Nuri madrasa in Damascus."

His eyebrows rise. "Arab medicine. Do you speak Arabic?"

"Enough to get by. I learnt a little Latin as well."

"Quite the scholar, then." I can see from his eyes that he is amazed at what his old fisherman friend has achieved. "Well, we have work for a doctor. We lost our own medic last week. Some of my men were wounded in our last little fracas," he nods back towards the town, "we need you to look at them. What do you say?" he is staring deep into my eyes.

"I say I can do nothing with my hands tied. Please release me."

"Of course, of course." He nods to the soldier who quickly unties me. It is a relief to flex my wrists again.

"Now take him to the wounded." His voice drops a tone. "When you are done report back to me. Understand?" I understand. As they lead me to where the injured lie I notice that other Janissaries are erecting tents. Clearly we are staying here for a while.

The wounds are not too bad. Mostly superficial lacerations. Some I need to sew but most only need simple dressings. One man has a fracture of his wrist with some displacement. With the help of his hefty fellows I set the bone. They are tough, these Janissaries, he doesn't make a murmur as I disimpact the fracture, pull it straight and strap it to a makeshift board to hold it still. I could have done with more effective splints and bandages but troops in the field do not appear to carry such supplies. Once finished I turn to my escort.

180

"Take me back to your Captain, please. I have to make my report." They lead me to a tent, set on its own in a shady area under the trees. Markos is inside seated at a trestle table.

"Come in doctor. Thank you, men. You can leave him with me." One of the soldiers steps forward and indicates that I should raise my arms. He then runs his hands all over me, searching, I suppose, for hidden weapons. Satisfied that I am safe he steps back, salutes and leaves the tent. Markos closes the entrance flap, turns towards me and wraps his arms around me in a firm hug. I respond.

"Ioánnis. Is it really you?" He stares at me intently. "This is unbelievable. How?"

"You too, Markos. How did you get here?"

"Sit down" he indicates a cushion on the floor. "I want to hear everything. Where have you been, what have been doing? Everything."

So I tell him. Everything from the night of the raid until now. Except that I do not mention the Turk. Even though I am overcome with joy at this meeting I am still not certain where his loyalties lie. For him to hear that I have murdered a Turk, albeit a brigand, might not be wise.

And then he tells his story. It is quite straightforward. He was taken away on the trireme, to the mainland. There all the boys were separated out and marched overland to Bursa to be enlisted into the Janissary Corps.

"It was a good training, Ioánnis. They were hard but we learnt fast. They took a liking to me which is how I have ended up here," with a nod of his head he indicates the captain's tent. "It's not such a bad life really. We are the privileged ones because we serve the Sultan direct."

I knew this about the Janissary Corps, they have a fearsome reputation. "So do you know what happened to Mama and Eleni? They were on the boat, weren't they?" He shook his head.

181

"I'm sorry. As I said we were separated out once we reached the mainland. I don't know what happened to them but I did hear, only a month ago, that there was a young Greek girl called Eleni in the Sultan's harem at Bursa. She might be your sister but it's a common enough name," his voice trails off. My upset must be visible to him. He puts his hand on my shoulder.

"We're on our way to Bursa. You will have to stay with us as doctor. Perhaps you can find out more when we get there but," and here he looks me straight in the eye, "don't ever attempt to get into the harem, or even make enquiries about it. That's certain death."

I nod. What he does not know is that certain death has no fear for me. It might even be an attraction. If, at least, I could find out what happened to Mama and Eleni I would be satisfied enough to welcome death.

We do not speak of his family, particularly we make no mention of Anna. Her death in the blazing house must be as much an agony for him as it is for me. I begin to understand how Markos has moved on. His is a new life so radically separated from his former as to protect him from the loss and pain. I can understand that but I have a chance to reach back into my old life, to reform what remains of my family. I cannot let that pass.

PERIIGIS TRITI

Chapter 19
Anatolia 1427

Now that I have some status as doctor to the unit I am allowed to travel unrestrained, no longer with my hands tied. Making our way across the high Anatolian plain I get to learn what this Janissary corps unit is doing here.

"We're the frontier troops, Doc" says one of the soldiers, speaking Greek to me, "we're the tough nuts."

It is a dangerous mission. The land is ostensibly part of the principality of the Karamanids. The Ottomans used to rule here but they lost all these frontier territories after their defeat at the hands of the Mongols at Ankara, twenty odd years ago. Technically they are at peace with the Karamanid ruler but it is necessary, at times, to flex their military muscle a bit. That is what this raid was about. Markos told me that there had been too much trouble from this area. Native Turkmen had been raiding caravans coming from the east. They needed to be taught a lesson so the Janissaries taught it to them. It was difficult to understand how my old gentle companion, Markos, could supervise terror of this kind. Most of the men of the town had been killed; the women and children were being taken off to Bursa. No doubt they would end up as slaves.

"It's a job that has to be done," says Markos. We are talking as we ride for they have issued the doctor with a gentle horse, just about within my capabilities as a rider. "This is my life now. I take orders, I give orders. We kill rather than be killed." I say nothing but it is hard to understand his brutal detachment.

As the days wear on and the journey extends he tells me more about his transformation from Christian goatherd to Janissary captain. On arrival in Bursa all the young men were collected together. "They put us through some punishing physical tests." he tells me, "They wanted to sort out the strongest. I was lucky; life back home, chasing goats up and down the hills, had kept me pretty fit. I had no difficulty in meeting the standard."

Once he had been selected he was taken to a small village, a day's journey from Bursa. "It was pretty primitive, even by our standards, Ioánnis. Dull, boring food and you had to shit in the fields." He was there for six months in order to learn Turkish. Then he was made to convert to Islam. "It has to be. No Christian is allowed to carry arms in the Ottoman state so I had to convert." I look at him quizzically.

He laughs. "I know what you're thinking, Ioánnis. Did they circumcise me?" I wince at the thought. "Well, yes, they did. Fortunately the imam had a very sharp knife. I was remodelled in an instant. Mind you, it bled like buggery and I walked with my legs apart for a week. It's fine now; all in good working order." He winks.

"And if you didn't want to covert?"

He pulls his finger across his throat and grins. "It's being a Janissary or nothing, Ioánnis. No choice really."

It is difficult not to admire the efficiency of the Ottomans. Quite straightforward in their deals, albeit ruthless. I suppose such directness is necessary to survive as a state. In my recent hermit-like seclusion I have ignored these realities of the world around me. Now I have been plunged straight back into the cauldron of events. My life is as much out of my control as was my little kaiki on the sea all those years back.

Markos is continuing. "Mind you there's a lot to be said for Islam. All us Janissaries are in the tarîkat, the following of Hacci Bektaş. He came from Muskara, that's the place back there."

"Hacci Bektaş , was he a Muslim?"

"Yes, but a mystic as well. They call them dervishes. It's a branch of Islam called Sufi."

"I know about that." I remembered my talks with Hassif about the Sufi mystic, al-Ghazali. Perhaps if Bektaşî-ism is a type

184

of mysticism, the gap between me and my former friend is not so great, though I never remember him being remotely interested in spiritual matters in the past. For the moment I say nothing about this.

"Where are we going now, Captain?" I have decided that it is safer to address him by his rank rather than his old Christian name.

"Konya first. That's about five days march. We can't go very fast with all these prisoners. It's a safe town and we can re-provision there. Then it's another week's journey to Bursa. A better road after Konya, more people on it as well."

As night falls I walk away from the camp. There is a slight breeze blowing and the air is chill. The sky is clear and starlit; the moon has yet to rise. I look back in the direction from which we had come. Nothing but flatness except that, away in the distance, I can see the snow-covered cone of a symmetrical mountain, still an awe-inspiring sight for me, particularly here. Under this same sky sits Gerasimos, wondering what has happened to me.

I could go back. I could easily slip away. I doubt that Markos would come after me. Go back to the peace, the structured life. I am forced to ask myself why it is that I am travelling with these Ottoman soldiers?

The truth is that I have not been at peace since hearing that Eleni might be in Bursa. And if Eleni, perhaps then Mama. Of course it may be another Eleni, it's a common enough name amongst Greeks. In any case if she is in the harem she would be so unreachable she might as well be dead. But there is a possibility that it is her and, in the face of that possibility, the certainty of a return to my previous pattern of life cannot compete. I have to choose the possibility.

MEROS TETARTON

Chapter 20
Bursa

As we approach Bursa the countryside grows less barren and plain. Orchards and green fields, streams running down from a nearby mountain, it is all very fertile and lush. We pass a huge camel-train and I can count at least sixty beasts. Bursa is a great trade centre. I remember dispatching goods from Damascus to this city when I worked for Kýrie Papadikis.

"Ioánnis!" Markos has ridden up alongside me. "We shall be going to the barracks in Bursa. I don't suggest you come with us unless you want to enlist," he laughs, "and I'm sure you don't want that." He hands me a bundle. "Take this, you'll find it useful." He spurs on his horse and leaves me behind. I rein in and one of the soldiers takes the horse's bridle as I dismount. He nods at me and grunts as I walk away.

We are in front of a vast, brand new mosque built, or so Markos told me, after most of the city had been destroyed by Timur's Mongol horde twenty-five years previously. I walk across to the ablution fountain and wash my face, neck and arms. Then I find a stone seat and open the bundle that Markos has given me. There is money; I am unfamiliar with the currency but it looks to be a generous amount. Then there is a list of names and streets, about seven in all. The names are in Turkish except for one in Arabic. These must be the names of contacts, people who might help me.

Finally I come across a small, smooth stone. On it is carved a hieroglyph that I do not recognise. Why has he given me this? And then I notice that the same hieroglyph is engraved next to the one Arabic name on the list.

I am hampered because I only understand a little Turkish and speak virtually nothing in the language. I wander away from the mosque towards the covered bazaar, the Bedestan. It is as crowded as all the bazaars I have ever been in. As I mingle with the shoppers, the arguing traders, the sellers, I can recognise Turkish, Arabic, Greek and another rough tongue that I take to be Turkoman dialect.

I am not as hampered as I thought I was. I stop at a food stall and buy some olives and peaches. At the next stall, I purchase a loaf of rough bread.

The day goes on. In a desultory fashion I wander through the streets of the city. There is much evidence of new building, some of it magnificent. Defeat by the Mongols must have been devastating but here, a quarter of a century later, the Ottoman Empire grows up again.

I find myself outside a large building which is neither a mosque nor a mausoleum. This must be the Sultan's palace. The gates are closed and two turbaned guards stand impassive in front of them. So, if she is alive, Eleni could be in there. For some minutes I stare at the gates wondering, hopelessly, whether I might see her. It is a foolish act; women of the harem are never going to parade themselves across the front courtyard. I turn away, conscious that the guards are becoming restless.

I look at the list that Markos gave me. The Arabic name is Ibn Al-Aswar. I cannot pronounce the street's name, it is in Turkish. I walk up and down until I can select a hopeful candidate, a young boy carrying a water gourd. In broken Turkish I can just about say "Please help me" then point to the street name. He squints at the name then grabs me by the arm to steer me at high speed through the crowds and down the hill. After ten minutes, by which time I am breathing heavily, we reach the entrance to a narrow street. It reminds me of the street of Kýrie Papadikis' house, narrow and dark.

He points down the street and is telling me something in Turkish. I shake my head to show that I cannot understand so he grabs the list from me and points at the Arab name. I nod assent and he grins broadly. We set off down the street and are soon in front of a closed door. There is no knocker so he beats on the door with his fist. Then he bows briefly and disappears.

It is quiet down here. Indistinct sounds of the bazaar drift down from above me. Nothing happens.

I begin to realise that the sun is going down. If this is a wild goose chase I am going to find myself with nowhere to go tonight. It is not looking too hopeful.

Then there is a creak and the door opens, but by only a small amount. I am aware of a dark figure behind the door. I speak in Arabic.

"Al salaam a'alaykum. Is Ibn Al-Aswar by any chance at home?" The figure replies in Arabic, an old woman's voice.

"Who is it that enquires?"

"My name is Ioánnis Papidikis. I was sent by," and then I struggle to remember Markos' Muslim name and my speech trails off.

"Wait there," and the door closes. Five minutes go by before it re-opens, this time fully. Standing there is a tall Arab. He wears white robes and has a patterned turban on his head. He is clean shaven except for a small, black, pointed beard.

"Al salaam a'alaykum." He bows, "I am Ibn Al-Aswar. Please come in." He steps aside to let me pass.

I am reminded again of the civility of an Arab welcome, the desert code; water with which to wash, refreshments and drinking water and settled on large, comfortable cushions. My spirits revive under the effect of such a welcome, which is what I have always received in Arab households.

He waits during all these preparations, patient and still. Finally he speaks.

"What brings you to my door, sir? In what way can I be of help?"

I do not reply but pass him the stone. He takes it and rests it on his open palm, staring at the hieroglyph that is engraved on its polished surface. There is a pause before he looks back at me.

"Where did you get this stone?"

"From Mustafa Hamîd," I remember the name, "except that I know him as Markos. We grew up together."

"Did you indeed?" his sonorous voice does not betray surprise but his eyebrows rise by a slight degree.

"He gave me your name," It was all that I could think of to say.

"Well, he is brave man, your boyhood friend. Being friends with me is sometimes a danger in this Turkish city," He waves his arm to indicate the rest of the city beyond his house. "But you are indeed welcome. We shall eat and then you can tell me your story."

Which I do, but in an expurgated fashion. Nonetheless I do tell him about Hassif and about my Arabic medical training. His eyebrows do more of a lift at that. But he is most interested to hear of the last three years in the Cappadocian desert. He questions me at some depth about that.

"I saw those caves once but I have never met a hermit who lived in them."

"Oh, I wasn't really a hermit. Gerasimos was the true hermit. I learnt a great deal from him."

"Indeed, and what was that?"

"Oh," and here I begin to struggle. What did Gerasimos actually teach me? It is difficult to express; I stumble over the words. "I suppose he taught me to be still."

Ibn Al-Aswar smiles broadly at this. "And can you be still? You seem pretty restless to me."

"I can but I am not settled. There are things I have to do."

Again he smiles. "We must talk again but now you must rest. Follow me, if you will."

He leads me to a small bedroom. It is cool and quiet. Before long I am asleep, but as so often happens it is a sleep punctuated with dreams. I cannot remember the content of the

190

dreams, rarely can I, but the feeling of restlessness is even more acute when I wake. The sun is already well up as I wash and dress. Aswar has lent me robes to replace my travel-worn apparel. Soon I look the perfect Arab.

He has already left the house. I wander through rooms. There are many books and manuscripts. He is a learned man, there is no doubt about that. I try to quiz the old lady when she brings me food but she is tight-lipped and uncommunicative.

Aswar returns in the late morning. He finds me seated in the small courtyard reading one of his books. He glances at it.

"Avicenna. You must be familiar with him."

"Yes, I am but I have never seen such a beautiful copy as this one." He smiles but does not respond. Instead we talk about my medical education, and Arabic medicine as a whole.

"What appealed, still does appeal to me," I say, "is how practical it is. It seems to base itself on clear observations, on positive science, rather than rely on a whole collection of inherited nonsense." This makes him laugh.

"I like that, inherited nonsense. That's very good." We talk on at length. He seems so well-versed I have to ask him whether he is a doctor.

He laughs. "Oh, no, not me. I'm not clever enough for that. I am a mere teacher."

It turns out that he is a senior professor at the theological college in the city. A large madrasa, well-endowed by the Sultan. "So, are you an imam?"

"No. Not an imam. I am a teacher of the tarîkat of Bektaşî." Of course, it falls into place, the link with Markos. This is the spiritual following adopted by the Janissaries that my old friend told me about. Difficult to equate such mysticism with the warrior class of the Janissaries. He is looking at me carefully, a slight smile on his lips.

"You know about Sufi?"

"A little. My friend told me something of it."

191

"Ah, the Janissaries. I'm not sure if all of them grasp the fundamentals but I think that Mustafa does more than most."

"Fundamentals?"

"Yes. We are followers of the Shi'ite Way and so we place more importance on the mystical than do our Sunni brothers. Most Muslims around here are Sunni but we all rub along fairly well.

"Yes. I am used to Sunni Islam. In Damascus the Mamluks insist on it. I don't remember there being any Shi'ites."

"No, there wouldn't be. You'll find more in Iran and elsewhere. Mind you, there is Sufi mysticism in Sunni Islam. Al-Ghazali was our great leader in that." There's that name again that I first heard from Hassif back in Kashaya.

"So can you tell me about Sufi mysticism?" I am beginning to wonder whether it had similarities to what I had been exploring with Gerasimos.

"In good time, Ioánnis. For the moment I must leave you. I have a seminar to attend. Mind you," he pauses, one hand raised to his mouth. I wait.

"No, maybe not today," he appears to be debating with himself. "Perhaps tomorrow you would like to attend a seminar. We are exploring emptiness."

"But I cannot speak Turkish. I wouldn't cope."

"That's not a problem. We converse in Arabic. I know you can manage that."

It is a challenging seminar. At the start Aswar outlines the four levels of knowledge of Alah. "These are the discourses," he addresses us in a firm voice. "The Makâlât of Hacci Bektaş." We are silent, awaiting enlightenment.

"A novice has to pass through four doors. The first of these is the Seriat. That is well known to us all; orthodox Islamic law. The second door is the Tarîkat, that is the teaching of the religious order. The third door is the Marifet, which is the mystical knowledge of Alah and the fourth door is the Hakîkat, the immediate experience of the essence of Reality."

As I listen my mind takes me back to my cave on the pinnacle, and even further back to my lessons with Father Ignatios all those years ago. There is an equivalence to this Sufi scheme. Father Ignatios taught me the laws, Christian doctrine, but we also explored religious knowledge in greater depth.

Brother Gerasimos taught me nothing more except how to be still, how to be open. In a way that was beginning to bring me to a mystical knowledge of God but it still feels very unclear to me. What is growing and growing within me is the negative way. God revealed not in what He is but in what He is not. That is an understanding that has taken root in me. If it is valid, and I truly believe that it is, then mystical knowledge of God is more likely to be un-knowledge. The mystical way is the way of emptying.

As for the Hakîkat, the fourth level, I cannot imagine what the 'immediate experience of the essence of Reality' can possibly be. It seems unobtainable, out of reach.

But aside from all these questions, I cannot turn away from what brought me to this city. The pressing need to find Eleni.

Chapter 21

The guards on the palace gate salute as Markos and I approach. My heart is in my mouth, a cold sweat on my brow. I feel more than uncomfortable in this uniform that Markos has found for me.

He barks something in Turkish and the gates are opened. The palace courtyard stretches before us. I swallow hard, trying not to vomit with the fear. Given half a chance I would turn back and run for it, but the thought that Eleni might be inside the palace overcomes the temptation to flee.

In the end I had put my confidence in Aswar. I told him of my need to find Eleni, and possibly Mama. By this time I had been a guest in his house, and a student at his seminars, for three weeks. I trusted him. The following day he had appeared with Markos. Together they outlined a plan. I was to disguise myself as a Janissary, a deception which included losing my beard. Markos had sufficient rank to get into the Palace. He could get me near the harem. After that I was on my own.

"You do understand, don't you, Ioánnis that if you are discovered you'll leave the palace without your head." Markos has become a very abrupt soldier. I nodded in assent but my mind jangled with fear.

We march across the courtyard and in through an imposing arched doorway. Inside it is cool and quiet, fountains everywhere, water as clear as crystal. There are groups of Janissaries scattered around the wide open space. Some are drilling with their large sabres. From the corner comes the sound of drums and a whining reed instrument.

Eventually we reach a large door that is firmly closed against us. With a nod of the head Markos indicates that this is it, the entrance to the harem. Under his breath he mutters, "You're

195

on your own now." In a moment he is gone. There is no sound now. I stare at the large, iron double-doors that mark the entrance to the harem. Above the door is the huge seal of the Emperor himself. I imagine the wrath of the Sultan Murad if he discovers that his harem has been breached by a young Greek. Fear rises in my gullet again. I swallow hard.

Above the seal is the inscription. *La ilaha illa-Uahu, Muhammad rasul allahì.* Only one God and Muhammad is his prophet. It is familiar to me, I have seen it emblazoned on mosques, on arches, on important buildings. A sequence of words that cements together whole empires. I have seen it in the Damascus of the Mamluks, the little church in the village of Kashaya, shared by Christian and Muslim worshippers, and here in Ottoman Bursa. One God and Muhammad is his prophet. Muhammad, singled out to be the transmitter of the Holy Qur'an. Muhammad, turning the unspokenness of God into language.

A sound from behind the door jerks me out of my musings. I stand well back, behind a pillar, not concealed but as unobtrusive as I can make myself.

The door swings open and a small group of people walk into the outer courtyard. They are led by a large man in flowing robes. He is fat and his hands and face are completely devoid of hair. From his waist hangs a long, curved sword. He is followed by two women who are totally veiled. They stand nervously at the door to allow the passage of another woman who has come up behind them.

This last woman is not veiled. She is middle-aged and attractive with auburn hair and striking features. Her eyes are alert and I am certain she has spotted me. I try to shrink back further but she has turned away and made no comment. She addresses the man in Turkish and sets off across the courtyard in the direction of the main gate. He, and the two veiled women, return through the iron doors which I hear locked behind me.

I act without thinking. In a moment I am marching across the courtyard like any other Janissary. I follow the woman at a

196

distance that will not draw her attention to me. She waits as the outer gate is opened and then she passes through to the city outside. With a salute to the guard I do the same.

As soon as I hear the gate clang shut behind me I am up beside her. I address her in Turkish.

"Excuse me, madam." She stops walking and turns towards me. Without smiling but showing no fear she replies,

"Can I help you, soldier?" Now I am stuck. I have run out of Turkish. I look at her more closely. She does not look Turkish, or Arab. I take a chance.

"Do you speak Greek, my lady?"

She smiles broadly and replies in Greek.

"Indeed I do, but what's this? A Janissary who cannot speak Turkish?" She takes a step towards me, as if to reinforce the challenge. I cannot find an answer but I must not be deterred.

"Please come with me!" I indicate a side-alley off the square but she stands firm.

"Would I be a fool to go down there with a Greek-speaking Janissary?" The hypothetical question amuses her for she laughs; an open, amused, unafraid laugh. Her eyes dance with delight.

"No, madam. I intend no harm. My name is Ioánnis Papadikis and I am not a Janissary." Slowly she looks me up and down. For a moment I feel exposed, like a skinned goat.

"Then it is a dangerous game that you are playing, Kýri Papadikis," she is definitely not a Turk, "but then all the best games are dangerous. You had better come with me but I suggest you lose that daft uniform and your weapon first." In a moment they are left behind a water cistern and in my plain tunic I am no longer a Janissary. I follow her bareheaded.

We walk for about fifteen minutes, travelling downhill through the city. It is obvious that she is well-known in the city; many people call out to her as she hurries past and are rewarded with a smile or even a wave. Eventually she stops and turns towards me. There is challenge in her look.

197

"I am trusting you, Kýri Papadikis. Am I being foolish?" Her eye is fixed on mine, it is disconcerting. I stammer

"No, no, not foolish. I mean no harm. I want help."

There is a pause as she scrutinises me. I must not look away, must not deflect this silent interrogation. She is not smiling now. I hold my breath, the city seems to still in this moment of decision.

"All right. I'll trust you. Come in."

We enter a small house. It is clear that she lives on her own. Soon we are seated and she has found me a cool drink, cool clear water that tastes of lemon and rose petals.

"My name is Miriam. You don't need to know more than that but it's pretty obvious that you want to hear more."

"I want to know why you were in the harem."

"And I want to know why you were trying to get into the harem." She waved away my protestations, "It was pretty obvious but why were you? You'd lose your head if you were caught, that is after they'd chopped your balls off first."

I am not going to show fear. "I think my sister is in there. I heard she might be," and I recount an expurgated account of what had happened on the island, how Eleni and Mama were taken as slaves.

"How long ago was this?"

"Ten years. I only heard about her a month ago. If it is her perhaps I could find my mother as well." She looks doubtful, her forehead furrowed.

"Ten years? So many people go missing for ever. The wars have been bad for all of us."

I ignore this, I do not want to hear it. "So then when I saw you come out of the harem,"

"You thought 'Aha, some inside information' didn't you?" I nodded. "You didn't stop to think what the Ottomans do to informants, did you? Especially Jewish informants; especially women." I mumble an apology, my head down but she appears not to hear it.

198

"If they're lucky, it's the bowstring. Quick and efficient. Otherwise tied up in a sack full of stones and dumped in the Sea of Marmara. Neither for me, thank you very much. Not even for a handsome young Greek."

"Do you want money? I could pay."

She jumps up. "Don't be so bloody offensive. Do you imagine that is all that is required. Just buy off the Jew?" She is angry now.

"I'm sorry. I'm truly sorry. I wasn't thinking, but you can see how desperate I am. Eleni may be the only member of my family left alive. I've got to find her." This had its effect. She sat down again and the fire went out of her eyes. For a few minutes we sat in silence. I sipped at my drink. She appeared lost in concentration. Finally she spoke.

"Well then. Listen to my story. My family, and there are plenty of them around here, are jewellery makers. We've lived in this city for hundreds of years, probably longer than most others that now think it's their city. Our work is highly prized and is traded all over the world.

"When the Sultan established his harem here in Bursa the ladies of the harem, his Sultanas, the kadins and the odalisques, became good patrons of our work. The only trouble was that they had to send out a eunuch to choose pieces for the ladies and those eunuchs did not have much of an eye for quality and good work. Eventually, and I think this came from the Sultana Valide, the Sultan's mother and the queen bee of the harem, they approached my father to see if someone, and of course it had to be a woman, could be found who might bring the pieces in. This was about ten years ago and my husband, Reuben, had just died." She noticed my look of concern, "Oh, it's all right. I've come to terms with it, mostly. He died of dysentery; there were many deaths in the city at that time.

"So I was put forward. I had to undergo a rigorous examination to see if I was a fit person to go into that place. I think those men fool themselves imagining that their women are cool and virtuous. It's anything but! Most people think that those eunuchs are flabby and impotent but at least half of them can still perform very well. The women make good use of them; no fear of impregnation and I'm told they can go on all night!" She laughs uproariously but I am taken aback by her candour, I blush.

"I'm sorry. Do I embarrass you?" She does not wait for a reply but continues with her tale. "Over the last ten years I have been in and out regularly but now I not only trade in jewellery. I take in news, gossip, tittle-tattle and they lap it up. I am treated like royalty when I go in there. It makes me laugh."

My spirits are rising. Surely this lively, resourceful woman is going to be able to help me.

"So you say her name was Eleni. Well, it won't be that now. It would have been changed to some Persian fancy, rose of spring or the like. In any case there are about three hundred women in there, many of them servant girls."

Just as quickly my heart sinks. It seems hopeless. Then I remember something. It might help.

"Have you seen a young girl who walks with a limp?" I remembered Eleni's accident and her dislocated hip. At this stage she might have developed stiffness in that hip and thus a limp.

"A limp ," she is thinking hard. "there might be. "

"She would have dark hair and be fifteen years old. Please think," the mounting desperation in my voice unsettles her.

"Hold on, hold on!" She pauses. "Yes, there is a girl who fits that description. She is an odalisque but I have not seen much of her. She's very beautiful though, shame about the limp."

"What do you mean, shame?"

"She'd never be chosen to be a gedikli, a maid-in-waiting to the Sultan. Probably just a servant of the chief eunuch." I feel my anger rising in me but have the sense to suppress it, for the moment at least.

"So how can I get to see her?" She looks at me, shocked, then roars with laughter.

"Oh, you poor ignorant Greek! Get to see her? Not a hope. These are the Ottomans we are dealing with. Not a hope."

I stare at her fixedly. "If that girl is my sister I intend to see her." The levity has gone. I think she has recognised my determination. Now it is her turn to retract.

"Yes. I do see that, though God knows how you are going to do it."

"I am going to do it with your help."

So we agree that, first of all, she will try to find out whether this girl with a limp is my sister, Eleni. Meanwhile she will think hard how a meeting could be arranged, even though she still regards it as impossible.

It is late when I slip out of Miriam's house; my head is throbbing with hopes and plans. She is right, it seems an impossible venture, but as I walk back to Aswar's house my mind wanders. There is no plan to my life, that I now acknowledge, but there is still purpose. All my energies, my efforts are now harnessed to the purpose of finding Eleni, if she still exists. She represents the one link to my family, to my old life. It is a link that I need, not because I want to return to that old life but rather that I need that link to define myself. I have tried to tell the story about myself as an orphan, deprived of family. I thought that I had been successful but ever since Markos told me that Eleni might be in Bursa the overpowering need to find her has been awakened.

So no plan but a burning purpose.

Miriam and I have agreed to meet again after she has been back into the harem. There has been no news from her, she has failed to find out about Eleni. I am frustrated.

"You have to be patient, Greek, I'm doing my best."

I fill my days with reading and attending seminars at the madrasa but it is hard to concentrate. The overwhelming purpose to seek out Eleni occupies the whole of my thinking. The idea that I might, at last, regain my family does not allow any space for meditating on Sufi mysticism or the four levels of Bektaşî-ism.

201

At our next meeting she has news. "I saw our limping lady today. I couldn't get to speak to her but one of the other odalisques told me she was Greek. Mind you, there are a lot of Greek girls in there so that may not be anything to go by." This investigation is being so slow and drawn out, I want to scream at her. Nevertheless I curb my frustration and offer polite thanks.

"That's all right, Greek," she has settled on this title, it seems to amuse her.

"Miriam, why are you doing this for me? Why are you risking everything for somebody you hardly know."

Her dark eyes burn into me and she raises her voice. "Why? Why do you ask me this? Why do you need to know? Can't you just accept my help without these questions?"

I step backwards in the face of this onslaught. "I don't know. I never understand why people want to help me."

"I have my reasons" she snaps. "And I'm keeping them to myself. Now get lost!"

"I'm sorry, Miriam. I'm sorry if I upset you." I daren't put another question to her.

"That's all right, Greek" she sounds grudging, "now, bugger off." That sounds more like the old Miriam.

It is a week later and she has news. When I meet her she is bubbling, almost hysterical. "Great news, Greek. I've discovered our limping girl used to be called Eleni. Now she is named Nesrine. I didn't speak to her myself but I had a good look at her. She is very beautiful and I think I can see the family likeness but don't you go thinking you're a handsome man, just because you have a beautiful sister." I am pleased to hear her laughter. So it is Eleni. It must be her. It must be true. I am exhilarated.

"I must see her, Miriam. I must see her."

Her face hardens. "You don't get it, do you, Greek? You cannot get in there, however much you dress up as a toy soldier. The only men ever allowed in have either had their balls chopped off or are doctors."

There was a sensation of the floor dropping from under me. "Doctors? Doctors go into the harem?"

"Well, the women can't come out and the Sultan wants to keep them in good shape," she pauses and spits. "But, young Greek, if you're thinking of pretending to be a doctor to get into the harem, put the idea straight out of your mind."

"But you don't understand! I am a doctor. I don't have to pretend." Now she really is stopped in her tracks.

"You, a doctor? How? When?"

"I trained in Damascus. Three years." There is a silence and then she screams at me.

"Why didn't you tell me, you blithering idiot!" but she is not so much angry as excited. Her eyes are alight with a fire of inspiration. "You, a doctor. You never know, there may be a possibility here." And then she is looking at me with a half-excited, half-quizzical expression, "You're not lying to me, are you, Ioánnis? I'll have your guts for washing lines if you are." She is laughing now. So am I. Something is passing between us in this moment.

"No, it really is true. I really am a doctor." I do not tell her how limited my clinical practice has been although I have amputated a leg. "Can this be a way to get in to see Eleni and rescue her?"

"I don't know. I must think. Get me a drink, I've got a possible idea." I busy myself with getting refreshments for both of us and return with a laden tray. She smiles at me, "There is an old physician, a Jew, who goes into the harem. He is the only doctor allowed in. His name is Abraham Levi. I have known him for years." She pauses, as if remembering. "He owes me a favour, though whether it is as big a one as this I am not certain. But it might work; I shall have to go and see him. Come back tomorrow, Greek physician." I start to thank her. "Shut up, Greek. I have done nothing yet. Now get lost!"

When I return the following evening she has an old man with her. Grey haired and grey bearded, he stands with a marked

203

stoop. One eye is opaque with cataract, the other is dark brown and inquisitive.

"This is Dr Abraham Levi, Greek. Dr Levi please meet Dr Ioánnis Papidikis."

"A Greek, eh," responds the old man. "Where did you learn your medicine, young man?"

"In Damascus, sir. At the al-Nuri madrasa." As so many do he shows surprise at the revelation.

"Arabic training? How did that come about?" I do not want to go into all this again. All I am concerned about is finding a way to see Eleni. "It's a long story, Doctor Levi, but it was a good training."

"No doubt, no doubt. And have you come to settle in Bursa? I am in need of an assistant these days."

"I don't know, sir. I don't have any plans, one way or another." He seems to accept this and turns to Miriam.

"Well now, Miriam my dear. Why is it that you have dragged an old man away from his fire and his evening rest?"

"I wanted you to meet Ioánnis, Doctor. I am hoping that you might be able to help him. When you hear the matter in full I think you will understand why I have approached you for your help."

"Well, let's hear it then. Let's hear the matter in full."

Between us Miriam and I recount the story that culminates with the tantalising possibility that I might have found my little sister, Eleni.

Then Miriam continues, "and I thought, Abraham, that you might want to help this young man, given the circumstances that brought you to this city." She is staring at him fixedly, as if she were willing the words out of him. He does not disappoint.

"Then you know what happened all that time ago?" She nods. "It was a long time ago, long before the invasion of Timur the Lame. I arrived from the north with nothing. I was on the run from the authorities. My life was in the greatest danger." He paused and wiped his rheumy eyes with an old kerchief. Already his story had resonances for me.

"It was your father, Miriam dear, who took me in. He arranged for a change of identity, he told everyone that I was his cousin from Baghdad. No-one doubted it. He arranged for my medical training and set me up as a doctor in the Jewish quarter. You were just a little girl at the time. You didn't suspect any of this."

"No, not at the time. When I was older my father told me the whole story, shortly before he died. I have told no-one else except Reuben, my husband, and he died with the secret intact."

Abraham Levi is turning to fix dark eyes on me. "So here is another fugitive. I think that, in the circumstances, I am bound to help you, young man." Miriam smiles.

And so we have a plan. Abraham is going to say that he is too ill to attend the harem; at his age this is not unlikely. He is going to present his young assistant, Benjamin, as a substitute; "that's you' Greek, but don't worry, you don't have to be circumcised." That way I can get into the harem.

But old Abraham emphasises that his help for me is in getting to see Eleni. "If you use your position as my assistant to spring her from the harem it will be certain death for you if they catch you and it will be very certain death for me too. I'm too old to be able to escape." If I am to release Eleni I have to find another way.

In the meantime Miriam is going to speak to Eleni and explain, without giving reasons why, that she should consult the doctor at his next visit. It is a risky scheme and could fail at any point. I have never been so nervous or so keyed-up.

My vetting at the palace is terrifying. I am interviewed by one of the viziers, an official wearing a large white turban and a daunting demeanour. He sits at a long, polished desk. I stand in front, flanked by two enormous guards, each one half a cubit taller than me. They both carry long sabres that glint in the late afternoon sun.

205

The vizier stares at me long and hard. "You are young for a doctor. Do you have evidence of your medical training?"

"I am sorry, Excellency. My papers were lost on my journey from Damascus."

"And why did you leave there?" He looks at me in a way that suggests he knows the reason why. How can he? My voice wavers, "There were no opportunities for a Jew there. I came north to find employment." Again he looks at me hard but says nothing. I begin to sweat. Am I going to be rejected? The length of the pause before he speaks again is disconcerting.

"Well, Dr Levi speaks highly of you," he indicates the testimonial that Abraham had given me, "and I trust him. You are approved; make your arrangements with the clerk." Immediately I am marched out to see the clerk who presents me with a document that authorises my entry to the harem. Back at Miriam's house I show it to her.

"Very impressive but don't forget, Greek, that it is still a very dangerous enterprise. Be very careful." She goes on to report that she has spoken to Eleni who appeared bemused but agreed to do as instructed.

It is the day of my visit. I feel uncomfortable in the dark robes of a physician. I stand before the iron doors once more, escorted by three Janissaries. The doors swing open, the Janissaries step back and I walk through. I am greeted by the chief eunuch who takes me through to an empty room with a couch in the centre. Thankfully he does not speak to me so I do not have to struggle with Turkish.

Women are brought to me, one at a time, escorted by a large Ethiopian eunuch. He does not stay in the room but a servant girl, or woman, does. The complaints and illnesses are, in the main, trivial and easily dealt with. My immediate impression is that most of them relate to boredom and enforced laziness.

Then another patient enters. She is accompanied by a very old female servant. The patient wears a veil and walks with a limp.

My heart skips more than one beat. I indicate a chair for her to sit. She sits down and removes her veil.

I can hardly breathe. I look her direct in the eyes, notice the dark hair, the line of her nose. She is a grown woman, a beautiful young woman but she is still my little sister, Eleni. I address her in Turkish. "How can I help you, madam?" I am conscious of the old lady in the corner but she appears not to hear so, in a quiet voice, I risk speaking Greek.

"Eleni?" She looks shocked and peers at me hard. It occurs to me that I have changed more than her.

"I'm sorry. Why do you call me Eleni?"

"Isn't it your name, your real name?

She flushes from the neck upwards. "How do you know? Who are you?"

"I am Ioánnis, your brother. Don't you recognise me?"

Her hand rises to her mouth. "Ioánnis? It can't be, I mean, how? Here?"

"Listen, Eleni, we haven't much time. You may not believe this but I am a doctor, a real doctor. We've got to be careful" with my eyes, I indicate the old woman in the corner of the room.

"That's all right. She is totally deaf."

"Well, good but it must look as if you are consulting me. Let's say it's to do with your hip. If you lie on the couch I will examine you and we can talk at the same time." By now Eleni has recovered from her shock and sees what has to be done.

As I examine her, I speak. "How did you come to be here? Tell me all."

Briefly she tells me her story. She and Mama were taken to a port on the mainland and herded into the slave market. She told of the degradation of being stripped naked and having to stand in the market place whilst potential buyers examined her body, her teeth and how she walked. At that time she did not have a limp, that had only developed later. She was bought by a Turk and then brought to Bursa to be admitted to the harem.

207

"It's not a bad life, Ioánnis. I am well looked after and I have good friends here."

I begin to worry that the plans I have been hatching for her escape may not gain her approval. "But we have to find a way to get you out of here." Her eyes drop and she examines her hands that are twisting in her lap. "Are you saying you want to stay here, Eleni?"

"It could be worse."

"But what about Mama, where is she? Don't you want to be with her?"

Her head drops. It seems as if she does not want to speak these words. "Mama died, Ioánnis, soon after we left the coast. She caught a fever and died on the road. The slave traders dug a shallow hole in the ground and buried her." Somehow I knew this was what she was going to tell me but the pain of it was like a knife turning in my gut.

"I'm sorry, Ioánnis, I'm sorry." She does not just mean about Mama. I can see that she is not going to leave, even if it can be engineered, which is unlikely.

Briefly I tell her of my journeying. As I relate the story it becomes apparent to me that I have come to an end. Yes, I have found the one member of my family that survives but she is as lost to me as before, more even. Before there was a potential of her as part of my life; not now if she is to remain in the harem for the rest of her life, a choice that I can see she has made.

"What will you do now, Ioánnis? Have you made contact with Anna?"

Anna! My voice cracks, "Anna! What do you mean? Anna is dead. She was burnt alive on the island." I am choked with rage and remorse. At first I do not notice that she is wide-eyed.

"No, she wasn't, Ioánnis. Anna was on the boat. Once we arrived at the port we were separated and I did not see her after that. But she didn't die." She was emphatic, her face creased in a way that reminded me so well of my little sister. "You haven't found her?" I shake my head dumbly for I am trying to

208

incorporate what I have just heard into the emotional turbulence of my mind. "She is probably somewhere. I heard tell that there were Greek slave traders at the market. They could have been heading for Constantinople."

Constantinople. Byzantium. The heart of what remains of the Roman Empire. Could it be that Anna is there, somewhere there? My life, which a few moments ago had seemed a void, is now filled with a new purpose, more pressing than any that preceded it. Already the compulsion is gaining strength, renewing itself as it rolls over and over in my mind. Anna.

It is hard, saying farewell to Eleni. I cannot touch her, there is no time to speak. The eunuch has returned and Eleni, veiled, leaves without a word. I am led out of the palace in a daze. I have to speak to Miriam, I am certain of that.

She is preparing a meal when I arrive, exotic aromas fill her small house. She turns, excitement in her eyes. She has changed from her hum-drum ordinary clothes and is wearing a long dress of deep blue material, dotted with glistening semi-precious stones that dance in the candlelight. Her dark hair hangs loose and glows with a sheen like the black of a raven. For the first time I see that she is beautiful, desirable. She takes my breath away.

"Well, you made it, Greek, and hopefully with your balls intact!" Suggestively she stares at my groin. I do not reply and her face changes to a look of concern. "Did it not work? What happened, Ioánnis?"

"It worked. I found her. It is Helena but I have lost her again."

She puts down the pot she is holding and walks across to me. She holds me in her arms. "I'm sorry. Lost again? Doesn't want to leave? I think I can understand that. Wouldn't do for me, mind you, but for some of them it is an asylum."

"It's because Mama is dead."

"Yes, probably so. It's the same for most of the women in that place. It becomes their home and their life." She moves toward the table where the food that she has been preparing is laid

209

out; sliced beef sausage, warm pickled cabbage, fruit and rough wine. At first I have little appetite but the food and the wine and the presence of this beautiful, benevolent woman combine to loosen the grip of my sadness. For the first time I am able to tell her the whole story of my life on the island, of my love for Anna and of believing that she had been burnt to death in the corsair raid. My voice begins to falter as I speak of the deaths and atrocities.

"How about you, Ioánnis? Were you unscathed?"

"A sabre cut to my arm," my voice tailed off.

"No more than that?"

I sense that she apprehends what I don't want to say. "There is more but I can't..."

"Can't?"

"Don't, Miriam." The tone of my voice has roughened. I feel threatened. A sense of panic rises in my gorge. Miriam says nothing and in that silence my agitation slips away.

"I was assaulted. By a large Turk. His companions held me down whilst he violated me." My head is in my hands; I dare not look at her.

"Ioánnis. Look at me." Reluctantly I lift my head to be met with a gaze of understanding and concern. At that moment something passes between us, a small but significant identification. She smiles "And now there is news, news that Anna may still be alive."

"Yes, I can't believe it. I have to find her."

"But news like that; Ioánnis, it turns you upside down. And all it is, well it's just that; news. Words and phrases, in this case one very short sentence. 'Anna is alive' or 'Anna may be alive'. A short enough tag to hang your life on, Ioánnis, but you are right to take that chance. I will pray that you are not disappointed."

She leaves me sitting at the table, my head in my hands. I fail to notice that she has left the room. In a few minutes she returns. I lift my head to look at her. She has changed and now wears an ankle-length shift and a pair of gold sandals. She stares at me directly, a smile lighting up her dark eyes. Now I begin to understand what she intends. I stand up, overtaken by a feeling of panic, and turn away from her. "No, Miriam!"

She stares at me for a moment, nonplussed. I sit down once more, my head in my hands. Through the open shutter I can hear the noises of the night drifting down from the city outside.

"What is it, Ioánnis? I don't want to hurt you." I cannot answer. "Is it Anna? The thought of Anna?"

I look up. I have to tell her. "Perhaps it is, but it is something else as well. That man I told you about, the Turk."

"The man who raped you." I wince at her explicit speaking.

"Yes, that man. I met him again some years later. It was down a dark alley in Damascus. I don't know what came over me. I was carrying a knife. I murdered him."

She whistled "You really are a dangerous Greek." Then she laughs "Bloody good job, too. All that he deserves."

"But perhaps you can see how I cannot come to terms with it all, being violated and then killing a man. I thought I could but you have awoken the whole thing once more. I feel filthy, I feel defiled and I am tortured with guilt. I had hidden from it until now."

She draws me to my feet. "Come here, Ioánnis, no more words." For a moment I am rooted to the spot. I was not expecting this. "Come on, Ioánnis," the arm is still extended. Eventually I stand and take her hand. She lifts my other hand, faces me then leads me through to a small bedroom. Swiftly and expertly she removes my clothes. I make no protest, it is as if I do not recognise what is happening. With a gentle smile on her face she pulls the shift over her head and stands naked in front of me. My mind is spinning now, struggling to recognise what is happening. I am remembering Anna; I am remembering the easy way I slipped the knife into Mahmout the Turk. I stand up and move towards her as she opens her arms towards me.

211

"Come to me, Ioánnis. Let me be your Anna, just for this night.". The touch of her gently curving body releases the pent-up frustration and sadness of the last few weeks. My head rests on her bare shoulder and I begin to cry. After a while she slips past me, lies down on the bed and pulls me on top of her.

"Come into me, Ioánnis. I need you in me."

When we have finished she kisses me and runs her fingers through my hair. "It's been so long, Ioánnis, so long on my own. For me the first time since Reuben died."

Lying and facing each other we sleep. Later there are further spells of love-making between passages of more sleep. I know, both of us know, that this will be the only night.

Early, before dawn, I dress. She turns towards me and kisses me as she whispers, "Good luck, Greek. Have a good life. Find Anna"

I slip out into the night.

PERIIGIS TETARTI

Chapter 22
Venice. 1438

The deck planks creak under my feet as the ship swings gently in the swell. I gaze out across the iridescent blue lagoon to the city beyond. Over to my left a flight of water birds takes to the air. Their ricocheting cries stretch the width of my view.

On the horizon I can see the towers, domes and large palaces of the city. I have heard much about this city. The old man has told me great tales of its history yet it is clear that he does not trust the people. Perhaps he is right, they are known to be a wily lot, opportunist raiders too. He says we shall see the great bronze horses that were stolen from our own city of Constantinople two hundred years ago. He holds out little hope of restitution.

He is down below, the old man. I told them that he should not travel; he is too old and too ill but It seems the Emperor insisted. Not that I have seen Emperor John on our journey, nor am likely to either. He has his own vessel. Well, not his own, the whole fleet is loaned to him by the Venetians. His barque must sail well for it reached here two days ahead of us. When we arrived it was moored by a long slip of land between the lagoon and the sea. No sign of Emperor John though.

I am worried about old Patriarch Joseph. He is more and more breathless. He struggles to get up the companion-way on to the deck so he has stayed below for the last two days, resting on his back. He appears to trust me. When I visit he is always gracious to me; surprising seeing that he is the leader of the True Church and I, an itinerant monk and medic. It amuses him to call me Lukas. The beloved physician, companion to St Paul.

"Come in, Doctor Lukas. See what you can do with this old hunk of flesh." That sets him off chuckling. I smile respectfully. Everybody loves Patriarch Joseph.

But when he talks of the forthcoming council his eyes light up with passion and, for a moment, the years fall off him. There is no doubt that he sees in these meetings the last chance to reunite a divided Church, once more for it to become a force in the world, and with it the salvation of our great city from the Ottoman Turks. He seems to have no doubts. I wish I could feel as optimistic but the signs are not good. I fear that the old man will not see his patriarchal seat again. Perhaps, in the circumstances, that will be a blessing for him.

My eye scans the horizon. There is little wind so we make very slow progress. As my gaze drifts the external space creates room in my mind, room for a narrative to form.

It is twelve years since I left Bursa; twelve years since I left Eleni in the harem; twelve years since I slipped away from Miriam's bed in the still light of early dawn. I left the town quickly before my intrusion into the harem might be discovered. Yet again I found myself a fugitive, unable to look anyone in the eye, suspicious of all.

I resumed my identity as an Arab. That seemed to be the safest way to travel, not that I knew where I was going. I assumed north was best, always north, north to Constantinople. I wondered where Markos might be. Perhaps he would help me; but then, the more I thought about it, the more I suspected that he was likely to be more of a danger than a help. Assuming the *persona* of a Janissary captain was not a cover or a protection for him; it was an identity that he had embraced wholeheartedly; and who could blame him? What loyalties did he have with his family all gone, or so he thought? Markos just had Markos to look after, no other ties.

It was clear to me that he did not know that Anna might still be alive for he had never mentioned it. I don't know whether I believed it either. I was beginning to think that it was futile, a

214

search for the unsearchable. Even in me there was a growing tendency to accept the world as it was, to abandon my past longings, my previous aspirations. Gerasimos had taught me about the acceptance of things as they are, a stillness which can bring serenity; but subsequent events had brought into stark relief the limits of my understanding. There was more to the nature of serenity than I had ever appreciated back then.

As I journeyed I could not get out of my mind that last, passionate night with Miriam. At times when I thought that searching for Anna was a fruitless task I imagined what might happen were I to return to Bursa and seek her out. My memory of that night conjured a cataclysm of emotions. In part there was guilt, a feeling that I had betrayed Anna. Yet again there was longing; Miriam had woken in me an understanding of how much I needed the reassurance of physical contact. Beyond that I was aware of something else, an awareness that was quite unexpected. The memories of that night are now linked with the night of the raid, with being raped by Mahmout the Turk. Her tenderness and her passion has taken away some of my sense of shame, of violation. Up until then I had thought that it was being buggered which had caused me the revulsion. Now I can see that it was the violence and the force that accompanied it which was the rape.

In some way it has also modified how I feel about murdering the rapist but I cannot, as yet, grasp how. Perhaps I am starting to come to terms with what I did, beginning to accept that it is part of me.

And now I have become a monk. I stare down into the water. Shoals of fish are darting about near the surface. I smile because I know how to cast a net that would land a good catch. That was back-breaking work in those days. The same routine, day after day. Perhaps there is serenity to be found in repetition. Perhaps I could go back to that, become a fisherman again, not a doctor, not a monk; simplify the tasks.

But I cannot let my life's direction go now. Since I arrived in Constantinople and was taken on as a physician there has been no turning back. Heaven knows I was needed. So many people had left. Parts of the city were deserted, there were great areas inside the city walls that were countryside; small, rundown villages being the only habitation. Admittedly there was plenty of activity around the Emperor's palace but even that exalted building was beginning to look decrepit.

We were always hungry. There was never enough food and mostly it was inedible. I present a gaunt figure nowadays. The cadaveric Brother Ignatios.

Ignatios, my new name; given when I became a monk. The Abbot approved it. I did not tell him of that other Ignatios, my dear old teacher who was slaughtered on the island. I adopted the name as a private homage to the old priest.

I am aware in my musings that I am censoring out the most significant event of my story. And as I am reminded a twist of agony touches my soul. My mind has tried to shut it away; partly protection but also an attempt to convince myself that what I heard that evening never happened.

I was shocked when I first arrived in the city, in Constantinople, a place I had so often imagined as rich, important and overpowering in its imperial splendour. I was travelling for several weeks on a journey that took me south west to the Dardanelles to cross the water into Europe. Al-Aswar had been generous to me and had left me with sufficient funds to pay my way. I paid for a crossing over the Hellespont on a flat bottomed cargo boat. Once on the other side it was many day's trek before I stood in front of the land walls of Theodosius, the impregnable defences of Constantinople, magnificent in their solidity. The main wall and towers did indeed seem unyielding but great stretches of the outer wall had collapsed. The brick-lined fosse that had been dug outside the walls was drained of water. Even so the whole defence looked solid to my inexpert eye. I stood before the ancient walls in awe, overwhelmed by the sense of permanence. They were not like the walls of Damascus that were breached by Timur the Lame and his horde. Mostly they reminded me of those other walls that enclose a holy space, the Monastery on the island of my birth. As I stared at them I became aware of how the religious realm appropriates power and permanence to itself. Its doctrines and its dogmas, its hierarchy of clerics generate a powerful and an oppressive hegemony. Four years in the Cappadocian desert with Gerasimos has had its effect.

I entered the city through a large gate, merging unobtrusively with a camel train that had arrived at the gates at the same time as me. It was a simple matter to slip in beside them.

Those first weeks in the city were difficult. Difficult to find food, difficult to find lodgings. Eventually I came across an old Greek lady, I call her Greek but she would insist that she was Roman. She let me a small room. The house was dilapidated, down a street but a stone's throw from Ayia Sophia.

Ayia Sophia. When I first saw Justinian's great church, with its beautiful dome soaring towards heaven, my breath was taken away. I stood in front of its magnificence, almost unable to take it in. But an even more overpowering experience greeted me when I entered the church. The rich colours of the mosaics, the opulence of the gold, the frescoes, the adornments and the sheer scale of the whole building overtook me. In one moment it confirmed the pre-eminence of the true Church. Surely there could be no doubting that this was God's place on earth. In its magnificence it cemented the religious *status quo*; there was no room for doubt. I was overwhelmed.

Standing under the huge dome I stared up at the vast mosaic of the Pantokrator . It made me recognise that my understanding of God had moved a long way from the traditional orthodoxy of my youth. Father Ignatios had started it, perhaps not realising what he was doing? On reflection I could see that, of course, he did. My discussions with Hasif in the little village of Kashaya, my years at the al-Nuri madrasa, my extraordinary three

217

years with Gerasimos in the Cappadocian desert and the teaching of Al-Aswar in Bursa had taken me far from the orthodoxy of my youth. This incredible building pitched me straight back to an old understanding. In the end it was not a fact that I welcomed. I almost came to resent the sense of oppression that I felt from the dome of Ayia Sophia.

As for the rest of the city it was sadly dilapidated. The Hippodrome was almost totally collapsed, none of the many other churches of the city conveyed the majesty of Ayia Sophia. Even the imperial palace at Blachernae was in desperate need of repair. A feeling of depression infected me. Now my life, my journeyings seemed even more pointless. Pointless to end up in this run-down mausoleum. I was succumbing to a feeling of hopelessness, an inner anger turned against myself that stultified everything that I thought or did.

But then, quite suddenly, my circumstances changed. My landlady, old Kýriaki Matsouki, discovered that I was a doctor.

"Doctors are needed here, Kýrie Papadikis. Most of them have left over the past few years."

"If that is the case I'd like to practice again. Can you put me in touch with anyone?" She promised to find out. A few days later she knocked on the door of my room.

"Kýrie Papadikis, I have someone who might take you on as an assistant. He is an old doctor who lives near the Pantokrator Monastery. His practice includes the people of that area," she frowned, "riff-raff mostly but he looks after the monks and nuns of the Monastery too. I think it would suit you well."

I visited him the very next day. Antonius Vangelis was a Greek, originally from the island of Lesbos so at least we had that, our upbringing, in common. He had worked in the city for thirty years. His methods of practice were very traditional, blood-letting was frequently employed, astrological calculations appeared very important to him. If I was to join him I doubted whether my methods, radically different from his, would fit in; we would be sure to clash sooner or later.

In effect it did not happen. He was a gracious old man who was quite prepared to let me have my head, just so long as I did not try to make him change his ways.

"I am an old man, Doctor Papadikis. I am a very old man; it is too late for me to learn new ways." By my smile he could see that I acknowledged that. We rubbed along well enough.

Working again as a doctor began to restructure my world, not only through the intellectual challenge of the work but also through the need to give something of myself back to the society which had adopted me. Rather than diminishing, it seemed to re-establish me; it allowed me to mould the narrative of my life at a time when the narrative had nearly run into the ground. Doctor Papadikis was a helpful *persona*, no doubt, but Ioánnis, and the story he told about his self, which formed his life, was the under-current that was allowed to develop once I started working as a doctor again.

MEROS PEMPTON

Chapter 23
Venice. 1438

We have started to move again. The city is getting closer. To our right I see the barque which carries the Emperor, both vessels making progress from the Lido to the city of Venice.

It excites me to think that I am going to see Venice. It was Venetians who ran our island. They built large, beautiful houses in the town around the Monastery. Their rule was relatively benign, taxes were reasonable (though Baba always complained bitterly but then, Baba complained about most things). Now I am going to see the city itself.

A flash of light from the direction of the city focuses my attention. I shield my eyes from the sun to see its source. One of the sailors is pointing in that direction and shouting.

"Look, it's the Bucintoro!" I strain to see and begin to make out the shape of a slender barge. Its superstructure is clothed in scarlet damask, twenty-four oarsmen propel it in a swift course that carves through the gentle swell. At one end is a raised deck on which is placed a solid, gold-encrusted throne. Now I can make out a figure seated on the throne. He wears sumptuous robes and a tall hat. This must be the Doge.

The Bucintoro and the Emperor's barque are closing fast. When they are within a couple of stones' throw of each other they come to a halt. A small skiff is sent out from the Doge's vessel to the Emperor's. I see a tall man in dark robes seated amidships. Soon he is boarding the Imperial vessel.

A stillness descends. The swell subsides and a hazy sun seems to cement the whole vista into place. I turn to one of the sailors.

"What is going on? Why have we stopped?" He shrugs his shoulders.

"No idea, brother. Some bit of bloody protocol, I expect."

After an hour the skiff returns. Shortly afterwards the Bucintoro is brought up to the Emperor's vessel and ropes are attached. Slowly, and with much straining of the oarsmen, the Emperor is towed in towards the city.

As we reach the entrance to the Grand Canal the splendour is revealed. No sign of the decrepitude of Constantinople, this city screams of wealth and power. We progress up the Grand Canal, finally mooring beside a magnificent palace. To the sound of a fanfare on eight silver trumpets the Emperor descends and disappears inside. Soon afterwards I help Patriarch Joseph to enter the same way and we are shown to our quarters. The old man is very tired but nonetheless excited by all that is happening.

Later that night I administer a sleeping draught to him. I sit with him as it exerts its effect, contemplating the sleeping figure; nothing more than a bag of bones. How is he going to survive the rigours of the forthcoming council? We are to meet in Ferrara, I am told. The Emperor and Patriarch on our side and the Latin Pope on the other. No Western Emperor though. I cannot help but feel foreboding about what is to happen. We may be the remnant of the Roman Empire on this earth but we seem weak and powerless, we have no strong cards to play.

Patriarch Joseph had explained the issues to me as we made our long sea voyage from Constantinople to this city on the lagoon. The main points of contention were clear: the Latins use of unleavened bread in the Holy Eucharist, the doctrine of purgatory and, above all, the hated *filioque* that the Western Church has inserted in the Nicene Creed.

"It is about the procession of the Holy Spirit, Doctor Lukas. It was all agreed at Nicaea a millennium ago but those Latins have altered it with no authority or justification."

"I remember a little about it," I replied. Father Ignatios had explained it to me once but that was many years ago. "The Holy Spirit who proceeds from the Father *and* the Son. That's what they say, isn't it?"

"Quite right, and with no justification. Adding in the words *and the Son* is deeply offensive." My face expresses the bemusement that I experience. "It's offensive because it downgrades the Holy Spirit, Brother Ignatios. Makes him a created being. That cannot be." I still struggle to understand.

Patriarch Joseph sighs. "Ah well. We are in no position to argue. We shall have to reach a compromise. We're good at that, us Orthodox. We know when to compromise."

Of course everyone knows that the real purpose of the forthcoming council is to enlist western help against the threat of the Turk. It is perfectly clear that that is why our Emperor John is here. The Ottoman threat is now pressing and terrifying. John is determined that he is not going to be the last Byzantine Emperor. If it takes an ignominious climb down over some piece of dogma like the *filioque* to enlist the help of the Western powers he is going to see that it happens.

I find my the cell allotted to me. It is small and sparse. I remove my monk's attire, tall black hat and a long black robe. Now a monk and a doctor, I still carry on my practice but from the Monastery nowadays. My time is evenly divided between monastic duties and medical tasks. I have settled into the routine. It gives a structure to my life, a structure that I needed when I finally realised that I had lost Anna.

I had been in Constantinople for three years. Despite my searches and enquiries there had been no sign of Anna. Then one day came news that turned my world upside down. I was dining with a family that had befriended me when I first arrived. On the particular evening in question there was another guest at the table, a Genoese merchant from Galata, across the Golden Horn. He was talking of his cousin.

223

"Silvio's a lucky man. He married a beautiful wife who used to be a servant to the Empress. It took some persuading, and not a little gold I have to say, to let her release her maid. I've never seen such a beauty as the Lady Anna."

I must have visibly started for heads turned towards me. I swallowed hard and fought to regain my composure.

"And when was this?" my voice was almost strangled.

"Oh, about three years ago I should think."

"Do they live in Galata?"

"No. I've lost touch. Silvio went abroad. I've no idea where he is now."

It may not be Anna, I told myself, seeking to quieten my panic. It's a common enough name. It can't be Anna. I try to sound non-committal.

"This Anna. Was she from Genoa as well?" He looked at me a little curiously.

"Oh no. Not Genoese. She was Greek."

Now I knew.

We make slow progress from Venice to Ferrara. The Emperor has done his best to make us an impressive procession but even the Imperial trappings are looking a little threadbare. I walk behind the Patriarch's litter. The old man is wearied by the journey but still has the energy to read his Bible.

"The Gospel of Ioánnis Theologos, Doctor Lukas. All that we need for salvation is here." I remember the old cave back on the island, the cave where my namesake received his revelations and dictated them to Prochuros, his scribe. My mind wanders from there to Father Ignatios. He and the Patriarch have much in common. In my love for this old man I remember how much I loved the other, the gentle priest who opened up my life for me.

As my thoughts wander back to the island I am brought up against the events of that terrible night. I remember the key that Father Ignatios gave me, my flight up the mountain and finally that

224

hidden ikon. I try to picture what it looked like as I walk along this muddy road. I am finding it hard to remember.

The sun is drying up the remnants of a rainstorm. Its heat is intense. As it burns into me I am taken even further back. Clambering over rocks, looking for a lost kid, the procession of the monks on the skyline, carrying a burden. Of course, it must have been that ikon. Being carried, and venerated, to the top of the mountain to be hidden from sight. I am reminded of the overpowering sense that I experienced all those years ago, the sense that what I was seeing was of supreme importance to my life. That perception has never left me.

But why on earth?

After the splendour of Venice Ferrara is a more ordinary city. It is raining when we arrive, in fact it rains for most of our stay. Our procession makes its way through the main gates of the city. The city wall is dilapidated, there are great gaps in its course and much of what stands is a wooden palisade, though inside there is evidence of much new building. The new quarter is laid out in a geometrical pattern which is quite striking to one who is used to the higgledy-piggledy streets of Arab cities and my home town on the island. We monks, and Patriarch Joseph, are accommodated in a Franciscan Monastery, only a stone's throw away from the central piazza.

The procession disperses and I escort the Patriarch to his cell. He looks relieved to be here at last. The Emperor has decreed that there shall be no discussion for four months. They say he wishes to allow time for the Western Princes to arrive. As yet not a single one of these has appeared.

Once I have settled old Joseph, and left him sleeping I wander up to the central piazza. I notice that the people I pass are staring at me. This is unusual; in Constantinople a monk is hardly noticed. It is quite the opposite here. A small boy, carrying a bucket upends it on his head and marches along behind me, mimicking my gait. Other children gather to laugh. I turn around

225

and with a big smile swap his bucket for my black klobuk, my monk's hat. His face reddens but then he shows off his new accoutrement to his fellows. There are cheers of delight, especially when I put the bucket on my own head.

Having finally retrieved my hat I cross the piazza to the Cathedral and stand in front of the great west end. The whole of this façade is clad in marble. There are three portals, the largest in the centre and two smaller ones on the south and the north. I stand in front of the central portal. Above it is an elaborately carved loggia containing a statue of the Mother and Child. Above that, carved in intricate detail is a scene which it is not difficult to identify; the day of Judgement.

I stand quite still as I examine this carving. The figures seem quite life-like. There it stands, above the door through which all worshippers enter, a perpetual reminder of what awaits them.

We are not used to this type of realism. Our apokalypses are distant and rarefied. This is quite different; it is immediate and it is designed to be terrifying. The more I look at it, the more I come to see what separates us, the Latins and us Orthodox, is much more than unleavened bread and the *filioque*. This display is about power. It is meant to threaten; it is designed to grasp and exert control. This is a way of forcing a reality on its adherents, to frighten them into submission.

And with that power goes an obsession with individual sin. That is what the doctrine of purgatory is all about. For the Latins, no-one can escape from the consequence of their individual sins; all is written down in the Book by the terrifying Recording Angel. Remission can be granted by the ecclesiastical authorities if it is earned by waging bloody crusades or paid for with money that stuffs the coffers of the priests.

That is not our way. We seek love, not retribution. Not for us the confessional, the penances. Acts done in love cannot be evil. I cannot think of the love that I received from Miriam, from Anna, without recognising the love of God. In my heart there is no distinction between the two.

I turn away for all this Latin hegemony has no effect on me. It would have done, in the past, but now I can see what this kind of religion is trying to do. To oppress me, to beat me down. I will not let it. In this revelation I recognise how much I have grown up, how much I have changed from that uncertain boy who was raped and dispossessed, to one who can now stand as a man.

Desultory weeks pass. Nothing is happening apart from some debates over minor matters, a dialectical flexing of the muscles. I am told that Pope Eugenius is not happy. He is footing the bills and they are not small. There are scores in our entourage, the Emperor's household; priests, academics, monks and servants, let alone the hundreds in the Latin contingent. It must be draining the Vatican's coffers.

Late one evening there is a knock on my cell door. I admit a worried looking servant.

"Brother Doctor. Your help is needed. One of the Emperor's guards is sick." His eyes stare at me with an intensity which signal his urgency. I put on my hat and pick up my bag of equipment. He guides me through the streets to a small barracks where the gate is opened for us.

"Up there," he points up a stone staircase. I can see a light coming from the chamber at the top. It is clear that he is not going to accompany me.

I climb the stairs and push open the rough door. By the flickering candlelight I see a man lying on a wooden bed. He is groaning gently. I place the back of my hand on his forehead. He has a high fever.

"Can you hear me? I am a doctor. What is your name?" All that I receive by way of a reply is a louder groan. I pull back the coarse sheet that covers him. Immediately I notice the large swellings in his groin. At that moment he is racked with a fit of coughing and a gobbet of blood-stained phlegm is propelled on to the floor beside him.

There is no doubt in my mind. Plague. I have not seen it before but was taught its presentation at the al-Nuri. I call for the servant. He appears in the doorway.

"Get this man water and fresh bedclothes. And call the captain." He runs off.

I see to the comfort of the suffering man and leave him some pain-killing powders. Then I meet the Captain in the square.

"It is the plague, Captain. You must seal off that room. No-one is to enter except one attendant who must wear a gown and mask at all times." The Captain quickly agrees. An epidemic amongst our delegation would be disastrous.

I return the following morning to find that the man has died. Already panic and fear is spreading amongst the Emperor's guard. The Captain looks seriously worried. "Can it be contained, doctor? My men are on the edge of deserting." I have no answer for him.

Over the next two weeks the plague does spread through the whole city of Ferrara. Mercifully our one soldier, who died within a day, was the only Greek to be affected. With no discussions going on, apart from a conclave that is half-heartedly debating the doctrine of purgatory, I wonder whether we shall all return home. Then comes news; we are to remove to the city of Florence, which is plague-free and whose city fathers are willing to meet the expenses of the delegations.

Immediately I am worried about the effect on the old man of another journey in the summer heat. He spends most of his time resting or sleeping. When I visit him he always enquires "Are they on to the *filioque* yet, Doctor Lukas?" as if he were saving himself until the fun starts.

Nothing on this earth could have prepared me for my first sight of Florence. Beautiful palazzos, magnificent churches, imposing towers with pennants streaming from their battlements and, over it all, the immense new dome of the Cathedral. In many ways it is a construction more magnificent than the dome of our own Ayia

228

Sophia but its dominance is not so much spiritual, it is architectural. There is something that is particularly secular about the splendour of this city. I am profoundly pessimistic at the prospect of our negotiation with the Latins. The contrast of this city and our own run-down, dilapidated Constantinople is too immediate to be ignored. What hope do we have?

Patriarch Joseph, along with the other monks in his party and me, are lodged in the Convent of San Marco. Our rooms are sparsely furnished but comfortable and we are waited on by the nuns in exemplary fashion. Old Joseph's spirits revive a little, he seems anxious to enter the fray.

The formal debates are to be held in the large church of Santa Maria Novella. Two huge, impressive thrones have been erected in the chancel, one for Pope Eugenius and one for Patriarch Joseph. The Emperor sits on another throne to the side, that is when he is present. More often than not he is absent. The word is that he finds more entertainment from hunting in the countryside around the city than in following the nuances of the interminable debates.

After a particularly long session of the Council I am summoned to the old man's cell. He is lying on his bed. His wispy grey beard lies bedraggled on the bed cover. His eyes are rheumy and tired. There is another man in the room, dark-haired and tall, dressed in Bishop's robes. I remember him from the council. Metropolitan Markos Eugenikos, Bishop of Ephesus. He glares at me as I enter, perhaps not understanding why a lowly monk has been summoned.

"This is my doctor, Bishop, the inestimable Doctor Lukas." The old man chuckles, never tiring of his little joke. I drop on one knee before the Bishop. He extends his right hand to me and I kiss the large ring on his fourth finger.

"Actually Brother Ignatios, your Grace; I am from the Monastery of the Pantokrator ."

"Ah, I know. The Hesychast hotspot. So, a monk and a physician. You are a useful man to have around, Brother Ignatios."

I glance across at the old man. He appears to have dropped off to sleep.

I have heard about Markos Eugenikos of Ephesus. He is proving to be the thorn in the flesh of our delegation. It is said that the Emperor wanted to send him home for the Bishop is proving doggedly obstructive, opposing all attempts to reach a compromise, particularly over the *filioque*. In particular he is vehemently opposed to our three most important delegates, Yiorgos Scholarios, the theologian, Yiorgos Gemistos Plethon, the brilliant philosopher from the Despotate of Mistra and Metropolitan Bessarion of Nicaea. These three are said to have considerable sympathy with the Latins, a fact which does not endear them to Bishop Markos.

"Did you hear today's debate, Brother Ignatios?" I nod. "Well, what did you make of it?" His tone is challenging. He wants to know whose side I am on. If the truth be told I had become quite lost in the arguments and counter-arguments of today's session. I know it is all about the Procession of the Holy Spirit and that everyone, with the exception of Bishop Markos, is trying to construct a formula of words that satisfies all parties.

"It's very complicated, or so it seems to me,"

He cuts across me. "Complicated! Complicated! Not at all. It's very simple. They had no right to introduce the *filioque*, no right at all. The sooner that we all agree that the better."

There could be something to admire in this intransigence but I am disturbed by his unbending self-assurance. I avert my eyes from his challenging gaze.

The old man has awoken and is mumbling quietly. I bend my head to hear clearer, "Markos, Markos. We have to agree." The tall man stiffens as he stares at the opposite wall, choosing not to look at old Joseph, "You must come with us. We have to agree."

The Bishop gives a slight bow to Patriarch Joseph. "Excuse me, your Grace. I have to go." He half-turns towards the door before he is halted by the raised voice of the old man who, seeming to have regained some of his strength, forces himself up on to his elbows.

"You are not to veto the agreement, Bishop. I will not allow it." He falls back on his pillow, weakened by this outburst. In reply Bishop Markos offers only a flat smile, turns on his heel and leaves the cell.

I look back at the older man, searching for clues in his face but finding none. His eyes are closed, his breathing is irregular. I am appalled at the Bishop's behaviour. He has no concern, nor even consideration, for his Patriarch. I kneel down beside his bed, my fingers find his pulse at the wrist. It is fluttering and irregular. I keep my hand there.

He opens one eye and looks up at me; a flicker of humour crosses his face.

"Beware those who are certain, Ignatios. They are far more dangerous than the uncertain." His smile widens and he allows himself a small chuckle, a sound like the creaking of a door.

"I will fetch you a draught for the night, Father. I will not be long."

He is asleep again when I return with the potion, a formula that usually settles him. I place it on the stool beside his bed and leave him for the night.

The following morning I find him sitting on his bed, still in his sleeping shift. He smiles weakly. "A thousand blessings, Doctor Lukas. There is no session of the council today. What a relief." I help him into his robes and we make our way to the convent church for Matins, a service that tactfully avoids the Nicene creed.

"I think I am up to a bit of a walk, Doctor Lukas," he says as we leave the church. We head for the cloisters. Already the heat of the day is impinging itself, making our progress slow. Patriarch Joseph supports himself on his staff and my arm. We make our way slowly enough for him to talk.

"What do you make of all this, Brother Ignatios? Are we not crazy to be wasting our time on this Council?" I shrug my shoulders for I do not know how to answer.

"When I was a young man I used to burn with zeal for the unity of the church. I suppose I was a bit like the Metropolitan of Ephesus. I was very certain in those days but the older I get, the more uncertain I become. Despite your administrations, which are much appreciated, young man," he smiles at me "I know my time is limited here." I begin to demur but he stops me, "No, no. I know it's true. I cannot go on for ever and this Council's wearing me out." He stops walking. For a moment there is silence. "You know what, brother? I have no idea what happens next, what happens after death. No, no idea. I used to have it very clear in my mind. Those Latins are very clear with all their complicated arrangements for purgatory. You know, it seems like building castles in the air, no substance. I have a strong suspicion that their after-life of purgatory is a super-structure designed to cement their power and income in this life." My mind runs back to that carving over the West Door of the Cathedral in Ferrara. "No, no idea," his voice trails off for a moment, then regains momentum "and I think I like it that way. Somehow it feels" he pauses, searching for the word, "truer than anything else. More authentic. I don't know why I think this way. This is heresy. Not many people I can say this to." He is getting more and more breathless, "Actually no-one except you, young man." We turn a corner in the cloister. "Let's sit down here, Brother Ignatios." He waves a weak hand towards a stone bench alongside the cloister wall. "Now you can tell me what you think."

"What I think? How can I say?"

"What do you think of this poor old man and his agnosticism? Does it not shock you?"

"No, it does not shock me. I'm not sure if I understand though."

"Nothing to understand, Doctor Lukas. Only to accept."

Can he know that his words are striking a chord with me, a chord that resonates with my memories of what I was taught by Father Ignatios, by Brother Gerasimos and Ibn Al-Aswar in Bursa? I hesitate to speak but his gentleness encourages me. I swallow hard and continue. "The things that you talk of make sense to me. I think my path has been taking me in your direction. When I hear these Latins speak of God they appear so confident. They seem to have him all worked out. It gives them great power."

"That's true. And it's that power that means they are going to triumph here. There is no hope for us unless we go along with them as best we can, whatever Bishop Eugenikos says. We have to try and capitulate with dignity. It is going to be very hard."

I look at the poor old man. He is sitting with his legs astride; he leans forward as he tries to encourage more breath into his weak frame, his lips are bluer than I have seen before. I know I have no medicines that will cure him but he does not look to me for curing. All I can do is care for him, not just by the medicines that I can administer to ease his symptoms but, more importantly, by hearing him, by accepting him.

Neither of us moves, neither speaks. The only sound to be heard is the gentle rasping of his breathing. I find a stillness coming upon me; into my head comes the Jesus prayer, 'Lord Jesus Christ, son of the living God, have mercy on me. Lord Jesus Christ, son of the living God, have mercy on me'. I allow it to roll over and over as I focus my mind within me, contain my outward self within the limits of my body. Bit by bit I experience less and less until I am in nothingness, a blessed place.

The bell of the convent church breaks into our stillness. Patriarch Joseph turns his head towards me and smiles. "Back into the world now, Doctor Lukas." I can see he understands. "Help me up. I must get back to my room. There's work to be done." I help him out of the cloisters and along to his room where a bundle of papers lies awaiting him. He nods at them. "Yesterday's proceedings; I have to go through them I suppose." He settles down at the small desk in the corner of the cell and I leave him to his reading.

It seemed such a simple step to take, to become a monk, back there in Constantinople where I practised medicine. My contacts with the monks of the Monastery of the Pantokrator had not just been medical transactions. In my discussions with them I was able to explore all the threads of belief that had drawn me out since my days on the island. I had not been aware that they had become interwoven into a cord that was pulling me towards a monastic vocation.

It was only in conversation with the head of the Monastery of the Pantokrator, Father Petras, that I was brought up against what I had hidden from myself.

"Doctor Papadikis, you are no ordinary doctor." I demurred but he continued "No, no ordinary doctor. You are searching, are you not?" He looked intently into my eyes. His gaze was unsettling. I wanted to look away but was unable to shift from his interrogatory look. "Searching. I think that you are more aware of your spiritual life than any other doctor I have ever known." I said nothing, not wanting to confirm or deny. "I think you need to consider your vocation, Doctor Papadikis. I believe that God has need of even greater things from you, greater than just your medical skills."

Eventually I found my tongue. "I am not sure that I understand you, Father." We talked on for a long time and bit-by-bit what he was suggesting began to fall into place. I was able to talk to him about my teaching from Father Ignatios, my experience of Islam from Hassif in Kashaya and Al-Aswar in Bursa, my extraordinary four years with Gerasimos in the Cappadocian desert. For the first time I was able to talk about my dawning understanding of a religious life that is contained within my own life, not relying on any objective, ruling reality from outside experience.

In response he said very little except "I think you should pray about this, Doctor Papadikis. Then we will talk some more."

I did pray about it, at least I tried to but no words came. I was confused. I could not find the words to pray it through. Again and again my thoughts turned to Anna. What I was contemplating involved undertaking a celibate life. Now I knew that Anna was married, was unobtainable; I could embrace the life of a monk. I thought that then and I think that now. My night of erotic passion with Miriam will never happen again, will remain as a memory only.

My mind was in turmoil with all these matters until I remembered Gerasimos; then it settled. Contemplation, and the Jesus Prayer, slowed down my fevered thinking. I became content to wait.

There were further conversations with the Abbot, mostly concerning other aspects of the monastic way of life. It was quite simple and straightforward, and its appeal was indubitable. In my conversations with Father Petras I never mentioned Anna, and my conviction that I had lost her for good. Nonetheless I wondered if he had guessed.

"In becoming a monk, Ioánnis, you are leaving behind all that holds you to your previous life. That does not mean that you cannot continue to practice your former skills, far from it. We need doctors as well as stone-masons, bakers or whatever. You would be a doctor-monk. No, what you leave is what would pull you back to your old life: attachments, longings, sadnesses." His eyes seemed to pierce through to the back of my soul; I had to look away. "They will need to be left behind. In your new life they will have no more hold over you."

I was glad to hear these words. Could this be the way to heal the anguish of the wound in my heart?

So one day, out of the blue, it became clear to me. My life was taking another turn and I did not understand how it had happened. Nevertheless I knew that I was to become a monk. The Abbot Petras agreed to accept me in the Monastery of the

Pantokrator. I was pleased to discover that this monastery was a centre of the Hesychast movement, the form of spirituality that I had learnt in Cappadocia. After a period as a novice I was admitted to the monastic community as a Rassophore. I was tonsured and clothed in the black habit and belt, an outer cassock, the Rasson, and a klobuk, the brimless hat with a veil. I was given my new name, Ignatios, starting with the same letter as my old. I settled in to the rhythm of my new community with alacrity. At last life was settled, my wanderings had ceased. I was finally on home ground.

And then had come the order to accompany the Patriarch Joseph in his delegation to the Council at Ferrara.

Chapter 24
Florence 1439

A quiet tap on my cell door interrupts my meditation. Irritated, I rise to see who it is. I swing the door open to reveal the cloaked figure of Master Yiorgos Scholarios, one of our chief delegates to the Council, standing in the corridor.

"May I come in, Father Ignatios?" I stand aside and he enters the spartan cell. "I am sorry to disturb you," he looks intently at me as if he knows what is in my mind, "but I need to speak to you urgently. May I sit down?" He looks around the cell. The only place that he could sit is the hard bed. I motion him towards it.

"The fact is, Father," by now he is seated on the edge of my bed, "with the death of dear Joseph our cause is threatened."

Patriarch Joseph's death had come as no surprise to me. His will to live simply ran out. Though he had no certainty as to what greeted him after death he appeared to trust that God, his God, would see him right. The oppression of the Council had become intolerable. In the end he died peacefully, lying in his bed. I held his hand and watched his face as his eyes closed, his expression unperturbed. He simply stopped breathing. I had sat there for hours after he was gone, remembering back to the island, to the dying Father Ignatios, remembering Baba too. That seemed natural; what was unnatural and disturbing was that the picture of Mahmout, lying dead in a deep red pool of his life-blood in that Damascus alleyway, kept intruding in my mind. Hatred was being elbowed out by guilt now. Guilt for what I had done and, inexplicably, guilt for what I had let him do to me. I try to clear my head of these memories.

"What is 'our cause', Master?" My presumptuous question is necessary for I need to know where he stands on the issues of the Council.

"There is only one cause, Ignatios. Only one. These debates are not really about purgatory, about unleavened bread, even about the *filioque*, they are all about one thing. Will these Latins come to our aid against the Turk? That's why the Emperor is here. He has no ambition to be the last of his kind. He wants these matters settled so that a Crusade can be raised to push back the Turks from our city once and for all. That will require help from all the West: Pope, Franks, Holy Roman Emperor; the lot of them."

"But at what cost to Orthodoxy? Are all our traditions, our inheritance as the true Church, to be trampled in the dust?" I could hear what Bishop Eugenikos of Ephesus would be saying. Master Scholarios frowns.

"I think we might find a compromise that would satisfy all parties. We have done that with all the matters of contention except the *filioque*. Metropolitan Bessarion is working on that but that is the reason that I need to see you." My face is unmoved. "You were very close to our dear late Patriarch, were you not?"

"I was his physician."

"Then he must have talked to you about all these matters." I am beginning to feel uncomfortable, understanding where this is taking us.

"Yes, well, he did talk to me a bit but...."

He looks at me benignly. "I know, I know. You are bound to maintain confidences. That is part of your calling as a doctor." I nod assent. "Don't worry, I do not need you to tell me what he said but I do need your help in one thing, something that is vital to what is happening in Council from here on." He pauses, as if to let this sink in. "Sit down next to me, Father Ignatios." He pats the edge of the bed, "Let me share a confidence with you." He turns so that he is looking straight into my eyes. His directness seems more friendly than challenging. "I know that Bishop Markos

238

Eugenikos had many talks with Patriarch Joseph. That was so, wasn't it?"

"Yes. That's true. He visited quite often."

"I thought so. This is the cause of the problem that we have. Bishop Markos is maintaining that the Patriarch was utterly opposed to any compromise on the *filioque*. If that were true, it would be difficult to get our delegation to accept the compromise."

"You mean the change of wording *'The Holy Spirit who proceeds from the Father through the Son'* as opposed to what the Latins say *'proceeds from the Father and the Son'*, the double procession."

"Absolutely. All of us would prefer that it was expunged altogether. We are with the Bishop of Ephesus on that but we would never get the agreement of the Latins. The Emperor insists that we get agreement, for all the reasons that I mentioned before. He is not concerned with the theological and ecclesiastical niceties, as he would see them; he is only concerned with the survival of our Empire," he allows himself a wry smile "not an unreasonable cause, I suppose." He continues, "What I need from you, Father Ignatios, is an indication as to whether the good Bishop's assertions are true. You don't need to break any confidences."

"But if I tell you what I know, Bishop Eugenikos is bound to hear of it. Knowing what I know of the Bishop I do not want to get on the wrong side of him."

"I think I can keep it from him." He is smoothing his bald pate as if to stir his mind into further activity. "You can rely on me for that."

A silence settles between us. I can hear calls from the street outside. A horse whinnies. He is looking at his feet, no longer at me. I see that I have to speak.

"Patriarch Joseph was no enthusiast for adopting the *filioque* but he was prepared to accept the compromise. I was with him each time that Bishop Eugenikos visited and I do not recognise the Bishop's accounts of what happened."

He jumps up. "Thank you, brother. That's all I need to hear. That will be a great help."

I raise my hand for I need to say more. "The Patriarch's greatest concern was neither the theological dispute, nor even the survival of the Empire; it was for truth. Towards the end he was abandoning elaborate constructions of belief and dogma. He used to say that they are simply language, the language we use to build our lives and therefore malleable and changeable. I think that he was moving towards some kind of emptiness, an absence, that's how he put it. I think he found truth there. It did not distress him. He died peacefully."

Master Scholarios has remained motionless. Eventually he moves to the door. He stops and turns to me. "Thank you, Ignatios. Not only have you been a help to me, you have opened my eyes a bit. Thank you." Once more he stoops to pass through the cell door and is gone.

I close the door slowly. Master Scholarios' visit has unsettled me. Did I accurately represent the Patriarch's views? I fear that I was too outspoken, perhaps I should have hedged more, watered down my account. I have an awful feeling that what I have said is going to cause trouble for me, despite his reassurances. With the Patriarch gone there is no-one I can turn to for counsel, at least no one I can trust.

The convent bell rings for vespers. I know I should attend but something prevents me. In any case I find the Latin observances uncomfortable, even though I can speak the language. I pull on my cloak and slip out of the cell. Other monks are making their way to the chapel. I join the throng until we reach the top of a wide flight of stairs. There is a large fresco of the Annunciation on the wall. The route to the chapel is down the steps where all the others are going. Instead I turn down an opposite corridor which takes me down to the library. I pass through the large room with its massive scriptoria bearing beautifully embellished manuscripts. I know there is a spiral staircase at the end which leads to a small outside door.

240

Within moments I am out in the street. There is no-one about. I stop for an instant to get my bearings. In the distance I can see the cathedral with its soaring dome. It floats above the other buildings of the city, a magnet to all that see it. I set off in its direction.

By now it is dark and I find myself in a narrow alleyway. I am not nervous, being well used to alleyways and darkness. Then up ahead I make out two dark shapes. As I approach I hear groans and cries. My eyes accustom to the gloom and I see another figure on the ground. The two assailants are kicking him hard, one is wielding a small club. He is swinging it wildly to augment the assault on the poor unfortunate on the ground.

I run towards them. "Hey!" I call. "Stop that!" For a moment they stop as they turn to see who it is that interrupts them. "Leave that man alone!"

One of the two peers towards me. "And who the fuck are you, monk? Mind your own fucking business or perhaps you want us to sort you out, too."

My heart is beating fast. "I said leave him alone." A long groan comes from the prostrate figure. His face looks badly beaten and dark blood is oozing fast from a scalp wound.

It takes me no time to realise that I have put myself in an impossible position. In years gone by I could have sorted these two out with my Damascus steel, an option no longer open to me.

The second man, the one carrying the club, is advancing towards me. "Come on then, monk. Try and stop us." His speech is slurred with drink. He takes a swing at me with the club but he is too clumsy and it is easy to duck and avoid the blow. In a flash I am overcome with a red rage. I cannot stop myself now. In one movement I catch him by the throat with my right hand and squeeze hard. I know how to find the right spot that will fell him. He begins to wilt at the knees but I hold on tight, increasing the pressure. Other people, attracted by the shouts, have appeared. They stare at me in amazement. Now the man is going black in the face but I do not let go. My burning anger has taken hold of me.

241

A young man in the group calls out, "Let him, go, Father! You're going to kill him." The urgency of his call is enough to bring me back to my senses and I release my grip. The assailant falls to the floor, unconscious. His partner stares in disbelief at the spectacle of his conspirator being dropped by a monk. I turn towards him but he lets out a cry, turns and runs.

Meanwhile the felon on the ground is regaining consciousness. I pick up the club and stand over him. He takes one look and flees as well.

Over in the corner the bundled body moves. I kneel down and lift his head. He is still conscious. One eye is badly swollen but he manages to open the other. He tries to speak but all he can produce are inarticulate groans.

"Don't try and talk. We must get you to somewhere safe. My name is Father Ignatios." Only then do I realise that he probably cannot understand a word of what I am saying. I am speaking in Greek for I know very little Italian. A thought occurs to me; in Latin I ask him. "Do you speak Latin?" He tries to speak but cannot so he nods assent. I continue in Latin. "Succurram tibi, ducemus in asylum." "Let me help you, we will get to a safe place."

We make slow progress down the dark alleyway but eventually we reach a small piazza. I call a passing man who turns and comes towards us. He looks startled to see my companion.

"Perugino. Is it you? Bloody hell. What has happened? Can I help you, Father. I know where he lives." This amount of Italian I could understand. Together we help Perugino across the piazza. On the far side is an imposing palazzo. Its façade is built in massive stone masonry with a large main portal of heavily carved wooden doors. Three storeys rise up to a heavy cornice that overhangs the whole façade. Who is this man who lives in such a magnificent casa?

I pull hard on the bell-handle beside the main door. Within moments the heavy door swings aside and the enquiring face of a servant peers round. He seems surprised to see a tall, Greek monk at the door and then he spies the injured man. "Perugino, my God! What has happened to you?"

My helper speaks for him. "He's been beaten up by two bastards down that alley over there." He indicates across the piazza with a nod of the head whilst still helping me to support Perugino. "Come on. Help us to get him inside. The servant and one of his fellows take over and I follow on. We pass through into a wide, colonnaded courtyard, overlooked by the windows of the first floor. Obviously many people live here because within moments there is a small crowd of helpers fussing around. Perugino is taken to an anticamera on the ground floor and laid on a day bed. Water and bandages appear and the women of the household vie with each other to bathe his wounds. I have to intervene.

"*Scusi*, I am a doctor. Please let me look at him." They step back in incredulity to see this bearded monk who maintains he is a doctor. I take no notice but busy myself with examining the wounded man. Close examination shows that he has no fractures. The face wounds are contusions only. The scalp wound has stopped bleeding and is clotting satisfactorily. He has multiple bruises over his body but there are no signs of internal injury that I can detect.

I speak to Perugino in Latin. "There are no serious injuries, no fractures. I will ask the women to bathe and bandage your wounds but before I do, what can you tell me about this attack? What was it all about? Did they steal your money?"

He manages to reply. His voice is quiet and cracked, his Latin is stilted.

"I know not who they were. I still retain my purse so it is certain that they were not robbers. They simply stopped me in the alleyway and set about me"

"Do you have enemies, people who have a grudge against you?"

"Who does not in this trade? There are always rivals, often jealousy," his voice falters; it is as if the effort of speaking is

243

draining more life force than he has to spare at this moment. He closes his one good eye.

"I will leave you to rest, Signor Perugino. Perhaps I will call to see you tomorrow." I discern a slight nod from the wounded man.

Outside the room I try to give instructions to the women in how to dress his wounds. I have to resort to mime when my limited Italian fails, a performance which causes them much amusement. It is only as I am about to leave that a figure steps out from the shadows of the colonnade.

"Father, a word." He speaks in Greek. He is elegantly dressed and that and his fine, aquiline features convey the impression of a man of authority. Around his neck he wears a heavy silver chain. I stop and turn.

"Signor."

"Thank you for rescuing Perugino. May I know your name?"

"Father Ignatios, Signor."

"And you must be part of the delegation at the Council?"

My eyes drop. "A very small part. I came as physician for our Patriarch, Joseph. Now that he has died I have little part to play."

"Yes. That was very sad indeed. He was a wise man." I say nothing so he continues. "Are we going to reach a conclusion; this Council I mean?"

"I am not qualified to say, signor. There is hope that some compromise might be reached."

"Your Emperor John needs that, does he not?" It is obvious that this man is well versed in the goings on in the Council and all the behind-the-scenes machinations. It would be wise for me to stay out of this.

"To whom have I the honour of addressing, and how did you come to learn Greek?" His Greek was quite intelligible even though much of the usage was archaic. He laughs, a round engaging laugh.

"It surprises you, doesn't it? There are quite a few of us who have studied Greek. Now that we are gaining access to the Greek texts of the masters we understand much more than what is fed to us by the scholastics. Their texts are bastardised and mutilated through copying down the ages. At last we can get nearer to the original Plato, the original Aristotle. These are exciting times for us."

My mind has gone back to the island, to the talks with old Father Ignatios. The same excitement felt by Anna and me when these ancient texts were opened up to us.

"I can understand something of what you must feel, Signor. May I know your name?"

"Ascharino Bottelini. My family is quite well-known in Florence."

"And this is your casa?"

"Indeed it is, humble abode that it is." I stared around at this central courtyard, the loggia and the balconies. Humble abode, indeed.

"And that poor man, Perugino. Does he live here?"

"Yes. I am his patron. He works for me."

"He talked about 'his trade'. What is that?"

"He is a painter. One of the best in Florence. I am lucky to have acquired his services. Mind you he is a difficult customer at times. This isn't the first scrape that he has got into." Scrape seemed an understatement for what had happened to the painter.

"So why was he attacked? Does he have enemies?"

"Not him so much; me. The attack was really against me." I looked at him hard but said nothing. "There are people in this city who would like me out of the way. They do not oppose me in public, they know they would get nowhere by doing that. No, they snipe away at me by trying to damage my household, my business and, through that, my life. One of those ways is to put my artist, Perugino, out of action. They know he is working on a new fresco for the Church of Santo Spirito, our family church. His work is brilliant and is bound to bring acclaim to me and my family and, thereby, my business enterprises. So they go for him."

"Do you know who these enemies are? Can they not be brought to account."

Again he laughs. "Yes, I know who they are but they are too clever to let me pin it on them. My hands are tied. But come on, brother, you must be tired. I must let you go. Take care on your way home and be careful not to let that strong right hand of yours overreach itself." He knows more than I think about the attack, that is obvious. I bow and take my leave.

Back in my cell at the convent I disrobe, splash some cold water on my face and then sit on the edge of my bed. The events of the evening play out in my mind. I stare at my right hand as I extend the fingers, then screw them tight into a ball. There is an anger in there that still fuels my behaviour. Being a monk has not changed that, however much I had hoped that it would. I feel ashamed at felling that man in the way I did but, behind that shame, there is a sense of release. It lets down the barriers on the hidden, inexplicable anger that I thought had gone many years ago. These feelings are disturbing me. I try and find some relief in sleep.

Soon after Matins I make my way to the Palazzo Bottelini. As I walk into the central courtyard women's faces appear over the balconies.

"It's the monk!"

"Quick, come and see."

"What a hero! What a man!"

"You can rescue me any day you like, sweetheart" Peals of raucous laughter ring around the courtyard. I keep my head down as a servant leads me to Perugino's quarters.

"Father Ignatios! How can I thank you?" Perugino is sitting up in bed. His face is a mess of bruising and lacerations, his scalp is swathed in bandages, his right arm is in a sling but he is smiling.

246

"Thanks are unnecessary, Signor Perugino. Let's take a look at you." Nothing untoward to find. They had obviously stamped hard on his right arm, hoping to put him out of action for a long time. It will be some time before he is wielding his brush again.

Surprisingly he appears inordinately cheerful. "I gather you had a talk with the Master."

"Yes, we did talk."

"In Greek, so he tells me. And here's me, condemned to talk to you in bloody Latin."

"It will be easier for me to learn Italian than for him to learn Greek, Signor Perugino."

He interrupts me. "Call me by my given name, Father. Angelo."

"Angelo. Right. I shall call you Angelo. I have been thinking, Angelo, that you are going to be laid up here for some time. Could you pass the time by teaching me Italian? Then we could converse more easily." The truth is that Latin is a ponderous language for everyday conversation.

His face lights up at my suggestion. "What an excellent idea. Let's make a start straightaway."

"I have to be at the Council this afternoon but that gives us an hour or so. In any case I think an hour is all that you can take in your present state of health."

So we embark on the task. It is not difficult. I pick up languages quickly and knowing Latin helps in understanding Italian. I revel in the musical rhythm of the language, quite different from Greek and Arabic.

Over the next few weeks Angelo's bruises heal whilst my Italian blossoms. By now I have no difficulty in conversing with shopkeepers and people in the street. A Greek monk speaking Italian seems to amuse the Florentines.

Transactions at the Council are moving on quickly now. The compromise over the *filioque* looks as if it is going to be agreed and all we Greeks are beginning to believe that we might be going home soon. One morning, on my visit to Angelo I

247

encounter Signor Bottelini again. I have not spoken to him since that first day.

"Brother Ignatios. How is our invalid?"

"No longer an invalid, Signor. He has nearly recovered."

"So he may be able to resume work on my fresco soon?" I smile. "Pretty soon, Signor Bottelini. He is very keen to get started again."

"Good, good." He rubs his hands together as if to induce further thought, much in the same way that Master Scholarios rubs his bald pate. "I wondered, Brother Ignatios, whether you could join us for dinner one day this week? I have a few friends who would like to meet you. They speak Greek as well, at least some of them do, but with your rapidly acquired ability to speak Italian maybe they will have no need." He allows a restrained smile.

"Thank you. I would be pleased to."

"Shall we say Thursday then?"

"Thursday would suit me well. I could come after Vespers."

"Excellent. I must say I do admire the way you Greek monks retain some of the pleasures of the flesh. Our pious Dominicans are such kill-joys."

"Our Lord dined regularly with others."

"Tax-collectors, prostitutes and sinners I seem to remember. Oh well, that about sums us up," and I can still hear his laugh as I disappear across the piazza.

The meeting of the Council this afternoon is ponderous. None of the main members from either side are there. The discussions are being conducted by monks, theologians and clerics. They are attempting to hammer out the wording of the final proclamation. As everything spoken has to be translated the whole process is drearily tedious.

I can see that the heat has gone out of the argument. We Greeks are going to capitulate on most issues before the Council, that is clear enough. The Greek delegation seems depressed and downcast. I wonder how this 'agreement' is going to sound when it is announced to the people back in Constantinople.

On my way out of Santa Maria Novella I come face-to-face with Mark Eugenikos, Metropolitan Bishop of Ephesus. I kneel and kiss his proffered ring.

"Well, Ignatios, do you think we have done good work here?" He indicates the Council with a disdainful nod of his head.

"I cannot say, your Grace."

"Or will not perhaps." The challenge is clear enough.

I try to turn away his attention. "Does your Grace have a view?"

"Your Grace certainly does," his voice has become firm and hard, "but he is not allowed to express it." I cannot think of what to say. "Struck dumb, eh, Father? You know what the Patriarch said to me and now it seems everyone knows what passed between old Joseph and me."

I avert my gaze. I have made an enemy here, of that I have no doubt. I cannot care greatly about what is being argued in the Council. In the end it seems pointless. The Christian world is moving towards the Latins. Byzantium is dying on its feet. I raise my head to face the Bishop.

"You know the truth, your Grace." Our conversation is ended.

Signor Bottelini's hospitality is lavish. The tables in his main sala are laden with fruit, exotic varieties that even I had not tasted before: cooked meats, sauces and wine, all of a quality that puts the rough Tuscan fare served at San Marco to shame. When I arrive most of the company are assembled. Their heads turn towards this bearded monk with black habit and tall kamilavkion on his head. Conversation quietens for a moment. Bottelini comes forward, smiling.

"Welcome, Father Ignatios. We are blessed by your presence." He turns to the other guests. "Friends, this is Father

Ignatios who, you may have heard, came to the rescue of my unfortunate painter, Perugino."

There are smiles of recognition. I move to join the company.

An elegant lady dressed in a flowing red robe speaks to me. "You have been at the Council, Father? Is there going to be agreement?"

I bow. "Yes, your ladyship. I believe that the proclamation will not be long in coming."

"I can't pretend to understand what it is all about." She speaks airily. "Something to do with the creed, is that right?" She turns away, her interest rapidly exhausted.

"Come, sit with us here." Signor Bottelini is calling from across the room. There are marble seats running alongside the windows of the room. Other chairs, wooden-carved and draped in sumptuous material are spread in a haphazard fashion to form a group. It is to one of them that Signor Bottelini directs me. I nod to the other seated men; some are elderly like Signor Bottelini but others are quite young, probably younger than me. I sense that their minds are sharp, sharper at least than the empty headed red-robed lady from whom I have just escaped.

"Father Ignatios, may I present Ambrogio Traversari," he indicates a grey-haired man in a monk's habit who is slowly rising to his feet. I rise too and we exchange bows. "Traversari is our Greek expert. He has been anxious to meet a scholar from Constantinople."

"Oh, I'm sorry, Signor," I bow again, "I am no scholar. There are others in our delegation who know much more of the Greek texts than I." Traversari has fixed me with a stern eye.

"But you, as a doctor, must be familiar with Aristotle, Hippocrates and others."

"That is true, sir, but I was trained in Arabic medicine," I notice a few eyebrows raised at this revelation, "I attended the medical college at the al-Nuri madrasa in Damascus. I read Galen in Arabic."

"And have you seen copies of Galen here, since you have been in Florence?"

"Yes, some. But it is nothing like the text that I learnt in Arabic. It seems greatly confused."

Traversari is becoming animated by what he is hearing. "Confused is right, doctor. It has been bastardised and deformed by repeated copying in the scriptoria of our monasteries. Some of the translations into Italian are done word-for-word by ignorant scribes who do not even read Greek or Latin. No wonder it is deformed. You are lucky to have had access to a pure version, translated by Arab scholars."

"I suppose I am. Certainly much of what I have read since being here in Florence makes little sense. For instance I have seen it attributed to Galen that the female uterus has seven chambers. That seems to me to be unlikely."

"Do you know differently then? Do you dissect?"

"No. Arabic medicine does not approve of the dissection of the human body. Galen himself derived his anatomy from animal dissection." I warm to the topic, pleased to see that I have their full attention. "I attended a dissection here just two weeks ago. It was held outside and I believe it only happens once a year. I mingled with the students to see what it was like."

"And what impression did it make on you."

"Not good at all. They laid open the body and one professor stood beside the corpse and read from his text of Galen. Having described a feature from the text the anatomist dug around and purported to demonstrate the feature in the body. At one point the professor read that there are connecting channels between the left and the right ventricles of the heart. The dissector removed the heart, opened it up and attempted to display the channels, which were clearly not there."

"I take it you were not impressed?"

I am enjoying the debate now. "No, not at all. It seems to me that if you want to know how man is constructed you go to the body first and the book afterwards."

251

Traversari smiled and turned to the others.

"I think we have the first humanist monk among us, gentlemen"

"Humanist? I don't know what you mean."

"It is a term we use generally for our endeavour. We seek to discover the classical writings, classical sculpture untainted by mistranslation or corruption. So when it comes to anatomy and medicine we believe that one goes to the body first, to the books after, just as you say."

I am flattered that my bit of homespun, island common sense should achieve such recognition. At that moment a servant summons us to eat. By now my interest is kindled and, with it, my appetite. I eat well and make the most of the wines that Signor Bottelini supplies.

A week has passed since the party at the Palazzo Bottelini. The Council remains bogged down in the minutiae of the declaration which, incidentally, is to be entitled *Laetentur coeli*, 'Let the heavens rejoice', an arrogant bit of triumphalism. Part of me would love to be on the way home but another part is intrigued by all that is happening in Florence. I want to stay for a while yet.

Signor Bottelino is keen that I attend his seminars again. "I call it my Academy, Father Ignatios, dedicated to the new learning." He paces about the room whenever he talks of it. "We need Greeks in our group. You have so much to teach us."

I feel out of my depth but, if I am, he is courteous enough not to point it out. I am quite relieved when he invites another member of our delegation, Yiorgos Gemistos Plethon, to join the debate. Plethon is a towering intellect and a Platonist. Some in our delegation maintain he is not a Christian at all. All I know is that he is a forceful advocate of union and a supporter of the Council's compromise over the *filioque*.

"Ah, Father Ignatios. I have heard so much about you. You looked after our dear departed Patriarch, did you not?" Whilst he is addressing me his eyes are darting around the room as if he has

252

other matters with which to concern himself. I find it disconcerting, to the extent that I do not reply. "A doctor and a monk. Where do you come from brother?"

"I trained in Damascus, sir. The al-Nuri madrasa."

His eyebrows raise slightly on hearing that and he stops his visual perambulation around the room. I have interested him for a moment.

"Damascus, eh. So an Arabic doctor. Well versed in Avicenna and Averroes, no doubt." Few lay Greeks would have known of these two masters of Arabic medicine but he had.

"Yes. Quite a contrast to the medicine I see being practised here."

"Quite right." His eyes are wandering off again. "Absolutely. Too much scholasticism here. Needs a good purge. Are you the man to do it?"

I am shocked at the suggestion. "Me, no certainly not. I'm just a monk. What can I do?" but he does not answer for his gaze had settled on a small figure in the corner. With a mumbled apology he has gone, heading down his next prey like a hawk falling on a rabbit. I breathe a sigh of relief. Too much contact with Plethon is not going to be good for my health.

I am aware of a short dark-haired man approaching from across the room. I turn towards him.

"Tell me, Father, you are Greek is that right?"

"Yes sir. I was born and brought up a Greek but that was many years ago." I do not welcome any more enquiries along these lines.

"I only ask because my wife is Greek. She speaks good Italian now but I have never been able to master Greek, it seems such a difficult language."

"I suppose that is so. I must say I have found Italian very easy to master."

"We are lucky," he laughs, "we speak the language of the Gods." I smile politely as he continues. "Yes, lucky indeed. Italian seems to be understood by most people."

"Do you travel much, sir?"

"Oh yes. I run a couple of trading ships, sailing out of Genoa."

A trader. Perhaps our paths might have crossed. "Have you ever traded with Damascus, at all?"

"Oh, once or twice. I try to avoid having to go there if I can. Too damned hot."

"Then perhaps you know a merchant called Papadikis that I once knew?"

"Papadikis? Yes of course. I met him the last time that I was in Damascus. Must have been a couple of years ago. Greek chap."

"That's him."

"I remember. Had to take my wife with me to translate. Very useful she was. I am sure he would have tied me up in knots if I had not got an interpreter. We struck a good deal in the end." He is smiling to himself at the memory. Somewhere at the back of my mind a door opens.

"By the way, may I ask your name, sir?" He pauses to return from his reverie. "Name? Oh, Father, I do beg your pardon; I never introduced myself. My name is Lorenzetti, Silvio Lorenzetti."

"Perugino!" My voice is constrained to a loud whisper that echoes round the church. "You must help me."

He is up above me on the scaffolding, now back at work on the fresco in Santo Spirito. He stares down at me.

"Help you, Ioánnis?"

"I met this man, Silvio Lorenzetti at your master's house. I think I know his wife."

He has turned back to the fresco and is applying paint to a prepared area of plaster.

"Ioánnis. I cannot talk now. I have to get this on before the plaster dries. I'll be finished within the hour."

254

I know that he cannot be diverted, however much I need to talk to him. I wait impatiently, staring at the fresco which is taking shape. I can now see that it is an *Adoration of the Magi*. A huge procession of the three kings and their retinue unfurls across the church wall. I notice that one of the kings, a bearded man with a fierce expression, riding a magnificent white horse, looks very much like our Emperor John. Then I begin to recognise other faces; the old Patriarch Joseph, Signor Bottelini and even Perugino himself who is staring out of the picture. There are still blank spaces but I notice that he is now working on a dark haired, bearded figure in a monk's hat and cloak; it is me.

I cannot wait. Since last night my mind has been racing. If this Silvio is the Silvio I heard of back in Constantinople then it means that Anna is here, or might be here, in this city of Florence. It must be that Silvio. How many Genoese traders have both that name and a Greek wife? The thoughts tumbled over and over themselves as I lay on my hard bed.

And then, in the cold farthest reaches of the night, those hours when life comes nearest to death, other thoughts came. I am now a monk, not just a novice but a Rassophore. I have undertaken to follow the monastic life and have been tonsured, four separate tufts of hair cut from my head in the shape of a cross have marked the irrevocable step that I have taken. I know that I have yet to take the vows but I am bound to follow the monastic way, to leave behind all my former desires and concerns. I thought that I had but, just as in my defence of Perugino, the old concerns and ways show that they have not truly gone away.

I cannot deny myself the chance to see if this mysterious Greek lady is indeed Anna. I cannot turn away from the chance of knowing that she lives. For so many years I thought that she had died. I cannot walk away now.

I leave the church and head towards the cathedral, trying to quieten my mind. What if I meet her, what can I say? The last time we met was when I was seventeen and now I am forty. Can feelings, attachments remain frozen, unchanged to be thawed out decades later?

I enter the cathedral. I can hear Mass being said in a side chapel. I slip past and make my way to the centre of the nave, right under the dome. I crane my neck to stare at the Pantokrator, so much like our own Ayia Sophia. I stare at his unswerving eyes. I should feel watched, judged, but I do not.

There is nothing there.

Chapter 25

I walk down the corridor. It is dark here, down in the depths of the palazzo, amongst the servants quarters. There is no-one around. In the dim light I can see that the door at the end is closed, a solid oak door decorated with metal studs. I know that if I go through this door there is no turning back. This will be the end of my search. I cannot think of the future, of where my passage through this door will lead. There is no future; this, in the end, is right for the present and that is all that the future is, an eternal present.

I turn the large round handle and feel it click free. For such a heavy door it requires little force to push it open.

Inside it is even darker. A single candle burns in the corner. The atmosphere feels close but, despite its heaviness, I detect a gentle fragrance, some perfume or other musk. As my eyes accustom themselves to the dark I can make out a figure seated in the corner, facing away from my gaze. Whoever it is, is quite still; a dark silk cloak prevents me from seeing whether this is a man or a woman. But then all doubts are dispelled as she speaks, her voice as gentle as the breeze.

"Ioánnis."

It is a sound from another world.

She stands and turns towards me, at the same time her hands slip the hood of her cloak from her head. In a way that is immediately recognisable she shakes her hair and it falls evenly over her shoulders. Dark, dark hair but now tinged with grey.

We are now face to face and my heart threatens to stop. I am staring into the eyes of the one that I have dreamed of, the one that I thought had died in the fire, the one that I have yearned for in torments of agony since the day I lost her.

257

"Anna?"

She smiles at me. "So you recognise me still. That's a relief. But look at you. What a powerful figure, and a monk. My Ioánnis a monk." Her stare is intense. "Have I left it too late to find you again?"

I cannot find words. I just gaze into her face, trying to force myself to believe that it is really her.

She lifts up her hands to unfasten her cloak. It slips off her shoulders, down into an inert bundle on the chair. She takes two steps towards me. Now we are very close. Her hand is lifted up to touch my beard.

"Quite a monk, my Ioánnis. For years I assumed you were dead. I grieved for you but I never forgot you."

At last I find words. "And I have never forgotten you, Anna. But you are alive. This is you?"

"No-one else," she laughs.

"And you are married now." A tightening ache is developing in my chest.

"Yes. I am married. And I have a son."

"A son."

She laughs. "Have you become a parrot as well as a monk, Ioánnis? Little Markos. He is twelve now. Just like his uncle." She turns away. "I wish I knew what had happened to my brother."

"But I know. I can tell you."

"You know? How do you know?" I recount to her my meeting with Markos and his position in the Janissary Guard.

"A captain, good heavens! I really need to see him again."

My heart sinks. Does she not realise how impossible that is? "I understand that, Anna, but he is with the Turks now. They are our enemies. That's why we are here in Florence. Our Emperor needs military help against the Turks."

"I thought you were here to talk all about the *filioque*, Ioánnis, " her voice is quieter, slower, "not to muster up a Crusade." It is not difficult to detect the irony in her voice.

"You remember our lessons with Father Ignatios, then?"

258

She snorts in amusement. "Of course I do, or is it only monks that are allowed to think about those things?"

"No, of course not. I'm sorry. Of course you remember old Father Ignatios. You were much more clever than me."

"I doubt that. What happened to Father Iggy? I never heard tell."

I pause before speaking. First Markos, now Father Ignatios. Am I for ever destined to be the bearer of bad news? "I'm sorry, Anna. He was killed in the raid. I found him dying from a stab wound."

Her face drops. "God rest his dear old soul, poor Father Iggy. I am sure he would have gone straight up, a good man like him." I nod and then I remember the key.

"As he was dying he gave me a key and told me to go to the church of Profitis Elias, you know the one on the top of the mountain. He must have thought I would be safe there. He wanted me to take you with me but by then I thought you had died"

"Did you go?" Her voice has become more breathless. She takes my hand in hers.

"Yes. Yes, I did. I ran up there in the dark, it was difficult to see but the light from the burning houses helped."

As if reminded she turns towards a fireplace in the corner of the room. Within moments she has a fire going, its flickering shadows dancing on the ceiling. She kneels down on a large rug that is set out in front of the fire. Now I can see her clearly. Anna, my Anna. If anything, more beautiful than when we were both young. She smiles at me.

"There is some wine on the table over there. Would you pour some for us?"

I do so and drink deeply, as if to celebrate our coming together. She sips from her goblet, her dark eyes always on me.

"It is so strange, Ioánnis, seeing you in those robes. Would you, at least, take off your cloak and came and sit with me?" I do as she bids and we settle down on the warm bear-skin. I look across at the door.

"I'm anxious, Anna. Will we not be disturbed?"

She puts her finger on my lips. "Shush, Ioánnis, darling. Perugino will see to it." I can imagine how much my painter friend must have enjoyed arranging this assignation. There is nothing that he enjoys more than to challenge my monkish persona. But then, he himself was rescued by some very un-monkish behaviour.

A slight breeze lifts the curtains at the window. The fire flares a little then dies down. We are quiet and still. There is so much that I need to tell her, so much I need to know of her but all such talk is stilled. We rest in the present moment, in our coming together again. Words are not needed for now. It is as if the decades since we were parted were but minutes. Decades that I believed her dead are collapsed into nothing more than moments of grief, now wiped away by this reunion. The years no longer matter, I sink into the eternity of the present.

Now we are naked. She is kneeling, facing the warmth of the fire. I kneel behind her, my arms around her waist. She turns towards me, "I have never forgotten that day by the Kalikatsoú, Ioánnis. Never. You have always been my one and only love."

"But what about your husband? Does he not mean the same to you?"

"He is older than I am, my love. For him, as for most Italians, marriage is for conceiving children. Once little Markos came along, and it was clear that there were not going to be any brothers and sisters, he changed. He left me alone." There is a sadness in her voice. It is difficult to understand how he could neglect her?

"Then." I pause and she fills the gap,

"That's right. I have been celibate for years now."

I fling my arms around her. "Anna, you poor, poor thing!"

Her voice takes on a steely edge, "Why poor? Do you not think I could be happy that way? And anyway, aren't you celibate? A monk."

"Yes, of course I am."

Her tone becomes gentle again. "And do you want to stay that way?"

"I could ask the same of you."

She looks me straight in the eye, "No. I want us to make love, Ioánnis. I want us to make love, the way we did by the Kalikatsoú. I want to forget all that has happened between then and now. We are here, now. Love me, Ioánnis" She lies back on the rug, her arms raised behind her head. Her breasts stand firm on her chest wall. She parts her legs, at the same time pulling me towards her, into her in a joyous reunion that obliterates time.

I do not know how many hours we spent in that room. After we had made love many times over, I fell asleep. When I wake, she is sleeping beside me, the both of us covered by her dark cloak. The fire is reduced to glimmering ashes, daylight creeps around the edge of the heavy curtains; I put my mouth to her ear.

"Anna. It is morning."

Slowly she opens her eyes and looks into mine. A smile spreads across her face and she stretches and yawns. "Good morning, Ioánnis. How is it with you?"

I kiss her on the lips, gently and slowly. "It is good, my darling. Very good." I draw her towards me under the cloak, hungry once more to feel her naked body against mine. She wraps herself around me and we kiss again.

Then she sits up and notices the daylight. "We must be going, Ioánnis. Perugino has arranged it. He will be here soon. You must stay here. I will go. Leave it until you hear the Cathedral bells ring, then you can get away. There is a small side-door at the end of the corridor. Take that and it will get you out into the street."

I pick up her hands. A desperation that is turning into panic is welling up inside me. "But Anna, when will I see you again. It must be soon."

She stands perfectly still. I drop her hands as she speaks, "Ioánnis. This is how it has to be. You are a monk. I am a wife and a mother. The die is cast." She starts to dress.

261

Now my voice is strangled, "No! Don't say that, I will give up everything just to have you. I'll renounce my vows. Don't say that, Anna!" She turns and lifts up her cloak. She drapes it over her shoulders and lifts the hood over her head. I am frozen.

"Goodbye Ioánnis. Goodbye my love." Before I can protest more she is gone. The heavy door closes behind her.

I stand there in desolation. To find her again only to lose her. Tidal waves of desperation flood my whole body; despair, anger then panic. Eventually a dull, empty nothingness inoculates me against them all. Emptiness, darkness. Nothing.

When I hear the Cathedral bells I pull on my habit and find my way out of the palazzo. Out in the street I see people about, going to Mass, buying bread, emptying slops. I feel separated, as if they are puppets in some masquerade. I am standing on the outside and watching. I can never be part of them, of their lives. I am outside.

I pull my cloak around me against the early morning chill and find my way back to the convent.

MEROS EKTON

It is the darkest point of the night, yet stretched across my field of view the torches of the enemy burn out the darkness. We have had plenty of opportunity to study their dispositions, the nearest tents are just two hundred and fifty paces from the city walls. I screw up my eyes, the easier to make out men huddled around camp fires.

Even the Sultan's tent, colourful and resplendent, is less than a mile away, perched on the hill of Maltepe. It makes a perfect vantage point; he can look down on us in the valley where the small river Lykos meanders its way under the walls and into the city. For centuries it has been known that this is the weak spot in what is otherwise an impenetrable chain of castles, turrets and walls; a defence that stretches four miles from the Palace of Blachernae in the north to the Sea of Marmara in the south; the great land walls of Theodosius. Four miles of a brick-lined fosse, then an outer wall, a terrace sixty feet wide and finally the vast inner walls that rise to forty feet in height. All along their length both walls are studded with towers and turrets.

It is these walls that have protected the city for over a thousand years, hurling back invading armies as a solid sea wall repels the storm waves of the ocean. It is this sense of permanence, of inviolability which has infected the minds of the people. In my twenty five years of living amongst them I cannot fail to be impressed by their hopeless fantasy, almost convinced of it myself.

That has all gone now. Forty days ago we stood on these same walls and watched as the Sultan deployed his weapons, the weapons that would make our walls shudder and shatter our invincibility; cannon.

Cannon have been used before. The Sultan's father, Murat, tried to break into the city in the siege of 1422. He failed but the cannon that he deployed on that occasion were tiny. Their projectiles simply bounced off the solid walls like the toy balls of children.

This time we watched as much larger weapons were trundled into place. They worried us but not as much as the news that had come from spies who had been watching the road from Edirne, the Sultan's capital away to the west of us. They spoke of a gigantic beast, a vast bronze cannon twenty-seven feet long with a mouthpiece so large that a man could climb into it. It was making its slow progress towards us, dragged by a hundred oxen and two hundred and fifty men. Never has such a weapon been seen in battle. Suddenly our battlements and walls seemed as vulnerable as butter.

Behind me, to the east, the first glimmerings of dawn are appearing. For once it is absolutely quiet. The few men around me on the rampart do not move, some are asleep, some sit with their backs leaning on the improvised battlements, barrels filled with earth.

We have been besieged for fifty three days now. Fifty three days of thunderous assault. The monster cannon, we have named it the Basilica, once manoeuvred into place, was horrifying. The sound of its detonation was as shattering to our morale as was the impact of the vast stone cannon-balls that it hurled against our outer wall. Soon gaps began to appear in our outer defence. During the nights the enemy had worked hard to fill the fosse. Our men on the ramparts could empty Greek fire on them, the ancient, secret weapon of the city and the enemy casualties from the burning material were enormous. Even so yet more men poured in. They filled the fosse with earth, timber, old tents, anything that they could lay their hands on. In the end we had no way of preventing them. The fosse became passable for them in four or five places.

We had to repair the damage caused by the cannon. Basilica could only fire seven times in a day but that was enough to inflict serious damage. Not every shot was accurate. One ball went straight over the walls and came down a mile inside the city, killing a group of civilians that were gathered in the street.

Then it became obvious that they had trouble with their vast weapon for it went silent for a day. I could see men working on it, smoke rising from a hastily constructed furnace. After two days it was back in action but only for a day. The following day it was silent. We never heard it fired again.

But the other cannon were nearly as devastating. The Ottomans had developed a technique of firing in threes which soon made holes in our defence. During the nights everyone, soldiers, civilians, monks alike worked hard on shoring up the gaps in the outer wall. We brought up earth from the base of the inner wall, stones, timber, brushwood, any material that could provide a temporary replacement. All through the nights teams of people would move what material they could find through the portals in the inner wall to the terrace between the two walls, the whole exercise being masterminded by our Genoese General Commander, Giovanni Giustiniani Longo.

When the mornings came the bombardment would recommence. It was then that we discovered that our soft ramparts were a better protection against the cannon balls than were the stone walls. The shots simply sank into the stockade but were unable to breach them.

A few days after the bombardment had started the enemy made a foray over one of our stockades. The fighting was fierce and they were soon beaten back. For a while our spirits lifted. Perhaps we would succeed, perhaps the siege would fail. I was not optimistic. The troops that Sultan Mehmet had sent on this foray were irregulars, poorly equipped and poorly trained. They were Christians from Hungary, Serbia and all around, here for the plunder. The people of Constantinople were yet to meet the Janissaries. I knew what Janissaries were like.

I see a small falcon dart across the line of the walls. In that moment its acrobatic flight brings back memories of my childhood on the island, sitting on the hillside with the goats, watching the falcons hunting in packs like wolves of the air. I should be there, in that halcyon memory, not in this gathering storm of destruction. It is only by chance that I have ended up in this doomed city. Ended up, for that is what it will be. All my wanderings of my life have brought me here to die on the end of an Ottoman sword.

And yet I do not flinch from that fate. There has been no meaning in my wanderings; yes, I did look for Eleni. Anna I discovered, not as a result of any search. Discovered and then lost again, this time for ever. No sense in my wanderings. I could have escaped from this city before the siege started but I didn't. There were plenty of ships leaving, carrying those rich enough to make their escape. The thought of going with them never crossed my mind. Staying here seems the right thing to do but, in the terms of my life so far, such a choice has no meaning at all.

About as meaningless as the great procession yesterday. For one day the Turks' bombardment had ceased, a blessed relief. All the people of the city followed the priests to the great church of Ayia Sophia. It has lain empty for years, since soon after our return from Florence, because of the dissension over unity with the Latins. The pro-unionists held one Latin mass there, unleavened bread and the *filioque* and all and since then the people have not gone near the place.

But yesterday there was unity in adversity. After celebrating the Eucharist a huge procession moved through the city, along the land walls of Theodosius, past the palace of Blachernae. All the church bells in the city rang continuously. Relics were reverently carried through the streets, prayers and psalms were chanted and the protectress of the city, the Hodegetria, was displayed for all to see. The Virgin who 'shows the way' painted, as it is believed, by Ayios Lukas, the beloved physician.

This ceremony was a last expression of the will of a broken city, the last remnant of the Empire of Rome. I was moved to tears even though I was unmoved by the metaphysics. My long odyssey has been mirrored in a gradual change in my perception of God. Now for me God is a God who is not, rather than this ancient God who is being implored and exhorted in the city's last gasp for salvation. I have left that God behind for he has no existence.

Standing here, knowing that out there is a man bearing a sword that will end my life, I feel at peace. It is an unexpected end but I have learnt, albeit slowly, not to expect, not to hope. There is enough peace in that.

I am jerked out of my reverie by a keening, nasal call that floats across from the tented army, the call to prayer. These Ottomans are a devout people, fearless in battle but still devout. Most people that I meet do not know or understand our enemy. Against all probability they believe that we shall be saved; it has always happened in the past. Yet there are some who are more pessimistic. They are convinced that our fate is sealed, our downfall being God's punishment for accepting the results of the Council of Florence.

It was a long journey back from Florence to the Holy City those fourteen years ago. Before I left I made one last visit to the church of Santo Spirito. Perugino had finished his fresco and I felt duty bound to go and see his completed work, even though my spirit was dull to the attractions of art, or of anything else for that matter.

The church was empty when I entered. All the scaffolding had been removed so that the fresco was revealed in its full extent. In the afternoon Italian sunlight the colours sparkled and danced. I followed the winding procession that was making its way to the infant Christ. There I was, a few paces behind the Emperor. Now

267

all the spaces had been filled in. Just behind the Emperor's horse were a few of his household. Then I noticed among them a dark-haired woman, her face turned and staring at the following figure of me. My heart froze. Perugino had painted Anna into the picture. And he had captured an unequivocal look on her face, a look of longing, of sadness, of regret and of a deep, deep love. Like Aeneas staring back at his Dido her gaze had separated us for ever.

Alone in that church, I wept.

We had to make most of the journey back to Constantinople overland which was dangerous; we were at risk from Serb bandits and the people along our way were unfriendly, even though we were fellow Christians. We were glad to see Constantinople again. When we arrived we learnt that the news had preceded us. We were not greeted with enthusiastic crowds, delighted that we had reached agreement with the Latins. No, quite the opposite, the people were enraged. There were crowds in the main square denouncing the proceedings of the Council. A copy of *Laetentur coeli*, the final document of the Council, was symbolically burned. Metropolitan Markos Eugenikos of Ephesus was hailed as a hero, Bessarion and Isidore were denounced as traitors.

I kept a low profile and returned to the Monastery. There I met Master Yiorgos Scholarios who had been talking with Abbot Petras.

"This was predictable, Father Ignatios. I knew the people would not accept it."

"Very few of us were happy with it, Master, but we had no choice."

"They say the Emperor is livid. After all that time and all that money it looks as if unity, and help from the Franks, is going down the drain."

"So where do you stand, Master?"

He indicated Abbot Petras' room from which he had first emerged. "I have been talking with the Abbot. I am to enter the order and denounce the proclamations of the Council." His face was set firm. His words were intended as a challenge to me.

"So where does that leave you, Master?"

"In a bit of peace, I trust."

He could not have been further off the mark. Taking the name of Gennadios, rather than being allowed to pursue his academic and theological pursuit in quiet and obscurity, he was adopted by the populace as their champion in rejecting the findings of the Council. He became the head of the anti-conciliarists, all those who rejected the conclusions of the Council. When Cardinal Isidore of Kiev, one of the leading conciliarists, appeared in the city some two years later he was denounced by Gennadios in a sermon that lasted from midday to night.

He was astute enough not to press me on where I stood in the anti-conciliarist debate. If the truth be told I was unsure myself. One thing, however, was obvious. The Council never had the desired effect of either achieving unity nor of uniting the Frankish princes against the Ottomans. There was one attempt at a Crusade about nine years ago but the weak western army was quickly routed by the Turks at Varna.

Up on the walls I unload the heavy pack that I have carried on my shoulder. It contains my medical instruments, dressings, absorbent gauze and sphagnum moss as well as some analgesics. I have no weapon, I am here for the wounded.

The numbers ranged against us are terrifying. It seems to me to be inevitable that we shall be overrun. Most of us know this but it does not affect morale. Yes, many of the rich have fled the city but the bulk of the population, achingly poor, have no option of escape. They are facing their fate with a simple courage. It has been a long journey for me, from the destruction of an island, all those years ago, to this final, impending destruction of the Holy City, an epoch-ending collapse. These days I am more resigned to where I find myself. The years have not just added greying hairs, aching joints and a collapsing face. They have brought with them a

269

small quotient of serenity which is unexpected. Sometimes I wonder if I am the same man as that young doctor-monk who sailed away to Florence those fifteen years past.

As the first rays of the sun light up the plain, casting the shadows of our vast walls towards the enemy encampment, the bombardment starts. Cannon hammer away at our defences. I can feel the shudder of the wall beneath my feet each time it is hit. Each time I brace myself to flee in case this is the volley which will collapse the wall under my feet.

Armed men are collecting behind the outer walls, their distribution is sparse. At some points the gates and portals that allow access from the city through the inner walls are guarded by two or three men at the most. It surely cannot be long now. I hold no hope that I will be spared, even though I am a monk and a doctor. This must truly be the end of my journey.

A volcanic shudder from below me startles me out of my reverie. I begin to feel the battlement shift. I grab my bag and run to my right, just in time to see the whole section of the wall on which I had been standing collapse down into a pile of rubble. At the same time I hear a huge shout from across the plain to the west. I look out and see them coming, vast hordes of men, running at a steady pace, only two hundred yards away. The moment has come.

To be any use I need to get off this battlement. I find a stone staircase and descend as fast as I can. The roar of the approaching Ottoman army is getting louder. Our own people are congregating by the breach in the wall. Some are clambering up the rubble pile with beams, planks and palisades in a vain attempt to repair the breach. I hear another cannon exploding, a small one, and one of the men on the breach is suddenly headless. His body stays upright for a brief moment before toppling over in a collapse of resignation, seeming to know that life without a head is pointless.

I set down my bag. Our men are climbing the breach now. I hear their calls.

"It's the Janissaries They're nearly on us!" Within moments they are in one-to-one combat. Steel blades flash in the early morning sun. I see limbs hacked from their torsos, men falling with fatal wounds. Our weapons and our body armour are adequate but the Ottomans outclass us. Over the top comes another banner and then the familiar headgear of the Janissaries. They pour down into the space between the walls and are coming towards me. A dark-haired captain leads them, his scimitar swinging from left to right. He comes straight for me. So this is the moment. All that has happened in the past, all that could have happened in the future, all that is irrelevant. Only the present moment is real.

I stand up, waiting for the sweep of the sword. My hands are by my side, my bag is on the floor beside me. All desire gone except one, that it should be quick.

My executioner is close enough now to look me in the eyes. I do not let my gaze drop. His sword is in the air, ready to swing.

And then he drops his weapon. He is staring at me. It is as if we are in a cocoon, sheltered from the noise, the screams, the death and destruction around us. He is staring at me intently and then he speaks to me in Greek. In his face I see a confusion.

"Bless me, father." I lift my hand as he lowers his head to kiss it.

"Blessings on you, my son."

He stands up and points downhill. "Get away! Quick. Go that way." I do not hesitate. More and more Ottomans are pouring over the breach. To stay here will be certain death. There is a portal open in front of me. In a moment I am through it.

Once inside the inner wall I find myself in a sea of people: soldiers, civilians, monks and nuns who are fleeing to the east along the Middle Way, heading for the church of Ayia Sophia. They are strangely silent even though the screams of battle can be heard from the terrace between the two land walls. For a moment I consider retracing my steps, returning to the conflict to help the

271

wounded but the Janissary's command was urgent and imperative. Get away.

Where to go? I pass the church of the Holy Apostles and turn down the street that leads to the Monastery of the Pankrator. There is no-one around and the main door is bolted. No sign of the porter. I beat on it with my fist.

"Open up. It is Father Ignatios. Quick man!"

There is a pause and then I hear the bolt shifted and the great door opens a fraction. The porter, looking terrified, is peering round the door.

"Quick! Let me in. It's quite safe." He says nothing but opens the door enough to allow me to enter. As I walk off towards the living quarters I hear the door crash shut behind me. Will it be solid enough to resist the Turks?

I am still carrying my bag and instruments. Quickly finding my cell I drop the bag on the floor. Then I hear a voice. "Ignatios. Is that you?" It is Gennadios, calling from his cell. I turn and walk down the corridor to the door of his quarters.

"Thank goodness, Ignatios. You're still alive."

"So far, but I cannot stay here."

"Why not? We'll be safe here."

"I doubt it, Brother. We ought to get away."

"But where? They tell me the wall is breached and the Turks are in the city. It'll be far more dangerous out there."

"Well. I'll stay put. If they do get in they will not be interested in a monk like me." I hope that is true but am not confident.

Just then we hear shouts and screams from the street outside. I turn to Gennadios. "Bolt your cell door and stay put, Brother. God be with you." I do not wait for his reply.

I know a side door of the Monastery that leads to a quiet street. I get the porter to let me out and slip away. After a few turns in the narrow alleyway I find a vantage point that overlooks the square in front of the Monastery. I can see two Genoese soldiers with their backs to the door of the Monastery, facing a

272

detachment of Anatolians. The Genoese fight bravely, refusing to flee. I see two Turks go down, one with a wound to his abdomen, the other with a deep gash to his shoulder. The others kick them aside in their anxiety to get at the Italians. Soon they are engulfed and I see two scimitars flash through the air to decapitate the brave pair. Bright blood spurts from their severed necks and the paved floor of the square is soon slippery and red.

Then I notice, huddled in the corner of the square, a group of women, some young, some old, accompanying five small children who are silent and pallid in the face of this violence. The Turks turn their attention on this group, prodding them to stand out in the centre of the square. I am paralysed with fear as to what is to happen. I cannot move but an anger begins to fill my sinews. My right arm burns with the need to hold a weapon. I long for my Damascene steel.

It is only then that I realise I have an advantage over them. They must be confused by all the alleyways and narrow streets of this city. I, on the other hand, know them like the back of my hand, particularly all those around the Monastery of the Pantokrator.

I stand up so that they can see me. My vantage point is above them. In Turkish I call out. "Hey! You!"

They turn to see who it is that is calling them.

"Leave those women alone, you fucking pigs!" I know that my jibe is sufficiently insulting. It has the desired effect. Three of them bellow something in Turcoman and run towards me. When they realise that they cannot reach me directly they plunge down a side-alley in an attempt to find me. That leaves just two in the square. I duck out of sight and find a way down into the square which will avoid my pursuers. I am out of sight until the moment that I burst into the square. One of the Turks is looking away from me, the other is watching the group of women. I am burning with anger now. I rejoice in the prospect of combat. I pick up one of the dead Genoese soldiers' swords and within a second I am on them. The feel of the hilt in my hand is strange. In an instant I

273

have become something I never thought I would be, a fighter. But there is no time to dwell on this transformation. I swing the blade hard down on the Turk. He has turned half towards me. It is a good sword, well looked after and sharp; it cuts off his left arm. I let out a shout of triumph as he falls to the ground, more blood despoiling the square. Now I step over him towards the other. He has only just noticed what has happened and his arms are down. With cool precision I run him through, just under the heart.

"Come on! Quick." I call to the women. There is still no time for reflection. I lead them out of the square, running. I am heading for Ayia Sophia; somehow I feel there must be safety there. I can find a route that will avoid the main thoroughfares where all the killing is going on. We pause for breath and one of the women speaks to me.

"Thank you for saving us, Father. Are you really a monk?" I turn away, not wanting to answer that question.

In around half an hour we are there. People are thronging towards the great church from all directions. Together we pour in through the main door.

Ahead of us, under the dome, is the great High Altar. The sight that greets us is appalling. There are women, prostitutes judging by their appearance, naked to the waist and dancing on the altar, egged on by a consignment of Ottoman troops. A rag-bag lot by the look of them, clearly not Janissaries. One of their number jumps up with the women and joins in the lewd dance. He tears off the skirt of one of the women and pulls her down on her back, stark naked. He is grabbing at his own breeches as she parts her legs to allow him to couple with her. His white buttocks bounce obscenely in time to the cheers of his fellow soldiers. Disgust makes me turn away only to notice another Ottoman soldier, not a Turk by the look of him, more likely a Serb or a Hungarian. He is chiselling away at a marble plaque set into the floor.

At this moment a tall, turbaned figure appears in the doorway. He is resplendently dressed in shining armour. This can

274

only be the Sultan Mehmet II himself. His face is creased with anger. He strides into the church and stops by the man who is chiselling away at the stone floor, trying to shift the marble plaque. He speaks a few words and then, in a flash, his sword has beheaded the looter.

Mehmet continues up towards the altar. The prostitutes and soldiers have shrunk away. He speaks to the captain of the guard who follows him and the Janissaries fan out to protect the altar and the rest of the building.

So this is our adversary. He is a striking figure, still young, with a hawk-like nose and cold, cold eyes. I had always known the Ottomans as a hard people, violent and bloodthirsty but he and the Janissary captain make me think that there may be another side to them, more honourable than my prejudice has painted them. I shrink back to the shadows but keep my eyes on the Sultan.

He calls for an imam to come forward. The cleric ascends the pulpit and, for the first time in its long history, the church resounds to the call of the muezzin, the call to prayer. In that moment over a thousand years of Christian history is demolished, a cataclysm far greater than the Latins' *filioque* could ever have been. The old, external God is finally dead. I see the Sultan climb up on the altar and then prostrate himself in prayer. Compared with the wrangles and dissension that have afflicted this church in the recent past, this act seems far more reverent and religious.

But I have little time to ponder this. The Sultan may be fair-minded but there are rather too many men in the city now who would be very happy to separate a monk's head from his shoulders. A little while ago I might have been resigned to death, almost happy to greet it. But, now that I have been reprieved, and having felt the weight of a sword back in my hand, my mind is on survival once more.

There is a small, hidden door in one corner of the base of the dome. I heard about this door from one of the other monks. It is concealed behind a screen. It takes a while to find it; it is a secret

275

door. Eventually I locate it and turn the handle. No-one is watching this corner of the building so I slip away unseen.

Down a circular staircase I come to another door. I push it open and there, in front of me, is the cistern that lies underneath Ayia Sophia, a small reservoir dotted around with pillars that support the floor of the church above. There is a small amount of light and I can make out a simple boat moored up alongside the low jetty on which I am standing. I climb into the boat and, using a long pole that I find on the jetty, propel myself away across the reservoir.

Few people know of this cistern, at least few know how to find it. The Emperor Justinian created it at the same time as he built the church above. After a while I reach another jetty and climb out. There is an entrance to a tunnel in front of me but there is no light down there. I creep along slowly, one hand on each side of the tunnel. Something live runs across my feet which makes me shudder.

It must be an hour before I finally reach a door. It requires all my strength and body weight to force it open enough to make space for me to pass through. In front is a metal ladder, fixed to the wall. I can see this ladder for there is light coming from above. I climb upwards, it must be the height of a building, and reach the top. There is a grating above my head. I push hard with my head and it swings upwards with a loud creak. Sunlight pours in and I take welcome gulps of fresh air. I lift my head slowly, I have no wish to run straight into an Ottoman sword. I look around to see where I am.

I am in open ground. I look behind me and see the city walls. I am outside the walls. To my right is a stretch of water, the Golden Horn. I can see Galata, the Genoese town, on the opposite shore. To my left I can see a pontoon that stretches across the Horn. I spot a few soldiers moving backwards and forwards on it.

There is no escape. I am sandwiched between the city walls and the Horn. Where can I go from here? I sit down on a low wall, my head in my hands.

Chapter 27

I don't hear them until they are on me. Rough hands grab me from behind. My head is forced down on to the wall, my hands gripped behind my back. I wait for the decapitating blade. A voice, in Greek, hisses in my ear.

"Keep your head down. Don't move." There is enough urgency in the voice to make me obey without questioning. I can hear the sounds of other men, the clatter of weapons, rough Turcoman voices that remind me of Cappodocia. One of them calls out.

"You got a fucking monk, have you? Trade him for one of these?" I cannot see what or who he was talking about but it was soon obvious.

"You'll get better fucking from her than sticking your dick up an old monk's asshole." There are guffaws of coarse laughter.

One of the men holding me down answers, "No thanks, friend, we've got plenty of those." I can hear the others walking off. With swift movements my wrists are tied. Only then do they allow me to stand up. Now I can see that they are Janissaries. We look very similar, despite my beard and their moustaches. They appear to be alone. One smiles at me.

"What's your name, Brother?" He still speaks in Greek.

"Father Ignatios."

"No. I mean your real name. Your given name."

"Oh, right. It's Ioánnis."

"That sounds better. Now, Ioánnis, I wonder if you know anything about a warrior monk, back up there," he nods towards the city, "finished off two of our Anatolian comrades. Very impressive." I keep still and silent, my head down. "No. I suppose not. Must be plenty of monks in that city."

279

I find my voice. "What are you going to do with me?"

"Don't worry, Ioánnis, your skin is safe. The Sultan has given orders for monks and nuns to be preserved. Not that everyone has taken notice of that. Nuns get a good price in the markets of Edirne and Bursa and, for some peculiar reason, those Turcomen have a particular predilection for celibate monks." This information has more resonance for me than he could ever imagine.

"Where are you going to take me, then?"

"We're camping over there tonight," he points across the Horn. "The Sultan has ordered the looting to stop tonight so it'll be safer to go back into the city tomorrow. Everyone will be sorting out their booty, there'll be no more fighting, except amongst themselves." He spat. "Come on, Father Ignatios, we can cross the water on that pontoon over there. Stay close to us and you'll be perfectly safe." I walk on between the two of them, glad of their protection.

After my wild episode in the square in front of the Monastery I have no wish to be returned to the Pantokrator so it is with some relief that I learn that both the church and the Monastery have been too damaged to be habitable. Instead I am taken to the Monastery that is attached to the church of the Holy Apostles. I am surprised to find that it is undamaged. Later I was to learn that the Sultan had placed a guard on it as soon as the city was entered, wishing to preserve at least one church. Inside its walls I meet other monks that I know, some from the Pantokrator. Between us we piece together an account of what has befallen the monks of the city. Nearly half, like me, are safe in the Holy Apostles. We hear of others who have been carried off as hostages and yet others who have died. I am distressed that there is no sign of my friend, Gennadios. No reports that he has been killed but, again, no one has seen him taken off either.

Within a few days some of the hostages are returned to us. They have been reclaimed from their captors by the Sultan as part of his one-fifth share of all booty grabbed in that wild day of looting.

"The vizier told us that the Holy Apostles is to continue as a church." The speaker is an old monk. He had escaped capture by hiding in a culvert.

"Ayia Sophia has become a mosque. Sultan Mehmet wants the city to continue with a Greek contingent, as well as Muslim. So the orthodox faith can continue."

A younger man speaks up. "That's all very well, Father, but how can the faith continue without Ayia Sophia and in the absence of a Patriarch?"

The old man slowly shakes his head. "When you've lived as long as I have, Brother, you will know that God is not dependent on buildings or people." The younger man is silent.

For two weeks we are isolated in the Monastery. The Sultan has placed a guard on the door, not only to keep us in but also to keep others out. Gradually the rhythm of monastic life is re-established but it is a pattern of life that frustrates me nowadays. Am I really to remain incarcerated in this tiny Orthodox enclave in a Muslim empire?

Thoughts like this are rolling around my head when they are interrupted by a knock on the cell door. I stand up and open it.

"Gennadios!" He steps forward, into the cell, a broad smile on his face. We embrace.

"Greetings, Father Ignatios. I am truly glad to find you here."

"And I you. I had thought that you had died. How did you get back here?"

He sits down on the edge of my bed. "It is a long story, Ignatios, but I think you may want to hear it", and so he unravels his narrative.

"I stayed in my cell when the city was invaded. Soon after you left me there the Ottoman forces battered down the door and looted the Monastery. Two large soldiers found me in my cell. One was about to slaughter me but he was restrained by his companion.

There was much frantic discussion between the two. I understood none of it. When they tied my hands and marched me out of the cell I knew I was being taken as a hostage. After two days the troops set out to the west, to Edirne, the Ottoman capital. There were many hostages, mostly young men and girls. A few monks like me but I was never close enough to speak to them. The soldiers made us travel fast. Arriving at the capital there was much bartering, buying and selling. I ended up as a man-servant in the house of an Arab horse dealer. They would not use either of my names, Gennadios or Yiorgos Scholarios. They insisted on giving me a damned Turkish name, Izmit. I cannot understand their language so it was difficult to know what they wanted me to do. I collected a great number of beatings. I could tell that things were restless in Edirne. The Sultan intends to make this city here the capital of his empire. They objected to that in Edirne, that much I could understand."

He stands up from my bed and looks out of the window of the cell. "Imagine that. This great imperial city to be reborn as the capital of another empire."

"So why were you brought back? Did they tell you what it was about?"

He turns to face me. "Yes, they have told me why I have been brought back here. The Vizier who came with a troop of Janissaries explained it all to me. The Sultan is determined that this city should accommodate many different peoples, Muslims, Armenians, Jews and, believe it or not, Christians. This church is to be the centre of the Greek Christian enclave. Some have survived here, others are being brought back on the order of the Sultan. We are to have religious freedom within the Ottoman state."

"But after all that has happened; thousands have been slaughtered. How can we live together?"

"It remains to be seen, Brother, but the Sultan is not necessarily the bloodthirsty conqueror that he has been made out to be. Mind you, that's what they call him now, Fahti Mehmet,

282

Mehmet the Conqueror." He pauses; he is clearly tired by his journey yet he continues with his tale.

"They're changing the name of the city too. No longer Constantinople, it is to be called Istanbul." New name, new ruler, new empire; it is not all unwelcome change.

"Father Ignatios, there is one thing more that the Sultan has decreed. He wants to appoint a new Greek Patriarch. That's why he has brought me back."

For a moment I fail to grasp what he is saying. My eyes widen as realisation dawns.

"You! You are to be the Patriarch? Is that what you are saying?"

He sits down again and nods his head. "That's what the Emperor wants. He does not want a unionist, too much association with the Latins. So he has chosen me."

I laugh out loud. "That's wonderful, Brother. That is really wonderful. You will be an excellent Patriarch. A Father of our church in the mould of dear old Joseph."

"I hope so, Ignatios. We have been too long without a Patriarch since the unionist Gregory fled to Rome two years ago."

"Absolutely. But how can you be commissioned without a Christian Emperor, now we know that Constantine died in the siege."

"The Sultan is going to do it himself. He is determined to be Sultan, or Emperor, to the Christians as much as to the Muslims."

My mind wanders back to the village of Kashaya; Muslims and Christians sharing the same church. Could we dare to hope that out of this cataclysm, out of this great Apokalypse, will emerge a new tolerance?

"I suppose there is no reason why he should not. God, Alah, Jehovah, all are but different aspects of one truth."

He stares at me intently. "You are further down that road than I ever realised, Ignatios." He could have been admonishing me but one look at his face suggested that he was not. A silence descends on us, broken only by Gennadios.

"But there is one thing I need to ask of you, Ignatios."

"Of me?"

"Yes. I shall need a secretary if I am to become Patriarch, and not just a secretary, an interpreter too. You know that I only have Greek and a smattering of Latin. You seem to have knowledge of many more tongues than I do."

I hesitate before answering, "I suppose that's right. I can certainly speak Arabic. Latin is well known to me and I have some Italian, but that is a bit rusty. It has been nearly fifteen years since I was in Italy."

"Yes, yes. But what about Turkish? That's the crucial one."

"I think I have a working knowledge. I can understand most of it; speaking it is more difficult."

"There will be meetings with the Sultan. I imagine that Turkish will be required."

The Sultan. Being secretary and interpreter to Gennadios as our new Patriarch would bring me up against Fahti Mehmet. It is a fearful thought. I remember the powerful, imposing man in Ayia Sophia, the beheading of a looter. Powerful and uncompromising.

Gennadios smiles at me. "No need for fear, brother. He is not going to appoint a Patriarch only to lop off his head shortly afterwards; or yours. Well, what do you say? Will you take the post?"

"What about my doctoring, Father?" As I speak I recognise that with so many changes in the air my medical practice has been running down. Nevertheless I will have to let it go completely if I am to take up the post of the Patriarch's secretary. It surprises me to find that contemplating the idea of leaving medicine behind is easier than I thought. For all these years, being a doctor has enabled me to define myself to myself. Now I am beginning to understand that such a construction is no longer needed. Like a heavy cloak I can let it slip off my shoulders. In some sort of way I am sitting lighter to my *persona*. It is a variety of freedom.

Gennadios says nothing, he just stares at me. Perhaps he knows that I have to resolve this myself. I incline my head. "Of course, Father Gennadios. It will be a great honour."

"Good, good." He is rubbing his hands together. "No more talk now. We'll meet tomorrow after Matins and sort out all the details."

"Details?"

"Oh, you know. Where you are going to work, who will be there to support you. The office of secretary to the Patriarch is a busy one."

"You think I can do it?"

"Well, if I can make a go of Patriarch, I am sure that you can make a success of being his secretary." He turns to leave, then turns back again.

"Just one thing, Ignatios," his forehead is creased for a moment. I wait. "You know those two soldiers killed outside the Pantokrator?"

"Yes, I had heard."

"Killed by a monk wielding a powerful sword." What is coming? He continues. "It seems that no-one knows who that monk was. He disappeared as quickly as he came." Still I remain silent, surely he is not going to reverse all that he has just offered me. I meet his gaze and am certain that he knows who that monk was. "I think it best that it remains that way; the unknown warrior-monk. Who knows, it could have been a phantom."

I swallow hard and am about to speak. He raises a finger.

"I should keep quiet, Brother," he speaks gently. "I know the Ottomans are not going to pursue it."

I am sure that the relief on my face must be obvious. He continues. "Mind you, if they had been Janissaries, the Sultan would not be nearly as tolerant. I don't suppose you carry a weapon, do you, Father Ignatios?"

I blush and the words tumble out, "No, no, of course not. And I never shall."

He smiles, "That's good. I don't think the Ottomans would welcome a Patriarch with an armed secretary."

I nod. "Goodnight, Father, and thank you."

"Sleep well, Ignatios. There is work to be done in the morning."

The enthronement of Gennadios as Patriarch is a bitter-sweet ceremony. The church of the Holy Apostles is bedecked with flowers and candles. Outside the streets that had been steeped in blood still carry the stench of death. The little Greek community that remains in the city is dazed by the conquest, the subsequent pillage and the influx into the city of thousands of new inhabitants. The muezzin rings out to call the Muslims to prayer. By order of the Sultan the church bells are silenced so the faithful are called to prayer with the semantron, the same wooden plank and mallet that I saw in Kashaya.

I have been preparing the order of commissioning that the Sultan will use. He has decreed that it will be spoken both in Greek and in Arabic. It is not a difficult task to put this together.

The ceremony itself encourages the little Christian community. No longer, in their perspective, is the perversion of the unionists going to destroy the beauty of the true faith, the true liturgy. The people respond with warmth and enthusiasm.

The Sultan has decreed that he will enter the church once all are assembled. He is an impressive figure as he passes through the narthex, wearing elegant robes and a snow-white turban. He is unsmiling; on his young face I can see signs of the heavy responsibility that he carries. His eyes are piercing, his gaze uncompromising. This is Fahti Mehmet, the conqueror of the eleven hundred year old Byzantine Empire.

Gennadios rises to the occasion; already he exudes the *gravitas* of a Patriarch. In his sermon he praises the magnanimity of the Sultan and speaks of the hope for all to live in peace. His

286

voice rings around the old church with an optimism that must cheer his hearers. He makes no mention of the unionists, no mention of the devastation of May the twenty-ninth. Gennadios is looking forward, not back. This pragmatic approach is just what is needed. The Sultan has been well advised to choose Gennadios.

The service over, a procession wends its way through the Greek quarter. The destruction to buildings all around is overwhelming. Gennadios is carried on a chair preceded by a simple wooden cross. He wears his monk's habit, no resplendent patriarchal robes. It is clear that he is identifying himself with the suffering, with the destruction. From time to time the procession stops so the Patriarch can bless the assembling crowds. Every now and then I see small consignments of the palace guard standing in doorways or gathered down side-alleys. The Sultan is making sure that there should be no disturbance. Eventually we end up at the Monastery and the people disperse, going quietly to their houses.

Inside I settle Gennadios in his new lodgings, suitable for a Patriarch. He looks tired.

"A good day, I believe, Ignatios, a good day."

"It is especially good that we have a Patriarch again after all this time. You could see that the people were pleased."

"I think they see the Sultan in a new light, don't you agree? Not quite the bloodthirsty tyrant we thought him to be."

I say nothing. It seems to me that if Fahti Mehmet needs to be bloodthirsty he would have no difficulty. I have seen and experienced more than Gennadios, shut up in his cell. But I say nothing.

Now that I work as secretary to Patriarch Gennadios I find that I am glad to be a doctor no longer. In many ways it is a relief to be freed of the expectations of sick people, however gratifying it is to do some good for them. In the end I am happy to put it all aside.

My life has become more ordered; I have time for my monastic devotions. I settle into the pattern of the daily offices. But now I find that the words of the liturgy, the communal

287

prayers addressed to God the Father, to Christ the Pantokrator, to the Holy Spirit seem to have lost much of their meaning. This is not because they have no meaning in themselves but more that the objects of the prayers and invocations are no longer objects. I find it difficult to express this because words of description all tend to objectify that which is not. With the taking leave of these transitional objects, God, Christ, the Holy Spirit, the focus moves away from them and settles on the liturgy and the prayers. Thus I take part in the offices, not because of a need to address an objective God, but because, in the end, it seems to be a right and worthwhile thing to do. Paradoxically, taking leave of an objective God makes the religious life more religious, it brings it back to the human dimension.

I suppose that I had the first inklings of this in the Cappodocian desert, learning and using the Jesus prayer. To start with I felt as if I was addressing both Jesus and God, they were solidly reified in my mind. 'Lord Jesus Christ, son of the living God, have mercy on me.' But after weeks of this discipline I began to find that the substantial was giving way to the spiritual. The prayer was bringing my focus away from the external world, away from external objects and limiting it within the confines of my body.

But then events intervened and I lost that sense, that heightened awareness that had left God behind.

It is a bright day in the spring of 1454. The sun streams into the chamber where Gennadios works. He is seated at a simple desk; I stand beside him.

There is a sharp knock at the door and it opens to reveal a young monk. His face is flushed and his stuttering speech betrays his agitation.

"Father, Father Gennadios. There is someone to see you."

"Yes, Brother. Is it important? Father Ignatios and I have much business to attend to," he waves a hand over the documents spread over his working desk.

288

"I think it is. He says he is from the Sultan."

Gennadios turns and looks at me, as if I might know what this visitation is all about. I shrug my shoulders.

"I think we'd better go and see, Father" says the Patriarch. "Lead the way, young man."

The visitor is in the ante-room. He stands as we enter. He is dressed in civilian Ottoman apparel; his turban is large and black. He is unsmiling.

"Good morning," says Gennadios making his way towards him. "I know you, don't I? The Sultan's vizier. You brought me back from Edirne, didn't you?"

The man inclines his head and then speaks. Gennadios looked confused, the man was speaking Turkish. I can just understand the gist of what he is saying.

"Father, he says you are to expect a visit from a certain man, he does not name him, after Vespers tomorrow evening. You are to wait in the side chapel," I was struggling to understand this man, "and you must be alone, apart from me."

"A mysterious request but I think I know who we can expect. Tell him that we shall be prepared."

This is even harder for me, listening was one thing, speaking Turkish is far more difficult. Nevertheless the vizier seems to grasp what I am saying. He gives a deep bow and leaves. We are alone.

"It's the Sultan, isn't it, Father Gennadios? He's the one who is coming. What can he want?"

Gennadios looks down at his feet and there is a short silence. "I really don't know, Ignatios. I really don't know." From his face I can see that he does not relish the prospect of meeting Fahti Mehmet again, but I am more intrigued than concerned.

The next day Gennadios gives orders that no monk is to go near the side chapel for two hours after Vespers. No-one seems surprised at this, at least no one questions it. During the Office I find it hard to focus my mind on my devotions. The sense of anticipation has been growing in me all day.

289

Vespers is concluded and Patriarch Gennadios leads the monks out of the church. As he passes me he takes me by the arm. Together we leave the church. Our brother monks turn right to return to the Monastery. Gennadios and I turn left, through an arch and into the chapel.

It is always quiet and peaceful in the chapel. The evening sun casts long shadows across the courtyard outside. A blackbird sings. In the distance I can hear the Muslim call to prayer echoing out over the city. The air is still and cool.

We enter the chapel. In the far corner I can make out a seated figure. Deep shadow makes it difficult to make out the figure's identity. Gennadios' step hesitates. I whisper to him "Come on, Father" and his pace picks up again. As our eyes adjust to the dark we can see that it is he, Sultan Mehmet, sitting on the stone bench. He is alone. He stands as we approach and makes a deep salaam to Gennadios. The Patriarch returns it and I join him. The Sultan indicates with his hand that we should sit. No word has yet been spoken.

For quite a few minutes we sit there in silence. He does not move a muscle. Out of the corner of my eye I can see the fixed expression, firm and decisive, not as tired as when I last saw him. Now he has the appearance of a man fully in control of himself. He frightens me and I turn away my gaze.

He speaks. He is using Arabic and is addressing me. "I believe, Father Secretary, that you speak Arabic."

"Yes, your Highness. I am quite fluent."

"Then we shall speak in Arabic and you can interpret for my good friend, Gennadios." When I translate this Gennadios' eyes widen at the way he is addressed. He visibly relaxes. The Sultan is continuing. "You must be wondering what this meeting is all about."

"Yes" replies Gennadios, "we have been speculating, but not to any useful effect."

The Sultan laughs. For the first time I can see some levity in his features, the laugh is quite innocent.

"Speculation. There's so much of that going around at the moment. My court is like a hive of bees, so much noise and so little thinking. That's why I have come here."

"Well, no noise here, is there, your Highness?"

"Gennadios, I want you to address me as Mehmet when we meet in private. You have no objection to me calling you Gennadios, have you?"

"No. None at all. Thank you, Mehmet."

The Sultan starts to wander around the little chapel. Gennadios walks beside him. I follow a little behind and between the two of them. The conversation begins to flow more freely.

"I need someone to talk with who understands what I understand. I am familiar with Plato and Aristotle. There is no one in the court that can debate these great Masters with me."

"I think I can do that, and Ignatios here is well-versed in the ancients as well in Arabic medicine." The Sultan stops in his tracks and turns his gaze on me.

"Are you indeed? Well then it will be a three-way debate, no less!" He laughs again.

And so, as the evening draws on, we talk. The Sultan has been taught well and our conversation stretches the brains of all three of us. Eventually he takes his leave and departs, leaving us tired but exhilarated.

These meetings become a regular, if not very frequent event. As we get to know each other better we become more open in our debate. It is having a healthy effect on Gennadios, better enabling him to carry out his role of Patriarch and leader of the little Greek community in the city.

The one subject that never seems to be discussed is God, or Alah. Mehmet always steers us away from the topic. Perhaps it is the Muslim sense that there is nothing that can be said about Alah; perhaps he sees it as a subject that will divide us. What is certain, however, is that he is a Muslim leader who is very ready to accommodate the Christian God, and the Jewish God for that matter. He demonstrates tolerance, even though he is a ruthless conqueror. It is a paradox which is difficult to fathom.

Bit by bit the Greek community in Constantinople, or Istanbul as we have to call it nowadays, is becoming re-established. There is still the greatest distrust of the Turks. Many people have left, to find a new life in Greek colonies in the Aegean. What interests me is the news that some have settled on my island, the island of the Monastery of Ayios Ioánnis Theologos.

I have not thought about the island for some years, not in any concentrated way. That part of my life is long gone yet, now when I hear it spoken of, a tug of attachment disturbs my inner soul. I have not completely left it behind. I try to recall it, the little hills, the villages, the bays and the proud, strong Monastery on the summit of the island, but it is becoming increasingly difficult to picture it. The strongest memory is one of slaughter, fire and destruction.

There is other news as well. One morning I am down by the Golden Horn. An Italian sea captain is sitting on a low bench that overlooks the harbour. His weathered face is staring across the Horn to the Genoese settlement of Galata, the home of Anna and her husband, Silvio Lorenzetti, all those years ago.

I sit down beside him. "Is trade good, now, Captain? Under the Turks, I mean."

He spits in the dust. "Could be better, could be worse. I make do." Clearly he is a man of few words. Something impels me to persist.

"Do you hear tell of Lorenzetti, Silvio Lorenzetti?" He looks at me and his face is both surprised and quizzical.

"Why do you ask, Father? Did you know him."

"I met him once." I try to sound non-committal. "Many years ago."

"Then you didn't hear that he died. Must have been at least five years ago. Apoplexy, I'm told."

"And his family?" I try hard to control the quaver in my voice.

"I'm not sure. The boy was grown up so I don't know where he's gone. They say his wife went into the Convent, somewhere out west I believe. That's all I know." I try to think of something to say but my voice is trapped in the tightness of my throat. I nod a farewell and walk back up to the monastery, my mind full of longing and despair.

It is in this mood of reflection that Gennadios finds me.

"Brother, we have work to do."

"I am sorry, Father. My mind was elsewhere."

He smiles, "That was obvious, Ignatios. Are you back from wherever it was that held you just then?"

I collect myself. "Yes, Father. So what is the task?" I start to sort through the documents on the desk.

"None of that, Ignatios my friend. That can wait."

I look up at him; he must see the surprise on my face. "Read this. I can't make it out properly." He hands me a scroll. I untie the fastening and unroll it. It is written in Turkish, there is not much writing but beneath is attached the great seal of the Sultan.

"Yes, Ignatios, it comes from Mehmet himself. Now all I need you to do is translate it." I scan the document. The calligraphy is fine, it is easy enough to read. I peruse it all. "Come on, Ignatios! What does it say? Don't keep me in suspense."

"Well, Father, as far as I can make out he wants you to write a treatise on Christianity, outlining where there are differences with Islam. That's all."

"That's all? That is a monster task. Why on earth does he want it, and why has he come to me?"

I speak quietly. "Perhaps he trusts you. He knows you will tell him the truth." I pause. "I think he wants to know the truth, Father."

Gennadios is fiddling with his pectoral cross. "You are probably right, brother. You are probably right."

The treatise proves to be at least as large a task as Gennadios had feared. He works on it day and night. Then he brings it to me and we debate the content, revise and rewrite. Sometimes he calls in one of the other brothers when there is a difficulty or an area of expertise which is foreign to Gennadios and me. We never let it be known for whom this treatise is being written.

Once the text is established I translate it from the Greek into Arabic. We have ascertained that that is acceptable to the Conqueror. One of his scribes can make a Turkish version if needs be.

It is a fine document when completed. A beautiful exposition of the orthodox, the true faith. I have been able to help him with the understanding of Islam. All that I have learnt in my past travels has been helpful.

"You know what surprises me?" Gennadios is staring at the completed document. "There is much more that we share than there is that divides us." Immediately my mind is taken back to the little village of Kashaya in the Lebanese mountains. He sighs. "It makes me wonder why we have to be at each other's throats so often." Then his face brightens up. "There we are, perhaps Mehmet and I can change all that. We must go and pray. Come on Brother."

The Sultan is pleased with the treatise. At his meetings with Gennadios, whom he calls 'my dear friend' nowadays, they discuss its content and the propositions that Gennadios has made. The discussion is free-flowing, ranging over not just the contents of the treatise but wider topics to do with the life of the city, the Sultan's ambitions, even some of his most private thoughts. All the time, however, he is careful to remain in control. I remind myself frequently, he is still the Conqueror.

Then one morning a messenger is at the Monastery door. I am summoned to the Sultan's residence in the Blachernae palace. Two Janissaries accompany the messenger and soon the four of us are to be seen marching through the streets, on our way to the palace. I am reminded of that other occasion, the time when I was escorted into the harem at Bursa. Now I appreciate how dangerous that escapade was. Miriam tried to make me see it but I was an impetuous youth in those days. I have been through enough since then to rid me of any such precocity.

I am expected. The great door swings open. As I walk into the palace I can see that there is still much damage from the siege, damaged stonework and holes in the ceiling. It does not seem like the palace of a great Conqueror.

A guard escorts me into a large room, empty except for the two of us. He retires and shuts the door. I feel a chill in my spine, standing in that large empty room. I can just hear the cries from the streets outside, the cooing of pigeons on the roof. On the wall facing me is a grill. I jump as I hear a voice from behind its bars.

"Good morning, Father Ignatios."

"Er, good morning." I peer at the grill but make out nothing.

"Stay there, please." I recognise the voice now. I should be used to this low tone.

"Yes, your Highness." I stand quite still. In a few moments a small door, close to the grill, opens and Sultan Mehmet emerges.

"Thank you for coming, Father Ignatios." I did not imagine that I had had much choice but I say nothing. "I have been reading Gennadios' treatise. A very excellent work and I suspect that there is something of Father Ignatios in it." I am about to demur but he raises a hand, "No, don't deny it. Gennadios is a brilliant man but I think you have given the treatise some depth. I suspect that you have helped to root it in real life. I like that." I mumble thanks, my head bowed.

"What intrigues me, what I want to know from you is where does it all come from. Where did you grasp all these matters?"

Can I possibly explain? He is a young man; much of what I have experienced is in a different world from his own. How can I explain?

"You are a Greek by birth, is that right?"

"Yes, your Highness. Both my parents were Greek."

His loud laughter comes as a shock. "Ha! Then we share something in common. My mother was Greek, a Greek slave. I can still remember her, she was truly beautiful." I cannot prevent myself from staring at him, I have to be careful, looking to see the Greekness in his face.

And then, quite unexpectedly and, as if out of my control, I start to speak. I talk without a break. I start to tell my story, beginning on the island, caring for the goats, my Baba, the fishing, Anna and old Father Ignatios, the raid, the sea journey to Lebanon, the village of Kashaya, Damascus and my medical training, murdering the Turk, the Cappodocian desert, finding Eleni in Bursa, coming to Constantinople, the journey to Ferrara and Florence, my meetings in Florence, finding Anna again, the return to Constantinople. I leave nothing out and throughout it all a burning anger keeps resurfacing, threatening to choke my narrative. He remains still and attentive. Eventually I stop.

There is a long silence. His eyes, which have rested on my face throughout, no longer seem forbidding. There is an unexpected gentleness as he speaks, "Thank you, Brother. Now I understand."

The audience is over and I leave quickly. Once in the familiar streets I slow my step. My heart is full. Now, with an epiphanic clarity, I can at last see the source of the inexplicable violence in my soul. In being encouraged to relive the narrative of my life until now I can see that I have never let my Baba go, he has retained a hold over me for all these years. Sultan Mehmet, a man half my age and from an alien culture, could see that. I need to let my Baba go, the man that I loved but who immured me in punishment and pain, the man whose blood was soaked up by the sand of the shoreline. I need to let him go, I need to forgive him.

Tears pour down my face. One thing is absolutely clear to me now.

I want to go home.

PERIIGIS PEMPTI

Chapter 28
The Island. 1458

The water is silky as it rolls over my shoulders. The cold tang of the brine complementing the blood warmth of my limbs. I strike out away from the shore in steady strokes. Stiffer, much stiffer, than I used to be the last time that I swam in this water with Anna those many years ago. Across the narrow strait I can see the familiar secluded beach. Dominating the shoreline behind me is the Kalikatsoú, now my home.

The early morning sun has little warmth in it. It shines on my face and reflects off the glimmering drops of water caught in my long grey beard.

I swim on. I feel as if I could swim for ever, to finally merge in the vast sea that has encompassed my life. Sinking downwards in an embrace of peace.

That is what my life has been; following where I am taken, no purpose except to move as I am willed. Have I been in control? Has anyone been in control? In the end it is in this journey that I have sought to find meaning for my life. Sought to find it but now, it seems, to no purpose.

Gennadios was good to me when I told him that I wanted to leave; to return to my home, to my island.

"I can understand that, Ignatios. This is not the place for you. I begin to wonder if it is the place for me." His face carried a worn, troubled look. "You can see how our brothers and sisters in this tiny Byzantine enclave are reverting to type. We are a disputatious lot. Even though we have seen off the unionists we still find matters to argue over or to fall out about. It's not for me, you know. More and more do I long for quiet and solitude. I'm not cut out to be a Patriarch."

"I can understand that, Father, but what can you do about it. The Sultan counts on you."

He waves his hand in a dismissive gesture. "I know, I know. I wish he didn't. He doesn't need me really. I suppose I shall have to persist, for the moment anyway." I sensed he did not want me to go but, such was his gentle way, he did not try to prevent me.

"I have written a letter for you to take to the Abbot of the Monastery of Ayios Ioánnis Theologos. I know him from my days as a scholar. I am sure he will welcome you in."

I had to wait for some weeks before I could find a passage. Then I heard of a Genoese trading ship that was stopping at the island, leaving at the start of the following month. I was impatient to go so was heartened when the day came. I packed my small bag, I had very few possessions, and went to find Gennadios.

"Farewell, Brother Ignatios." The old man had tears in his eyes as he clasped me to him. "God go with you." I could not speak, my throat felt knotted up. I nodded, turned and walked away. It was yet another leaving.

There were few people about as I walked through the city and down to the Horn where the ship was tied up; muttered greetings from the few Christians that I met, uncomprehending stares from the Turks. I was beginning to look like an old monk, with my hair greying, my walk stilted; becoming invisible.

The voyage was uneventful. A strong north wind blew for three days and the fat little caravel made good progress through the warm Aegean Sea. As I stared down at the deep blue water I thought back to that extraordinary journey that I made in my little kaiki with its single sail all those years ago. Taking to sea in that way was lunacy, I can see that now. Difficult to bring back the boy I was then though; the boy that responded without thinking to a compulsion that was neither sensible nor logical. A compulsion that spoke one message, 'move on'. Now I was experiencing a demand that was equally as strong but this time it was drawing me home. It was marking the end of my odyssey. Like that other Odysseus, who crossed these same waters, I was going home but not to a Penelope, to a faithful lover. Anna, my Penelope, was lost for ever, of that I was sure.

My vessel was a cargo ship and I was the only passenger. The rest of the people on board were Genoese crew. Some of them had fought under the Genoese general, Giustiniani, at the Siege. They were reluctant to talk when I spoke to them about that terrible time. They had little affection for the city that they were leaving.

I was left to myself for most of the time. It felt good to be on the water again, to feel the salt spray on my face. We sped through the Dardanelles with a good following wind; there were two brief stops at Chios and Lesbos and then we set course for the island.

We were some way off when I first saw the Monastery. Those huge, grey walls perched high above the island still had the power to intimidate me. As we came closer the familiar summit of Mount Profitis Elias hove into view; within the hour we were tying up at the quayside of the little port. The sun sparkled on the water of the bay. I looked across the harbour to the small beach where I had stumbled over the body of my father. It was disorientating to see a place that had only existed in my dreams these last forty years; and to be forced to think about him once more. As I stared across the bay I recalled his roughness and his cruelty. I remembered how he beat my mother as well as me. Once again the anger grew in me, an anger that I had taken away from the island, an anger that led me to kill both Mahmout the Turk and those two Anatolian soldiers outside the Pankrator Monastery. Now I was there, at the spot where I last saw his mutilated body, staring at that small patch of greying sand and in that moment I felt the anger slip away. It simply went, leached away as the waves cleanse the sand, dissolving his blood, and my anger, in the neutrality of the ocean.

Now, at last, I could feel the loss of my father. I remembered how his life emptied away whilst I tried to staunch the flow of blood with my shirt, the recognition going from his eyes before I could tell him that I loved him, that I forgave him for what he had done to me.

And for all the years since then those feelings had been hidden, buried by the restlessness of the rest of my life. It was only in this returning that my heart had been prised open. As the sailors strained to propel us into dock I turned away from the ship's rail, left only with an aching sorrow.

On land once more I looked about me. The first impression was obvious, it could not be ignored; poverty. It was clear that the island had suffered since the raid. There were still burnt out shells of cottages. There were a few fishing boats beached in front of the town. They were in a pitiable condition, ironwork rusting under the hot sun. I saw an old lady sitting beside some tattered nets. Would I know her? Would she recognise me?

I walked towards her. She looked up. There was no recognition in her eyes. She crossed herself.

"Bless me, Father." I obliged in the expected fashion. Then I stared at her closely. Was there something that I recognised in her features? "May I ask your name, Kýria?"

"Eleftheria, that's my name, Eleftheria." I did not remember her. She must have been at least ten years older than me.

"Do you recognise me, Kýria Eleftheria?" She screwed up her eyes hard as she peered at me. I could tell that she was thinking 'one monk's just like any other'. In a dull voice she replied.

"Sorry, Father. I don't know you."

"I lived here once, up there near the Monastery. My name was Ioánnis. I left the island after the raid." She crossed herself again. "My father was a fisherman."

She turned away, muttering. It was exasperating.

"Do you not remember me?" My voice was raised.

"I don't remember before the raid. Don't want to," she called over her retreating shoulder. It was clear that I was not going to glean any more from her. I could see that the raid had

300

had a devastating effect on her, it was not difficult to imagine how. There was no point in persisting. I resolved from then on to keep my former identity a secret.

"Thank you, Kýria." Head down she shuffled off towards a tumble-down cottage above the beach. I turned on my heel and made my way towards the path that led up to the Monastery.

There was a reassurance in treading the stone pathway that led up to the Monastery of Ayios Ioánnis Theologos. Eucalyptus trees shaded the way but the midday sun was still hot enough to beat on my back. I was conscious of being stiffer than I used to be. Strange, I did not remember this in Constantinople.

It took an hour to reach the heavy doors of the Monastery. I remembered how, during the raid, the women and children were denied sanctuary by the monks. I still hold a vestige of anger at the thought of that. It has made me sceptical about the humanity of some of my brother monks.

The Monastery still seemed more like a fortress than a house of God. As I stared at the walls I wondered how they would cope with the Basilica, that monstrous cannon that demolished the walls of the Holy City. Would that massive weapon smash these walls down in the way that it blasted its way into the world's most strongly protected city? Not much point really. These walls were built to keep out pirates. Pirates were unlikely to turn up with a twenty-seven foot monster. Nevertheless a part of me would have liked to see them brought down. Such defences were inappropriate; they were buttressing an old, autocratic religion. I would have cheerfully lit the fuse of the giant Basilica were it turned on these walls.

The doors swung open. I showed my letter to the monk on the gate and within minutes was shown to the ante-chamber of the Abbot's quarters. I settled down on a white wall-seat and regained my breath. I could feel a pulse throbbing in my throat.

It was peaceful there. I sat, unmoving, for what seemed like a long time. Eventually the door opened and the Abbot appeared. He was a short man with long reddish hair. He must have been ten years younger than me. He wore an analavos, the full length mantle joined at the neck. On his head he had a koukoulion, the soft hat embroidered with the instruments of the passion, both mantle and hat a mark of authority, an expropriation of powerlessness by the powerful.

"Come in, Father Ignatios. Come in." He stepped back to allow me to enter. It was a simple white-washed room; above his desk hung an ancient ikon of Ioánnis Theologos. A small, open window gave a view over the port below and, beyond that, out to the blue sea. The nearby islands were lost in the midday heat haze. He indicated a chair.

"Sit down, please, Father." I did as he bade and waited whilst he read through my letter of introduction from Gennadios.

"It seems you were much appreciated by our venerable Patriarch." I nodded my head, more in a gesture of dissembling than of agreement. He read on.

After a minute or so he put the letter down and looked up at me. "So this is coming home, then, Father?"

"Yes." I was reticent to talk about this.

"Coming home, yes indeed. You were brought up on this island?"

"Yes. But I left when I was seventeen."

"Left? What was the reason for that?"

"Perhaps you don't remember, Father. The pirate raid."

"Oh, that. I have heard about that." His tone was almost dismissive. "I did not come here myself until ten years ago. I was on the Holy Mountain of Athos before I came here. So you left then. Why was that?"

The repeated question was impertinent and unthinking. It was difficult to control my annoyance. "My father and brother were killed. My mother and sister were carried off."

"Oh. I am sorry. How clumsy of me. That must have been terrible." I said nothing. "I'm not sure if I understand why, Father Ignatios, in the face of all these terrible events, you want to return.

302

Were you not happy in the Patriarch's Monastery in Constantinople?"

My face was set. "This is my home." There was nothing more to be said.

He was now shuffling documents on his desk. "Quite so, quite so. Well now, we shall be privileged to have you in our community. I shall ask Brother Petros to show you your cell." He came forward and kissed me on both cheeks. "Welcome to the Monastery of Ayios Ioánnis Theologos, Father Ignatios." He stepped back as a young monk appeared in the doorway. "Brother Petros, this is Father Ignatios who has come to join us. Would you show him to the vacant cell upstairs?" The young monk nodded and led the way for me to follow. I paused for a moment and turned back to the Abbot. I was not smiling. "I'd appreciate it if you would keep all that we have talked about to yourself, Father."

His face expressed surprise as he waited before speaking. "Of course, Brother, of course."

It was not difficult to fall into the pattern of life in the Monastery. It was very similar to the Holy Apostles in Constantinople but now I was freed of the duties of secretary to the Patriarch. I had more time for contemplation, more time to think, more time to pray. I was able to re-establish my use of the Jesus prayer, 'Lord Jesus Christ, son of the living God, have mercy on me'. Now it was taking me further into the depths of Hesychast meditation than I had ever been before. Not a depth that was represented by any entity; more a nothingness, a deep emptiness.

But after a few months living in community I began to experience a restlessness. It was almost an irritation, not with my brother monks for most of them tried hard to live in a loving community. I began to think about the solitude of my time in the Cappodocian desert. Yes, little Gerasimos was there but his presence was not overpowering; in truth it was quite the opposite. Those three years in that strange environment began to seem like an oasis in my otherwise turbulent life. I had not sought them out, they just appeared in the way that so many of the events that led me on appeared. My mind pondered the experience of those three years. I became aware that that was the happiest, the most tranquil, part of my life. Could I recapture that experience?

And then I remembered the Kalikatsoú, the huge rock the size of two houses piled on top of each other, on the beach only two miles from here. I remembered the meeting with Anna there, how we had explored the rock, finding caves that had once been inhabited. Just like the rock-caves of the Cappodocian desert. I began to formulate a plan.

The Abbot was surprised at my request. "You want to become an eremitic? That is an unusual request." I could believe this. In my few months in the Monastery I had become aware that worldly matters assumed an importance at least as great as spiritual matters in this community. I had to escape. That was why the memory of the Kalikatsoú rock came back to me. I could practice the eremitic way, the life of a hermit, right here on the island.

It was agreed between us that I should move to the rock and live there for six days of the week. On the Sabbath I would return to the Monastery to take part in the Eucharist. I would live simply, mostly bread, cheese, water and fruit. On my Sabbath return I could join with the other monks in their main meal. Some might have thought that regime oppressive; for me it was in all ways satisfactory.

It is some three years now that I have lived the eremitic life. Each morning I rise before the sun and for an hour I pray and recite the office. Then I make my way down to the beach and swim. It helps my stiffness, swimming every day. There is never anyone else about. Occasionally I see boats returning to the port after a night's fishing, their lanterns swinging from the stern posts. The low morning sun from the east soon blackens out my view.

This morning my mind is empty. I concentrate on each stroke, feel the water being pushed behind, enjoying the buoyancy of the clear, velvet liquid. Now I feel part of it, part of the ocean rather than an interloper. It is as if the water around me merges into the water within me. Now the limits of my body have extended, now they are the limits of the ocean. Except that there are no limits to the ocean. It is limitless; it is as if I am being sunk into infinitude, incorporated into the endless. It is a sensation like no other. I try to hold myself in the feeling.

A call echoes over the water, disturbing me back with a jolt. I turn and look across to the beach. There is a figure in black standing there, she is waving and calling.

"Father, Father!"

Reluctantly I swim back to the beach. I lift myself out of the water and stand in front of her, a shivering, dripping old greybeard, dressed in a wet shift.

"Bless me, Father." She stoops and holds out her hand. I place my right hand, still wet, in hers and mutter the blessing. She kisses my salty hand.

"Thank you, Father. I have brought you some things." If she notices my surprise she does not betray it. Wondering I dry myself and put on my habit and sandals which had been lying on the beach. She leads me back to the Kalikatsoú where she has left me a basket. I can see pomegranates, lemons, goat's cheese and bread.

"Bless you, Kýria."

"It's nothing, Father. We have more than we can eat."

"No, it is a Christian act. Thank you."

"Keep the basket, Father. I shall return next Friday". She turns on her heel and sets off along the strand. I watch her walking slowly along the edge of the sea towards the village, less than a mile away. The light shimmers off the water.

True to her word, the following Friday the woman is back. The empty basket is exchanged for one brim filled with fruit, bread, cheese and, on this occasion, fish.

I want to express my gratitude. "Kýria, this is most generous of you." She frowns and mutters something which I cannot catch.

305

"I'm sorry. What was that?"

"It's a tithe."

"A tithe?"

"Yes. This is my tithe, my family's tithe. Our priest told us we should always give away a tithe. There are no scoundrels in our village that I want to give it to so I give it to you. You're a holy man, aren't you, Father? Why shouldn't I give it to you?"

I am nonplussed as to how to reply. In the end I say nothing. She is looking more closely at me.

"Don't I know you, Father? Your face looks familiar."

"Oh, probably not." I prefer that the truth remains hidden.

"I'm sure I do. Take away that grey beard and you look just like a man I once knew."

"Who was that?"

"His name was Yiorgos . He lived up there." She indicates up the hill towards the Monastery. "Used to have a fishing boat, but you can't be him. He was killed in the raid."

"The raid?"

"Yes, the pirate raid. Forty years ago. Did you not know about it?"

"I have heard since, but I wasn't here in those days." Why am I lying? Why not let her know that Yiorgos was my father, that I have returned to my home. Perhaps it is an instinctive caution. Perhaps her perception, her acceptance of this tall, grey bearded hermit would be disturbed if she were to hear that he once was Ioánnis, the little goatherd whom she saw playing in the streets all those years ago.

"Thank you again, Kýria. May I know your name?"

"Irini, Irini Mangrioti."

"Well, thank you once more Kýria Mangrioti."

I watch her on her walk back to the village. She is probably ten years older than me. I try to remember a young woman called Irini but cannot place her.

Later I sit at the cave mouth. This is my favourite spot. It reminds me of my cave in Cappadocia. Looking out to sea, to my

306

right the narrow strait that separates the lonely beach from the mainland. Up to my left, beyond the village, rises the hill on which perches the Monastery.

I fix my eyes on the horizon and then let them relax. I am looking at both everything and nothing. Without my willing it the Jesus prayer starts. It comes more easily now, the discipline of the last three years has had its effect. Bit by bit my attentiveness becomes encompassed within the limits of my body. Now I am experiencing my own self but no longer is that self any kind of an entity. If I hold myself steady I experience it as nothing, an active nothing but with no objective substance, no ontological reality. It is as if I could slip into the nothingness that is all reality.

The moment is held but soon is gone. I return to the Jesus prayer. It has never stopped. It brings me back to the here and now. It leaves me with strange feelings. On the one hand a sense of happiness, on the other a disturbance. The happiness is a deep happiness, a recognition that I have found home at last. Home is this rock by the sea, home is what is nothing; yet, conversely, is everything. Home is the absence of desire, the obliteration of past and future.

But yet there is also a disturbance; a giddying breathlessness when I become aware of the very presentness of my existence. In the past I have always defined myself by what I have been, what I hope to be in the future. No longer, for now there is nothing more than the present.

Overpowered by all this, all I can do is give thanks to God and turn to preparing my food. The fish is good, the bread is fresh. I sit and eat and reflect just how much my life has moved; only this time it is an inward move, in contrast to my previous outward journeyings. Outwardly I am static, inwardly I move.

And now, when I give thanks to God, I have no conception of any reality. Absolutely none. God is not sitting there, waiting for my thanks. The God that I worship now has no substance, only an absence. That is what this odyssey has taught me. Bit by bit he has left me or, to be more accurate, I have left him.

But still I worship God. I thank him, I pray to him. I feel as close to him as a lover. The excitement of my long journey into the absence of the deity retains that erotic energy that I experienced all those years ago when I heard Father Ignatios talk about the wedding at Cana. It is an eroticism that found expression with Anna, and also with Miriam. *Eros* and *agape* coexist. It would be difficult to explain this to the Abbot. Gennadios might have understood. For certain Al-Aswar in Bursa would. He would know what I mean.

Now the weeks stretch into months which, in their turn, stretch into years. The pattern of my life is unchanged. Nothing drives me on, everything has become settled, it is neither good nor yet not good. It is what is and I can accept that.

Kýria Mangrioti still visits me weekly. She has become more relaxed in my presence and is taking a proprietary interest in replacing my worn-out clothes and attending to the untidiness of my cave. I think she is rather proud of having her own hermit to domesticate. She continues to talk to me very directly.

"Father Ignatios. What can I do about my son?"

I look perplexed. "Tell me about your son, Kýria."

"Well, he seems to have lost interest in his work. His wife says he does nothing at home."

"Do they have children?"

"Yes. Two girls. Growing up now. Beautiful girls."

"And how does he take that?"

"Take what?"

"His daughters growing up."

She pauses, her face looks troubled. "I don't know. I hadn't thought," her voice trails off.

"Can you remember when he grew up, Kýria Irini?"

She is enlivened. "Oh, yes. He was a handful; wouldn't do a thing we asked him. A real rebel."

308

"So his growing up was stormy. Now his daughters are growing up and he must remember his time. Perhaps he feels that he might lose them." There is a silence for a while. I hear a gull call above us.

"I never thought of that, Father."

"Maybe you should speak with him. Can't do any harm, can it?"

"No. It wouldn't do any harm," she is silent again, as if her perception might have shifted. Then she stands up. "Thank you, Father. I'll do that."

It is a few weeks before she speaks of it again and then it is to tell me that she has talked with her son, as I had suggested, and now things seem better. He is more like his usual self.

Emboldened by bringing this one problem, she begins to tell me of other of her difficulties. Mostly they are family matters and none of them are of any great consequence. Nevertheless they are the stuff of daily life, the upsets which make that life difficult at times. Rarely do I speak of God to her; it seems, in a way, to be inappropriate to do so.

As time goes on she starts to tell me of her neighbours' problems. This is difficult because I cannot deal with them at third hand.

"Perhaps you had better ask her to come here." She has just told me of a young widow who is in a dilemma. The widow comes and I listen to the story of her attraction to a young fisherman who is already married. Matters like these seem outside my sphere. There is little that I think I can offer but what little I do say sometimes helps, a surprise to me.

Gradually, over the years, the numbers of people making their way to the old hermit of the Kalikatsoú increase. I am beginning to find my solitude being threatened. Not that I want to turn them away but my prime purpose is to be an eremitic. It seems strange that I am sought after for advice on matters, marriage, children, neighbours, of which I have no expertise. Perhaps they see me as different, foolishly different. After all, who would seek to live in a draughty cave beside the sea, surviving on meagre rations and with nothing to do. Perhaps that is it, I am perceived as a fool. I do not mind, you can say anything to a fool.

I have to admit it that living in this degree of privation is now taking its toll. I can feel old age creeping up on me like some insidious companion. My stiffness is worsening. Nowadays the climb up to the Monastery every Sunday becomes more and more of a trial. I take to missing it out from time to time, offering a vacuous excuse the next time I see the Abbot. He is very tolerant. I misjudged him at that first meeting many years ago. These days he has matured into a gentle, understanding pastor.

So, for most of the time, I am alone. Kýria Mangrioti makes sure that I am not over-troubled with petitioners from the village. She seems to enjoy the role of hermit-protector; I am happy to let her adopt it.

As if to undermine my spiritual journey my bladder starts to give me trouble. Bit by bit when I piss the stream is getting weaker. Then when it stops I have to stand and wait for the late dribble. It wakes me through the night, an overpowering urgency to pee which is rewarded by less than a cupful of piss. I learn to adapt my pattern of contemplation, practising my piddling prayers. Prayers after I have been woken by my bladder, prayers whilst I stand and wait for the stream to come. It puts the whole business into context.

And now I frequently sleep in the day. Mostly when I am sitting up. Irini finds me like this one day. I wake with a start.

"Bless me, Father. Are you all right? For a moment I thought you had died."

I laugh. "No, not yet, Irini. Sometimes I wonder myself." To be honest when I wake like this I am uncertain whether I am alive or not alive. The distinction seems blurred; in any case it hardly seems to matter. It is at such times that I find myself away from myself. At times like this, memories of Anna, and also Miriam, return; the erotic excitement that stems from the desire for the loved one has always been with me, ever since Anna

310

revealed herself to me as a young man. For most of the last half-century it has lain hidden but it has not been inactive. It has had a life of its own erupting at those few moments of passion that I spent with Anna and with Miriam. It has not gone away, it still lives within me.

Now I see that the excitement it brings is the same excitement of discovery that I have felt in those other parts of my life. I experienced it when I learnt from Father Ignatios, I was enthralled by it in my years in Cappadocia. That opening of the eyes brought with it an exhilaration that is the same as discovering the loved one.

And now, in these recent eremitical years I have, at last, been able to discover God as my lover. The erotic closeness with her femaleness is the same, it seeks a union that is finally satisfying. No domination, no overpowering reality, the God that I love is absent; that is a truth into which I can sink, sink with joy.

For now I understand that my journey is nearly over. I have reached a place where I can quietly and happily live. Now I can worship, now I can pray, now I can give thanks, solely because those acts feel as if they are the right things to do for their own sake. No longer are they bidden by some other, their justification is in themselves alone. They are entirely and completely human acts, undertaken because they seem right. My faith has, in the end, brought me back to humanity. Now I can see that old Father Ignatios understood that; Al-Aswar understood it as well. In Florence I saw this understanding of humanity struggling to emerge from the stranglehold of the Latin church.

Yet they are not ideas, nor yet another philosophy amongst others. They are un-ideas, the true destiny of the negative way. They have led me to a point where 'nothing' is good, where 'nothing' does not matter, where absence is all-encompassing.

A small falcon cuts through the air in front of me. Suddenly all is clear. It is a falcon, rejoicing in the moment of flight, unaware of anything except this one moment. A moment that will be followed by other moments, each equally immanent.

311

Just as for the falcon there is no God so, for now, there is no God for me. In the now, the eternal present, the absence has become complete. It is nothing less than bliss.

I fall on my knees and praise God. It is the only thing to do.

MEROS EVDOMON

Chapter 29
1474

The Abbot welcomed me back to the Monastery.

"I have to confess that we have worried about you, Ignatios, down there in that draughty rock. Your eremitic years have been a blessing to the Monastery but it is good to have you back amongst us."

I mumbled a few words of thanks. They lodged me in my old cell. The view from the window is pleasing. On clear days I can make out the mountains of the mainland, the land of the Ottomans. Some days I wonder how things are with Fahti Mehmet, a ruthless conqueror but a good man. There are times when I miss him.

As I stare across the ocean, without willing it, the whole journey of my life runs through my mind. Is this cell where it will end? Nowadays I am having to use the tubes to empty my bladder more and more. I know I cannot go on like this for ever.

Then one morning, a day when I piss well, a blessed act which always restores my equanimity, I am taken with a plan. Before Matins I make my way out of the Monastery and down the track to the south. I reach a divide in the path. One track, to the right, goes down to the Convent of the Evangelismos, home of the ikon-making nuns. I take the path to the left. It leads across rough terrain, scattered with thistles. I look up and there, above me, is the steep slope of Mountt Profitis Elias, the slope that leads to the whitewashed church on the summit. I slip my hand into the pocket of my habit. The small key is there. The key that I have carried with me ever since I was given it by the mortally wounded priest, Father Ignatios. Now a second Ignatios is going to carry it back.

I start to climb the slope. It is exhausting work and soon I am panting for breath. My legs ache intolerably; I have to stop. I find a rock on which to sit and rest. From here I can see the Kalikatsoú and the vibrating shimmers of light from the waters of the bay. I can just make out two swimmers; they are crossing the strait, heading for the secluded beach. A boy and a girl. I smile indulgently as I remember the swim that Anna and I made across that little strait. Now there is no sense of regret in the memories stirred by the sight of the pair; even from here I can see that they enjoy the awareness of each other, just as Anna and I did. The act of making love was an expression of the divine, no more, no less. It was an act of immanence, of union with the here and now. A blessed state, I can see that now.

And then a new sensation overtakes me. From the centre of my chest I feel a tightness. It slowly increases and then, as if it had never come, fades to nothing. I must move on.

It requires three more stops before I am in reach of the top. Now the journey has truly come full circle. This is where it all started, decades ago. This is where a fisherman's son, bereaved, abused and confused, fled into a world that he never dreamt he would inhabit. Not just an external world of violence, of compassion, of learning, but an internal world in which, finally, he has found a place to be.

It is warm. I hardly notice that my cloak slips off my shoulders to lie in a crumpled heap on the ground. I take the last few steps to reach the church and the tightness in my chest returns, only this time it is stronger, now experienced as pain. My vision has become blurred but I can see enough to find the trap door in the floor. I pull the key from the pocket of my habit and bend forward. The pain increases, now it is moving up into my throat. I turn the key in the lock and slowly lift the door. The hinges are rusted but, with an extreme effort that brings on more pain and constriction, I manage to force it open.

I look down inside. There it is, wrapped in a rough cloth, obviously untouched since I last saw it, sixty years ago. I reach

314

down, the pain is trying to stop me but I persist and eventually it shifts. As I remove the cloth the gold glitters in the sun. This was the ikon carried up here all those years ago. It must have been made at the Evangelismos convent but was never displayed, carried up here to be hidden away. Of course it had to be here. No ikon could be secreted away except on holy ground. No ikon, however shocking, could be destroyed. That is why it is here.

I remember seeing it that night, the night of the raid. Old Ignatios wanted me to find it. I did not understand why, even when I looked at it.

Now I do. I stare at the ikon. I see Ayios Ioánnis Theologos, sitting in his grotto on this very island over one thousand years ago. He is not looking up but is staring into the middle distance. His message is coming from within him; not an external theophany, the voice of an external God, that he was simply expected to dictate to his scribe. That is what is different about this ikon, different enough to be shocking. That is why it had to be hidden away. I read the inscription. *In the beginning was the word*. Faith, belief, understanding, God, all is rooted in language, human language. It cannot escape from language, cannot get outside language however much it might try, cannot escape from humanity, that is the truth that the ikon-maker apprehended. Quite simply religion is in the end created by us, of value for its own sake and for its own sake alone. In the end, immanent.

I stare at the ikon, stare at old Ioánnis. In the end I am him once more. I was Ignatios so that I could follow the search that Father Ignatios demanded of me. Now I am at the end, I am Ioánnis once more. Ioánnis, the cave dweller.

The pain drives up in my chest like the blade of a sword. I know what it is. My head is dizzy. I fall to the ground, forehead resting in the dust. I know this is the end. There is no fear, no regret. This is the final absolute merging into nothingness. It is as it should be.

315

Chapter 30

The young goatherd was busy throwing stones at a tree stump. His charges were quietly grazing on the slope below him. He did not notice the black-cloaked figure making slow progress up the mountain behind him; not, at least, until the climber was half-way up. The boy raised his arm to shade his eyes, the better to see. The figure was going up towards the church. As far as he could see he was a monk. He looked very old, judging by the speed at which he was climbing.

The goats would look after themselves. He scrambled off after the figure, unsure as to why he was doing so. He saw the old monk disappear into the church.

The boy was a nimble runner, well-used to getting about this terrain. Soon he was near the top. In front of him was a black shape; stooping down he saw that it was a cloak, a good one by the look of it. He picked it up. The old monk would want it.

As he reached the church he saw a figure on the ground. It looked as if he was praying. He was bent prostrate, his forehead pressed to the ground, absolutely still.

The boy coughed, anxious that he might be disturbing the old monk in his prayers. There was no movement. He took a pace towards the old man.

"Bless me, Father." Still no response.

Tentatively he walked over to the figure. Then with mounting horror he noticed the extreme pallor of the monk's face, the staring eyes with no life in them, the lack of breathing.

He put out a hand to touch the recumbent figure. The contact was enough to tip the body over. It fell to its side and lay in the dust. He jumped back. Now he was certain. The monk was dead.

317

He turned and ran. Ran down the mountain. Ran to get help. Ran to get away.

But he kept hold of the cloak. It had been left for him.

They buried Father Ignatios in a grave hewn out of the rocky top of Mount Profitis Elias. The Abbot and all the monks of the Monastery made the pilgrimage up to the summit. In addition there were many ordinary people from the island who wanted to honour this old hermit by attending his funeral. None of them knew that he was once Ioánnis, son of Yiorgos . That was the secret that had died with him. His gravestone, set in the ground, simply read '*Ignatios, monk and hermit*'.

The crowds had gone. Mount Profitis Elias stood alone in the late afternoon sun. There was no one around to see the figure that made its way up from the convent of the Evangelismos. The dark shape walked up to where the path divides and then took the steep slope up the small mountain. Reaching the summit there was still no one to see the old nun who made her way around the church to where the burial had lately taken place. Her face was lined with the concerns of years.

She carried flowers in her hand, stems of pink oleander. Her long hair, uniformly grey, was bunched up under her skufia. She stood and read the inscription, then bent forward and placed the flowers on the stone. Her lips moved quietly. "Goodbye my dear, my love, my Ioánnis."

She stayed there until the reddened evening sun had sunk into the deep blue, infinite and encompassing ocean.

TELOS

318

TIMELINE

1347	Bayezid I, Ottoman Sultan annexes Karaman Province, part of Anatolia
1402	Battle of Ankara. Timur the Lame defeats the Ottoman army
1403	Bayezid commits suicide. Civil war between his sons
	Timur sacks Bursa and Smyrna then returns to Samarkand
1413	Ottoman empire reunited
1425	Byzantine Emperor John VIII Paleologos crowned in Constantinople
1436	Brunelleschi's dome of the Cathedral in Florence completed
1439	Council of Florence
1444	Battle of Varna. Crusading army defeated by Ottomans, marking the end of the Crusades
1448	John Paleologos dies. Succeeded by his brother, Constantine XI
1453	Constantinople besieged and falls to the Ottoman Sultan, Mehmet II. End of the Byzantine Empire
1481	Mehmet II dies

GLOSSARY

Alah	Arabic (and some Eastern Christian) term for God
'Alah akbar' (ar.)	known as the takbīr, it means 'God is Great'
al-Ghazali (1058-1111)	a Persian theologian, philosopher and Sufi mystic
al-Nuri	the famous mosque in Damascus
'al salaam a'alaykum' (ar.)	Arabic spoken greeting
anticamera(it.)	antechamber
analavos (gr.)	a garment worn by the highest order of Orthodox monks
Ananias	in the biblical account of Paul's conversion, he comes to Straight Street in Damascus to meet Paul
apophatic theology	a theology that asserts that the only things that can be said of God are negative such as infinite, immeasurable, etc
agape	Christian love for one another
Avicenna 980-1037	a Persian polymath and the foremost physician of his time. His *Canon of Medicine* was translated into Latin and remained in use in the West for 700 years
Ayios (f. Ayia) (gr.)	Saint
Baba (gr.)	father, daddy
Barlaam the Calabrian 1290-1348	a monk and scholar from Calabria in Southern Italy who opposed the hesychast (q.v.) movement
bedestan (ar.)	a covered bazaar
Buccintoro (it.)	the gold-covered barge used by the Doge of Venice
casa (it.)	a large house
cenobitic	members of monastic orders that live in community (as opposed to eremitic (q.v.)
defteron/i (gr.)	second
Dimashq (ar.)	Damascus
eremetic	Monastic order practised in solitude i.e.as a hermit
ekton (gr.)	sixth
eros	sexual love

320

evdomon (gr.)	seventh
filioque (lat.)	an insertion into the Creed concerning the Holy Spirit proceeding from the Father *and* the Son which was greatly resented by the Orthodox Church
fosse	the deep, wide, man-made ditch in front of the outer walls of Constantinople
gedikli (gr.)	a maid-in-waiting to the Sultan, one of the highest ranks in the Ottoman seraglio
Gregorios Naziansos 329-389	St Gregory of Naziansus, one of the three Cappadocian Fathers (along with Basil the Great and Gregory of Nyssa). A great theologian, he became Bishop of Constantinople
Hacci Bektaş	an Islamic mystic, humanist and philosopher who was born in Iran but lived in Anatolia in the 13ᵗʰ Century. He is the eponym of the Bektaşhi Sufi order
Hakîkat	in Sufism, the fourth and highest level of the knowledge of Alah, the immediate experience of the essence of reality
hegemony	dominance by one particular group
hesychasm (gr.)	an eremetic(q.v.) mysticism revived in the Byzantine church in the 13th Century. 'Hesychia' means quietude
Hodegetria (gr.)	literally: "she who shows the Way", an ikonographic depiction of the Theotokos(q.v.) holding the child Jesus at her side while pointing to him as the source of salvation for mankind. The most venerated ikon of this kind, regarded as the original, was displayed in the Monastery of the Panayia Hodegetria in Constantinople, which was built especially to contain it. It was said to have been brought back from the Holy Land by Eudocia, the Empress of Theodosius II (408-50), and to have been painted by Saint Luke

Ioánnis (gr.)	John
Ioánnis Damascene 676-749	St John of Damascus. An Arab Christian born in Damascus. He became chief administrator to the caliph at that city before becoming a monk. He was best known for his opposition to the ikonoclasts and his exposition of apophatic theology (q.v.)
Ioánnis Prodromos	John the Baptist (lit. 'the Forerunner')
Ioánnis Theologos	John the Divine supposed author of the Gospel, Epistles and Book of Revelation
Ikon (gr.)	An image in traditional Byzantine style of Jesus or a holy person that is used ceremonially and venerated in the Orthodox Church. Ikons were made in a proscribed fashion with the appropriate observances of prayer and liturgy
Ikonostasis (gr.)	A screen bearing ikons(q.v.) that separates the sanctuary or altar from the nave in some Orthodox churches
kadife (tk.)	an Islamic woven velvet. Bursa was a centre for the production of such cloth
kadin (tk)	in the Ottoman seraglio, one of four woman allowed for the Sultan by Islamic law
Kalikatsoú (gr.)	(lit. *the Cormorant.*) The name of a large rock on the shore of the Island, once used as a hermitage
kalimera (gr.)	good morning
kamilavkion (gr.)	a monk's stiff cylindrical head covering, similar to a stovepipe hat but without a brim
Karaminids	a nation of Turkmen occupying south-east Anatolia. They were regularly at war with the Ottoman Turks
kathisma (gr.)	a hermitage
kaiki (gr.)	a small wooden fishing boat used for centuries in the Aegean, propelled by oars or a rudimentary sail
Kristos (gr.)	The Messiah

koukoulion (gr.)	a soft, embroidered hat, developed from a cowl, worn by the Abbot of a monastery or the most senior monks
Laetentur coeli (lat.)	The title of the document (lit. 'Let the heaven's rejoice') that was drawn up at the end of the Council of Florence in 1439. It's intention was to unify the Byzantine (Orthodox) Church with the Latin Church, a task it failed to achieve
Latins	a term used by the Orthodox church to refer to members of the Western Church, headed by the Pope of Rome
madrasa (ar.)	a Muslim college, usually located within a mosque.
Makâlât	discourses
Mamre, oak of	a common ikon subject depicting Abraham and the angelic visitors
Mamluks	a regime established and maintained by emancipated white military slaves, chiefly Circassians from the Causucus, who ruled Egypt as a sultanate from 1250 until 1517, and in Syria from 1260 to 1516
Marifet (gr.)	in Sufism, the third level of the knowledge of Alah, mystical knowledge
meltemi (gr.)	a strong north-easterly wind that tends to blow through the Aegean in the summer months
meros (gr.)	a part or portion
narthex (gr.)	a railed-off antechamber or porch at the western end of some (especially early and Orthodox) churches
odalisque (tk.)	a female slave or concubine in the seraglio of the Ottoman Sultan
ontological	a theology that asserts concrete reality to God
Pantokrator (gr.)	the artistic impression of Christ as judge
Pentateuch	the first five books of the Jewish bible
pempton/i (gr.)	fifth
periigis (gr.)	a journey, a wandering
proton/i (gr.)	first

Rassophore (gr.)	the first degree of monasticism in the Orthodox Church, after the novice.(*lit.* 'robe bearer')
sala (it.)	a chamber in a large house
semantron	a long piece of timber which is struck with a hammer, used as a substitute for bells in religious communities to call the worshippers to prayer
seraglio (tk.)	the Ottoman name for a harem
Serîat (tk.)	in Sufism, the first level of the knowledge of Alah, orthodox Islamic law
shi'ite (ar.)	an adherent of the Shia branch of Islam. Shi'ites believe that Muhammad divinely ordained his cousin and son-in-law Ali in accordance with the command of God to be the next Caliph, making Ali and his direct descendants Muhammad's successors (c.f. Sunni)
skufia (tk.)	a soft-sided black brimless hat worn by both monks and nuns in the Greek Orthodox Church
Straight Street	a street in Damascus where Ananias (in the biblical account of Paul's conversion) went to meet the Apostle
stylite	an ascetic who lives on the top of a pillar. The most famous was St Simeon Stylites (390-459) who lived near Aleppo
suk (ar.)	bazaar
Sultana (tk.)	wife of the Sultan
Sultana valide (tk.)	the Sultan's mother, usually the head of the seraglio
sunni (ar.)	the branch of Islam that adheres to the elected succession of the Caliph from the Prophet (c.f. Shi'ite)
Sura (ar.)	a chapter of the Holy Qu'ran
tarîkat (tk.)	a mystic religious order, an order of dervishes
tetarton/i (gr.)	fourth
telos (gr.)	end
theophany	the visible manifestation of God to humankind

Theotokos (gr.)	a title given to the Virgin Mary in the Greek Orthodox Church (lit. 'God-bearer')
Timur the Lame 1336-1405	Mongol leader and conqueror. (Marlowe's Tamburlaine the Great.)
triton/i (gr.)	third
Turkmen	Turkic people originating from central and west Asia

BIBLIOGRAPHY

Writers of historical fiction should always remember that we stand on the shoulders of giants, historians whose laborious study and painstaking research illuminates the past for us. I am grateful to very many such, too numerous to list exhaustively. However I would mention the following which you may want to seek out if you are interested in finding out more about this fascinating century.

Paul Strathern. *The Medici – Godfathers of the Renaissance.* Jonathan Cape, London 2003

George Holmes. *The Florentine Enlightenment – 1400-1450.* OUP, Oxford 1969

Steven Runciman. *The Fall of Constantinople 1453.* Cambridge University Press, Cambridge 1963

Roger Crowley. *Constantinople. The last great siege 1453.* Faber and Faber, London 2005

John Baggley. *Doors of Perception – icons and their spiritual significance.* St Vladimir's Seminary Press, New York 1995

Tom Stone. *Patmos.* Lycabettus Press, Athens, 1984

Halil Inalcik. *The Ottoman Empire. The Classical Age 1300-1600.* Phoenix, London 1973

ACKNOWLEDGMENTS

I am indebted to so many people who have helped me in the writing and production of this book, none more so than my indefatigable editor, John May. His encouragement, his critical appraisal and his unflagging enthusiasm have been spot-on (a favourite phrase of his). Without him there would be no book.

Once again Barbara Powell has cheerfully undertaken the huge task of converting my scribble into a clean typed manuscript. I am also deeply grateful to Liz Colman who meticulously proof read the text and to Paraskevas and Claire Mangriotis who helped me with Greek nomenclature and usage. Jean and Andrew Smith kindly helped me with my schoolboy Latin.

Sarah Dunant, an encourager if there ever was one, was generous enough to read an early draft and to make cogent and appropriate criticisms which did much to improve the end result. However whatever failings this frail vessel has are entirely down to me and not to her.

I am most grateful to the staff of the Bodleian Library in Oxford for their help in my researches into the background to this book. The Bodleian is a wonderful place and I was in danger of disappearing without trace into the research. It was very seductive.

One of the undoubted features of my previous book, *Beyond the Silence*, was the cover design by Annie Pickering-Pick and her daughter Sera. I have been very lucky that they have done the same for this book. I think you will agree that the end result is quite exceptional. I am also indebted to Annie for the design of the map which will, I hope, help the reader follow the course of Ioánnis's journeyings.

Stephen Maslen kindly let me read his thesis on John of Damascus and Al-Ghazali and was generous enough to discuss many of the issues that have arisen from it.

Ed, to whom I dedicate this book, is my oldest friend and has, over more than 45 years, been a source of ideas and controversy which has always kept me intrigued and challenged. We had been out on a walk discussing Christian unity. His view was that the split of the Reformed Church was as nothing compared with the schism of the Council of Florence. At that time I had never heard about such a Council but I had to find out. Out of that came this book.

Finally my thanks and love are due to Jill who, as ever, has been an encourager and also an inerrant sounding-board throughout the long process from first inspiration to publication.

Andrew Chapman
Bredon 2012